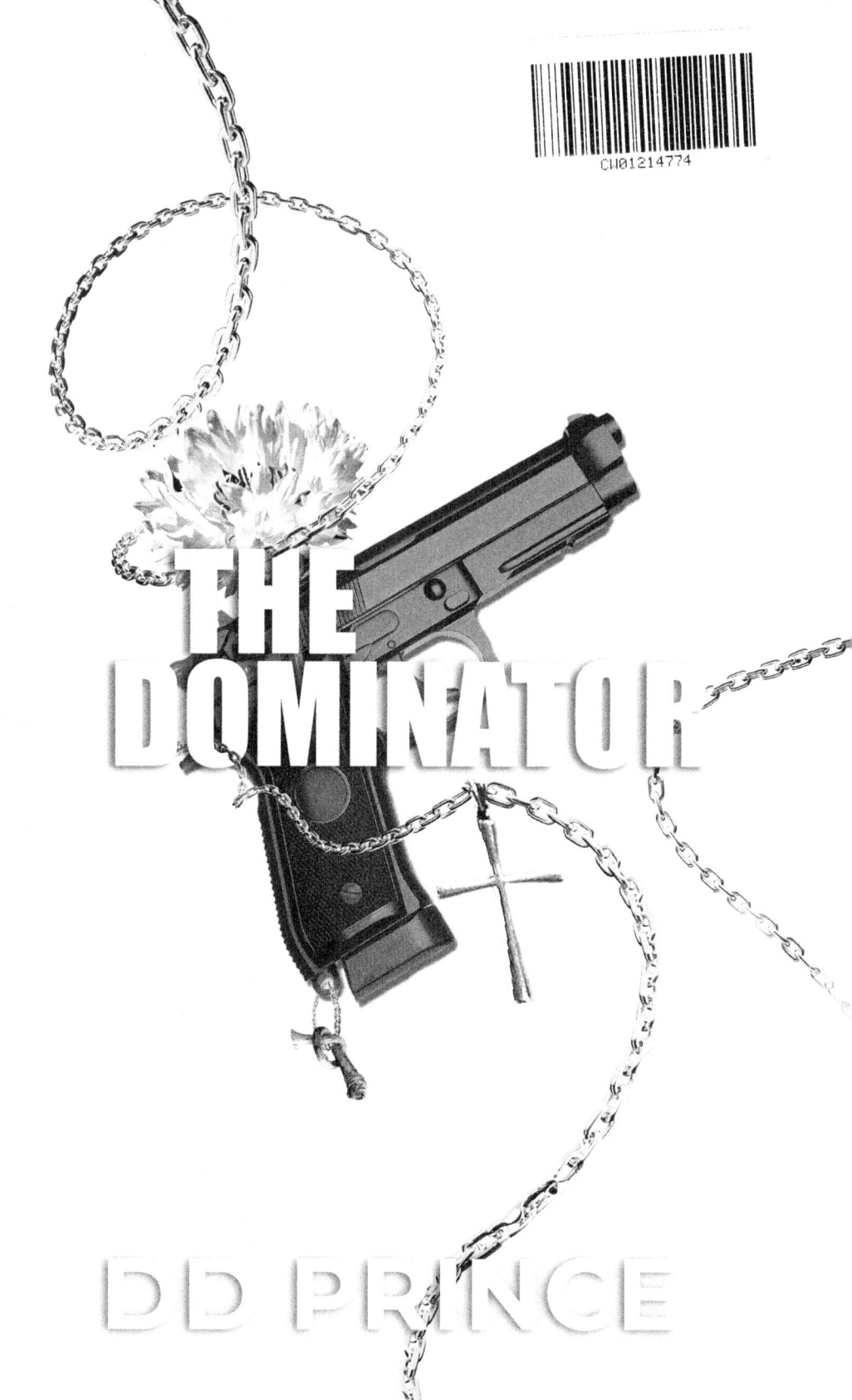

THE DOMINATOR
Book 1 - The Dominator Series
Copyright © 2024 DD PRINCE
THIRD EDITION

First edition published in 2015
DDPRINCE.COM

All rights reserved. No part of this publication may be reproduced, distributed, or transmitted in any form or by any means, including photocopying, recording, or other electronic or mechanical methods, without the prior written permission of the publisher, except in the case of brief quotations embodied in critical reviews and certain other noncommercial uses permitted by copyright law.

This is a fictional story, the product of the author's imagination. Copyrights are the property of their respective owners.

Copyright ©2015, 2024 DD PRINCE.

Contents

Content Warning:	vii
Chapter 1	1
Chapter 2	13
Chapter 3	39
Chapter 4	69
Chapter 5	141
Chapter 6	169
Chapter 7	179
Chapter 8	213
Chapter 9	229
Chapter 10	301
Chapter 11	311
Chapter 12	373
Chapter 13	403
Chapter 14	439
Chapter 15	475
Chapter 16	501
Chapter 17	525
Chapter 18	537
Epilogue	539
The End	543
The Dominator Playlist	545
End of Book Notes:	547
About the Author	549
Follow Me	551
Books By DD Prince	553

Dedication

I dedicate this book to myself.
I marinated in this story for years and years before finally finishing and finding a bit of bravery to put it out there.
This is, I hope, a few hours of entertainment for you.
To me, it's so much more.
I used this book to change my life. To live my dream.
I hope you find the courage to leave your comfort zone and live your dreams, too.
This book is also for Tommy and Tia, who are very real to me after occupying space in my brain for my entire adult life and a few years before that, too.

Content Warning:

This work of fiction is a dark mafia romance with scenes and situations that those who do not enjoy the genre may find disturbing.
It contains graphic situations, violence, and difficult mental territory including organized crime, arranged marriage, and tough physical, sexual, and psychological subjects. If you are not a dark romance and antihero lover, this might not be the book for you.

If you've ever wanted the villain to get the girl, this could be your series.

Further information is available on the author's website.

1

Tommy

"Her name is Athena. They call her Tia. She's yours if you want her."

"Mine?"

"Yeah, yours." Pop waved his hand dismissively. "For whatever."

I was sitting in my father's office absorbing this news, news that this *Athena* was coming to me as a gift from my father, that he's taking her as payment for unpaid debts.

Pop said he was about to have the news of the payment arrangement conveyed to her father and then I could do what I wanted with her.

"For whatever" meant I could put her on the streets under one of the pimps on our downline. I could also opt to send her overseas and pocket the profits.

We had connections in a variety of industries, including those of the seedy underworld. We had fingers in less-than-wholesome pies. Looking at her photo I knew she'd fetch more on the black market than the debt her daddy owed. Way more.

We receive commissions based on a variety of pursuits. Some call us mafia. I don't like that word. You might say I say tomato, you say tom-atto and while it's all the same fruit, of course, there are many varieties of tomatoes. We're businessmen. We have businesses we fully own and those we own a stake in.

Not all of what we do is legal, but it's not all shady business deals and gambling debts, either. The way it's set up creates multiple layers and plenty of income streams. Money flows to the family coffers from a variety of areas like security, construction, retail and wholesale businesses. There are gray areas, too, like security, protection, and of course loansharking, prostitution, and drugs. We mostly deal in organics rather than chemicals, and it's only a small part of our business.

Yes, organized crime exists in the 21st century. No, it's not always as glamorous as it's portrayed on screens but it's not always as seedy, either. It's a living. Some days are fairly ordinary. Some days are a rush. Some days we have to make tough decisions. I'd had to make many difficult decisions so far and I was sure there would be many more ahead of me, especially given that I'd soon be sitting at the helm of the family empire.

My father had humble beginnings as a working guy who was respected and connected around town. He and his best friend, a guy also connected – even more connected that Pop – started a construction company. It did well; they were smart and resourceful. Over time, they saw the need for a number of other services and had the capital to begin expansions so they could better provide for their family without paying half their earnings in taxes. The company has grown by leaps and bounds in the past thirty years.

After the construction company got off the ground, he opened a coffee shop. He now has six of those coffee shops and it's moving to a franchising model in the next five to seven months. He's a partner in some restaurants, some hotels, plus a few nightclubs. Some of those clubs have backroom card games; some that deal in big money.

Drugs and druggies, alcohol and alcoholics, hookers, nymphos, bookies, gamblers, loan sharks... they'll always be out there. Why shouldn't we profit from it? We have the brains and the brawn and the green. And because of that we've got the cars, the houses, the fat bank accounts, and the high tax brackets so we look above-board to the tax man and have the fat rainy day funds in our mattresses, attics, basements, whatever. We do regular shit. We also do bad shit.

Why bust our chops for a bit better than minimum wage and work like a dog until we're ready to drop to put a meager amount of money into a retirement plan we may never get to spend? Successful men get between what men want and the source.

That's what we do. You want to bet on the races? We can help. You want to get your rocks off, find someone to cater to your fetishes? We'll hook you up. You need money to pay off your gambling debts or start up a new venture? Guess, what? We can help there, too.

It all fits together nicely, like a puzzle. People need protection. People need money. People need help from builders to build those businesses they want us investing in, so we do the investing *and* we do the building. And people need vices so at the end of a hard day they've had a little fun.

And because men can have too much of a good thing and get caught up in the sins of the flesh and the thrill of the bet it can get dirty. Some don't pay their debts. Some need to be dealt with. Sometimes people get greedy and try to take from us. We have to make tough decisions. People come to play; they must be prepared to pay. We show our enemies and those who want our profits that we aren't to be trifled with.

I'm twenty-nine, Pop's namesake, and I'm inches away from taking over the family business. This is how we feed and protect ourselves and the ones who count on us. We take that seriously. If people borrow money, they have to pay their debts. We prefer cash as our currency of choice, of course, but sometimes creative financing comes into play when someone can't pay.

My family may be wealthy, but I've earned my stripes, too. Pop didn't believe in sticking a silver spoon in my mouth when he had to claw his way up. He made sure I had to do the same. He calls it character-building. My brother and I both call him a hard ass.

I started at the bottom at fourteen and worked my way up, buying my own condo with cash I earned by the time I was nineteen. I've done hard work. Dirty work. No one can say that I don't *legit* deserve to sit in my father's chair when that day comes.

Sitting in my father's office and getting told he was handing over a flesh payment on a debt to me was intriguing, to say the least. I'd never seen him take this kind of payment before.

Telling me I could do "whatever" was a game. My father wanted me to keep her for myself. My cock twitched looking at her photo. Long, silky-looking chestnut brown hair, big jade green eyes, beautiful skin, full lips, fit yet curvy. Soft-looking.

"Why are you letting the guy pay like this? This isn't our style. There's more to it. Spill."

Pop shrugged. "This was my choice, not his. Too many questions, Tommy. Just think of it as a gift. A bonus for all your hard work. Look at her."

He pushed the picture closer. My Pop didn't like questions, that was for damn sure. I guess I inherited that quality from him. But, I needed to know the details, particularly because he was probably only a few key decisions away from retiring. He didn't look ready to retire; he's only in his mid-fifties and looks like he's forty. But Pop worked hard to build his empire and says he wants to reap the fruits of that labor before he's too old to fully enjoy it.

"What kind of guy gives his daughter up for debts? The debt is measly," I said.

He looked reflective and a long moment passed.

"Pop?"

"I bought his debt. There's history. Long family history. This guy! He..." He waved his hand. "He was like one of those, what do you call... fan girls. He tried to crawl up all our asses and worm his way into the business. He was always a liability, so he didn't get the time of day. He disrespected me many years ago. He took something from me. He paid a price. But I don't know that his price was enough." He tapped his temple with his index finger. "And some nights I still lay awake thinking about what he took from me. This daughter, she's all he's got of any value. And look at her. I'm thinking she's young, she's beautiful, you could make her yours. Marry her, maybe. Your call, I know, but that's what I think. It'd be a shame to put her to work or sell her off. I saw opportunity. I acted. Two birds, one stone. Pay this guy back by taking his last thing of value. Take her to pay his paltry debt and help our family move forward."

He shrugged like it was no biggie, but was looking at me studiously. I could see it *was* a big deal.

I shook my head, exasperated. This was Pop's way. He was telling me this *Tia* could be mine to do with what I wanted, dropping his suggestion of *"marry her, maybe"* was his way of suggesting it without outright demanding it. If I didn't, he'd be disappointed. People know better than to disappoint my father. I also know bonuses aren't in his vocabulary, so he isn't giving her to me as a bonus. He's got plans. But, my father knows better than to tell me what to do outright. When he really wants me to do something, he does it like this.

"Married, Pop? Who says I'm ready to get married?"

"Tommy, my boy, you're almost thirty. By your age I had a couple kids and was on my second wife. You don't truly become a man until you start a family of your own. A family man needs to take over the company. You decide who you marry, of course, and this girl, she's part Irish, half Italian. She's beautiful and she's young. She can be molded into what you need her to be. Taking a wife don't mean you can't still have your fun, my boy."

"I'll think it over."

This was the best way to handle my father. He'd nudged about me getting married, but never this bluntly. I'd been prepped and primed to take over this company ever since I could remember. He'd drilled a lot into my head over the years and I'd jumped through hoops to prove I was worthy. Not just to him, also to myself.

I figured I'd already proven I was a man many times to my father with tests I'd passed, decisions I'd made, problems I'd taken care of, opportunities and profit I'd brought the business. He knew I had what it took. But, my pop was a demanding prick and I'd paid the hefty price of being his son many, *many* times. In his mind, I should show everyone: his associates, his enemies...that I'm a family man, ready to take the helm. An old-school way of thinking but that was how it was with Pop.

Putting me and my brother at the bottom of the ladder like any other soldier that worked for him ensured we'd earn respect. Evidently, he'd decided I needed to take one more step on this journey before he'd be willing to hand over the keys to the kingdom.

But married? He'd talked about me being married in a *"someday when you're married"* or *"someday when you're a father", "someday when you run this business",* way for years but I'd never given getting married much thought. Pop certainly enjoyed being married, he got married often, though despite his love for walking down the aisle, he wasn't a man who believed in any sort of marriage sanctity.

Me? Women were a means to an end for me. I had a healthy sexual appetite with as much action as I wanted. I didn't do relationships. Didn't want to; never needed to. I never had the desire to get serious or be monogamous. I knew women liked the way I look and of course loved the money, the power. I hadn't met anyone I cared enough about to take things to any level beyond physical. I hadn't ruled it out; I just hadn't had the urge. I was Thomas Ferrano Jr., a force to be reckoned with in and out of the boardroom, the boxing ring, the bedroom, and more, and I'd been busy my whole life, proving myself, focused on the business.

I liked control in and out of the bedroom and was partial to rough play. Very partial. I had my pick of playthings to suit whatever my fancy was on any given day. Blonde, brunette, redhead, Black, Asian. Pop threw in the bit about this Tia being half Italian as if it was a factor. I didn't give a shit about that. Regardless, I'd certainly never met someone I'd wanted to marry or even date seriously. Dating someone and getting serious? That'd feel too much like giving up control to me. Not interested.

Rarely was I interested in even having the same woman twice. Who needed a woman nagging me, thinking she could tell me what she didn't want me doing, asking me inane questions that I couldn't be bothered to answer? I had no biological clock niggling at me yet for kids, either. I had nieces and nephews through my two sisters and the kids were great, but they weren't my problem on a daily basis. Being Uncle Tommy was just fine by me.

Married? Sheesh. I knew how Pop's brain worked and to him it was a necessity. I'd need to do it to get what I wanted. Full control. I wanted control in all areas of my life and since Pop was slipping just left of his prime, it was time. Pop was missing the boat on opportunities that could make us a lot of money and get us out of the small-time game in a few areas. I could take the company to greater heights with more profit and lower risk. If I had to get married to get him to give me the keys to the kingdom and for me to not have to run business decisions by him, maybe that's what I'd have to do.

He and I butted heads a lot. I guess what everyone says is true; we're a lot alike. As head of the business, I'd want to think about an heir to take over for me some day, rather than promoting one of my nephews.

My buddy and business associate, John, was married with kids. He and I got hammered the other night at the sex club we both belong to and a conversation came up about my lack of desire to hook up with one girl night after night. He'd talked about how amazing it was to have a submissive wife who would do anything he wanted. Because she ached to please him. I argued there was no shortage of women in the club who'd pant in heat when I approached them. Johnny said I didn't get it, didn't understand what I was missing, how amazing it was to have her complete trust and commitment.

Johnny played at the club and his wife was cool with it. His wife liked threesomes, even. And she didn't tell him what to do. She yielded to him. He told me there were relationship parameters and he knew what her limits were and said he had loads of room to play.

I'd laughed, slapped him on the shoulder, and said, "See Johnny, that's where you and I differ. The only way in the world that'd go down for me is if there were no limits, no safe words."

Control. Full control. I looked at the photo in front of me again and the way she looked... I thought about control. I thought about controlling the business, being in full control of my own destiny, and I couldn't help but think about controlling her.

Pop was watching me mull things over. *Fuck.*

I looked at him, conceding. "I'll meet her. We'll see."

My father got that look on his face that he gets when everything is falling into place. That look was one of the very few things that could chill me to the bone.

Tia

I'm young but I've been called an old soul more than once. As my high school graduation and nineteenth birthday loomed, all I'd been thinking about is the fact I was officially grown up. Ready to strike out on my own. Sort of. It was time to transition out of foster care into my first apartment.

My foster parents have been wonderful to me for the past five and a half years and they'd gone above and beyond, arranging for me to rent the apartment above the garage at my foster mom's parents' home. My own space, but still close to people who are like family, the only family I've had for years.

Because I've been a ward of the court for the past few years and I'll continue my education, I'll have an income supplement through college while my tuition is paid for.

Nona and Nono Caruso have been like I'd expect real grandparents would be to me and the half a dozen girls that live with Rose and Cal Crenshaw at the moment. I'll be the fifth girl to move into the garage apartment. The family has been fostering for years and they have helped countless teen girls have a home and a stable family for at least a little while.

While I could've opted to move out and finish my victory lap of high school from my own place on my eighteenth birthday, the Crenshaws invited me to stay. Being an only child who embraced this busy, hectic, and crazy house full of laughter and love, I was happy to stay the extra year.

I've been in foster care since I was nine and was moved around a lot before finding home here. My mother committed suicide when I was small, and that led to my already troubled father falling completely off the rails.

His partying and gambling intensified after her death. That, coupled with his inability to hold down a job was amplified without my mom around. Dad tried to move me in with his sister, my Aunt Carol, one night after being beaten up pretty badly (in front of me) by loan sharks, but she'd said, "Not a chance."

She actually said that *right* in front of me. Shame on her. And shame on Dad for asking her in front of me, knowing it was unlikely she'd agree. Not only did she refuse, she also reported him to Social Services for neglect.

They took temporary custody of me so he could get his life together, but he never managed to do that long enough to get me back.

Dad seemed like he wanted to try a few times – he'd go long periods of time without seeing me and then he'd turn up for a visit, tell me he was doing better. Sometimes, he would even do a visit two months in a row, but inevitably over the past nine+ years, the more common pattern was for him to get my hopes up and then let me down and disappear for months at a time. I stopped having expectations of him a long time ago. Becoming a ward of the court made it simpler. They stopped trying to make him try.

This foster home has been, by far, the most nurturing of all. Not only do they go out of their way to make their home a real home, but whatever isn't provided that me or the other girls need through the "system" they take out of their own pockets.

Three years ago, Rose and Cal bought bicycles out of their own pockets for Christmas gifts for all of us. Two years ago, they took us to Disney World on their dime. They are amazing people and they've helped so many girls get their lives together. I hope to repay them someday. Karma is definitely on their side.

Rose, a sweet round woman with a heart of gold, tells me all the payment she wants is my happiness and success. And for me to continue to be a part of their family. Come for Christmas; come for special dinners on my birthday when I don't have other plans. Have them at my wedding someday. Think of them as my family.

They have one son and one daughter. Their autistic son is one of my favorite people in the world. Their daughter, Ruby, is my best friend. She still has a year left of high school, otherwise we'd just get a place together.

I'm starting college next Fall for social work, to make a difference in the lives of other kids who might otherwise fall between the cracks. So many do, and many blame the system. I've had a great social worker all along who has always cared about my safety and happiness. I aim to follow in her footsteps.

I wouldn't say I've been the perfect student or foster child. I make mistakes. Boys. Partying. Skipping school. But, for the most part, I try to be responsible. I know what I want from life and I'm grateful for the blessings I have.

Of course I miss my mom. I wouldn't say she was a happy person and clearly her unhappiness ran deeper than I knew. I also wish Dad could've pulled his life together. While he was never all that responsible before she died, he was really, really messed up afterwards.

Although I don't know how often he checks messages, I've sent him a Facebook message to tell him about high school grad and left a ticket at the office with his name on it. I'm not counting on him making it, he's never made it to any school plays, birthday parties, or anything else I've asked him to attend. When Dad shows up it's generally very random. Some wonder why I bother to go out of my way, but I guess I've never given up on him. I've always wanted to believe that people are redeemable.

2

Graduation day! It was *the* day for me and two of my foster sisters, so mayhem at the Crenshaw house, but in the best way. I was ready, my hair in a sleek updo that everyone said makes me look like a pin-up model. Bright red lips, smoky eyes. Rose told me I look twenty-five instead of nineteen. I feel like I'm older, anyway; always have, probably partly due to being almost on my own for the better part of a year at nine years old.

After Mom died, Dad would leave me alone for hours at a time, sometimes overnight, while he nipped out to run his errands. I learned how to make simple meals at that age, to cook and clean up after myself. I even paid the electric bill once after finding a disconnection notice taped to our apartment door. It was a rare occasion that my dad's wallet had been full of cash, so while he slept off a bender, I walked the three blocks to the bank and paid it.

Social services hadn't looked too kindly on that explanation, though when I was interviewed and told them I could get myself off to school, make my own breakfast, pack my own lunch, and that I'd even paid bills at the bank with money from Daddy's card games.

Yeah, that had gone over so well that they hauled me into care. It didn't help that they found me at home alone with almost no food in the fridge other than some dried out Chinese take-out, but a case of beer in the fridge and nothing but some saltines and beer nuts in the cupboard. The green mat had still been on the dining room table from a poker game Dad had hosted two nights before. It was littered with crushed beer cans and overflowing ashtrays. He'd always told me to stay in my locked room during those games and touch nothing on that table if his poker stuff was left out. The games were often on school nights.

Dad turned up drunk in the middle of the social services meeting and blubbered like a baby. Mom's death ruined him, and I felt like I had to take care of him for her. Lord knew he couldn't take care of me. I guessed that was what made me an old soul, the fact that I had to be.

Anyway, here I was, wishing my parents could see me get handed my diploma, graduating on the honor roll. I doubted Dad would make it. Rose, Cal, and Susie (my social worker) would all be there for me and that was enough.

After the ceremony, we'd have a celebratory meal at Rose and Cal's and there was a school dance planned after that. My ex-boyfriend Nick had been lingering all week and I wasn't looking forward to seeing him tonight but knew he'd be there.

I'd dumped him a month ago, because I found out he was selling drugs from his gas station job. His customers would buy gas and when they came in to pay, he'd slip them dope. I wanted no part of that. I had no desire to build my future with a guy who would put his future in jeopardy. He was a loser. I didn't like to think of my dad as a loser but in reality, that's what he was. I wasn't about to get tied down with a loser of a boyfriend, too.

Nick was a twenty-two-year-old gorgeous, long-haired, tattooed, and leather jacket-wearing *bad boy*. I was attracted to the look and the swagger of bad boys for some reason, but when it all came down to it, they'd get dumped as soon as they showed me their true *bad boy* colors. While I was attracted to them like a moth to a flame, it didn't last. I didn't want to waste my time on someone going nowhere but downhill.

As I got dressed for grad, I thought about the guy that had come into the ice cream parlor I worked at the other day. He came in while I was working my last shift and he was well-dressed, as sexy as a movie star, and carried himself with confidence. He was so tall and strong-looking. A hundred percent grown-up male and very different from Nick. Older. Somewhere near thirty, and he gave me tummy flutters like I'd never had before. What would it be like to date a man who oozed sex appeal *and* maturity?

As me and my foster sisters got ready for our big day, they were giddy and giggling. I was deep in thought about the guy I'd been thinking of as the ice cream parlor hottie. I barely stopped thinking about him the past two days and nights. But, as that had been my last day at that job the chances of seeing him again were small. He flirted with me, but I behaved like a deer in the headlights. I wished I was older, more confident, and that I'd given him my phone number. I was so *over* guys that were like Nick.

I knew Nick was trying to get my attention because he knew that tomorrow I'd be moving into my own apartment. He wanted *alone time* with me. He and I had done the *alone* thing plenty of times and I didn't need to go down that road again. It wasn't exactly symbiotic.

Nick wanted to attend the graduation ceremony, but I only had a limited number of tickets to give out and since I had no one but Dad, I'd given my extra tickets to the other girls who had guests.

I was ready for new things. A new place, college in the fall, and new opportunities. Maybe a new guy, too. One who was ready to be a man, not a boy living in a one-bedroom apartment shared with two other guys who rotated using the bedroom when they had girls over (with the never-innovative sock on the doorknob as the clue that the room was "in use". *Gross.*).

We'd done it in there once and... *never again*. We'd done it a few times in his car, but it was certainly not very fulfilling! Neither the car nor that bedroom had been cleaned in months. He undoubtedly saw my upcoming apartment as an 'in'. *Wrong.* He'd already texted me today, trying to get me to agree to 'talk' later tonight.

* * *

As I walked up on the podium to receive my diploma, I had the surprise of my life. Dad was in the audience, a big smile on his face. He was seated beside Rose, who was chatting softly to him while snapping pictures of me. Nick was sitting directly behind my dad, dressed up and smiling at me, too. I avoided his gaze, tried not to think about how handsome he looked. Looks weren't everything. Why was he even here? I bet Ruby found him a ticket; she'd been trying to get us back together for days like it was her mission in life.

After the ceremony was over, I was in the school's courtyard for photos, and Dad rushed to me. He looked good. I'd only ever seen him in a suit once, at Mom's funeral, and this was that same suit. He had his dirty-blond hair gelled back and he smelled like expensive cologne. Seeing him like this reminded me of how he sometimes was before Mom died. His green eyes sparkled. He was good-looking for his age. Everyone said I had his eyes. He'd never been perfect, but we did things together. He taught me to cook, I'd hang out with him while he tinkered with his car. When I was small, he'd hold me high in the air with an airplane ride to bed. He'd read bedtime stories with such effort and emotion, doing different voices for every character. He wasn't the perfect father or husband before she died but after she died, he was a shell of a man who tried to drink and gamble away his pain. Seeing him here today, trying for me, I felt a burst of affection for him.

He swung me around in a giant hug, making me squeal. "Athena! I'm so proud. You look all grown up. Look at you. Someone take our picture!" He called out to the rest of our group and Rose hurried over with her camera.

Susie, my social worker, eyed my dad warily. I knew she'd lost patience with him over the years. Getting me to agree to be a ward of the courts made her life so much easier because she didn't have to continually try to reach him to find out what was what with him, to get him involved in decisions that needed to be made, and so forth. When he lost his parental rights, it had been eleven months since he'd made contact. He always managed to miss birthdays.

It hurt that he could go that length of time without checking on me, leaving others to raise me. It hurt, but I wasn't the sort lash out about it. I always just thought of him as broken. Who wouldn't be broken after finding their wife dead in a tub with slit wrists?

I was supposed to have been picked up from school after a field trip that required parents to pick up the kids late since we were back at 7:00 at night. Nobody showed up. I sat in the principal's office for hours while they tried to find someone to pick me up. The principal had been huffy and snippy, too, clearly with plans for the evening that had to be canceled due to this poor little neglected girl who hadn't been picked up from school.

Finally, my Aunt Carol had come along and brought me to her home. She didn't give me an explanation, treating me like kids should be seen and not heard. She did, however, not even try to lower her voice to stop me from overhearing her on the phone as she told someone she was *stuck* watching me for the evening because my father was a wreck, mourning his dead wife who'd killed herself. What a way for me to find out.

She never bothered with me all these years, just wrote me off. Mom hadn't had any family step up either. I heard she had an older brother, but it seemed she was a bit of a black sheep with her family because I never met anyone from that side and no one sought me out after she died.

* * *

So, here Dad was, all smiles for the camera, looking well-fed, well-groomed, and yet there was a weird aura about him, something in his eyes, a nervousness in his laugh. He seemed off, like there was something shifty going on. He kept checking his phone and looking around suspiciously. When everyone had gotten their fill of camera flashes in their eyes, Rose tried to corral everyone so we could go back to her house where a big buffet and gifts were waiting.

"Please join us, Gregory," she said to my dad.

"I'd love to!" he beamed. "Tia, ride with me. We can catch up on the way."

Did he have something to tell me? It'd been ages since I'd seen him and while I was happy he was here, I knew something wasn't quite right.

He had a decent enough car, surprisingly. We drove through a coffee shop drive-thru for Dad to get a coffee and me to get an iced cappuccino and then we parked so Dad could get out and have a cigarette first, saying he wouldn't smoke in the car with me.

"Thanks so much for coming, Dad."

"Like I'd miss it!"

He gave me an *are you kidding* look. As if he hadn't missed most other milestones in my life so far.

"What's new, then? You working?" I asked.

He nodded. "Yeah, I've been working at an auto parts place for about seven months. I do parts counter, a few minor repairs. Got a nice apartment. Got myself a nice girlfriend, too. You'll like her. Sadie. She's a schoolteacher. Teaches kindergarten. This is her car."

"Really? That's awesome." It'd been the longest he'd held down a job for ages and this was the first relationship he'd ever told me about. He evidently knew what was going on with me already; I'd filled him in with my Facebook message where I'd invited him to come to the grad ceremony.

"Something off, though, Dad? You seem stressed."

He nodded quickly and lifted the lid off his coffee and took a sip. "Yeah, we need to talk."

I frowned. "Okay..."

He sat at a picnic table outside the coffee shop and picked at a loose thread on his suit pants. "I'm in some trouble. Chickens coming home to roost, sort of thing."

My heart lurched. "What kind of trouble?"

He let out a heavy sigh. "I have old debts from when I was gambling. I haven't gambled in a long time, Tia. I go to a support group. The debt was sold to someone high up in organized crime, someone who hates my guts and has a vendetta from years back. He's decided to make life... difficult."

I nodded, urging him to continue, feeling dread spread through my gut.

"I need to figure this out, find a way to get them paid. They've already given me an extension, but they want a marker. I just need a few days to sort this out. I was hoping you could help me."

"How? How could I help you?" I didn't have any money. Well, $248 in my savings account from my job at the ice cream parlor, but that was it.

"You need to be my marker," he said, resigned.

"Your what?"

"Yeah. I know it's not ideal, but I have a plan to clear it up and then there won't be anything else. This is the last loose end from my old life, Tia. I'm really sorry to drag you into this, but I have no choice."

"Dad..." I began.

I noticed a black SUV pull in beside us. The passenger window rolled down and a guy in the passenger seat wearing dark sunglasses eyed us.

"Tia, it's just for a few days. I have a plan, I..." He glanced over his shoulder and then his shoulders slumped.

"Dad, you can't expect me to...who are these people? What on earth have you gotten yourself into?"

Dad's face took on a look of desperation. "Sweet pea, I'm sorry. I've been such a fuck up."

He hadn't called me that since I was little, since before Mom died.

"You need to go with these guys. Trust me. I'll make this better. It'll be better."

"It's my high school *fucking* graduation!" I shrieked, looking to the SUV. Was this them?

Dad blanched. I've never sworn at him, never raised my voice at him. I've always treated him like he's fragile. The front passenger and rear passenger doors of the black SUV opened and burly men dressed in expensive suits looked out at us.

"Problem, O'Connor?" One in the back seat asked in a gravelly voice.

"Naw, no. Not at all. Not at all. We just need one minute." Dad was like a stuttering fool. "Tia, please," his eyes pleaded with me.

"Dad." I folded my arms. I could not believe he came to my grad to set me up to be his "marker". This was the only reason he came!

Burly guy from the front passenger seat lifted his shades off. "We need to go, O'Connor."

I took a step back as the two of them got out, leaving their doors opened, revealing a big Black dude in the back and a younger, pissed-off but hot blond guy in a suit in the driver's seat.

Dad leaned forward and took my hands in his. His face had a look of desperation that made my scalp prickle. "They'll kill me," he whispered.

What the...?

What would make him use *me* as a marker? Did he think they wouldn't kill *me*? Did he think they wouldn't hurt me? How much money did he owe these guys and how would he even pay them off?

He'd let me down countless times. In the early days of foster care, he'd promise that his life was almost together enough to gain custody again. He'd promise to take me places, buy me things – I never needed or wanted things, but he always tossed promises around and he never *ever* kept them. Why would I believe him now? Why would he put me at risk and even make this an option?

"Just hang tight. They'll keep you comfortably in a luxury hotel suite or something like that. You'll be fine. Look at it like a little getaway."

I tilted my head at my father, dumbfounded. This couldn't be real. Back at Rose and Cal's, they were waiting for me. There was a big, beautiful cake congratulating me, Mia, and Bethany for graduating.

Ruby, her brother Connor, the other girls, and everyone's friends and some relatives were all there. There was a table filled with everyone's favorite foods. There were graduation gifts. Tonight, there was a dance and all my friends would be there.

He was ruining this; ruining a pivotal day that I'd worked so hard for. I was a nearly straight A student. I was on the motherfucking honor roll! I'd beaten the odds despite my screwed-up childhood with a loser father and a mom lost to suicide. I didn't deserve this. A combination of pain and rage rose in me.

"Athena, sweet pea; trust me." His eyes implored me.

"How much do you owe? Do you even have a way to pay them back?"

He nodded. "It's not out of my reach, and I have a plan."

"It must be pretty bad for them to want human collateral, Dad. What'll they do to me if you don't pay?"

He put his hands on my shoulders and said, "I just need you to trust me."

I held my breath. Burly man number one and burly man number two seemed like they were staring me down from behind their *Men-In-Black* sunglasses.

I was about to open my mouth to say *No, no way* was I agreeing to this, but then the blond driver got out of the vehicle and rounded it.

He strode to the passenger side where this standoff was happening, took my elbow and ushered me into the SUV, his mouth in a tight line. Burly guy number two was standing by the opened the back door. It happened so fast that I was in the vehicle before I had a chance to protest.

"In!" Blond guy was dressed like he was ready for a GQ photo-shoot. He blurted this at the goons with a grumbled, "For fuck sakes" then he gave Dad a chilling death stare.

Before I had a chance to react, *angry hot guy* got back into the driver's seat and we were pulling away from Dad, who was standing with his hands in his pockets watching the SUV pull away.

I was sandwiched in between backseat burly guy two and the scary-looking Black dude. I glanced over my shoulder out the window to see Dad take a sip of his coffee and dial a number on his phone. Backseat burly guy passed the guy on the other side of me my seatbelt and he fastened it for me.

I frowned. Dad had looked so flippant, so nonchalant as he dialed that number and sipped his coffee. What on earth? I was so flabbergasted I couldn't even think straight.

Half an hour ago, I was graduating from high school.

Now I was some kind of marker for my father's gambling debt. Now I was in an SUV with a bunch of scary looking men heading, where?

No one was saying anything. Nobody even looked at me. The blond guy was radiating a pissed-off vibe as he drove, and there was a sports event of some kind on the radio. I gulped hard and stared straight ahead, saying a silent prayer.

Tommy

It'd been a couple of weeks since Pop had told me about Tia O'Connor. A long couple of weeks.

I'd given the matter thought, like I'd promised him. In fact, I thought about it more than I'd care to admit because the more thought I gave it, the more it made sense. Getting married meant getting handed the keys to all of it. It meant I wouldn't be second guessed, it meant I'd be in total control.

The idea of owning a woman did things to me. I couldn't deny that I'd been thinking about the fact that in addition to being in control of the business, I'd be in control of her. Owning this girl, having her available for my every whim, it was stirring something in me. And did I have whims.

Something about the idea of a girl who was mine, a girl who probably hadn't already had dozens of sexual partners – it appealed to me on a deep level, a level so deep I was having trouble shaking what felt like cravings; the things I was imagining doing to her. Naw, I wasn't deprived but I certainly was depraved.

I'd dreamt about her almost every night since seeing her picture. Filthy dreams. I woke up every night a few times as a rule, anyway, but since seeing her picture I'd woken up sweaty, with a hard-on, after delicious dreams of her across my knee getting spanked and fingered, dreams of her wrists tied to my headboard, dreams of her on her knees in front of me, taking my cock into that gorgeous mouth with her hands tied behind her back with one of my belts.

It got even worse after I managed to gather intel about her because in addition to the way she looked, she had other qualities I liked. I decided to check out the goods myself, in person, because I'd put one of my men on detail to watch her and report her activities. After a week, he came to me with the report and some photos.

I'd probably never defined what my 'type' was before this, but I now knew. She had a smokin' hot body and though she was younger than I'd normally go for, she didn't look her age. I knew where she lived, where she worked, where she spent her time, who her friends were, and I knew what sort of person she was.

My man had taken candid photos of her at school, at play in the pool in her foster parents' back yard (in a barely-there string bikini). My cock twitched at the thought of her in that tiny bikini. Her silky, chestnut, shampoo commercial hair fell three quarters of the way down her back with bangs that swept gently across her forehead, and I'd been imagining wrapping the long length of her hair around my fist and pulling her head toward my cock. I imagined taking handfuls of it while I did her from behind.

She had the sort of lips women paid to upgrade to. While looking at her file, my jaw tightened at the fact that my man had taken this photo of her, looked at her in those scraps of material. I felt like a possessive prick, wanting to knock him out for even looking at her. She was semi-sexually active but not slutty. She was on birth control, but had no boyfriend for the past month or so.

Earl told me there was a punk ex-boyfriend sniffing around, trying to get her attention. She was giving him the brush-off. I had video of him trying to talk to her over a fence while she was in that bikini. She seemed like she could be a cock tease. She had a bit of sass, but not enough to come across like a bitch. No, it was just enough to make me want to bring her to heel.

The girl hadn't had it easy; her old man was a piece of shit, by the sounds of it. She worked part-time at an ice cream shop near the foster home and did some volunteer work at the animal shelter as well as at a nearby old folks' home. She wasn't a typical nineteen-year-old girl out to party and spend, and that appealed to me, too.

After way too much attention spent looking at videos of her and flipping through a file of photos and general intel, I decided to stroll in and size up the potential chemistry in person. Regardless of what she looked like, I needed to know if there would be any sort of spark before moving forward.

Yeah, most would say I should just let her go, let her go live her life. If I was a nice guy that's what I'd do. There were girls out there that I'd already been with who'd be more than happy to wear my ring and sleep in my bed. But I guess I'm not a nice guy. The thing was that Pop had a claim on her so either I took the gift, or he'd give her to someone else. Either way, she was now Ferrano family property. That was my justification, as twisted as that was. If I had to get married, she might as well become mine.

Yeah, I know; I guess I'm not even a little bit of a good guy.

* * *

Bells jingled over the door to the small store as I walked in. Music played and it had a fifties diner theme going with a long white counter flanked by a dozen or so red and chrome stools and half a dozen little red tables, some for two, some for four, in front of a big window that looked out to the busy street. She was working alone; the shop was empty except for a prepubescent kid playing on his handheld game system at the counter while nursing a drink and making an annoying slurping sound as it was obviously just a few ice cubes rattling around in the bottom of the cup. I gave him the 'scram' stare and jerked my chin toward the door. The kid gulped, grabbed his skateboard, and took off.

I stood at the counter and watched her. She was up on a footstool stocking a shelf above her head with small boxes of ice cream cones. She was humming along to the song on the radio, her arms over her head making her tank top ride up, showing her bare lower back and two sexy dimples at the base of her spine. My pants suddenly felt tight as I looked at the juicy heart-shaped ass popping from those tight low-rider jeans. And the knowledge that it was mine? In that moment, with that knowledge, I had to take a deep breath to stop myself from taking her right then and there.

She turned around and smiled at me expectantly. Then she instantly blushed. Yeah, I had that effect on women. Nope, she didn't look like a teenager in person, either. She looked closer to mid-twenties. Her pictures didn't even do justice; she was fucking beautiful.

"Can I help you?" she beamed and quickly moistened her full pink lips with the tip of her tongue, eying me in a way that I liked. It wasn't the look of a woman hunting man prey, which was a complete turn-off for me. No, this was shyness and anticipation. This was a girl tingling at the idea that the guy in front of her could be remotely interested in her. Clearly, she had no clue how beautiful she was. And obviously, she liked what she saw when she looked at me.

"I hope so." I smirked at her.

She climbed down and straightened her black tank top, pulling it down slightly to cover her midriff but resulting in revealing just the scalloped tops of the cups of a lace black bra and (probably unintentionally) giving me an even better view of her cleavage. Great rack. Full C-cup, maybe even a D.

"What do you recommend?"

She flushed even pinker and it was clear she'd seen where my eyes had landed. "Umm, we have ice cream, cold drinks. If you want something hot I can do coffee, hot chocolate, cappuccino..." She trailed off.

Hot. Yeah, I'd like something hot.

"Surprise me," I told her.

She chewed her lip shyly. "Well, what do you like?"

"I see plenty that I like. What do you like?" I asked, widening my eyes at her and then trailed my gaze from her eyes to her mouth, down to her hips, and then back up. I did this slowly, being very obvious that I was checking her out.

"Hmm." She smiled at me and eyed me up and down, too. "Hungry or thirsty?"

Mm.

"Hungry," I said.

"We don't have much for food, really. Popcorn, nachos, ice cream?" she suggested.

"What flavor?" I asked her.

"There's a list up there." She motioned behind herself.

"What's your favorite flavor?" I asked.

"Call me weird but I really just love plain old vanilla." She shrugged.

I almost laughed at her. My face split into a grin. I bet she did. I bet vanilla was all she'd been exposed to so far.

"You are weird," I said.

She wrinkled her nose at me and fuck, but it was adorable.

"Vanilla, when there are so many flavors to choose from?" I

drummed my fingertips on the counter, staring into the ice cream freezer, "Bah, vanilla sounds like a good start." I sat on a stool.

"One scoop or two?" she asked, flushing even pinker. I wondered if she picked up on the double entendre.

"Two." I was eyeing her luscious round tits.

"Cup or cone?" she asked.

"Cone." I raised a brow.

"Sugar cone?"

"Oh yeah," I said low and gave her another grin.

She gulped, fumbled, and got the ice cream for me. Then she put a cherry right in the middle of the top scoop. A fucking cherry. I could've come in my pants right then and there.

"That's three bucks," she said, holding it out to me with both hands demurely, but something flirty in those eyes. Gorgeous eyes. Jade green, long and thick black lashes.

Oh, it'd be a lot more than three bucks. I could buck all fucking night if I had her in my bed.

I put a twenty in her hand, then grabbed her wrist for a second before she could turn to the cash register. I told her to keep the change and then wiggled the tip of my tongue against the cherry and winked at her before letting go of her wrist. Then, I walked out.

I used the tip of my tongue to scoop the cherry into my mouth and dropped the cone in the trash bin outside the shop and glanced in the window. She was staring at me, mouth open. After a few flicks of the tongue behind my teeth I pulled out the stem and showed her that it was now knotted and then put it between my teeth, winked, and got into my car and drove directly to my father's office, tonguing that stem while I drove.

I didn't knock; I strolled right in, interrupting a phone call and ignoring the four other people sitting there with him at a conference table, one of them my brother.

Pop looked up at me and put his hand over the mouthpiece of the phone.

"Tia O'Connor? Make it happen," I told him, dropping the knotted cherry stem into the trash can beside the table.

"On it," he answered with a huge smile and then lifted his chin at Dario, my brother. Dare got up and cracked his knuckles.

"Let's go," Dare said to Bruce, Gus, and Earl, who were all sitting there with him.

Later that night, Dare called me and told me he'd visited Greg O'Connor and told him the score. He walked in and told him Tom Ferrano was calling in his debt. If he didn't have cash on the spot he was to hand over his daughter Tia, that Tia would be presented to Thomas Ferrano Jr. as potential marriage material and that if marriage didn't happen she'd remain Ferrano property in order to clear his debt. Dario had brought muscle with him, expecting resistance even though Pop told him not to bother.

O'Connor hadn't even seemed all that surprised, according to Dare. Said he knew that my father wasn't done with him yet and had a feeling this day would come. He said my father had warned a few weeks prior that Tia might be the payback for what'd happened *back in the day*, whenever and whatever that was.

O'Connor told my brother it was almost a relief that the day had come, and that Tom had chosen to handle things this way because he'd been carrying around the worry for years. What the fuck? Piece of shit. Whatever the beef was between him and my pop, he wasn't gonna even try to barter or fight for his daughter? What a sorry excuse for a father, for a man.

Of course, she was already mine in my head, so there was nothing he could do even if he had the money to pay the debt, but that the man wasn't even trying? He'd get zero respect from me.

Dare thought it was funny that Pop had done this to get me married off and said he was surprised that I was going through with it. I shrugged it off, told him it was a means to an end. We joked about the fact that he'd be next. I'd seen Dare date plenty; he got a lot of female attention and had even been engaged already, but she'd broken his heart and in return he'd broken the jaw of the guy she was fucking as well as bankrupted the guy's family's business. Since then he was about as interested in settling down as I was.

I saw Pop the next evening at dinner at his house with him, my two sisters, their families, and Pop's wife, wife number four if I hadn't lost count yet, and Pop told me on the side that he'd told O'Connor years back that he'd have his daughter someday. I tried to ask questions but got the brush off.

Why that son of a bitch didn't leave the country to protect his little girl was beyond me. I mean, we had reach across borders, but if you'd at least tried to get out of his line of sight maybe you'd have somewhat of a chance of getting off his radar. I knew O'Connor had left his kid to rot in foster homes right under my pop's nose while he put cocaine up his own nose, while he repeatedly bet all his earnings on the horses and in card games, while he paid next to no attention to his kid whatsoever. Knowing Pop was threatening his little girl, how could he stay around here?

I didn't know what the beef between Pop and O'Connor was about, but it had to be a pretty big beef for Pop to let a wound fester for years and then decide that the payment would come in the form of about 120 pounds of flesh. For whatever the reason was, I'd be getting that flesh in my hands right after she graduated from high school. It was all arranged. Dare would pick her up and deliver her to me.

Tia

The SUV stopped in front of a gatehouse and when the gates opened, continued up a semicircle driveway to park in front of a gorgeous Tudor-style house. A mansion, really. I clutched my purse close and when the SUV emptied, the Black, scary dude reached for my hand and helped me out. He gave me a little smile.

Hm, not so scary, really. Now that he'd smiled at me, he reminded me a little of Michael Clarke Duncan. The guy from the Green Mile isn't scary, just misunderstood. Maybe this guy wasn't scary. The other two *were* scary, though. Burly Number Two from the back seat looked a tad like Lou Ferrigno, *the Incredible Hulk*. Burly One looked like a total criminal – Sopranos or Godfather henchman type – angry dark eyes, uni-brow, deep acne scars on his cheeks. All three of them were imposing-looking men. The blond driver in the front looked little less scary, but his attitude was scarier than all the other guys. He was in maybe his mid-20s and while he was extremely good-looking, wearing an expensive suit, he looked pissed off and impatient. He seemed like the one in charge.

The Michael Clarke Duncan-looking dude finished helping me out of the SUV and *blond angry hot guy* motioned for me to follow him. I did, dread filling me.

I was on a gated property with several big, scary guys and I'd bet money they all carried guns. The blond guy led me through a big foyer into a room down a long hallway and rapped on a door.

"Come in," a man answered from the other side.

The three men waited in the hall while the blond guy opened the door and signaled for me to walk ahead of him. My heart felt like it was in my throat.

I was inside a large office with a man sitting behind a large executive-style desk. He had salt and pepper hair and light brown eyes. He was fit and handsome for his age, kind of George Clooney-ish. He wore a suit and had an air about him that said businessman or hot shot lawyer. But Dad said he was mafia, a mobster.

A guy in a mansion with all these thugs or whatever was buying debts from bookies? It didn't add up. How big could Dad's debt actually be? Who would front him more than a few hundred dollars on a poker game, knowing he wasn't capable of earning much more than the minimum wage?

"Athena, I'm Thomas Ferrano. Call me Tom for now. Please sit." He motioned toward a chair in front of his desk.

I sat. His name sounded familiar. His face sort of seemed familiar, too.

"Aren't you lovely? You graduated high school today, I hear. Congratulations."

I stared at him. Words won't form on my lips.

His gaze narrowed. "No need to be rude."

I shook my head, "I'm not trying to be rude. I'm just a bit overwhelmed. Thank you. For the congrats."

He nodded, curtly. "Dario, get a bottle of water for Athena."

Angry hot blond guy nodded and left the room.

"So, I take it your father filled you in? Why don't you tell me what he said to you, ah? He used to have an unfortunate habit of leaving out important facts. Maybe he still does."

Boy, did I know that.

Blond guy, Dario, returned quickly with a bottle of water and handed it to me, then left the office.

"Um thanks." I took a sip. "I haven't seen much of my father in years. He turned up today at my high school graduation and told me I had to be a marker for a few days so he could get money together to clear up a gambling debt."

Thomas Ferrano laughed. "Interesting spin."

My heart plummeted. Spin? If that wasn't the truth, what was?

"Isn't that the truth?" I asked, starting to tremble.

"Not exactly. Your father owes me a rather large debt, one I'm not sure he can ever actually repay." He looked at me expectantly.

"Why am I here, then?"

"Let's say you've been drafted." He smirked.

Huh?

"My son Tommy needs to get married. He hasn't found *Miss Perfect* yet. Your father owes me a great deal. I've agreed to consider writing off the debt if my son decides you're *Miss Perfect*."

I started to laugh. "Am I being punk'd?"

"Excuse me?" he asked and I knew, then, that he was serious.

"I don't understand." The room began to slowly turn. I was white-knuckled, gripping the arms of the chair I sat in.

"Simple, really. As of now you are property of the Ferrano family."

If my chin wasn't touching the floor right now, it must be awfully close. Had I been transported back to the dark ages? I didn't know what to say. I was totally and utterly gob smacked.

"So, I've arranged for you to be transported to Tommy's home. There, you two can get acquainted and go from there, see if this is an amicable arrangement for him."

For him? For him?

"What?" I can't fathom this. "No."

Don't I have to agree to this? I don't agree to this. He raised his index finger and his eyes narrowed. He took on a much more menacing look. "Listen carefully. This meeting, the one between you and my son, if it doesn't go well it won't bode well for your father and it may not bode well for you, either. We have many options available for where you could go. I think you'd prefer ending up with my son over the alternatives. We're a wealthy and powerful family so you could be in a much worse position, believe me. I'd advise you to cooperate. You're in an enviable position, Athena. I'll be seeing you soon. Tommy's brother will drive you. Dario!"

Enviable? Was this man whacked in the head?

The door opened and Dario popped his head in.

"Take Athena to your brother. Athena, don't be difficult. I wouldn't advise it. It was nice to see you again. You've grown up to be a lovely girl. An almost dead ringer for your mother."

He gave me a big smile. My blood ran cold.

My mother? This man knew my mother? See me again? When had he seen me before? This man was scary. The brother was scary. Their thugs or whatever they were --- really scary. Was I in the middle of the fricking dark ages or what? An arranged marriage to a mafia kingpin's son to save my father's life? This was nuts! If I was asleep, I wanted to wake up right now!

Dario led me back out to the SUV and two of the other guys got in, too. One had apparently opted out of this leg of the drive. They thought they needed muscle to get me from point A to point B, evidently. Were they afraid I'd try to run? I didn't know what the heck I was dealing with here so no, I wasn't about to run now before sussing things out. I didn't want to end up dead. I didn't want Dad to end up dead.

Did Dad really sell me out like this? I mean, he was a lousy father, for sure, but did he really sell me to the mafia in exchange for payment of his old gambling debts? Not a marker. Not temporarily. Sold, like chattel. Married off. No way. He was capable of a lot, but this? Surely not. This was North America and the 21st century. This kind of stuff didn't happen.

I combed through my memory. The name Ferrano rang bells. Was he known in the city as a mafia guy? Where had I heard his name from?

What might've been about ten minutes later, the SUV was pulling up in front of another set of gates. The drive had been quiet, more sports, I figured out was soccer, on the radio and no talking other than a "Woo" and a "Yes!" in unison from angry driver, err Dario, and burly guy number two (number one had opted out) on what must've been a goa. It'd all been white noise to me due to my state of mind.

"Wait here," Dario told me after getting past the gate and then he walked into the house alone. Me and the muscle sat in awkward silence.

My purse started ringing my ringtone for Ruby.

"Hand it over," Burly two ordered gruffly, and I knew he meant business.

I took my cell phone out and handed it to him.

Tommy

Dare was inside my doorway, "I come bearing gifts. I deliver your bride."

He gave a gallant bow and then snickered. I'd just gotten home and had known they'd be along soon.

I rolled my eyes. "Fucking Pop."

He laughed, leaning against the wall. "She's a looker, bro. He did good."

"Don't look at my bride." I punched his shoulder playfully. "And just you wait. I'm sure he's lining up someone for you to marry next."

"Since you'll be head of the family, I think that means you get to pick, doesn't it?"

I threw my head back and let out an evil laugh. "Oh yeah. And just you wait!"

"I'll go get her," he told me, grinning. He knew I'd have his back. Truth be told, he couldn't wait for Pop to head out to pasture. Dare and I had plans for taking the family business to the next level together. We were half-brothers and five years apart, but we'd grown up together and were alike in many ways. He was the only other person I'd 100% trust to have my back. I didn't even trust my father 100%.

I didn't think he'd set out to do harm to me intentionally, but I knew that we were all pawns, to a degree, and that his idea of having my back and Dare's idea of the same would diverge.

"Put her in my bedroom and lock the door," I said and wiggled my eyebrows. Then I walked into my office to tie up a few loose ends before the big reveal. I didn't know much about her yet but, from what I did know so far, I guessed that she wouldn't have taken the news of today lightly. I was anticipating, even hoping for some resistance and looking fucking forward to it.

Tia

The guy with my phone gave it to Dario when he came back to the SUV.

"Let's go," Dario said to me with a chin jerk.

I couldn't run. The gate was shut. Would I run, though, if it wasn't? Thomas Ferrano threatened me, pretty much saying Dad was a goner if I didn't cooperate, and maybe me, too. But, what would happen to me here?

I followed Dario into a large house, feeling a little shaky and *a lot* queasy. I couldn't help but notice the architectural details of the place. It looked like a pretty hacienda, had an orange terra cotta roof, white parging with archways. There were loads of flowers everywhere. Climbing vines, overflowing baskets.

Inside the front door was a foyer that opened to a staircase directly to my left and a long hallway under an arch to my right. This was the kind of house Mom and I used to talk about having, a hacienda and beautiful gardens. It was her dream to live in a house like this and it'd become my dream, too. I shivered at the thought of my mom, unable to fathom how she'd feel about all this.

"Follow me," Dario led the way up the stairs, down a long hall with several closed doors to a set of double doors, and then opened them both and walked in. I followed inside.

"Bag?" he motioned.

I hesitated.

"I'll give your bag and phone to Tommy. He'll decide when you can have them back."

I was trembling. I couldn't help it. I was in a big master suite with a king-size bed, about to be left for someone who thought they had a claim on me. I was supposed to be at a party celebrating the end of my childhood and the beginning of life as an adult. An adult with choices, a future, independence.

This was not that. This was something else. This something else was bad. Possibly very bad. He nodded politely, reached over to the bedside table and picked up a cordless phone, and then he left with it. I let out a big breath, as if I'd been holding it in for hours. I had to keep my cool somehow. If I had a freak out, there was no telling what would happen to me. If I kept my cool I could suss everything out and then make a calculated decision about what to do.

I surveyed the room. It was nice, luxurious, even. Soft dove gray walls, big dark wood furniture, lots of leather, exposed beam ceilings with ceiling fans. It didn't really match the hacienda theme outside, and I wouldn't say it was my taste, but it was nice. There was a big difference from this room to the kind of room I was used to. The small room I'd shared with Bethany was small, containing two twin loft beds with desks underneath, drawers for stairs. Here was a room I was expected to share with a man. I cringed, looking at the bed, fearing what I'd be expected to do. I knew nothing about this Tommy. All I knew was that I was in a pickle of a situation, and I didn't know how I'd get myself out.

Rose, Cal, and everyone must've been worried about me right now. Or had Dad made up an excuse? They'd probably report me missing if they didn't hear from me in a few hours. They knew how stoked I was about this party. Rose had made my favorite artichoke and spinach dip as well as mozzarella sticks plus a plethora of appetizers that the other girls had requested. There was a huge cake for us, two thirds vanilla and a third chocolate because me and Mia preferred vanilla and Beth preferred chocolate. Cal had suggested three separate cakes or cupcakes with icing slathered all over to hold them all together but we were all so close we wanted the same cake. Rose had said she had our photos put on in icing. I never saw my cake. A tear slid down my cheek. Then I heard the doorknob turn and I dashed it away and held the others back. I put my lips together and stood still, back straight, took a deep breath, and waited.

3

Tommy

When I opened the door and saw her standing there, I wanted to capture the moment in time. It went from her being stoic, trying to hide her fear, standing tall and rigid in a gorgeous, clingy black dress, high heels, her hair up in a sophisticated style, to the flash of recognition that led to her forehead crinkling and her eyes staring at me accusingly.

I stepped in, closed the door behind myself, and I stood there, waiting for her to say something.

Tia

Oh my God. OH MY GOD! The hottie from the ice cream parlor. I couldn't believe this! I told my friends about him and how gorgeous he was to the point that the subject had been banned because they got sick of my going on and on about him. I'd fricking dreamt about him, about him and his cherry stem-tying tongue. And here he was. This was him.

He's tall. Like really tall, six foot three, six foot four, maybe. Caramel brown kind of curly, kind of messy-on-purpose hair, chiseled face, light brown, sort of whiskey-colored, eyes. He resembles his father. His mouth? Drool-worthy. He had a bit of a five o'clock shadow just like the other day. He was standing in a suit, a black suit with a dark blue dress shirt and no tie. That suit fit him very well. He looked like a million dollars. Five million dollars. He has to be close to ten years older than me. He has to be the sexiest fricking man I've ever laid eyes on. Ever. But What.The.Fuck?

If this were ancient times or whenever arranged marriages were common and I'd been brought up to know that I'd someday have an arranged marriage, I'd have been thrilled at what was standing in front of me.

Obviously, I'd been betrothed to a wealthy gorgeous man. It could be worse. A lot worse. But this wasn't ancient times. I'm not thrilled. I'm freaked right the heck out. Not only are my choices being taken away and not only am I under threat, but this is a fricking mafia family. What the heck?

"Athena," he said, a little smirk on his face. That meeting at the ice cream parlor was so obviously no accident.

I stood still, totally in shock.

"Tommy Ferrano," he said. "Nice to officially meet you." He extended his hand.

I snickered and folded my arms. He gave me a little smile and pulled his hand back without reacting, then proceeded to circle me. Circle me! Fear prickled my scalp because I suddenly felt like prey; felt like a piece of meat. That's exactly how he circled me.

"So, I'm told you're missing a party right now, one that's important to you," he said, meeting my eyes with his and stopping directly in front of me. Close to me. Too close. In my personal space, really.

I nodded slightly, feeling my skin heat up under his appraisal.

Damn, he was tall, broad, and authoritative. I felt like I was at a huge disadvantage.

I was. Of course, I was; I was standing here in his space. Not just his space, his bedroom.

"Come; I'll drive you."

He stepped back and opened the door with a sweep of his hand, motioning for me to go on ahead of him. Confused, I walked out. When I got to the bottom of the stairs, I saw my purse on a table beside a big brass bowl with multiple sets of keys in it. He grabbed a set of keys and passed me my purse. He reached into his front pants pocket and pulled out my phone and passed it to me, his finger brushing my hand as he did. He gave me a little smile, eyes sparkling with what looked like mischief. I swallowed hard.

Once outside, he hit a button on his keychain and one of four garage doors opened. He put his hand on the small of my back and led me toward it. I flinched at the contact, but let him lead me there. He opened the passenger door to a black convertible sports car for me and closed it after I was in and then got into the driver's seat and proceeded to back out of the garage, turning around and then driving forward down the driveway, through the now opened gate.

Talk about uncomfortable! He was so nonchalant, and I knew this wasn't a situation that called for nonchalance. The brother had locked me up, took my phone, treated me like a prisoner. The father had threatened me. I'd been surrounded by burly goons up until now. But Ice Cream Parlor Hottie, err Tommy, was being the exact opposite. Even still, I was more uncomfortable than even before because this was him. This was the guy who's going to decide my fate. And he was going to mess with my head; I knew it. He'd already come into my work and flirted with me, which was obviously no coincidence, and now he was here, with all the power, and dropping me off at my house with my phone, like it was nothing, like it was no big deal.

I just sat, frozen, with my hands in my lap, absorbing the fact that control over my own life had been snatched away from me. He was inches away from me, of course, and I could smell his cologne, which smelled leathery, spicy, a bit musky. He smelled good, not like the guys I knew who practically bathed in Axe. This man wore just enough. He had this presence, this masculinity and authority I couldn't even put into words. I had no idea what to say, where to even start. So, I just sat there.

Around fifteen minutes later, when we were in front of Rose and Cal's, he finally broke the silence.

"Say nothing about any of this to the Crenshaws or anyone else," he said, leaning over close, uncomfortably close, looking in my eyes. "I'll pick you up here in three hours. And so you know, Tia, obedience is rewarded; defiance is punished. Remember that." He winked at me and flashed his watch at me, showing me the time.

I'm sure I must've looked at him like he'd lost his mind. I didn't know what to say, so I got out of the car, feeling like something slowly crawled up my spine. I felt his eyes on me, watching me, until I entered the house. I looked back before entering and the way he was staring at me made my blood run cold. Gorgeous or not, he was obviously a very dangerous man, and I had no frame of reference for this situation. I needed to think.

How would I get a chance to think, though? I had three hours in a house bustling with activity, people everywhere. Kids that live here, graduating kids, their family members, Rose, Cal, the grandparents. I heard Ruby shouting my name. I couldn't tell any of them what was going on with me, no way.

"Where were you?" she cried out, running to me, her dark ringlets bouncing. Rose was behind her, looking expectantly and cautiously at me.

"I'm sorry, I..." I didn't know how to finish; I almost started to cry.

Rose rushed over and threw her arms around me. "It's okay darling, come; let's get something to eat." She directed me to the dining room table, which was covered with dishes of food, people swarming it. She probably just assumed my father had disappointed me. She didn't push for answers.

God, but I loved this family. I didn't know what to say. I had no idea what awaited me in three hours' time, but I knew one thing for sure – *fear*. I was afraid.

Mia bounded over to us. "Did you find your hottie and take off on us for a romp?"

She and Bethany laughed but Ruby was eyeing me suspiciously. If they only knew.

Tommy Ferrano had come into my work and had checked me out, made himself known to me, had flirted with me, even. How long had this been planned for? Where was my dad now? I didn't even have a phone number to call and ask him what was going on. The look on his face as I pulled away was of defeat but then two seconds later it was as if nothing happened. Drinking coffee, talking on the phone, not looking devastated. Was it all for show? And Mr. Ferrano had acted like the whole marker thing was just a ploy by Dad. What was the real story here? Who was I dealing with, really?

I excused myself to the bathroom and sent Dad a Facebook message from my phone, demanding he call or text me immediately.

> **Dad! What on earth? These guys say I have to marry the mafia guy's son to clear your debt. MARRY! And if I don't do it, we could be what? Dead? And if he doesn't like me, I still don't get to go home, they have 'other' options. WTF? Please tell me this is a prank, Dad. Write ASAP, come to the house (I'll be here 3 hrs.), or call my cell! After that I guess I'm back at Tommy Ferrano's house (but they may take my phone again). It's on the corner of Jane St. and River Rd.**

I knew, after Mom died, that Dad had dealings with less than desirables. Maybe he did before, too.

I remembered people coming to the door for money after Mom died. I remembered hiding in my room during the poker games in our apartment when things would sometimes get loud and out of control. More than once I'd seen Dad with bruises on his face and blackened eyes. I vividly recalled his jaw being wired shut after a night when he'd left me alone the whole night and came back in the morning, unable to talk. I'd also had guys bust in behind me when coming home from school one day and beat Dad up right in front of me, calling him a lowlife deadbeat. What was I in for here?

Dad had always been fascinated with the mob world. Like, crazy-fascinated. He and I used to watch mob movies and he'd give me a running commentary with facts throughout, about real-life mobsters, about parallels, about code of conduct, hierarchies, and so forth. He watched mob movies, mob documentaries, and the mafia came up in conversation all the time. I never got the fascination but remember my mother getting pissed about him letting me watch *The Godfather* when I was about six. I was here, but not enjoying my graduation party. Despite the laughter and the fun everyone else was having, I was in my own head, but couldn't delve deep enough to ponder my fate because the reality might be too difficult to face. I just felt numb and disjointed.

I kept staring at the clock and time was flying. I knew he'd be back for me and didn't know what'd be in store for me tonight. How would I tell everyone I wasn't going to the dance? Tomorrow was the day I was supposed to be moving into Nono and Nona's. My room here was already almost totally packed.

"You okay, sweetheart?" Cal put his arm around me as Rose served everyone generous slices of the large, beautiful cake with our three smiling faces on it. Susie was smiling at me with a sad look on her face. She probably figured Dad had disappointed me, too.

"Mm hm." I tried not to choke up.

"We are so proud of you. You're always a part of our family, okay?" He kissed my temple and moved away.

I nodded. He wasn't usually the touchy-feely sort. My heart sank. I stepped out onto the porch and saw that Tommy Ferrano was there, parked on the street, waiting for me. I didn't know if he was just half an hour early or if he hadn't even left. I didn't know if I should go to the car or go back inside and enjoy what might be my last thirty minutes of freedom.

"Tia, come! Open your graduation gifts!" Ruby called from the family room.

Tommy

Damn that douchebag Greg O'Connor. It pissed me off that he'd do this to his kid. Pop had already told me that he'd broken the news to Tia that she wasn't just a marker to be held temporarily, like her father had said. She was now property of the Ferrano family. My property, if I wanted her.

When I'd seen her in my bedroom it took everything in me to not rip her clothes off, throw her on the bed, and take her. She'd been mine from the minute Pop had told me about her and it didn't take long for me to feel it down to my bones. I hadn't even been with anyone since seeing her face that first time. I had zero desire to touch anyone. Anyone but her. And because I typically had pussy at my disposal every single day and it'd been weeks, I was on fire for this girl. She'd be in big trouble if I couldn't bring this need in me to heel.

I thought about taking my frustrations out on someone else, to lock it down, save her from me, but I didn't want anyone else. I didn't even think I'd get hard for anyone else because I was looking forward to having her that much.

She'd stood there looking surprised, then confused, then defiant, and I couldn't wait to get her back to my place, to my bed, where we could explore a variety of her emotions together. Fear, submission, satisfaction.

Now she was on the porch of the Crenshaw house, staring at me sitting in my car. I tilted my seat back to show her I was in no hurry. She disappeared into the house.

Tia

I told Rose, Cal, and Ruby that I had something to take care of and that I didn't know when I'd be back. Rose and Cal assumed it was just to do with my dad and, as usual, gave me space. Ruby pummeled me with questions.

"I can't, Ruby. I can't talk about it."

"When will you be at the dance? Nick texted me and he really wants to see you."

"I don't know. I'll try. But if I don't come, don't worry."

"If you don't come? If you don't come! This is the last hurrah before you become a grown up. What do you mean if you don't come?"

She was in hysterics. It was time for me to leave.

"I have to go," I said, pulling her into a quick hug, "I'll be back ASAP. Okay?"

Mia and Bethany were approaching, so I decided to make my exit *tout de suite* before the questions started coming at me rapid-fire.

Ruby looked so confused. It wasn't like me to leave her in the dark. I hated to walk away, and I hoped she wouldn't follow me. I didn't know what to say. I was confused, myself!

I left the porch and walked toward the car. Tommy brought his seat back upright and stepped out to open the passenger door. I got in and when he closed it, I glanced over my shoulder at the house and saw Ruby and Rose watching me from the front door with confusion on their faces. Of course they were confused. I was getting into an expensive convertible with a man they'd never met.

I put my seatbelt on. Tommy turned the ignition and drove off. I sat, frozen, numb, not sure what to say or do. Then we approached Nick on the street, jaywalking, heading toward Rose and Cal's house. He made eye contact with me and then his jaw dropped because Tommy sped up and then swerved to just miss hitting him. My eyes shot to Tommy who was staring straight ahead, a devious smirk on his face. Did he know who Nick was to me?

Tommy

When we got back to my house, she followed me back upstairs to my bedroom without a word, until the door was closed. Then she dropped her purse on the floor and her fists balled up. Now she was shooting imaginary daggers at me from her eyes.

"Would you please tell me what's going on?" she blurted. "The story my father told me is very different from what your father told me. And your father didn't say much. You've gotta admit, this is not normal."

I removed my suit jacket, dropped it on the bed, rolled up my sleeves, sat on the sofa that was in front of the bed, and propped my arms on the back of it. "Sit."

"I'd rather not," she said, staring at the ink on my left forearm. She swallowed hard. She was trying to hide that she was intimidated.

Her legs went on for miles in that tight black dress. She wore heels and damn, she had a smokin' body. The temperature in the room rose as we sized one another up. I undid my top shirt button and moistened my lips.

"What's going on here is this." I leaned forward, resting my forearms on my thighs, looking at her face. "Your father owes my father something and he's paid that debt off using you as currency." This was all I knew, although I did plan to get to the bottom of it. I shrugged like it was no big deal.

"Why would anyone pay a debt with a person? And I'm not my father's property; he had no right to agree to those terms."

I liked how she was looking me right in the eye. I smiled at her.

"So, your father arranged a marriage?" she continued, "And even more strange, you agreed. And my father agreed to this as well?"

I mulled the question over for a moment. "Not exactly."

"Then what, exactly?"

She was on the verge of losing her temper. I wanted that. I wanted her to lose her temper so I could bring her in line. I could barely stand waiting for that moment of realization – that moment when she got an inkling of what she was *in* for.

"We've had no real resistance from your father. He handed you over willingly, knowing you might be married into my family and that you might not be. Even said it was a bit of a relief. My father would like to see me married before he retires and hands over the helm of the family business. I haven't agreed to anything. He's given you to me as an option."

"What if I refuse? Wait, what do you mean a relief?"

"This isn't up to you," I answered.

She winced, "Um, yeah, it is. You can't force someone to marry you."

"Can't I?" I gave her a smile.

Her forehead crinkled. "Then what if you don't take that option?"

I tapped my index finger on my lips for a moment, assessing her body language. She shuffled uncomfortably, no doubt dying to get out of those heels and away from me. I didn't want her out of the shoes. I wanted her in them, them and nothing else. I wanted those heels up behind my ears.

"Then I'd get to decide what happens to you instead."

She let out a slow breath. "And what would that be?"

I smiled, "Could be any number of things."

"Like?"

I snickered. She was trying to mask her anger and fear underneath a bit of snark, but she was failing.

"Could I be... killed?" she asked me.

I raised my brows. "Or worse."

Confusion swept over her face. She didn't know what I meant. She doesn't know there are things worse than death. She doesn't know that many women sold into slavery wished for death because of the hell that was their existence.

"So you're having trouble finding someone to marry?" She eyed me up and down as if I was something she scraped off her shoe. "That's why you're doing this?"

"Not exactly."

Tia

He sat on that couch staring at me like he wanted to have me for breakfast. He was, to me, what a cunning devil might look like if he were disguised as a handsome man. Oozing with sex appeal and danger. And deception. And more danger. And arrogance.

He'd come into the ice cream parlor on my last day there and flirted with me. Today, he looked like the same guy, but acted different – almost like he was the evil twin. His eyes and his overall demeanor were vastly different. The light and playfulness in his eyes wasn't there. There was intensity instead, something I could only describe as a sort of darkness, or evil.

His body was broad and muscular, but not bulky. His arms were muscled and because his sleeves were rolled up to the elbows, I could see swirly tribal-looking tattoos on his forearm. His jaw was tight as he assessed me. I didn't know what to do with myself. I didn't know if I should try to reason with him, to plead for him to let me go, or to sit and shut up, and wait see what his next move would be.

I couldn't take this pain in my feet any longer. I sat on the bed, leaned over, and loosened my shoes. My feet were freaking killing me. I wasn't used to walking in heels this high. I'd wanted to look grown up for my high school grad and they definitely helped with that, adding to my 5'4" height. I let them dangle and one fell to the floor. I flexed my toes in relief. I looked up and he was staring at my legs.

I wanted to ask 'what, exactly?' again but suspected I wouldn't get a straight answer, so I said, "I'm, uh, I'm expected tonight at a graduation party. And tomorrow I'm supposed to move into my own apartment, and–"

He cut me off. "Obviously, things have changed."

I opened my mouth, but nothing came out.

"If there's anything important from your old life, it can be picked up. Or we don't look back and I replace everything." He was still looking at my legs.

"So, that means..." I wasn't getting it. Did this mean he wanted to marry me? He didn't even know me!

"Let's see how this goes, call it a trial engagement," he said, answering my unspoken question. "There are some ground rules. I'll fill you in on those shortly. Right now, I have something to do. It's best you stay here until I go over the rules with you."

"Wait, trial engagement? What if I refuse?"

He snickered and then raised a brow at me challengingly. "You don't want me to answer that."

I believed that. A chill crawled up my spine. "So, I'm your fiancée now? Just like that?"

He grinned. "Just like that." He got up, and left. He just left me sitting on the bed.

I heard a text alert on my phone. I pulled it out of my purse. Nick.

Can't wait to c u tonite ;) U looked hot today. So who the fuck was that asshole in the convertible?

The door swung back open, and Tommy snatched my phone from my hand. "You can have a phone after we go over the rules." His eyes were a bit crazed as he looked at the screen and then put my phone into his pocket. "You won't be seeing Nick again."

The door shut.

Trial engagement? Based on what, on an order from a mafia godfather? No romantic candlelit dinner with a guy who loved me, down on one knee in candlelight, telling me he wanted to spend the rest of his life with me. Nope. Instead I got a forced engagement with underlying threats. Lovely. What now, though? How could I get out of this without getting hurt or killed or without Dad getting hurt or killed?

Tommy

Her phone rang a little while later with the name, "Mia" on it. I ignored it. Then a text came through from the name "Bethany" with

"Where the bleep r u and who was THAT who you left with?" I shut it off. My own phone rang immediately afterwards. I glanced at the screen and debated rejecting the call, but shook my head and answered, "Yeah, Pop?"

"Well?"

"Well, what?"

"Who do you think will win the playoffs? Shit, what do you think I mean? What about the girl?"

"I haven't decided yet," I answered.

"Of course, you have, Tommy. Please. Like I don't know you. You tell me you really haven't decided and I'll be–"

I cut him off, "Pop, give me five minutes, will ya?"

"I'll give you a few days. Dinner Sunday at my house. If you're keeping her, bring her with you. Then we'll celebrate. If you come alone...well..."

I had things to do. The sooner they were done, the sooner I'd be back in my bedroom with her.

"Gotta go, Pop."

"Okay, my boy," he said, and I could almost see his cocky smile through the phone.

I ended the call.

Tia

I was pacing. What else could I do? I was in this bedroom, waiting for him to come and tell me what his rules were. Rules. Pff. I couldn't believe this.

A million thoughts flitted through my brain, and I couldn't think straight. All I could do was pace back and forth and back and forth. I could try to walk out and leave, but what would happen if I did? All the scary dudes and the gates and everything made me think it'd just be a waste of my time. But there had to be a way out of this. Could I reason with this guy?

Tommy

I stepped into the bedroom a few hours later. She was in my bed, watching TV. The sight of this girl in my bed stirred my sex drive *big time*. She'd taken her hair down and it hung down her back like a glossy curtain. Her shoes were on the floor; she had her feet tucked under herself. She was against my pillows, hugging one against herself. Her eyes were a little puffy, most of her make-up gone. She'd been crying.

Her eyes widened at the sight of me as I strolled to the other side of the bed and sat down beside her. I could see she was trying to stay frozen in place but she was failing. Trembling. I reached into my pocket and pulled out a heart-shaped ring box. I set it down between us. She stared at the box like it might bite her.

"You're not ready to wear it yet, that's fine. I'll put it on the table. We'll discuss later. Our engagement's contingent on several things; we'll see how it goes. In the meantime, there are a few rules. Want a drink? We can discuss."

She closed her eyes and nodded. A tear slid down her cheek. She was chewing her juicy-looking bottom lip. I was so fucking turned on right now.

Before I could calculate the move, the back of my hand touched the tear. She winced. Involuntarily, I groaned low in my throat. It must've sounded like a growl to her. Goosebumps rose on her arms. I pulled my hand back, got up, then walked to the wet bar, dropping the ring box on the dresser on the way.

My room was pretty self-contained with a small fridge, a fully stocked bar, an office area, sitting area, ensuite bathroom, and doors that led to a balcony that had a hot tub and stairs that led down to the backyard where there was a pool and patio. Pop had bought me this house and presented it to me a few months ago on my 29th birthday as a surprise. I had the money to buy my own house, with cash even, but had been content living in the condo. In hindsight, I should've known that this, the engagement, was the next step. It had five other bedrooms, quarters for staff, and a two-bedroom pool house. Why did I need all this space unless I was starting a family? I was still getting used to having people around all the time.

He'd been inching me toward taking the next step and now was gifting me a bride so I could easily step in to be handed the reins. I was thinking it'd be my wedding and his retirement party all on the same day.

I poured two glasses of red wine and handed her one. She now sat with her legs dangling over the edge of my bed with a look on her face that told me she was trying to hold it together despite wanting to fall apart. This trait would serve her well as my wife. Through her black stockings I could see that her toes were painted red, the same as her fingertips. The same as the shade her lips had been when she arrived. Her lipstick was gone. I could barely restrain myself. I couldn't wait to taste those lips and make those toes curl.

"Come." I grabbed her hand and led her to the sofa. She pulled her hand away but sat beside me.

"It's unfortunate that your father put you in this situation," I said, "And I have no respect for what he did. But that said, this is the situation. You were given to me as a gift. That makes you mine."

She blanched. My heartrate picked up pace with excitement; I wouldn't show her that excitement yet, though.

"So, it's important to me that you understand and follow my rules. Not following these rules is dangerous. Deadly."

She kept her eyes focused on the carpet.

"Rule number one, I own you."

Shock flashed across her face as her eyes met mine. I felt it in the groin, so I said it again.

"This means exactly what it sounds like. I own you. You're mine. Mine to do what I want with. This means you obey my orders. If not, you face consequences. Being mine means that if I want you marrying me and I choose to give you everything that's mine, that's what happens. If it means keeping you in my bedroom and using you however I want, never letting you see the light of day, that's what it means. If it means shipping you off somewhere and selling you to a pimp in Bangkok or Tijuana who wants to turn you into a five-dollar whore that's what it means. You need to understand the gravity here and come to terms with this as soon as possible. The sooner the better. Any privilege or comfort you get is because I allow it. I can take it away. All of it. Do you understand?"

She didn't answer. She looked down at the floor and her chin started quivering.

"The concept of ownership might be foreign to you but it's a concept you need to learn fast. Tia, look at me."

She looked up and what I saw in her eyes was pure and utter defiance. Perfect. A muscle in my cheek involuntarily twitched. I wasn't ready to reveal all my cards yet, but she needed a glimpse. And I wanted to push her, see what she'd do.

I stood up and continued, "Because I own you, I'll do what I want to you. Since you chose not to answer my question, I'll reiterate: if that means that I want you to wear my ring and have my babies with the run of this house, you'll do it. If it means you simply stay tied to my bed until I get tired of fucking you, so be it. I'm in charge. You obey me, things go well. You defy me? They don't."

Fear flickered in her eyes for a beat, but she continued to stare up at me, right into my eyes, trying to be brave. I liked it. I liked it a lot. Yeah, I'm a sick fucker. And the only thing scarier than a sick fucker is a sick fucker with power. If I was going to have to marry to get all the power I'd damn well get as much pleasure as possible from it. Fear and defiance rolled up in one? She was perfect. Maybe that's why I'd waited so long. This was coming for me. Her.

Yeah, Dare was right; Pop did do good with this choice for me. In the moment I was feeling something new. Bliss? She was mine and I felt it deep inside. John Lewis was right about the rush here. I'd never felt this level of excitement, this sense of ownership with a woman before. I was standing in front of her, towering over her, and I was going to wipe that defiance right off her face.

"Do you understand?"

She didn't answer. Her eyes narrowed.

I snickered and continued,

"I'll let it sink in for a moment, then. Rule number two, you reveal nothing to anyone about anything that you see, hear, or suspect to do with my business activities, my family, my personal life, or my preferences. You don't discuss me with people outside of my family or my house and you don't disclose information about me or what happens in this house or especially in this bedroom with anyone. The rules are simple. I'm in charge and you keep your mouth shut. The rest we will figure out as we go. I hope you're a smart enough girl that I don't need to lay out consequences. Hearing about who I am, you probably have an idea of what I'm capable of. If you don't, you will soon enough. You shouldn't test your limits with me. I'm not a patient guy and I like doling out punishments. A lot."

She closed her eyes. Now she was trembling not so subtly. Fuck, my cock was straining against my pants. I sipped my wine, put it down, then strode over to close the blinds on the doors that led to the deck. When I turned back around to look at her, she sat holding the wineglass, eyes squeezed shut tight. Then she took a deep breath, looked up, and stared me right in the eye. The girl hadn't said anything yet, but she had balls. I could see it. I looked forward to some sparring.

I unbuttoned my shirt the rest of the way and shrugged to let it drop. Her eyes never wavered from mine, but I saw her swallow hard. I sauntered toward her.

She shakily raised the glass of wine to her lips and tipped it back and drank it all at once. Then she slammed the glass down on the coffee table and stood. She eyed me from head to toe to head again. It made my heartrate pick up. She was ready to fight with me.

Tia

I summoned as much inner strength as I could muster, despite wanting to cower and weep, and I glared at him. I glared hard.

"If you think for one fucking second that you can just steal my life from me you've got another–"

He cut me off, physically. In an instant, he lunged from several feet away to in front of me, and then his hand was on my throat. He used his grip to press me against a wall. He towered over me, staring down at me, breathing heavily, his lips an inch from my temple. He wasn't squeezing, but the grip was possessive, making a point.

"You are so fucking sexy," he said slowly in a low and scary voice, his eyes burning into me.

His body was flush against mine, and his erection poked me in the abdomen. "I can't wait to be inside of you."

Holy shit. I forgot how to breathe for a second.

I finally gulped against his hand and tried to regain my bearings. I was breathless, totally surprised, and pretty much petrified. I tried to slink away from him, but he tightened the grip on my throat just a little. My hands came up and I tried to pull on his wrist to get him to let go. He wasn't cutting off my air supply, but it was firm and scary. His jaw tightened. My nails dug into his wrist until I drew blood. His eyes darted down and when he saw the blood, I saw something shift in his gaze.

"I was about to dare you to give me a reason, but it looks like you just did."

He let go of my throat and hauled me by the arm to the bed, then threw me down on it so I was on my stomach. He instantly climbed onto me, and pinned my arms above my head. I let out a groaning protest and tried to struggle. I felt his dick digging into my ass. Oh no. Please no.

He let one hand go and caught both of my wrists in the other hand, re-pinning them to the bed. His free hand ripped my dress upwards so that the part that was covering my bottom tore. Humiliation, mortification, the plethora of emotions flooded through me.

Underneath that dress was a pair of black lace stay-up stockings. I also had on a black lace thong so my dress wouldn't have underwear lines. I never thought when I'd put them on they'd put me in peril. I thought, I'm about to become an adult, I'm going to dress like one. Now I regretted that with every fiber of my being because it meant that Tommy Ferrano was looking at my might-as-well-be bare ass, looking at lingerie on me, and I was helpless to do anything about it. I was totally pinned.

"Look at this…" He palmed at my rear end and snapped the thong quickly.

"No! Don't!" I screeched. His palm was hot. Or maybe my skin was hot. I didn't know which. He rubbed it for a second.

His mouth was right against my ear and hot breath tickled me, so I squirmed, and then he growled low in his throat. "You're a very naughty girl telling me *no*." Then his hand wedged under my hips and he cupped me between the legs. I gasped. I felt a finger dip into the panties and touch my opening. Oh no. God, no.

He groaned. "How come you're wet down here, Tia?" He let out a little chuckle, a supremely pleased one. "Could it be? Do you enjoy being overpowered?"

I squeezed my eyes shut tight, and held my breath. His finger circled leisurely and then I felt him gyrate ever so slightly against my behind.

"You do. Fuck. And you're all mine." His tongue was now tracing from my earlobe up the ridge of my ear. "How did I get this lucky?"

"Not karma, that's for sure, asshole. And I will never, do you hear me, never ever be yours." I grunted this, trying to squirm away. Why did I say that? Why was I provoking him?

I was infuriated at the idea of my future being ripped away from me and crumpled up like a sheet of paper. I was furious with my father for doing this or for doing nothing about this. I was mad at myself for not being stronger, not finding a way to get this guy off of me.

I was also mad because he was right, I was wet down there. And I didn't understand why my body was reacting like this. Yes, this was the super-hot guy from the ice cream parlor who made me melt when he tongued that cherry provocatively. And okay, this was the same guy I'd rubbed myself thinking about that same night and the next night, imagining being under his body. But I imagined nothing like this.

I'd been wrong, so wrong, to fantasize about this guy. This was a dangerous man who had me pinned to his bed, who'd grabbed my throat, ripped my graduation dress, who threatened me. Who'd said he *owned* me. Who'd said scary things that were a nightmare come true to any woman.

"You're disgusting," I spat.

His finger left and his weight was no longer on me but then he slapped me hard on the ass. I shrieked. Then he slapped my ass again and then stuck his finger in me again. I frowned and held my breath.

"Oh, but you are mine," he whispered, "I like your spirit, Tia. And I look forward to breaking it."

Despair crested over me at those words. He let go of me then and he was off the bed. I whimpered, devastation filling me, but I stayed still. He stood behind me; I could hear him breathing heavily.

A long moment passed, and then I heard a zipper. Oh no. No, no. I scrambled up and tried to bolt for the door. He was fast. He caught me by the arm and walked me back to the bed and pushed me down.

"I'm not gonna fuck you tonight, Tia," he said, watching me scramble up to the headboard. "You can relax."

He kicked off his shoes, toed off his socks and then dropped his suit pants, leaving him in just a tight pair of black boxer briefs. He fetched the dark blue shirt he'd been wearing earlier and tossed it at me. It landed beside me. He looked so calm. How could he be so calm with what he was doing to me? What kind of sick psycho was I dealing with?

"You can sleep in that. Hurry back." Smirking, he motioned with his chin toward what I'd already discovered was the bathroom door on the opposite end of the room. He stood there, arms folded. He looked even better without clothes than I'd imagined, not that it was comforting – not one bit. His tattoo traveled from just above his wrist up his arm and over his shoulder. He was strong, muscular, someone I'd have a lot of trouble fighting off.

He eyed me hungrily. "Like what you see, Tia?"

I shook my head. "Not at all." I grabbed the shirt and headed for the bathroom, hearing him laugh at me as I closed the door.

I sat on the floor against the door for the longest time, crying face buried in my knees, ass on the cold floor. I heard a door. Maybe he was gone.

I took off my ripped dress, removed my stockings, which now had a big snag in them, kept my bra and underwear on, and put the blue dress shirt on. I caught my reflection in the mirror. I looked horrible. Tear tracks and black eye makeup streaks on my cheeks, my eyes all red, my hair a disheveled mess.

I washed my face with hot water and a fluffy white washcloth that had been on the vanity and then hung my clothes up on a hook beside the shower stall. This bathroom was luxurious. The whole master suite was. And I couldn't wait until I could try to forget it existed.

The shirt smelled like his cologne. It felt foreign to have that scent on me. I felt bile rise in my throat at the idea of it, the idea of him clothing me in things that smelled like him. It seemed so... primitive.

Taking two big breaths, I hesitantly stepped back out into the room, hoping by some miracle that he'd left. He hadn't. The lights flicked off, but not before I caught a glimpse of his form in the bed. He was sitting up, the blankets down around his waist. He was waiting for me.

Tommy

I flicked the lamp off a second after she came out. When I saw her wearing my shirt, I thought I'd combust. I needed to turn the light off to regain my composure. She looked edible. I decided that second that it'd be a rule that she'd sleep either naked, with me wrapped around her, or in the clothes I'd worn that day, so she'd smell like me, either way.

Where these sudden possessive feelings had come from was a mystery. But the second I decided to accept her as a gift I instantly became obsessed with the idea of having someone who was mine. Just mine. It didn't make sense because I could easily find someone who wanted to be mine, but the minute Pop told her she was mine, something in me had changed. I never wanted that before. That I'd wanted her to smell like she was mine must be some primal instinct.

"New rule. Rule number three: you either wear something I've worn when you get ready for bed, or you sleep nude. Get in." I moved to the center of the bed and lifted the covers to welcome her into them. She stood, frozen in her tracks.

"Do I have to come get you?" I asked.

She stood there, not moving, so I flicked the lamp back on and got out of the bed. She backed up, holding her palm out at me.

"Can't I please sleep alone? I don't know you."

"No. It's time to get to know me. Don't worry; I'm not fucking you. Yet. We're just sleeping together." I loved that she was saying *please*.

She let out a whimper and covered her mouth to try to stifle it. Gone was the defiance she'd had in her eyes. She was crumbling.

"Get in. Or I'll put you here myself."

She shook her head at me, blowing her hair out of her eyes. I reached for her hand. She flinched, didn't take it, and then walked around to the other side of the bed and climbed in, staying as close to the edge of it as she could. She did a karate chop move down the middle of the blankets. She was trying to draw a boundary line. Fucking adorable.

I got back in and slid over, obliterating her Berlin wall, then climbed on top of her. I pinned her wrists above her head and nuzzled into the crook of her neck. I ran my nose up the length of her throat until my mouth was at her ear. She smelled amazing. She smelled like me, but like a woman, too. Her throat smelled like vanilla and cherries. Of all things. She stiffened under me.

Tia

He ran his nose up and down my neck, burying it in my hair. His hand travelled up my leg and then it landed on my hip. He dug his fingers in and then his nose trailed down my throat and across the opening of the shirt. He undid a button and then another button... with his teeth.

"Please don't," I whispered into the dark, pulling my hands from his grip and putting them out to stop him. He pinned them above my head, this time tighter. My eyes were adjusting. Then his nose was in my cleavage.

"Big day for you today, huh?" I felt the hum of his lips against the skin between my breasts. If I weren't so petrified, I'd have been turned on. He was obviously attempting to be seductive.

"You could say that." I tried to be sarcastic, but my voice came out in barely more than a whisper.

He lifted his head and let go of my wrists. His fingertips grazed my lower lip and I winced.

"Relax, I've said I'm not going to fuck you tonight," he said to me, his voice so deep it felt like it vibrated inside me. Then he rolled over onto his back. I tried to stay as still as possible but was shaking like a leaf.

He continued, "But I want something tonight from you."

I winced again, trying to stop my mind and heart from racing. "What?"

"I want you to crawl into my arms and I want you to relax, like you wanna be here. If you can do that for me tonight, sleep curled up against me, I won't fuck you." He stopped for a moment and then continued, "If you don't do what I ask, you're getting fucked hard and rough." He put his hands, fingers laced, behind his head, flexing his biceps and looking at me expectantly.

"You're crazy." I breathed. What a maniac. This was messed up!

He reached over and flicked the lamp back off. "Well?"

I took a deep breath. "You're, like, fucked in the head, aren't you?"

Stupid, Tia. Why would I say something like that to him?

"Yeah, and I have a gun," he announced. "Who gives the crazy guy a gun? Oh yeah, and a goodnight kiss; I want that, too. Keep me waiting and my list of demands may keep growing."

I was wide-eyed. Gob smacked. I heard an impatient-sounding huff and then I was gob smacked *and* scared. I got the impression he wanted me to give him a reason to take me against my will and / or show me his gun. I wanted neither, so I scampered over to him and then hesitated. He pulled me into an embrace, my head falling onto his chest. Both of his arms were tight around me. He kissed the top of my head and his palm slowly slid down my back until it rested on my rear end. He was hard, all over.

"Relax," he whispered against my hair and then he kissed my forehead.

"Get your hand off my..." I started and he moved his warm hand up to my waist before I could finish the threat that hadn't quite formed on my tongue yet, pulling the shirt up with it. I could hear him breathing hard. I could feel his heartbeat and it felt like it was racing. I squeezed my eyes shut tight and gulped. How bizarre to have my head on the chest of the man from the ice cream parlor, the man I'd had on my mind the past few days. But this wasn't that guy, that guy was from my fantasy. This guy looked just like him, but looks were where similarities ended. He'd behaved in a way I'd never imagined. The fact that this guy had taken 'ownership' of me and had forced me to lay here with him was repulsive.

"Don't tell me not to touch what's mine again. You get a pass tonight because of the day you've had, but don't make the mistake of thinking whether or not we fuck is anything but my decision to make."

I squeezed my eyes shut tighter. This was a nightmare. A horrible nightmare. He started to stroke my hair.

"No. Don't," I said.

"Tell me no or say don't one more time and the deal is off, Tia."

His hand trailed back down to my ass. He drummed his fingers on it, letting me know he was waiting for me to protest. I clamped my mouth shut. I believed him, so I made myself shut up and stay still. Every muscle in my body wanted to sprint, to run, to scream, to fight, to kick, to scratch, but I just stayed there, trembling.

"Now kiss me," he said.

I chewed my cheek and kept my eyes shut tight, like that'd help.

"Naw, I'll kiss you. I've been dying to taste these lips since that day I walked into that ice cream shop."

He flipped me over onto my back and then he was on me, his lips were on my lips, his body hard against me. He touched my lips softly with his at first and his lips were soft but strong. He got my bottom lip between his lips and he sucked on it. I couldn't breathe. He made an "Mm" sound against my mouth, then said, "You didn't kiss back, but I'll give you a pass tonight."

Then he flipped back so that I was again on top of him. His hands were on me, one on my lower back and the other in my hair. My cheek was against his chest, his legs were parted, and our pelvises were touching. He was rock-hard. If I could see myself, I'm sure that I'd see that my eyes were bugging out of my head.

His fingers massaged my scalp; he was playing with my hair a little. After a long moment of silence, I started to take stock of the day. The day that I'd been so excited about for so long had taken such a turn, one I wouldn't have guessed would happen in a million years, a trillion years. Right now, I should be at a party, getting tipsy. I should be cheers'ing with my friends about the fact that we'd made it through high school and should be comforting poor Ruby who had another year before she could go off to college.

I should be getting geared up to move out on my own, buy my own groceries, have full control over the remote. Living in a foster home filled to the brim with kids meant you almost never had control of the TV. It'd always been a democracy there where regular compromises had to be made on what would be watched. It meant if you didn't tackle the bag of cookies on grocery shopping day the only snacks around until next week was fruit. It meant hustle and bustle and loudness, occasional spats, frequent cold showers because someone else used up all the hot, but lots and lots of hijinks, and so much laughter.

I should be excited about the next chapter in my life. Another chapter was starting, though. Only, it was one I hadn't anticipated. Instead of having the night I should be having I was in the arms of a criminal. My life was at stake. My father's life was at stake. Either I got to be married to this criminal, got to be his unwilling sex slave, or got shipped off to be someone else's sex slave.

If anyone had told me that morning I'd spend the night in the bed and in the arms of Ice Cream Parlor Hottie in his hacienda style house, I'd have told them they were nuts, but the very idea of it would've melted my panties off. I'd never have been able to predict what'd wound up transpiring.

I guess the moral of the story was, Be Careful What You Wish For.

I was exhausted in mind and body. I had somehow gone from trembling to completely still against him. He was holding me in strong arms like I was something precious. What a contradiction!

His hand occasionally moved either up or down my back and every once in a while, I'd feel his lips or fingers moving in my hair. A whimper involuntarily escaped my lips and then he was pulling my leg up at the knee to drape it over him. I was pretty much totally on top of him, trying hard to ignore the erection poking me against my inner thigh. I tried to ignore what was happening despite the fact that it was scaring the heck out of me. I worried that the longer I lay here awake the more likely he would do something sexual. I decided I should try to sleep. I just wanted this day over. I had no idea what tomorrow would bring, but today had kicked me upside the head and it needed to just be done.

I cried softly, tears dropping onto his naked chest. He just stroked my head and my back as if he was the solution, not the problem. Then he took my right hand and held it against his chest over his heart, not letting go. His left hand was moving up and down my back. My left hand was at my side, clenched into a fist, my cheek on his bare chest.

I don't know how long I lay there crying on him in a puddle of tears while he stroked my hair and my back and rhythmically stroked my fingers with his thumb on his chest against his loudly beating heart, but eventually I felt my eyes droop. This beast was comforting me by holding me and stroking me and somehow it was working. I guessed it was working because it had to work. My fist loosened and my breathing started to even out. I had to act like I had no problem lying with my body on his or else he'd take me against my will. Or maybe I just shut down out of being totally, completely, devastatingly overwhelmed.

Tommy

She felt so fucking good in my arms. I was a 'wham, bam, fuck off, ma'am' kind of guy. Not one to spoon a chick after I fucked her, not one to snuggle up with. Not ever. I'd always just left after sex, never subscribed to the whole 'aftercare' bit after a scene. Why did this feel so good, so right? Why did I make this deal with her tonight? The answer in my head was crystal clear. Because she was mine. I hadn't even fucked her yet, but she was already mine; I knew deep down that it was my job to look after her so that's what I wanted to do. Right now, holding her, her sleeping on me, felt so fucking right. I was jumping ahead to a result I wanted, but that I wasn't patient enough to wait to earn.

I was surprised at myself, my actions. Earlier today I couldn't wait to fuck her. Couldn't wait to tear those panties down and plunge into her, holding her by the hair while I showed her who she belonged to. When she got mouthy with me I wanted to haul her over my knee and spank her until she begged for mercy. Now, I just wanted to comfort her. I wanted that even though I knew being here with me was the source of her tears.

Her life had shattered into a million pieces by that douchebag of a father of hers. Right now, I just wanted her to stop trembling and fall asleep in my arms. I wanted those stress lines off her pretty face.

I felt a warm tingling in me as I heard her breathing even out. A while later, I touched her cheek and when I did, she, obviously asleep, nuzzled into me, like she did wanna be here. I let out a long breath and closed my eyes, deciding that while Greg O'Connor had paid his debt to my father, now he owed me something. I gritted my teeth. I was gonna make him pay dearly for doing this to her.

4

Tia

Sensation woke me. Sensation between my legs. What was happening? I opened my eyes. I was in Tommy Ferrano's bed, on my back. Daylight. Then it hit me that he was nestled between my legs with his mouth on me *down there*. Holy crap.

I tensed up. I couldn't see him since he was under the blankets, but he had my hips in his hands and his tongue was flicking down there, on my clit. He was doing to me what he'd done to that cherry. Fuck!

My panties were sliding down, down, down, and off. No one had ever done this to me. Truthfully, I was the only one who had ever given myself an orgasm and I always stopped probably a bit short because the intensity always frightened me. The few sexual partners I'd had were more interested in getting themselves off than even figuring out where the clit was.

But, Tommy Ferrano was in between my legs, tongue swirling around my girlie parts, and my eyes were rolling into the back of my head. He sure knew where *it* was. And I was about to go off like a hand grenade with the pin pulled out.

Holy shit, that felt intense! He flicked the covers off and now I didn't just feel it, I could see it. He looked up at me, twirled his tongue, sucked inward, and then he gave me the sexiest smile I'd ever seen in my whole damn life. He was the ice cream parlor guy right now, my fantasy come true. Messy bedhead, twinkling pale brown eyes looking sparkly almost like quartz, all muscles and a potently male scent coming off him. Was I dreaming? My head rolled back and my back arched, letting out a squeak as sensation rolled through me.

Tommy

She was like heaven, wrapped tight around my tongue. She had a tight shaved pussy that, when I spread her folds apart, was so pink and perfect that taking those panties off felt like Christmas morning. She tasted a little like pineapple. What was even more amazing was the way she was responding. I'd woken up at dawn with her sprawled across me, looking, feeling, and smelling gorgeous.

It was the longest uninterrupted sleep that I could remember. I was always up two or three times a night, but I'd slept seven hours straight and woke up with this goddess draped over me, her silky hair fanned out across my shoulder, her fingertips touching one of my nipples. Her hot palm had skated across my skin and she'd let out a sleepy moan as I'd run my fingers through her hair.

So, I flipped her over and kissed my way down the shirt and nestled between her legs while I pushed those silky black panties down.

She was so responsive, moaning in her sleep and spreading her legs for me. She tasted so good, sounded so sweet when she moaned, and she was mine, moaning for me. Something about that just called to me on a deep level.

When her eyes had opened and she looked so flushed, but didn't pull away, instead arched and let out that hard shudder and high pitched "Ah!" it was perfection. My hand slid up under the shirt and cupped a breast, feeling the silky tip harden under my touch. Fuck, I had to be inside of her. Now.

Tia

After giving me the most intense orgasm I'd ever had and the only orgasm I've ever had *not* alone, he rose up my body and settled directly on top of me, looking at me with a smile on his face. I was wide-eyed and probably red-faced, and more than anything, I was freaking scared. The earth had just shattered, and I was in pieces. He'd caught me off guard, doing this to me while I slept. And I was afraid because I didn't know what was next.

He reached down, not breaking eye contact with me, and freed his erection from his underwear. I was about to protest, but in an instant, he pushed inside of me, hard and to the root. His eyes sparkled as I winced.

"Not a virgin," he whispered, "but close."

I shut my eyes and chewed my lip, absorbing the feel of him and at the same time continuing to let the horror sink in.

"Tell me, baby girl," he whispered huskily in my ear. "Anybody ever make you come like that?"

I would've gulped, but I couldn't swallow. My face was beet-red, I was sure, but I had goose bumps everywhere, too.

"Good," he whispered against my forehead and then kissed it.

"Might as well have been a virgin then. I want to gut anyone who has had their sorry excuse for a cock inside you." He grabbed my chin, forcing me to look at him, then said, "Play your cards right and this big, hard cock is the only one you'll ever have inside you again."

The seriousness on his face struck fear down in my gut. Then his tongue was in my mouth. I wanted to pull away. I didn't want to taste myself on him. But, he wasn't letting me move. He kept pushing deep into me down below, his tongue tracing across my lips, darting inside. His lips were strong, demanding.

"Wrap your arms and legs around me, baby," he whispered.

I was frozen.

"Now," he grunted and my arms and legs obeyed him. I didn't want this but if I fought it I was sure it would turn violent and happen anyway.

"Ah, you feel so good Athena; you *are* a goddess. You're so fucking tight."

He grunted those words into my neck, and I just lay there, letting him do that to me. I felt like I was splitting in two. Half of me felt what he was doing to me, and it felt good, *so* good. This must be what sex was really supposed to feel like, except that it was missing the emotional component and probably shouldn't have this fear component. Under my hands, I felt his muscles ripple. Under my calves I felt his butt clench as he drove into me. His body was so muscular and strong. This wasn't a boy; this was a man, a man who knew how to make me feel good, a man I was petrified of.

The other half of me wanted to float away somewhere else. If I'd risen above my body and looked down, I'd have seen that my eyes were staring at the ceiling, wet with unshed tears. This sensation in my body was real, and it was intense, but it wasn't what I wanted to feel. I wanted to disappear into thin air. I thought back to my fantasies about him and felt real remorse for ever wanting to be underneath him. I started to sob. Loud.

He started pushing harder and harder and then gyrated his hips and hit something inside of me that made me jolt. My mouth was wide open as I let out a moan and staggered breaths. My legs were shaking. Hard. He grabbed me roughly by the hair and held my cheek to his cheek. I let out a cry of pain and then he came inside of me, moaning loud and the sound of that, it made every nerve in my body prickle. Then he fell limply onto me, out of breath.

"Fuck!" he growled into my ear, and then nuzzled hard all over my face and neck and chest, rubbing his rough stubbly face all over me. It made goose bumps rise all over my body again. He ripped the shirt I had on wide open and sucked one of my nipples into his mouth and moaned loudly. Then he let go and gathered me to him and flipped over, holding me tight against his side, brushing my hair away from my face with his fingertips on one hand and sliding his fingers from behind though the moisture between my legs with the other hand. I shuddered.

"Good morning, gorgeous." His voice was husky, sleepy. He leaned over so I could see his face and gave me a dazzling smile while he kept rubbing with his fingers. His fluid was leaking out of me as he continued to rub rhythmically back and forth over the seam of my vagina and spreading it all over that area.

I started breathing shallowly again as sensation began to rebuild. I think my eyes were rolling back into my head again and I was inches away from coming again. I fisted the bed sheet. But then he pulled his hand away, "Naw, you've had enough for now. Wouldn't wanna spoil you. But I could get used to waking up like this, huh?" He kissed me behind my earlobe and then sucked my earlobe into his mouth for a second and made a victorious-sounding growl in my ear.

I think I must've looked back at him like he was an alien or something because he waited for a beat, eyeing me, then burst out laughing. He gave my bottom a stinging slap while biting his lower lip, and then pulled away from me.

"Aren't you full of surprises?" he asked, crawling backwards out of the bed until he stood at the foot of it and looked down at me, naked and his body glistening a little bit with sweat, "I know vanilla is your favorite flavor, but just so you know, that's probably the one and only time you'll ever get it." He winked at me and sauntered, naked, to the bathroom. I heard the shower spring to life.

I bolted upright, feeling my heart pound against my chest. My eyes scanned the room.

I have got to get out of here. Could I make a run for it now and get away from this psycho?

My dress was in his bathroom, ripped. My shoes were still here on the floor, but all I had on was his blue dress shirt. I threw the covers back and my panties were still around one of my ankles. I pulled them out of the mess of tangled-up sheets and hurried to his walk-in closet, where I rifled through drawer after drawer, looking for pants. I found a drawer of t-shirts, so took one and put it on. I took another and wiped away the mess between my legs. I threw it toward a hamper and it missed. I yanked on a pair of Tommy's track pants rolling the cuffs up until they were to my knees. I decided to abandon my killer heels. I never wanted to see them again after the day I'd had wearing them. The water was still running and my vagina was still throbbing with raw sensation.

I grabbed my purse from where it'd been tossed on the floor last night, darted out of the bedroom, tying the drawstring around the waist of the pants as I ran, and took off down the stairs. I unlocked a deadbolt on the front door and then dashed out. The house alarm started instantly and piercingly betraying me. Then I saw the Michael Clarke Duncan-looking guy leaning against a car, doing something on his phone. His chin lifted and then he was looking right at me.

My heart thudded wildly. Damn it; I hadn't thought this through. He quirked his eyebrows up, clearly aware I was trying to escape and probably taking in my disheveled appearance and probably frantic look. This place was gated all the way around, by the looks of it. The guy stepped away from the car and headed in my direction.

I couldn't see how I'd get out with the property being gated and even if I'd found a way out, would I be sentencing my father to a terrible fate? I didn't know the whole story and one wrong move and it could mean he'd be dead. I'd be an orphan without ever finding out the whole story.

I certainly didn't want to piss this big guy off, so I put my head down, turned around, and headed back into the house.

When I closed the door, I leaned against it, breathless. My mind raced. What could I do? I needed to get out of here. Maybe find a phone and call the police? But that might get me killed, too. Or shipped off to some foreign land to be a sex worker.

I stood there for I don't know how long, my hands over my ears, and not knowing what to do and then he was coming down the stairs, holding his phone to his ear and wearing just a towel. He casually strolled past me and pushed buttons on a panel on the wall by the door. The alarm's screeching halted. He looked at me with what looked like an amused look on his face.

"Thanks. Yep, got it under control." He ended his call. "Looks like you tripped the alarm on your way out for a stroll, huh? Nice outfit."

He stopped in front of me.

I was sure I was quite the sight barefoot in his track pants, which I could've swum in, and a way-too-big men's t-shirt with no bra underneath. Where the heck was my bra? I'd gone to sleep with it on last night. I covered my chest with my arms and blew my hair out of my face.

"Why don't you go get a shower and I'll have my housekeeper get some breakfast together for us."

I gave a little nod, wide-eyed and started to head for the stairs. As I passed him, he caught me by my upper arm and leaned in,

"Don't try that again." His grip tightened painfully. "You get a pass because you pleased me so well this morning. But, try that again, you won't be able to sit down for a week." There wasn't a trace of humor in his eyes; his expression shook me right to the core.

I swallowed hard. This man was beautiful outside but obviously hideously ugly on the inside. He smirked like he'd read my mind and let go of my arm. I went upstairs and took a shower.

I scrubbed myself for at least twenty minutes, almost frantically.

I tried to wash him away, but I could swear I still smelled the sex on myself.

When I came out of the bathroom wrapped in a towel, I noticed clothes on the end of the bed, which had been made. There was a stack of ladies' t-shirts and tank tops, a pile of several new pairs of underwear with the tags still on. Yoga pants, a pair of capri yoga pants, and a pair of denim shorts sat in a neat stack. I got dressed and sat on the bed and combed my hair with the small hairbrush from my purse. Thankfully, the tank had a built-in bra. Not ideal on its own for a bigger chest like mine, but better than nothing.

Someone knocked and then opened the door. An attractive Latina woman was in the doorway. She looked to be in her early to mid-forties, about my size with shoulder-length wavy dark hair with copper highlights all through it.

"Oh good, they fit. I'm Sarah Martinez. I'm your housekeeper. Welcome, Miss O'Connor. I've put your underthings in the wash. The dress can't likely be saved, I'm afraid, but I'll see what I can do with it. You can borrow those things until your things arrive. The panties, they're new; you can keep those."

Her kindness was sort of disarming. She reached out and shook my hand. She stared at my left hand for a second, probably noting I wasn't wearing a ring. Had she actually come into the bathroom while I was showering to get my dirty clothes?

"Thank you," I managed to say.

"I know it's all unconventional," she whispered, lifting her chin toward the heart-shaped box on the dresser, "but I'm so happy to see him settling down. I'm here for you and at your service. If there are changes you want to make after the wedding, I'm happy to be accommodating. Don't hesitate to come to me for anything, okay? We must talk but we'll do it later." She had a mild accent and her tone was conspiratory. She winked at me.

I nodded slowly, not sure what to make of her. If she knew the circumstances under which I was here and knew how this family operated and still chose to work here she couldn't possibly be a good person. I couldn't trust her. I wouldn't trust her.

"Come; breakfast is waiting."

I stood up. She linked arms with me like we were bosom buddies and led me downstairs, saying, "All those rooms are bedrooms. There are five and each has an adjoining bathroom, except the room that'll be the nursery. That has a door adjoining to the master suite in through the walk-in closet." She gave me a squeeze. *What the heck?*

She led me through a big modern kitchen and then out some sliding doors onto a patio area where Tommy was sitting at a table, reading a newspaper with coffee in front of him.

He tucked his phone in his jeans pocket. He was Mr. Casual today, dressed in a pair of button-fly faded jeans and a tight black t-shirt. His still damp hair was pushed back with his sunglasses. He was barefoot. How could he be so attractive and yet be willing to be put in an arranged marriage? I suspected with his family being criminals, he couldn't get a woman to agree to marry him. Either that or he was so ugly on the inside that no one cared how good he looked on the outside.

"Sit," Ms. Martinez told me. "I'll bring you coffee. Or tea? What do you prefer?"

"Um, coffee, please. Milk with three sugars."

"Three? Oh, that's bad." She waved her hand dismissively. "I'll wean you off."

Tommy glanced up from his paper at me. "She's a sugar hater. She weaned me off a few months ago. Didn't tell me until 2 weeks after I'd been drinking it with no sugar."

"Sugar is evil!" she replied, waving her finger at him. He rolled his eyes.

I sat across the table from him. He was smiling, staring at the paper with what looked like not a care in the world. No, no cares. He had a prisoner here and had tricked me into giving him sex this morning by starting something when I was asleep, but now he didn't have a care in the world. Too bad I didn't have it as easy.

Ms. Martinez brought me a coffee. When I sipped it, it tasted sugary enough. She winked at me, "I gave you three today, but bit by bit I'll cut back and then you won't even miss it."

How poetic. Tommy had promised me that I wouldn't have my favorite vanilla after today and she was promising to wean me off sugar. Obviously, by his statement and by the way he'd spanked me and pulled my hair, he was a kinky sonofabitch so vanilla sex was off the menu. Would I soon stop missing my freedom and everything else I loved because I'd be weaned off? Would I ever stop missing vanilla ice cream? Freedom was something I was missing already.

There was the illusion of freedom in front of me. The patio area was nice. Spanish themed, mosaic tiles, big infinity pool that overlooked a lush-looking forest. I wondered what the drop was like on the other side of the pool. Could I escape through the forest? I was in a big giant cell. A ginormous cell with an infinity pool and servants.

"Tia?" Tommy's voice broke my daze.

My attention snapped to him. Ms. Martinez was putting a plate of scrambled eggs, toast, and fruit in front of me. Then she went back inside.

"I'm leaving. I've got work. You'll behave?"

I think I nodded a little, I wasn't even sure. I could hardly look at him, after what he'd done to me. After how I'd participated. I knew my face was red, I could feel it.

"Uh, you want your things picked up at your old place or are we starting over?"

I was shocked at the question. "I, um... I have to talk to them, tell them, uh..." Tell them what?

"I'll take care of it. I'll have your things brought here. Then whatever else you need, I'll arrange." He got up, pulled me up to standing and took me into his arms. "Be a good girl," he said and poked me gently on the nose, "No phone calls yet and no attempts to run." I caught sight of his hand; it was covered in scratches from our scuffle last night. He saw that I'd noticed and smiled devilishly at me and then touched his lips to mine. His tongue darted in as he hauled me closer. I didn't react, I didn't respond. I guess was in shock. He let go of me and then said, "Watch her." I glanced behind him and the Michael Clarke Duncan guy was standing in the doorway. I guess I had a babysitter.

I robotically dropped back to sitting and stared at my plate. Ms. Martinez sat down with a cup of coffee,

"Shoo Earl!" she said to him, annoyed. He backed away. She sat down and put her coffee in front of herself. "He can go. Leave us girls to talk. Food not okay?"

"I...I uh, haven't tried it."

"Eat. I'll keep you company." She took a sip of her coffee. "Are you okay?"

I stared, dumbfounded at her, then finally answered, "Not really."

"Tell. Tell me everything." She leaned forward and propped her chin on her palm, her elbow on the table. She stared at me with big brown doe eyes.

I winced.

"You don't trust me. I understand. I'm a stranger to you. Let me talk while you eat. We'll become friends in no time."

I took a bite of cubed melon from the plate.

"I've been with the family since Tommy was a small boy. His mother died when he was just a boy. The Ferrano family hired me to look after him. I was an illegal alien with no future. I'd been smuggled into the country by a nasty piece of shit who wanted to work me and my family to death in payment for getting us into the states. Mr. Ferrano, Tommy's father, Tom, he broke up the operation that was ruining lives of a lot of people. He freed dozens of people treated like slaves. In thanks to him I offered to work here for their family for nothing; they saved us, a lot of us. Of course, they have paid me generously all these years, anyway. He got me citizenship, too. I stayed anyway; I wanted to be surrounded by people who cared."

"Slaves? They saved you from slavery?" I shook my head, a sour look on my face.

She continued, "This family, they don't play everything by the books. But, they did a lot for me. There are a lot of people out there like them, don't kid yourself. They don't all get called by the same names but there are some very bad people out there disguised as good people and there are people who do bad things sometimes but are not bad, they do what they need to do. This family, what you see is what you get. They did good for me."

She pointed her thumb at her chest, "And for my parents." She looked up, kissed her fingertips and pointed them at the sky, "They've become family to me." She motioned to my plate again. "Please, Chiquita; you need to eat."

I took a bite of food. She kept talking.

"Tommy is the oldest of four. He's taking over the family business after he marries you. He has big responsibilities. Big. This means you will have an important position. He's like a son to me, you know? I have no kids but his mother died and so I was like his mother. We're like family. You're resistant to this. I know a bit about your father. I know that he gave you to pay them. Having a man like this for your father, what he did was a blessing. Better to be with the Ferrano family than a man like that." She spat the word 'that' out with a grimace.

I was shocked. "I'm a prisoner, Mrs. Martinez. How is this better?"

"Call me Sarah. Better to be a prisoner of a good man than an evil one. Tommy is a good man. You'll see. Underneath all his – you'll see."

I shook my head. "I wasn't imprisoned by my father. He left me in foster care for years. I was free but he came and he – and Tommy is forcing me into –" I stopped talking. I didn't want to say another word. *Rule number two.*

"Your fiancé will provide for you, keep you safe, give you a family, an amazing loving family. Maybe you don't think this is what you want but you will be very blessed. I know he has dark tendencies, but I think the right woman will bring him into the light. He's had much pain in his life so far. He's had a lot to prove. He's beautiful outside; he just needs love to help create some beauty inside where he feels ugly. You'll see."

How promising. Ugh.

I sipped the coffee and stared out at the forest beyond the pool. I was done listening to her. This was pointless.

"I hope we can be friends. You can come to me if you need anything."

Yeah, she's loyal to him, to them. I won't go to her for a thing. I stared, unseeing, ahead of me.

She must've picked up on my vibe because she left me alone then, patting me first on the shoulder and saying something softly in Spanish. I ate a bit, but it was tasteless and pointless. I was worrying about Rose, Cal and everyone who would be worried about me. I don't know if 'worry' was the right word for the emotions I was feeling about my dad, though. He had really done it this time. And Tommy said he'd take care of things with Rose and Cal but I hadn't a clue what that meant. I felt sick about it.

Would Dad try to get me out? Tommy's father had certainly said different. How could Dad have looked so calm when he watched them drive away with me?

It started to rain, so I wandered back into the house. Mrs. Martinez was cleaning the kitchen. She piped up. "Tour of the house?"

"Actually, I'd like to lie down. I don't feel all that great." I couldn't care less about a tour of my prison.

"Do you need something? Painkillers, tea, anything like that?"

"I just need a nap. Thank you, Mrs. Martinez."

"I'm not married. And call me Sarah."

I nodded, then I went back upstairs to Tommy's room and got under the covers. I felt dirty in his bed, the bed where he'd screwed me that morning. The bed where I'd let him do that to me without fighting back. The bed that smelled like him and smelled like sex. I thanked my lucky stars, if I had any, (I probably didn't) that I wasn't going to get pregnant from this morning's activities since he hadn't worn a condom. I rubbed my arm, feeling the small birth control implant that was there. I only hoped that Tommy Ferrano didn't have any STDs.

I woke up a few hours later, feeling no better. I wandered over to the wet bar Tommy had gotten wine from the previous night and opened the mini fridge. It was stocked with bottled water and had several wine bottles plus a few bottles of beer. I got a bottle of water and then wandered into the bathroom and found a bottle of Tylenol in the medicine cabinet. I took two of them, hoping they'd save me from this excruciating tension headache, and then I climbed back into the bed. My eyes landed on the heart-shaped box. It had been moved from the dresser to right beside me on the bedside table. My eyes flew up to the ceiling so fast that it was like I was trying to unsee the box. I didn't even want to think about that box. What I needed to think about was how to get out of this mess.

*　*　*

When it got dark the door opened and I thought it'd be Sarah Martinez again as she'd looked in on me and tried to engage in conversation at least three times. But this time, it was him. I looked up from the bed, where I'd been all day. He stood over me, staring.

"Honey, I'm home." He was smiling, probably thinking he was funny. I looked back to the television. My whole body was tense, locked tight.

"Sarah has dinner ready for us." His tone was gentle.

I shrugged.

"I need to talk to you about a few things so maybe up here is better. It's more private. I'll bring it up."

I chewed my lower lip and didn't give him anything.

He sat on the edge of the bed and flicked the lamp on, "I'm gonna try to be patient with you, but I won't tolerate this for long." His eyebrows were up and he looked serious but not angry. I blinked at him a few slow times and then rolled my eyes and looked back to the TV, trying to give off a 'whatever' vibe.

Suddenly, he hauled me up to standing. Now his eyes were cold and angry-looking and he had my chin in his grasp. "I don't appreciate being ignored," he told me, "You'd be smart to remember that."

"I wasn't ignoring you. I know you're here."

"I don't appreciate the attitude, then."

"I don't appreciate being kept prisoner," I said softly, pushing my palms against his chest to get him to let go of me. How dare he think he can just manhandle me!

He let go of me and I sat back on the bed, ignoring the fact that he was looking at me like I was a piece of meat.

"I'll go get dinner for us," he said.

"Not hungry," I muttered.

"Fine, suit yourself. You can wait until tomorrow to find out about the fate of your father, your belongings, and to find out what's happened with your foster family."

He let me go and left the room and I sank down into the pillows like they were the pits of despair.

I silently prayed nothing had happened to any of them, biting back tears and stared off into space until it got darker and darker. I eventually slept.

* * *

He was in bed with me, kissing my neck. My eyes bolted open and I squirmed away. He caught me and stopped me.

"Out of these clothes," he ordered.

My eyes bulged. Oh no. I shoved him away and he caught my wrist.

"Hey! I told you obedience is rewarded. But you haven't been very obedient this evening, have you? Are you going to take them off or will I have to do it?"

"Go fuck yourself," I muttered under my breath. I don't know what possessed my mouth to say that but I instantly regretted it.

Covers were flung back and then he yanked the pants off me, pulling the underwear down with them. I tried to struggle, but it felt like I was a flailing toddler and he was a giant. Then the tank top was yanked over my head while I was simultaneously pulled over his lap. He was in a pair of silky boxers and I felt his erection poking me in the upper abdomen. One hand was on my upper back and the other on my ass, fingers digging in.

"Apologize for saying that to me," he demanded softly. So softly it was frightening. His voice was laced with menace.

I held my mouth shut. It was a weird position, being naked over his lap, feeling his erection digging into me like this. His breathing was heavy. He slapped my ass hard. I cringed at the pain and tried to get away, but he had a firm hold of me.

"Apologize," he repeated in a still soft but even more menacing tone.

I pursed my lips. Forget this. I wasn't apologizing to him for being shocked when he demanded I get naked. I tried to struggle to get out of his grasp again. Another slap. This one was harder.

"Ready to apologize yet?" he demanded, his voice still quiet but his tone even harder. The sick asshole was getting off on this so much. Spanking me, it was turning him on. I didn't care; I wasn't giving in. This was my life, my freedom, I couldn't just give in, give up everything.

"Answer me, Athena," he sang out, sounding impatient. Another slap.

Ow! My ass was on fire. He wanted to do this. This was going to happen to me no matter what, tonight; I just knew it.

"I love the way your body jerks against my cock when I spank you, baby." His voice had gone husky.

Suddenly, he pried my legs open and plunged a finger into me hard. It was excruciating.

"Not wet tonight, Tia?" He tsk tsk'd at me, "That's disappointing."

"I hate you," I cried out into the sheets, tears streaming down my face. "Sick fuck!"

He sat motionless for a moment and I didn't know what was coming next so I just stayed still. He leaned forward, still gripping me, and I heard the bedside table's drawer open, then heard a pop sound, like a cap popping off something. I felt something slimy down there. He was rubbing something on me down there. Damn him, was he –? He was! He was lubricating me.

He slapped my ass again, and I jumped, still in his firm hold, but then he plunged his fingers in again and pumped them in and out a few times before pinching my clit.

"So tight, Athena," he muttered. His finger prodded at my rear hole.

Oh heck, no. I tried to scramble away and he tried to grip me but his fingers were now slippery from the lube, so I managed to get off his lap. I took a tumble to the rug and then tried to scamper away, feeling the rug slice across my knee like sandpaper. I wasn't fast enough. He caught my ankle in his grip and the rug sliced again as he dragged me backwards. Then he was pinning me to the floor.

"Here's how this is going to go," he told me, calmly, crazily calm. His hot breath tickled the back of my neck, "You're going to do your best to please me and make up for this poor attitude tonight."

He gathered my hair at the nape of my neck and pulled a little so that my chest was off the floor. I pushed my hands into the rug to support myself, whimpering.

"Right now, you can please me by apologizing."

He grabbed my ass and then started rubbing his hand up and down.

"Tia?" He was letting me know he was waiting and I suspected, ready to strike again. He squeezed my rear end.

"Sorry," I spat, hating my life with a passion.

"You want me to make you come again, baby? You'd better do better than that," he whispered.

I couldn't even think. My brain was filled with a list of expletives, but I held my tongue.

"Hm?" He slapped my ass again.

I was going to be full of welts in the morning. And my knees were on fire from rug burn.

"I'm sorry," I whimpered, thinking *I hate you, I hate you, I fucking hate you.* I didn't want him to make me come; I wanted him to stop and go away.

"That's better," he said, then started to trail light kisses up and down my spine. "Good girl," he murmured against my skin. "Good girls get to come."

I wanted to cry out, to shout *no*, but I was immobile. His hand cupped me and he started to circle my clit with his fingers again. The moisture was there. It wasn't mine, but it was there and I guess that's why my body started to respond. My ass was so sore, I was so scared, and yet I was starting to breathe heavier.

"I love that sound. Music to my ears. Training you might be easier than I thought. From now on, if I spank your ass, I want you wet. It makes me very happy when you're wet and trust me, you want me happy with you." He whispered this into my ear and then nibbled roughly on my earlobe, before flipping to his back so I was straddling him.

"Do you want my cock inside you, baby?" he asked, pulling at my hips and then sliding slowly into me.

"I hate you, I hate you, I fucking hate you!" I cried, shaking my head frantically, wanting desperately to get away.

His eyes radiated danger as he slid the rest of the way in, a muscle working in his jaw. "Oh fuck, yeah." He began to tweak my nipples, making them go harder as he pulled up to sitting, still inside me, and holding my back tight, then attacking my neck hungrily with his mouth, nipping, suckling, kissing.

"I need to feel you come around me, Tia," he mumbled into my hair as he rubbed tiny circles with his thumb between my legs, while pushing in and out of me.

Fuck, but it was building. I didn't understand it. I went from pushing him away to digging my nails into his chest as I pushed. But then I felt my body clench around him involuntarily as he kept the rhythm going, pushing inside of me, kissing me, rubbing at my center. He slapped my ass again and then squeezed it, his angle making him hit that sensitive place inside me again, making me go off like a cannon. I screamed as the orgasm gripped me and twisted me up in knots. Now I was digging my nails into his back and pulling him to me.

He groaned my name and then it was over. I'd uncoiled like a spring and now I was boneless. We were both covered with sweat, my ass was probably covered in welts, my knees raw and bleeding from the carpet, his chest and back probably covered in claw marks.

He abruptly grabbed me by the chin and declared, "I'm gonna fucking marry you!"

He kissed me hard, closed-mouthed, but possessively, and then lifted me up, still straddling him and gently put me on the bed. I winced in pain as soon as my bottom touched the sheets.

"Turn over," he told me. "Stay there."

I rolled over onto my stomach, filled with despair, silently crying, tears streaming down my face, onto the bed. I saw a light go on and realized he'd gone to the bathroom. He came back and slathered some cream all over my sore bottom. Then he moved away and I heard the water running in the bathroom.

He climbed into bed beside me, leaned over, and ran his fingers through my hair gently, then pulled my torso on top of his body. I tried to pull away, but he gripped me tighter, "Uh-uh," he warned. Tears burned in my eyes and I went limp and just let him pull me close.

What the heck? I came harder than I'd ever come and it happened the second he slapped me that final time. What kind of twisted, hellish rabbit hole was he dragging me into? He refused to let me go despite that I tried to worm away, so I silently cried myself to sleep on top of him, dripping tears all over his probably scratched up chest. And all the while he said nothing, just lay still, stroking my hair. I could feel that he loved every single minute of it. Sick bastard.

As I started to drift off to sleep, I heard him say, "I'll take good care of you, baby. You're doing good. *So* good."

What on earth was I in for with this man?

Tommy

I stared down at her face while she slept diagonally across my chest, no blankets on as her bare ass had been covered in cream. She was so fucking perfect. The fight was something I'd wanted, needed, and she gave it to me. But, it infuriated me when I'd found her dry unlike last night.

The way she responded after that couldn't have been more amazing. She was already giving me everything I craved, and I knew that I could easily take her down the roads I wanted to travel down. I could take her there, get what I needed, and then comfort and care for her afterwards. But, what I was doing niggled at me. And that meant I was losing control. And I had to slow down, so I didn't break her too far.

The crying herself to sleep on top of me was the fucking cherry on the top. I'd never wanted that before. When I was done, I was done. But with her, I wanted to hold her afterwards, feel her tears hit my chest, whisper comforting words into her ear. I could break her down and then care for her after, and the feeling when she went soft in my arms and fell asleep…

Yeah, I'd made her cry but because she was mine, I'd comfort her afterwards. It was a beautiful thing. A twisted but beautiful thing. She was right, I was a sick fuck.

I'd been with plenty of women who'd let me tie them up, who'd loved when I slapped or whipped them, but they'd never affected me like this. The BDSM club I'd joined a few years back made it so that I always got just what I wanted without having to look too far. I'd go in, give a look, maybe have a drink with a woman, sometimes two women. Sometimes I'd just lift my chin at a woman and it was enough for her to know. I'd walk out and leave, someone would follow, I'd get what I wanted, and it'd be over. They were usually way too fucking eager so sometimes, depending on what I was in the mood for, I had to fuck with their heads and make them afraid... see the fear to get me hard.

Some were so seasoned at the lifestyle that it just wasn't a challenge for me because there was no fear, only anticipation. I enjoyed the cat and mouse game, but it had to feel real. Sometimes I had to go what some might call a little too far to get the result I wanted and then when it was over, I never wanted to go back for seconds.

Until now, I guess I never knew what I really needed. This girl, this gift to me that was sound asleep on top of me was so responsive. She was the perfect amount of defiant and afraid at the same time. And she was mine. All mine.

I'd give her everything. She'd want for nothing. I'd give her everything she wanted and I'd avenge her with anyone who'd ever crossed her, including her sorry excuse for a father. I'd never wanted to give a woman so much before. I'd never wanted to take so much from her at the same time. I wanted her to give me everything she had, every emotion.

I went to sleep filled with emotions I'd never had before. Possessiveness, need, and fear. Fear of what, I didn't know.

* * *

In the middle of the night I woke up to a scream. I bolted upright. She was thrashing beside me, in the throes of some nightmare, probably a nightmare about me.

I grabbed her. "Athena!"

She half woke up, confused. I pulled her against me and kissed her forehead. "It's okay, baby. I've got you."

She was stiff in my arms, trembling, having trouble shaking whatever she'd dreamt about. She tried to pull away, but I wouldn't let her go. I cooed in her ear, stroked her back, and kissed her over and over. When she finally stopped fighting, but cried herself back to sleep on me I lay awake in deep in thought for a long time, a strange emotion swelling in my chest. Finally, she went completely soft and I heard her breathing even out, so I closed my eyes.

I made her stay. She didn't want me. Suddenly I wanted to be the source of the comfort, the one she reached for, not the source of nightmares. I slept like shit.

* * *

I woke up with her laying on top of me, her head on my chest and her leg draped over my thigh. I gingerly got out of bed before she woke. I saw her backside was still pink, still covered in my fingerprints and I caught sight of one of her knees and it was all scraped-looking, I guess from when I dragged her back to me across the carpet. I felt a strange pull in me. I didn't want to see her eyes open. I couldn't explain why, but I just didn't wanna see sadness in them and suspected that's exactly what I'd see. I was gone before she was awake. I'd grabbed my gym bag, a garment bag that had a dry-cleaned suit in it and tossed a clean pair of jeans and pair of dress shoes into the bag, then headed out.

* * *

I called the house at around 10:30.

"What's she doing?" I asked Sarah. I was waiting at one of our coffee shops for someone and that someone was late. Not impressed. I glanced at my watch and tapped my foot impatiently.

"She's not so good. She's been crying. You really need to be gentler, give her time to—"

"I didn't ask *how* she's doing, I asked *what* she's doing," I snapped.

I could almost hear the disapproval through the dead air.

"Mind your own fucking business, Sarah. What's she doing?"

"She's watching television in your room. I just checked on her and brought her coffee and breakfast. She won't get out of bed."

I switched the phone off without saying goodbye.

* * *

That night I got back late, but she was still awake. She was in my bed, staring at the TV when I opened the door. She didn't look at me. I walked into the bathroom and undressed. When I came back her eyes were closed, but I knew she wasn't asleep. I got a drink and stood over the bed, watching her while slowly sipping from a glass of whiskey.

Tia

Go away, go away; leave me alone.

I wanted to say this, but I didn't. I was quiet. I knew he was standing over me, but I kept my eyes closed and tried to breathe evenly, to will him to go away. Then I felt the covers sliding away from my still-fully dressed body. I was in more of Sarah's clothes, a pair of jean shorts and a blue tank top. She'd gone out and bought me a bra, some face wash, a toothbrush and she later found my bra from grad day in with Tommy's laundry.

Now I felt the breeze from the air conditioning on my skin and I heard the sound of ice cubes tinkling in a glass. The television was switched off and I felt his hand land on my ankle. He ran his palm up along my leg directly up to my hip. I wanted to keep pretending to sleep, but I involuntarily shivered at his touch.

"You're not following my directions very well," he said softly. I opened my eyes to see him lean over and tug the buttonhole of the shorts, releasing the button. I curled up into a ball. I heard more ice cubes tinkling.

"If I'm not here to give you something to wear to bed I want you waiting for me, naked. Get undressed."

"Leave me alone," I said softly.

"Get out of those clothes or I'll do it."

Then he's gonna have to do it, because I'm not submitting to him. No way. I curled into a tighter ball, feeling my pulse begin to race as the bed depressed. He was hovering over me.

"You've got a chance to behave. Follow my directions and I won't punish you."

I stayed still.

"Undress," he repeated softly.

"Let me go. Please." I started to tremble hard.

"Let you go?"

Tommy

"Please?"

She looked at me and looked so vulnerable. Every nerve in my body was awake. I liked seeing the word *please* on her lips.

"Why would I do that?"

"Because you don't need to do this. I'm sure that you can find someone to m-marry you. It doesn't have to be me. We don't know each other and I–"

Tia

"But you're already mine," he told me, and there was something unreadable to me in his eyes. But then it registered. It felt like my fate was sealed.

Devastation filled me. It was like getting a death sentence. He'd slammed the proverbial gavel on the desk. He believed he owned me, and he wasn't going to let me go. He was going to play his sick games with me and continue to use me. He'd get off on my tears, on spanking me, on forcing me, and he'd enjoy every minute of it.

And I would come undone one stitch at a time. I already felt like I was a wreck.

Something passed between us, an exchange of knowing looks. I knew then that he wasn't going to let me go and I was pretty sure he knew I was having that epiphany. A slow smile spread across his face.

"Might as well get undressed," he said.

Might as well? *No.* I glared at him.

"Tell ya what, baby girl, let's make a deal. Get undressed and spread those gorgeous legs for me willingly and we can have your favorite vanilla tonight. Don't and it'll have much more flavor, my kinda flavor. Tonight, it's your decision."

I was queasy.

He leaned over and put the drink on the nightstand, then caught the hem of my tank top in his grasp and started to lift it.

"I guess I'm doing this myself. Then I'm using this shirt to tie you to the headboard so you can't move while I fuck you. Last chance, because I'm feeling generous. Take your clothes off and you don't have to be tied to my bed."

Tommy

I let go of her to see what she'd do. She swallowed hard and stared up at the ceiling and then shuddered and tried to mask a whimper with a deep breath, but it broke and she choked instead. She crossed her arms over her belly and then slowly lifted the tank up and over her head. Now she was in a bra and unbuttoned jean shorts. She put the shirt on the bed. *Yes.*

"Stand up," I ordered, "and undress slowly for me."

I leaned back onto an elbow and watched her get out of bed and slowly take off her jean shorts. She had no idea how alluring she was. She wasn't moving slowly to tease me, but she was teasing me all the same.

She let them drop to the floor and stepped out of them. Now she was in a lacy white bra and V-cut matching panties. She stood there, crossing her chest with her arms, looking so vanilla, looking so fucking beautiful, like a bride on her wedding night. *So mine.*

"The rest," I said and waited.

She just stood there, eyes filled with wet, trembling.

I waited. She continued to just stand there.

"Tia."

"I can't," she said.

"Fine. Then it's rocky road, baby girl."

She remained still, but with a resigned look.

While I usually preferred rocky road sex to vanilla sex, tonight I wanted her to submit to me without a fight. It was a first. I wanted cool, creamy, sweet vanilla from her. As creamy and sweet as the lacy bra and panties she was wearing. I wanted her to respond to me awake the way she'd been doing while she was asleep. And I wanted her to moan for me, to wrap her arms around me, to voluntarily kiss me, to moan my name. It was bizarre, but it was what I'd been craving all day.

"But I can't," she said again to the ceiling.

I shrugged and stood up. She quickly took a step back. I took a step forward and she backed up some more, so I reached out and grabbed her panties at the hips and then hooked my thumbs into the waistband and pulled them down while simultaneously pulling her closer. I caught a whiff of her throat, her hair. My nose touched her jaw and I inhaled her scent deeply, then caught the band of her bra in one hand and snapped it unclasped. I pulled it off her and then gave her ass a hard slap, making her thrust forward against me. I liked that. I slapped her ass again, then grabbed it and squeezed. She whimpered and took a tumble but I caught her by the hips. She reached up like she was going to slap me in the face, but I caught her wrist in my left hand and then slapped her ass again with my right. It sent her breasts right against me and I pulled her tight to me while squeezing her ass cheeks, digging my fingertips in, eliciting a squeal from her.

I loosened my grip, but before she had a chance to back away again, I heaved her up into my arms and carried her the few paces back to the bed and quickly fastened her left arm to my headboard with the bra and grabbed the tank top and fastened her other arm to the headboard with that. She was panting; I could see that she was freaked out, and I was so fucking hard it felt like I'd blow my load any second. I took a few steadying breaths.

"Look at you now. You could've cooperated, but now look what we've had to do. Put you in your place. Looks like your place is here, tied to my bed, baby girl. You're exactly where you belong."

She wouldn't look at me. She looked fucking beautiful naked and tied to my headboard and I couldn't wait to sink into her. I leaned over and my tongue flicked over a nipple. She gasped and pulled on the restraints. Both nipples were rock hard.

"You're not going anywhere. Not ever," I said.

Her face was filled with horror at my words. It was as if until tonight she thought of this as a problem that she just had to figure out the solution to and now she knew that I was serious about this game and that I was 100% in charge. I licked her nipple again and then blew on it gently, watching goose bumps rise on her skin.

"Do you not want this" I asked innocently.

She shook her head vehemently.

"No?" I prodded.

She shook her head again, "Of course I don't." She was speaking all breathy and her eyes were wide.

"Tell you what," I said, "If I touch your pussy and it's not wet, I'll untie you and let you go to sleep."

She swallowed hard and squeezed her eyes shut tight. I watched her chest heave up and down for a moment.

"But if you're wet when I put my fingers inside you, after I fuck you good and hard, you wrap your body tight around me for the rest of the night and you kiss me goodnight first. You don't make me ask for it. Deal?"

"You're a pig. Sick in the head," she spat.

I smiled, "We've already established that. So let's see here."

I put my index finger to her bottom lip and tugged it downward so that when I let go her mouth was in a sexy pout. She moistened her lips, sucked in her bottom lip, and fixed her eyes on the ceiling.

"Look at me," I demanded and pulled at her chin until she did.

I gave my best smoldering look and a little smile as my finger trailed down her throat, between her breasts, and then darted back up and circled a nipple. Then my finger resumed its journey downward, slowly, just below her navel. She was holding her breath, but still looking at me.

I trailed my finger further, down her pelvis and then stopped over her clit. I exerted a little pressure on it and watched as her eyes changed, pupils grew larger. She was so inexperienced and so totally enthralled, so easy to seduce. I could feel the air charge with electricity. She wanted to fight, she'd tried through sheer will to find what I was doing repulsive, but it wasn't working.

I drew light tiny clockwise circles with my index finger on her clit and then flicked my wrist and plunged two fingers into her hard and fast, and fuck me but she was soaked.

Tia

When his fingers drove into me I saw white light in my mind. I was dizzy with arousal. What on earth was wrong with me? This was the enemy here. This was the man holding me captive, a man who'd been playing games with me the last few days, and who was now getting this kind of response from my body. I was mortified. Mortified didn't even begin to describe it.

He didn't look at me with smugness after getting his fingers into me so easily. Instead it was like someone had struck a match and his whisky-colored eyes were suddenly on fire.

"I'm gonna fuck you so hard," he told me. And then, he kissed me. He kissed me hard, possessively, and then he was leaning over me, bracing himself in a one-handed push-up stance, and in a split second, his fingers were gone and his cock was there instead. He pushed it in hard and smiled at me.

"This?" he reached between us and rubbed my clit, "Mine."

I tried to pull away but was stuck, restrained. Pulling only made the material cut into my wrists. He kissed behind my earlobe and grabbed a nipple and squeezed it hard. I whimpered.

"And this is mine," he said into my ear and then sucked on my lobe while tweaking the nipple. Then he wedged that hand under my bottom and squeezed a cheek. "Your ass... your sexy little ass... *so* mine."

I was breathing hard and my heartbeat was so fast. He started to pick up his rhythm and pushed hard and deep into me over and over. Then his hand caressed my face and he kissed me sweetly. "These sexy lips are mine, too." I think I started to kiss him back, I don't know. My head was fuzzy, almost like I was drunk or something. I felt like my body was all nerve endings and they were all buzzing, alive with sensation.

"Oh yeah, kiss me baby," he said.

Shit, I guess I had kissed him back. *Shit, shit*! He was rubbing my clit again, and I started to feel the sensations rise. Oh no. I'm going to have an orgasm. And he's going to think I like this. He's going to think tying me to his bed is the sort of thing I like. I don't like this, and I don't want this, like... *at all*. So, why is my body responding like this? Why don't I just spit in his face?

Maybe it was because I knew couldn't stop my body from responding. I was suddenly limp, letting sensation take over.

I'd been fighting so hard, trying so hard to hold myself together, to think about how to get out of this in a way that wouldn't endanger me or my dad, to not show him how weak I really felt, but right now, having my arms tied... it made it easier to deal with this. It was easier to let him make me come, because I had no choice. It didn't make sense but it made total sense. I had no choice. He was going to make me come. The sooner I let myself feel it, the sooner it'd be over. I didn't have to fight. Fighting was futile.

Sensation crested for a second and then came back, overflowing. I moaned hard as the shuddering sensations wove through my every cell. I went from tight and shaky to lax but still trembling because I just let the sensations take over. I gave in to it.

He started to plunge harder and faster and harder and faster still, and then he had my head in his grasp, kissing me and pulling my hair a little. And then he grunted my name as he spilled into me.

"Yeah Tia! Oh fuck, baby," he groaned, trailing kisses from my lips to my chin, and downward until his mouth landed right on my girlie parts. He gently kissed there and nuzzled in. I was dumbstruck. He leaned up and started untying my wrists. My arms were numb. So was the rest of me.

He pulled me against him, and I started to shiver. The blankets were all on the floor. He didn't take the shivering as a cue to get them.

"Blanket?" I rasped, my voice barely a croak.

"Naw," he answered huskily, "You can use my body to keep warm."

I was shivering and my teeth started to actually chatter. I think I was in shock. He pulled me tighter to his body and wrapped his arms around me. After a few minutes I actually sank into his warmth. I had no choice. I had to close my eyes and get away from these intense emotions I was having. He rubbed up and down my rear end. I had welts there and it felt bruised, hurt so much to have them touched. I whimpered.

"Go to sleep, baby. I'll keep you warm," he whispered and kissed my temple.

Good God. I was coming undone. Another stitch gone.

Tommy

I woke up first in the morning and she was wrapped around me, her head on my chest, her left hand under my shoulder blade and her right arm draped around me. I'd be thinking about last night all day. Thinking about what I'd do to her tonight. I could do her right now, actually, but I'd overslept and had an early meeting to dash to. I rolled away and got the comforter from the floor and wrapped it around her. Her eyes opened and for a split second she stared at me dreamily. Then it was as if she realized who I was and who I wasn't. Her expression dropped and her eyes frosted over. I felt a pang in my chest. I pushed it away.

"See ya later, sweet girl. Be good." I tucked her in and kissed her forehead. Then I headed to the shower. She was buried under blankets as I got back out so she was either asleep or hiding from me. I got dressed in the walk-in closet and then left the room.

* * *

I called Sarah at noon, "What's she doing?"

"She's in bed."

"Still?"

"Mm hm." She sounded judgmental. "Red eyes. Won't talk."

"I'll be home at six to pick her up and take her out. Make sure she's ready. I've called over to Donna's for a dress and shoes and things for her. Help her, yeah?"

"Yes, Sir." Her reply was laced with sarcasm.

I hung up. Fucking Sarah thought she had a right to interfere. I waved at the barista to bring me a refill.

Tia

Ms. Martinez, Sarah, was standing over me, telling me I had to get up and get dressed. She had a garment bag draped over her arm and was holding two department store bags, too.

"You and Tommy have a date tonight." She beamed at me. "I've run you a bath. Go bathe, shave your legs and underarms, and shampoo and then I'll help you get ready with your hair and make-up. I'll get some teabags to get the puffiness out of those eyes. I saw the dress and it looks like he's taking you somewhere nice! It's from a shop owned by a friend of the family and you're going to look so gorgeous, Chiquita." She clapped her hands together.

Was she for fricking real?

She left the room and I slowly got to my feet. I got a head rush before I practically stumbled into the bathroom. I couldn't sit in the bath. It was hot. Too hot for my sore ass and it'd definitely make my scraped-up knees hurt, too. Just as I was about to climb in the shower stall, she rushed into the bathroom and stopped in her tracks when she saw my naked rear end.

"Do you mind?" I breathed, grabbing a towel and covering myself.

Her face contorted. "Who did that to you? Was that – " She stopped and her hand covered her mouth.

I didn't answer her. I got into the stall and shut the door. She left in a huff. Rule number two was to keep my mouth shut and I didn't need another punishment.

I couldn't seem to feel clean. At all. No amount of soap and running water could erase what he'd done to my body and my mind in the past few days.

After my shower, Sarah blow dried my hair and then put it in hot rollers and put makeup on my face. She cleaned the now chipping red nail polish off my fingers and toes and then did a French manicure on both. Then she threaded my eyebrows like a pro, all without talking to me, with her lips in a tight line.

The results were as professional-looking as any salon I'd ever been to. Not that I'd been to many. Not that I cared about looking good for Tommy. I was in a red slip dress and kitten heeled black sandals that were thankfully not nearly as high as the fuck-me shoes I'd worn to grad. I didn't wanna look good for him; I wanted to be invisible to him. I wished I was in a burlap sack and rain boots so he wouldn't even look twice at me.

Sarah had given me some aloe gel with lidocaine to spread on my backside and my rug burn so that it'd help numb me. She hadn't asked any more questions, but her lips were pursed tight when she'd passed me the bottle of gel, and said, "For your..." She motioned to her own behind and said nothing else.

When I was ready, she beamed, "You're pretty as a picture." Sarah glanced at her wristwatch. "Okay, he'll be here soon. Something to drink first?"

I shook my head at her. I didn't have any desire to go out on a date with this guy. How could I be in public and pretend to be okay with all of this? I wondered, idly, if he'd update me on the situation with my dad, with Rose and Cal. All day yesterday I'd worried about all of them but today I was pretty numb about even that. I was mad at myself, mad for responding to him sexually. I didn't want to think about it, yet I couldn't stop thinking I might be some kind of mutant. Was I just in shock from everything that had happened in the past few days? Was it all self-preservation?

I started to think that all this was all my fault. Karmic justice. I'd always been drawn to romance novels where the hero was roguish, I'd loved the part in Gone with the Wind where Rhett carried Scarlett up to bed against her will and she was all happy in the morning.

I'd even once had a kind of dark fantasy and I'd beat myself up for it afterwards. I'd been touching myself, imagining the drummer of my favorite band but it wasn't all romance in the fantasy. As I'd touched myself my fantasy morphed from him and me in his dressing room having rough hair-pulling sex against the wall to the whole band coming in, holding me down while they took turns. That was the hardest I'd made myself come, ever, and after that, maybe the guilt over that fantasy was why I'd always stopped touching myself when I started to come, culling the orgasm or something.

I'd never wanted to let my mind go there after that. I'd told myself that it was so wrong to even fantasize about when that was the sort of thing that happened to real women, women who'd be broken after something like that. Was I a mutant for responding to that sort of behavior? Now I was imprisoned in a sexually abusive forced relationship. Maybe it served me right.

Tommy

She stepped out of the house looking gorgeous. Her long, dark hair fell in soft waves today and she wore a sexy little red dress with thin straps over her bare shoulders. She had bare legs, heeled sandals, and when she got into the passenger seat of my car, my hand instantly travelled up her leg, under her dress.

She squirmed, red-faced.

"Don't be shy. Kiss me." I leaned over.

She sat stiffly in the seat and wouldn't look in my direction.

Earl and Sarah were standing on the front steps, eyes on us.

I gritted my teeth and squeezed her leg a little then whispered, "Kiss me, Athena. My staff are watching." I glanced at her knees, they were both rug-burnt and scabbed over. I felt myself get hard, remembering her on her knees on my bedroom floor.

She flashed a look of confusion at me and then glanced at Earl and Sarah, then back at me.

"You actually want everyone to think I'm okay with all of this?" The challenge in her eyes got me harder. Her full lips were bright red and glossy, like raspberries. Juicy-looking raspberries.

"They know I'm a prisoner here. No one expects me to kiss you."

"Kiss me." I leaned in, "Kiss me now and make it good." I caressed her cheek gently. "Don't disappoint me."

She swallowed hard, got a supremely sour look on her face, then leaned over, raked her fingers through my hair and dragged my mouth to hers. She plunged her tongue into my mouth and she was obviously trying for shock value. She let out a little gasp as my hand travelled up further until I cupped her between the legs.

"Good girl," I smirked and then let go of her and turned the ignition.

She'd summoned courage and had tried to shock me, but I'd turned the tables on her. I suppressed the urge to bust up laughing.

She seemed to withdraw into herself as I drove to the restaurant. She needed help to snap out of it.

"Your things from the foster home have been brought in. They're in the basement. You can head down tomorrow and look through them and decide what you need to keep."

Her breath caught. "Okay."

I knew by her face that she wanted to ask me questions. She didn't. She just sat there, hands folded in her lap, staring ahead.

"Your foster parents have been debriefed," I offered.

Her head snapped to my direction. "They know the truth?"

"As much as they need to know. They know that you've moved in with me. They know who I am and they know not to ask questions."

She swallowed hard. "Please tell me that you haven't threatened them."

"They've been cautioned against contacting you or anyone else about the matter."

She looked lost in thought for the rest of the drive. She hadn't asked me about her father, the piece of shit. Maybe she knew enough to know he wasn't worth the trouble of asking. I hadn't done anything about him yet. I was quietly having him tailed by my private eye and looking into his past first. I wanted to know what my father's beef was. Then I'd decide what to do about him.

I pulled into the restaurant parking lot and turned the car off. "There's something else."

Tia

He was staring at me, looking like he was considering what he'd say next.

"What?" I whispered, feeling dread spread through me.

"I want to compromise with you about tonight. Have a nice evening together."

I waited for him to continue. He scratched his jaw, looking like he was pondering something.

Finally, he spoke. "Tonight, I want you to look at this as if it's just a date. Just two people having dinner. Get to know me. Try to be open-minded about enjoying the evening."

I gave him a *yeah right* look.

"I mean it. I'll reward your obedience."

His eyes were flirty. I didn't want flirty. But he rewards obedience, he punishes defiance. I had been punished already and knew that to be true, for sure. This guy loved mind games, that much was obvious. Making me snuggle in exchange for not getting raped, offering me vanilla sex if I complied, raping me, restraining me, and now making me pretend to be on a date and be happy about it?

I swallowed hard, "How will I be rewarded?"

He looked thoughtful for a second. "We'll see."

I thought back to our first night together. He wanted me to pretend to be happy about lying in his arms in order to have him not touch me sexually. This seemed like it was a lot like that. But it was probably a trick, too, because when I'd woken up the next morning, he was doing sexual things to me anyway, taking advantage of the fact that my guard was down. What was his trick this time?

"Why would I trust you after you tricked me that first night?"

"Whoa, that wasn't a trick. I kept my word. I didn't fuck you that night. In the morning you were rubbing your sweet body all over me and I just responded. I'm just a red-blooded man."

I rolled my eyes. He was so full of it. As if I'd rub all over him.

"I'm trusting you," he said, touching my hair, twirling a curl with his index finger. "I'm taking you out in public with me when you could make a scene, when you could try to run away from me. I think you know that it'd be very stupid to do either. I think you know you're lucky that you're not still tied to my bed. I'm trusting that you won't do anything stupid. Compromise. I'm trusting you. You give me some of that back."

I backed away, not wanting him to touch me and hating that this was a veiled warning for me to not try to get away tonight. It had occurred to me, of course it had. I could sneak out the bathroom window. I could hope someone else was in the bathroom and tell someone in the bathroom that they needed to call the cops. But I hadn't hatched a real plan because I didn't know how to do it without putting Dad and the Crenshaws at risk.

What choice did I have about this little game, though? He was repeatedly letting me know he was in charge, and I didn't feel like I had much choice in the role I'd play.

I'd had fleeting thoughts in the past about joining the community theatre. Maybe I could just look at this night as being in a play, playing a role. Couldn't I? Could I pull it off? I wasn't sure if I was capable.

"I don't like to talk consequences, Tia, because it's usually not necessary. Most people who know me know what they put at stake when they cross me. But maybe you and I should have that conversation. Just this once."

"We don't need to have that conversation," I said, not wanting him to make it impossible for me to play this role tonight. But by the look in his eyes, I think he wanted to scare me. And he was. Every hair on my body was at attention.

"Let's just say this, then. Let's just say that all you hold dear is at stake with me, Tia. Now, tomorrow, twenty years from now. Always. I don't forget debts and won't forgive betrayal. Capeche?"

Tommy

This was going to be a fun experiment. I'd get to see what she was made of. Could she be convincing, or would it take some work to get her to be as perfect outside of the bedroom as she was in it?

Now she seemed like she was trying to mentally prepare herself as we sat parked while I checked my voicemail messages. When I got out of the car and reached to open her door, I held an index finger up, signaling her to wait while I walked around and opened the door for her. She got out of the car and looked up at me.

"Chivalry should be shot dead and pissed on." She flashed a look of disgust at me.

"And why is that?" I was taken aback.

"Because it's one of the things that keeps women oppressed."

I was a little shocked at her comment and her brashness.

She flashed a smile at me. "This is me. The real me."

I laughed, a big open-mouthed laugh. She looked embarrassed.

"Well, I guess I'm an old-fashioned guy. I'll be oppressing you every chance I get. Opening the door for you is something you should look on as a gift, my treating you like a queen. My queen."

Her face was red. I kissed her on the temple and held my arm out. She hesitantly took it.

The maître d greeted me excitedly. "Mr. Tommy, so nice to see you!"

"Augustus, this is Tia."

He lamented for nearly thirty seconds about how gorgeous she was and how nice it was to meet her. Yeah, she was beautiful, but he was laying it on a bit thick.

I gave him a look. He pulled himself together and kissed her hand and led us to a table, then immediately brought over a bottle of red wine and poured glasses for us. A waiter brought bread to the table and menus were presented. He spoke to me in Italian about the specials prepared for the evening. When they were gone I leaned over and reached for her hand and skimmed my thumb across her knuckles. She didn't pull away and her face revealed nothing but a warm-looking smile. I returned the smile, giving her a look that showed I was pleased with her.

Tia

We were sitting across the table from one another at a really romantic Italian restaurant with red and white checkered tablecloths, soft lighting, candles, and I'd decided to try to pretend that I was on a date with the guy from the ice cream parlor.

I figured it'd be the only way I could pull off the feat of acting like I was happy or even open-minded about being in his company. I didn't think I could pull off acting like I was happy to be sitting here with Tommy Ferrano, the guy who had done all those awful things to me, so I tried, instead, to rewind the clock in my head and pretend that the gorgeous hunk from the ice cream parlor hadn't morphed into the sadistic criminal who'd threatened to sell me into slavery.

I decided that this wasn't the guy holding me for some ransom that could never be paid. This wasn't the guy who'd spanked me, getting off on my pain, who'd tricked me into sex and then forced sex on me. This man didn't tie me to his bed and screw me, making me cry from embarrassment at responding to him. I tried my hardest to rewind my brain to when I first saw him.

What if I could be here in this nice restaurant with the gorgeous guy from the ice cream parlor who'd given me an outrageous tip, who'd flirted with me, who'd winked at me with some unspoken promise? That'd be nice. That unspoken promise wasn't going to be a nightmare. This was just a date. My loved ones hadn't been threatened, my future hadn't been stolen, and I wasn't being forced to sleep in the bed and the arms of a criminal. I wasn't being forced into anything. Thinking like this was the only way I figured I could pull it off.

"Mind if I order for you?" he asked me, caressing the back of my hand with his thumb.

There was light in his eyes, not darkness, making it easier for me to pretend.

"Sure," I said, "Just no shellfish. I'm highly allergic."

He nodded, then he spoke Italian to the waiter.

"I heard you're half Italian. You speak it?" he asked after the order was taken.

"No, my mom was Italian, but she never taught me. She only spoke it in the house when she was yelling at my dad or using it to keep some secret from me talking on the phone. We never understood her, but knew when she spoke Italian someone was either about to get something good or get in trouble." I laughed a little, and then I knew my face sobered, thinking about her, about my dad.

"I ordered us the lasagna. The lasagna here is to die for." Tommy tried to change the subject. "The only lasagna better was my mother's. She never passed the recipe on before she died, but my sister Tessa does pretty good."

"I think my mom was the only Italian woman in the world who

couldn't cook," I said, smiling, but Dad could cook. Between Dad and Rose, I'd learned to cook, too.

Dad had shown me how to make meals seemingly from nothing. When the fridge and pantry had been nearly bare at times he'd come up with gourmet concoctions. I'd watch and had started to make suggestions for spices or additions to the meals based on what I could find in the cupboard or freezer. We joked that we could make anything taste gourmet with a little of Dad's secret spice blend.

The waiter brought warm bread and an antipasto platter. It smelled mouth-watering and for the first time in days I was actually hungry. It all tasted as good as it smelled, "Oh, this is so good!" I exclaimed and Tommy looked happy. He kind of smiled like ice cream parlor guy, looking insanely attractive. He wore jeans but with a black button-down dress shirt today under a blazer and the top few buttons were down. I could see a little of his chest. There was a thick silver chain on his neck with a crucifix of about two inches long on it. I felt a pang in my gut, reminding me that it was just wishful thinking that this wasn't what I was pretending it was, that this wasn't a real date with that guy that I'd daydreamed about.

After it was over, he wouldn't walk me to my door at my new apartment and kiss me goodnight before we'd go our separate ways. If only. If only after tonight I could dream about our second date. I'd call my friends and we'd talk about the date for hours. If only…

Tommy

Watching her eat was a beautiful thing. Sarah had complained that she'd barely eaten anything since arriving. She was talkative, too; nothing too in-depth, but we conversed about the food, the restaurant, and the mood was light. She seemed carefree.

But then staring into her dessert, she started to take on the look of someone with the weight of the world on her shoulders.

My phone rang just before I delved into my dessert. I answered.

"Tommy! We've got a huge problem. Huge!" It was Luciana, my sister.

"Is it the baby?" I exclaimed into the phone. Tia looked up at me from her tiramisu.

"No; we have a big problem because I've just heard the news, news that did not come from you. You're engaged! I'm going to punch you in the nuts for letting me find out from someone else. How could you?"

I let out a little huff. "Seriously, Luc?"

"Yes, seriously! Q'uest que fuck, Tommy?"

"It's not official yet so no nut-punching, all right? I'm not alone. Tia and I are out for dinner. I'll call you later."

"Bring her Sunday for dinner to Pop's. We need to meet her. I've got Tess here. She agrees."

"That was already part of the plan," I answered. "Gotta go."

Tia was looking at me curiously. I shrugged. "My sisters just found out about you. They're anxious to meet you. Sunday there's dinner at my Pop's. We're expected. You get to have the whole Ferrano experience all at once." I rolled my eyes.

Her eyes widened fractionally, then she said, "Tell me about them."

"Well, there's Contessa - Tessa, she's, ah, 22, has two boys, aged one and almost three. There's Dario - Dare, you met him, he's 24 and single, then there's Luciana, Luc, she's 22 also. She and Tess are like 10 months apart, and she's pregnant with her third. She has two-year-old twin girls."

"Uncle Tommy? You're the oldest?"

I smirked at her, feeling a twinge at my name on her lips. That might've been the first time she'd said it. "That's me. Thomas

Vincent Ferrano Jr. 29. The three of them are my half siblings. Pop remarried after my mother died. That marriage didn't last though, so he got married again. That didn't last either. Now he's on wife number four. Lisa is the same age as Dare. She's good friends with the girls."

Tia winced.

"Yeah. That didn't go over well at first. Everyone's over it. Pop's a real ladies' man."

She shuffled uneasily in her seat. I looked at her curiously.

"I'm so full," she said, putting her fork down.

I signaled for the waiter to bring the bill. "Wanna take a walk? Walk off all these carbs?"

"Great idea." She smiled at me. Her smile seemed genuine. She was a damn fine actress so far. This was good to know.

Not far away, I pulled into the parking lot for the beach. It was close to sunset and the weather was perfect for a stroll. As she got out of the car I grabbed her hand and held it as we walked. We got to the sand and she stopped, reached for and then held onto my shoulder, then pulled the strap off an ankle, let that shoe drop off, and then let go of me to get the other shoe off. She bent and looped the straps around her index finger to carry them and I grabbed her free hand again and kissed each of her knuckles.

She looked up at me and smiled. "Thanks for dinner, Tommy."

My name again. Another twinge. And that smile seemed real. I felt a pang of annoyance that it seemed so real. I think I must've frowned at her because she swallowed hard and chewed her bottom lip, looking down. I took a few steadying breaths to push my pissed-off attitude away. I lifted my necklace out of my shirt and fingered the crucifix on it as we walked in silence. I caught a look on her face that made me realize I was squeezing her hand too tight. I loosened it and her expression softened.

A tiny fur ball of a golden retriever puppy bounded right up to her and started licking her calves. She let go of my hand and dropped to her knees, dropping her shoes and pulling the pup into her lap.

"Oh my goodness!"

The dog licked at the air, furiously, wanting to lick her face. She held him back at arm's length but giggled. A kid, probably around ten, ran up to us with a leash in his hand and it still had the collar attached to it. Obviously, the pup had squirmed right out of his collar.

"Sorry!" the kid said. "Marley!"

"Oh, it's okay!" Tia exclaimed. "He's so cute; how old is he?"

The kid shrugged. The dog couldn't be any more than eight or nine weeks old. Tia was scratching him behind both ears while he licked her arms. Her red dress was covered in wet and dry sand and she didn't seem to care in the least.

The kid leaned over and tried to get the collar over the pup's head, but the dog was having none of it. He took off into the water. The kid shouted at the dog and Tia laughed, calling out, "He's a water dog, he can't help it!"

The kid's father came running up, out of breath. The dog had obviously gone on a good run. The guy looked at the dog swimming in the water like it was his worst nightmare come true.

"Hang on," Tia called to him and then she lifted a thick stick up off the beach and tossed it toward the dog. It landed in the water beside the pup and he immediately swam to it and caught it between his teeth. Tia started slapping her legs, "Come here, Marley, come here! Fetch!" The dog swam toward her with the stick in his mouth.

"You're a genius!" the kid's father exclaimed.

"I love goldens. They can't resist two things. Water and retrieving."

Yeah, and he can't resist beautiful girls. She was laughing harder, carefree. It was a beautiful sound.

I shook my head, taking it all in, a grin on my face. She flashed a smile at me and it was so gorgeous and seemed so genuine that I felt a strange pain pierce my chest.

The dog bounded toward Tia again and then shook hard, getting all of us wet. Tia squealed like she loved it. The dad went to grab the dog.

"Wait!" Tia told him. We have to let him fetch it at least once more. Can I? He'd think I was a liar if we just let you chain him without a fetch."

The guy laughed and shrugged. My face hurt from my perma-grin. She didn't want the dog to think she was tricking him. I shook my head at that.

"Marley, drop it!" she demanded with authority, and pointed at the ground. The pup held tight to the stick for a second and then dropped the stick in front of her and panted enthusiastically at her. She swiped it and flung it into the water and squealed with glee as the dog took off back into the water. "He's so smart already."

As soon as she slapped her legs, "Marley!" he swam back. The little boy took the stick from the dog and threw it into the water again and I grabbed her hand and whispered in her ear, "Let's make our getaway."

"Bye," she said to the guy and his kid and waved at the dog who was swimming back toward us. She actually waved *bye* to the dog. I shook my head.

She was walking along, a spring in her step, holding my hand, smiling. I'd somehow wound up carrying her sandals in my free hand, and the sun was setting. It was like something out of a chick flick. I had to kiss her and take full advantage of this moment right fucking now.

We were in an area with no one else around. I stopped and took in a big breath. She looked at me. Then she swallowed hard, looking freaked out.

I brushed some sand off her cheek with my thumb, then leaned down and sucked in her bottom lip. She hesitated at first, but a second after my lips touched hers, she started to melt into me. I wrapped my arms around her waist and pulled her closer, kissing her deeply. She was responding.

The sun was setting, leaving the sky orange and pink. Birds were on the horizon, and I was filled with emotion.

"Marry me," I said, caught up in the moment.

Stupid beach at fucking sunset. I felt like such a cliché. But clichés are clichés for a reason, I guess. She looked up at me, her jade eyes full of alarm.

"Marry me," I repeated. "I want that ring on your finger." I felt like the fucking Grinch who stole Christmas after his heart had grown three sizes.

She swallowed hard. She was searching her brain for a reply, and I saw fear in her eyes. She didn't want to say the wrong thing, but she certainly didn't want to say yes, either. For the first time, the fear on her face didn't send a thrill up my spine and through my pants. I kissed her again, kissed her in a way that could be called claiming as much as it could be called kissing and she responded with a little moan into my mouth, and then her hands came up and her fingers wove into my hair and it felt like she was really in the kiss and in the moment with me.

But despite how convincing she was, she had to still be just acting and I was trying my damnedest to not let it piss me off and ruin this moment. But, it nagged at me. For her, this was just self-preservation. I pulled away and looked at her accusingly.

Tia

Until he said, "Marry me", he was Ice Cream Parlor Hottie. Somehow, I'd managed to convince myself of that and it had made things not so difficult, other than a few awkward moments. I thought I was doing okay, and I did start to forget who he really was there for a bit.

But then when he looked at me with that scary hunger in his eyes, he was suddenly the guy that had slapped me and scared me and tied me up, who'd threatened me and everyone I loved.

Thankfully, he'd broken the awkwardness when I didn't answer his proposal, if you could call it a proposal, since he more demanded than asked. He broke the tension by kissing me again. The way he kissed me...wow. I'd gone weak in the knees. How could he make me feel like that one minute and fill me with hate a moment later? Then he glared at me for a second like I'd done something wrong, and before I could process it, we were walking hand in hand back toward the car. I wasn't sure what would happen when we got back to his house. He was walking too fast and I got a stitch in my side.

He waited, looking broody while I washed the sand off my feet in a small fountain near the parking lot and then walked on the hot pavement to the car. He tossed my shoes into the back seat and got in the car and started it.

He was quiet all the way back to his house. I kept seeing his jaw muscles flexing as he drove. My heart was racing; the suspense was freaking me out.

When he pulled the car into his driveway and got out, I didn't know whether or not to sit there and wait or get out. I reached for my shoes and then looked at him as he slammed his door.

"What, you want chivalry now?" He quirked his eyebrows up at me.

I opened my mouth, but nothing came out. He started to laugh. I cracked a smile, embarrassed, and then got out of the car and followed him into the house. I wasn't sure if the laugh was cynical or if he was just teasing me. I was having trouble getting a read on him.

"What happened to you?" Sarah, standing in the front hall, looked at me like I was something the cat had dragged in. Tommy was arming the house alarm.

"Wrestling on the beach with a golden retriever puppy," I said and shrugged. I caught my reflection in a mirror on the wall in the foyer. My hair was windblown and I was barefoot without an ounce of lipstick remaining on my mouth and my eye makeup was a little bit raccoonish. "Oh, I'm a mess!"

She smiled, looking surprised and pleased.

"No, you're beautiful. You can punch the clock, Sarah." Tommy said. "I don't need anything else tonight. Where's Earl?"

"He's out back. I'll tell him you're in." She was smiling at him with a sort of goofy grin.

"All right. I don't need to see him; I just wanted to know if it was him on patrol. Lock the door on your way through the kitchen."

"All right. And yes, until midnight, then Marco relieves him." Her smile was still big.

"All right." He looked at her strangely.

Patrol. There were men here, guarding. Were they doing more than making sure I wasn't escaping? I'd seen enough mafia movies to know that most organized crime families considered themselves under threat from some enemy or another most of the time.

"Let's go," he said to me and took my hand, moving us to head up the stairs, leaving her standing there still smiling goofily.

Following him up to the master bedroom felt ominous. The instant I shut the door behind myself, he pinned me against it. He wasn't touching me with his hands as both palms were flat against the door, but his hips were against me and I was stuck. He was breathing heavily, looking down at me. I looked up into his eyes and swallowed hard. It seemed like an eternity passed before he finally spoke.

"So?" he breathed.

He threw his suit jacket on the floor and then undid the silver chain around his neck and tucked it into his pants pocket. Then he undid the buttons of the dress shirt and shook it off, and held it in his hand. He did all this while continuing to pin me with his hips. I felt his erection against my stomach.

I took a deep breath. I was torn between wanting to stare at his beautifully sculpted naked upper body and looking away due to the darkening look in his eyes. Obviously, our little date was over and now he was back to being himself. Ice Cream Parlor Hottie was long gone, if he'd ever even been there at all.

"Think you passed tonight?"

I regarded him for a second, trying to read his eyes. They were smoldering with something. Was it passion? Was it anger? Was it both? Whatever it was, it made me bristle.

"I..." I started to answer but was lost for words.

"You're a damn fine actress," he said, shaking his head, and then he caressed my cheek with just a graze of the back of his hand. The touch was gentle, but the look on his face – it wasn't. I felt heat coming off his body and it left me lightheaded. Speechless.

"Aren't you the perfect little liar?" He looked upset.

Oh no.

"How am I a liar? I wasn't lying," I whispered.

He looked at me with disbelief. His face looked on the verge of turning from upset to a sneer and a sneer couldn't possibly bode well for me.

"I was pretending," I said quickly, feeling like I was in very dangerous territory.

"What's the difference?" He frowned at me. "There's no difference."

"You told me to behave a certain way and I did. What did I do wrong?" I was trying to not sound snarky. I was trying to not provoke him.

"Nothing. You were perfect." He looked at me with sourness.

Tommy

Why was I so pissed off?

Because if this girl could, on a dime, play me like this, make it feel that real, I was in serious fucking trouble. She'd already dinged my armor somehow. She was looking up at me with huge eyes and a trembling bottom lip asking what she'd done wrong and truthfully, I didn't know how to answer her because she'd done just what I'd told her to do. She'd done a masterful job of acting like she wanted to be with me. I felt guilt sweep through me. I didn't fucking like it.

"Do you really want to know what the difference is?" she asked me.

"Yeah, why don't you enlighten me?"

I needed a fucking drink.

Tia

"I pretended you were the guy from the ice cream parlor," I said quickly.

He looked at me weirdly for a second, and then it started to dawn on him, I think.

I continued. "When you came into the ice cream parlor, when you flirted with me, I fell into total crush mode. I thought, wow Tia, imagine if this gorgeous man, not a boy, a man, took you on a date? What would that be like? I imagined what I wanted it to be like. A nice restaurant instead of fast food. All dressed up. Romantic. I thought about you for days. You were on my mind right up until I graduated. When I met you for the second time you shattered that image, that fantasy. Shattered it. Tonight, it felt like my life was on the line and I couldn't lie, couldn't pretend to like you, not after everything that's happened. So," I took a deep breath, "I tried to rewind things. I pretended you were him... the guy I first fantasized about, how I'd thought you might be." I swallowed and then continued in barely more than a whisper, "and the date was kind of like I'd imagined and you kind of were like that, too."

His expression dropped. He was two inches from my face and he just stared at me. He stared at me for the longest time. I didn't look away. I just leaned against the door.

I finally spoke, "Tommy, please don't hurt me tonight." It came out in a flurry of words, almost like two words, his name and then the rest.

He dropped the shirt on the floor and slowly backed away from me, palms up, like I might shoot, then he was at the bar, pouring whiskey in a glass and he drank it straight in one gulp, then slammed the glass on the bar. I flinched, but stayed put. He poured another few inches in the glass and downed that, too. Then he was staring at me and I couldn't get a read on him. Finally, he slammed the glass down again and strode over to me.

Here we go. I felt sick to my stomach. I felt like I was gonna throw up.

"Go to bed, Tia. Your reward for this evening's exemplary behavior is that you don't have to sleep with me tonight. Excuse me."

Startled, I stepped away from the door.

He left.

I stood, chin to the floor for a moment, then I walked over to the bar, and shakily poured a bit of whiskey into a glass and I downed it. It burned like a sonofabitch.

I got ready for bed, washing the remnants of my ruined make-up off and putting on his dress shirt from the floor.

I tossed and turned almost all night. I thought about Cal and Rose, I thought about the Carusos' apartment, thought about my friends, about school in the Fall, and most of all I pondered the enigma that was Tommy Ferrano. I didn't know what to make of him, of the events of the evening. I lay there, lost in thought, torn between stressing about my future and remembering the way that kiss on the beach at sunset felt.

Wearing his shirt with his scent on it felt so intimate; it was almost like he was beside me and that scent was Ice Cream Parlor Hottie to me. Not the gangster, the abusive jerk, but the guy who'd kissed me like I'd never been kissed in my life, who'd smiled at me, who'd laughed at the puppy, held my hand while we walked down the beach, carried my shoes.

I fell asleep probably just before dawn, so slept late. I glanced at the small clock on Tommy's nightstand and it was 11:30. I sat up and stretched. I got up, used the bathroom, took a shower, and put on his bathrobe, which was hanging up on the back of the bathroom door. It was just the tiniest bit damp around the collar, telling me he must've used it today. He must've showered in here while I slept. It felt too intimate wearing it. I changed my mind and got out of it, staying in just the towel while I brushed my teeth. I then dressed in more of Sarah's clothes and made my way downstairs, finding Sarah on a stool at the kitchen island doing something on her phone, laughing.

"Hi," I said, hesitantly.

She waved me over and showed me a picture of a bunch of old men in Speedo bathing suits with some silly caption below it. I didn't even read what it said; I just scrunched up my nose at the image and backed away.

She cackled all the way to the coffee maker and brewed a cup for me. I watched her put in two full and then three quarters of a spoonful of sugar. Yep, the weaning off had begun. She stirred it and passed it to me.

"Today I'm going grocery shopping. Anything you fancy, let me know and I'll add it to my list. Tell me what you like to eat. What do you want for breakfast today?"

"Nothing, I'm not hungry. And um..." I so did not want to have this conversation. It would mean I was settling in here.

"I'll get you cereal, at least, so you have something in your stomach. I'll get you some more clothes to wear. What do you like to eat in the mornings? What are your favorite foods? What do you like to drink?"

I was about to tell her that Tommy said my belongings were downstairs, so I didn't need any more clothes, but her phone rang and she picked it up.

"Yes, Sir?" She mouthed the name Tommy at me.

I backed away from her and walked through the kitchen to the dining room where there were more patio doors. I took my coffee outside to the patio.

A moment later she came out. "He says I should bring you grocery shopping. We'll go after your coffee and breakfast. He had this delivered for you."

She passed me an Apple iPhone box. The shrink-wrap was loose. I put it on the table and held my lips tight together.

"What do you want to eat? I'll make you something. At least have some cereal? Open it. There's a message."

"Cereal's fine; thanks."

She disappeared into the house.

There was a black iPhone and when I turned it on, there was a text message alert. I opened the text, which said it was from "T".

"Keep this phone with you at all times in case I need to reach you. It only dials to me and won't make any other calls. I'll be home @10-11. Behave."

I said 'whatever' aloud then I put it down. I liked my phone. I didn't know where my phone even was. Why did I have to use this phone? I wanted to throw it in the pool accidentally-on-purpose.

Sarah came out with a bowl of cereal for me.

"Sugar Crisp?" I asked.

She smiled. "Is that okay?"

I hadn't had a bowl of Sugar Crisp since my mom walked the earth. I started to bawl. Hard. Ugly cry. She sat down and wrapped her arms around me and let me howl it out. Damn, but it felt good to wail. I think I went on for fifteen minutes until I was doing that stuttered breathing thing. She just let me. She just sat with me and patted my back and stroked my hair and let me cry it out. She was about the age Mom would've been if she hadn't died. God, I missed having a mother.

Rose was amazing and I'd had some other amazing women help raise me, but I really, really wanted my mom. Mom wouldn't have let Dad sell me to the mafia. If that's what he'd done.

By the time I let her go, my cereal had gone soggy. She got me another bowl, telling me that she always kept it on hand because it was Tommy's favorite. I told her through the last of the tears that I wouldn't hold that against the Sugar Crisp and she laughed at me and rubbed big circles around my back with her palm. Mom used to rub my back like that.

Tommy

My phone rang, interrupting a meeting – a meeting that was dragging on enough as it was, and I didn't need something else slowing it down. It was Sarah. I declined the call. Then I got a sinking feeling about Tia. I had seen her in my bed that morning and it'd stirred something in me that I couldn't put my finger on. She'd been asleep in my shirt, the blankets kicked off, giving me a raging hard-on.

She'd been on my side of the bed, snuggled in to my pillow. I wondered if the only reason she stayed cuddled up against me at night instead of rolling away was because I was on her preferred side of the bed. But seeing her in my shirt just hit me hard. I had to stop myself from climbing on top of her. I got a quick shower and had left before she woke up. I was about to call back and then Sarah called again.

"Excuse me," I said to Dare and to the three men I was sitting with, brokering a deal for a very lucrative upcoming construction project. I answered and stepped away, asking, "What is it?"

"That girl just spent twenty-five minutes crying on my shoulder like her life was over. She won't talk, just keeps crying. What are you doing to her?"

The fuck?

I ended the call without a word. For fuck sakes. Few people in the world dared talk to me that way. Unfortunately, Sarah was one of them.

My head was barely in the rest of the meeting. Thankfully, Dare picked up the slack. By the time it was over I knew that Sarah and Tia would be out shopping. I called Earl to check in and make sure everything was okay.

Tia

Grocery shopping with a six-foot-six mean-looking Black guy in a suit along with a sweet Latina woman who never shut her mouth for more than five seconds was interesting. It broke up the boredom of lying in my torture chamber (a.k.a. his room), at least.

I was quiet, just pushed the cart while Sarah filled it and talked about recipes, about prices, about what was in season, while she asked me questions about whether or not I preferred crunchy or smooth peanut butter, about whether I liked fruit bottom or stirred yogurt. She told me what Tommy liked to eat, like I cared. But this was a diversion, at least, from the pit of despair I'd been in.

Earl was on the phone, saying, "Yes, Sir. No, no problems, Sir. Yes, Sir. Right, Sir. Fine, Sir. Bye, Sir."

Fuck off and die, Sir, I thought to myself, or so I thought, but guessed I had actually muttered it aloud because Earl was staring at me with a funny little smile.

I tried to smile back; I definitely blushed. I was grateful I wasn't being babysat by burly number one or burly number two or Tommy's very intense angry brother. I guess I kind of liked Earl so far. He seemed nice. He had kind eyes. As kind and nice, I guess, as a guy can be who's helping another guy hold me prisoner.

As my neck was coming around to face forward after smiling at him I saw my foster mother push an empty shopping cart past me. Rose! She made eye contact briefly, and then kept going. This wasn't her neighborhood. She glanced back at me and subtly made the sign language sign for toilet.

I knew a bit of sign language because last year we'd had a deaf girl named Shelly live with us for four months. They were four hellish months because she was a nasty piece of work that brought too much drama to the house. Me and the other girls threw a little "Ding dong the witch is dead" party with chanting and everything when she was relocated.

Rose wasn't happy about our celebration at the time, lecturing about being patient, trying to be helpful, and turning the other cheek, yada yada, but that girl had stolen something or another (clothes, money, books) from every one of us, had spread lies about Bethany at school and online, and she was just really unpleasant. Anyway, I knew a few signs because of that.

I waited until we turned another corner and then tried to be nonchalant. "Is there a public bathroom in this store?" I asked Sarah, careful not to look at Earl.

She pointed behind us. "Yeah, back by the customer service desk."

"Okay, I'll meet you in ice cream in five?"

She smiled at me, "You want ice cream?"

I smiled back and nodded. "Be right back."

Earl said something to her and she took the cart from me. He followed me to the bathroom. I felt my face get hot. I didn't make eye contact with him. Thankfully, he at least waited outside the door.

The bathroom had two regular stalls and one wheelchair one. I saw Rose's feet in the wheelchair one, so pulled the handle and stepped in. She grabbed me and clutched me tight against her.

I tried not to make a sound but wanted to fall apart.

"Let's go. Quick!" she said.

I put my finger to my lips and pointed at the door. "Bodyguard," I whispered.

She gasped and covered her mouth, then said, "I've been so worried. Are you okay?" her voice was barely above a whisper, "You don't look well."

I nodded and dashed the tears off my face.

She said, "I don't know much but I know when something is fishy. A man came to see me to tell me you were in protective custody temporarily, that your father was in trouble but the police were keeping you safe. He gave some cockamamie story with too many holes in it, so I called the police. I had written down the license plate and gave it to them."

My hand came up to cover my mouth. Oh fuck. Oh no. Oh fuck.

"They transferred me to a cop who took down the information and said he'd call me back. Someone else called and it didn't feel right. They were giving us the brush off, like you'd just run off with a boyfriend or something. Something wasn't right. This wasn't you. I called Susie. She started poking around and then I got another visit, from a man who said you were now engaged to a powerful man and that you had moved on with your life. When I balked because, hey, I know you...he said we'd all be in danger if we continued to try to interfere. He said if we stayed out of it we might get invited to the wedding and get to have a relationship with you. If we didn't, we might need to find a new house to live in because old houses like ours often had electrical fires. Can you imagine? Cal was close to the house as he left with your things, I had him follow. This morning I decided to wait at that house for them and saw them leave with you, so I followed. Susie thinks you're in trouble with the mob because of your father. Is it true? She said he's been associated with the mafia over the years according to her contacts in the police department."

"Oh Rose, this is too dangerous!" I was trying to keep my voice low. I didn't have much time. "Listen," I said, "These are dangerous people. I don't want you and Cal getting mixed up in this. I'm okay. I'm fine. Please don't do anything else, please just–"

"You are not fine!" Her voice was getting too loud.

"Shh," I winced, clutching her biceps.

There was a loud knock on the door. I flushed the toilet and signaled for her to *shh*.

"Miss O'Connor?" Earl was inside the ladies' room right outside the stall door. Shit.

I started to open it and tried to squeeze out without revealing that Rose was in there with me. It was no use. He pulled the door open and came face to face with her.

"Is everything okay, Miss O'Connor?" Earl asked, looking at her instead of me.

"It's fine," I breathed. "Let's go." I looked back, giving Rose a desperate look. "I'm fine. It's okay. I'll be in touch, okay?"

She shook her head at me and turned her attention to Earl. "What do you people think you're doing? You can't just–"

"Please!" I exclaimed, "I'll be in touch. Don't, okay? Don't put your family at risk. Trust me. I'll be fine."

Earl's eyes narrowed at me and then at her. He reached for my elbow and gently ushered me forward.

"You're part of our family, Tia," Rose choked out.

"I love you," I said to her. "Thank you for everything. Everything. I'll be in touch, okay?"

Tears welled up in her eyes and she covered her mouth with her hand.

As we stepped out Earl said, "Take my arm, Miss O'Connor."

I did. He ushered me directly out of the store and to the Jeep he'd driven us there in. He opened the back door, and I got in. He got into the driver's seat, then dialed a number and held the phone. Then he hung up and dialed again and held the phone and looking pissed off, punched at the screen to dial again. Then he dialed yet again.

"Sir, there's been an incident. It's under control, but the foster mother followed us to the supermarket and got Miss O'Connor into the bathroom and I broke up a conversation."

He was quiet for a minute and then stepped out of the Jeep and closed the door. He moved several feet away to finish his conversation. By the look on his face he looked like he was getting raked over the coals. He made another call and talked with a cold look on his face and then seemed like he was getting in an argument with someone.

When he got back into the car he dialed another number. "Miss. Martinez, we're in the car due to a problem, security breach; you're almost done there? Wrap it up immediately. No, per Mr. Ferrano. It's urgent. Or, I take Miss O'Connor home and you either wait until I have relief to come back for you or you take a cab."

He paused, then continued by biting off. "No, I will not ask her that…. fine…" He leaned back and asked me, "What kind of ice cream?"

I let out a half laugh, half cry. He shrugged kind of apologetically. I shook my head.

"She says surprise her," he snapped, ending the call.

He pulled out and left Sarah at the supermarket and drove me back to Tommy's house. That phone started ringing from my pocket. I took it out.

"T" calling. Great. I stared at it. After the third ring, Earl cleared his throat. After the fourth ring, he said, "I'd answer that, Miss."

I didn't. I couldn't do anything but stare at the screen. It stopped at five rings. Then Earl's phone started ringing and he said a mix of Yes Sirs and No Sirs all the way back. When we pulled inside the gate, which Earl appeared to have engaged somehow from within the vehicle, he stopped in front of the gate and sat there for what seemed like the longest time. He dialed the phone and said, "What's your

ETA? Shit. Can't do it. Won't work. No, that's not the plan. Can't. We'll have to reschedule."

He growled a sound of frustration into the phone and then hung it up and finally drove in through the area between the gates.

"You can go ahead, Miss. O'Connor. I'm instructed to come with you, keep you company until Mr. Ferrano returns."

I nodded and opened the car door and followed him into the house.

I sat at a stool at the kitchen island and folded my hands in front of me. I was dizzy.

Please don't hurt them, please don't hurt them. It was a chant inside my head, and I said it over and over and over.

"Do you want something to drink? Some tea?" Earl asked me. He seemed really uncomfortable.

I nodded. He put his suit jacket on the back of the chair, loosened his tie, and then rolled up the sleeves of his shirt and filled the kettle.

"I didn't have anything to do with that," I whispered. "They're good people. Please tell me they won't be hurt."

"Tommy will find a way to get them to back off. Don't fret," he said softly, then put the kettle on its base and turned it on.

He stepped into the dining room when his phone vibrated. I couldn't hear his conversation. A moment later, he returned and then filled a tea pot and put it on the island with two cups, the sugar, and the milk.

A few minutes later we were drinking tea and saying nothing. Finally, he fetched a newspaper from another room and handed me the entertainment section and opened the sports section.

After just a few minutes I heard noise and it wasn't what I'd hoped for, which would've been Sarah coming in with the groceries. Instead, it was Tommy who was leaned in the doorway of the kitchen, eyes narrow and on me.

"That's all for now," he said.

Earl left the room.

"Upstairs," Tommy said to me very calmly and then turned on his heel.

I was frozen in place. He looked back over his shoulder at me. "Now."

I slowly rose and then followed, taking slow and shaky breaths, wishing I could disappear.

Inside the master bedroom, he sat on the bed and untied his black leather shoes. When he took them off, he then took his tie and his blazer off, followed by taking cufflinks out.

He looked even more dressed up than usual. Great, this incident got him pulled from an important meeting; that should put him in a fine mood.

He took his silver crucifix necklace off and put it on the nightstand and removed his shirt before he tossed it on the bed. Then he stood and undid his belt. He was looking at me with intensity; biting down on his bottom lip as he did this. My heart rate picked up and my throat felt dry. He had the halved belt in his hands and he jerked his hands to make it snap loudly. This made me jolt and shudder.

"So," he said to me. "Care to explain what happened in the store today?"

I blanched. He had to already know what had happened from Earl.

"I saw Rose in the bathroom. She followed us. She was just worried. I told her to back off. She will." My voice was small, weak, I was quaking.

"Yeah, Rosalie Crenshaw and Susan DeLong are making inquiries. It needs to stop."

"I-I told her I was fine, to back off." I was not at all comfortable with the name dropping, that he obviously had information on them. I kept my eyes on the belt while bile rose in my throat.

"Yeah, you said."

"What are you gonna do?" My chin trembled.

"You want to know what I'm gonna do?" His eyes were challenging me.

"I want to know you're not going to do anything to... to them. I've talked to her, it'll be fine. She..." I didn't know how to finish that, to find the words to make him leave them alone.

He sighed, then pinched the bridge over his nose. "I do not need this hassle."

I stood still, not knowing what he wanted me up here for. It was still the afternoon and he was undressing in front of me so of course I didn't feel like, based on his track record so far, that this was going to go well.

"Come here," he told me, dropping the belt on the bed beside him.

I blew out a slow breath. "Listen," I said and took a step back.

He raised his eyebrows. "Here."

I stepped up in front of him. He grabbed the back of my knees and pulled me even closer.

"I had to come all the way home in the middle of a busy workday to deal with you, so you're going to make it worth my while," he said and the tone of voice and expression on his face were scary. Beyond scary.

He caressed the back of my leg softly. I tried to step back, but he grabbed my hips.

"Did you disobey me?" His fingers dug in.

"No." I whispered, my voice hoarse, gaze fixed on the ceiling.

"You snuck off to talk to her; what did you say?"

"I just kept telling her I'm fine and not to worry."

One of his hands slid up and down my thigh. Suddenly both of his hands were pushing the pants I was wearing down, taking the underwear with them. I tried to back up.

"You refused to answer my call. Stop," he commended.

I froze.

"Take your shirt off," he ordered.

I chewed the inside of my cheek. No way.

"Now," he added.

I shook my head.

"Are you telling me *no*?"

I stared at the ceiling, trying hard to not cry.

He yanked the pants the rest of the way down, then stood up, towering over me and hauling the t-shirt I was wearing over my head, leaving me in just my bra. Then he undid it, too, and yanked it off. He did all of this methodically and then he stopped and tipped my chin up so I'd have to look at him. He was so intimidating. Bigger, stronger, such an intense look on his face. I was a quaking mess. I covered my chest with my arms. He dropped his pants. I held back the tears that were threatening.

"I've done nothing wrong," I said to the ceiling.

His eyes were on me, glaring at me, making me want to cower. "I told you to come to me and you hesitated. I told you to take off your shirt and you hesitated. I think you need to learn a little bit about following directions." His eyes burned into me with anger. He was scaring the fuck out of me.

"You don't hesitate when I tell you to do something. You do it. And when I call, you answer the fucking phone. Understand?"

I stepped back, stepping out of the pants that were pooled at my feet. He stepped forward. I stepped back again and again and then my back hit the wall. He came up directly against me and grabbed my wrists and held them against the wall above my head.

"Disobey me again; I dare ya."

He stared for a moment and then let go, grabbed my breasts and raked his fingers over my nipples roughly.

My now free hands pushed at him and for a split second he let me go and then my hands came up to cover myself. He smirked, then leaned forward and hauled me over his shoulder and then dropped me on the bed.

"On all fours, now," he said. He pointed at the mattress. I shook my head and a whimper came out.

"Oh, another refusal? Did you forget rules one and two today, Tia? Not obeying me and discussing me with someone else?"

"I didn't discuss you."

"But you agree that you disobeyed me?"

"Please don't." My heart hammered against my chest wall.

He leaned toward me. "On all fours. Now. If you're going to be a disobedient bitch, I'll fuck you like one." He picked up the belt from beside me. I started to whimper and cower. He smirked. He looked so evil, so like he was loving every minute of this. Part of me was ready to just do what he said to make things easier, but something rose in me.

No. No, I wasn't going to just be a victim here, let him beat me. This sick and twisted man could not just take me over and over like this. I may not have been a strong person but I certainly wasn't this weak, was I? I backed up against the headboard watching him move closer, a sickening glint in his eye.

Right then, right there, I was so done. Totally done dealing with this prick. I leaned over to the nightstand and grabbed for the lamp and bashed it on his head.

"Fuck you!" I screamed. He looked dazed for about a second. Unfortunately, it wasn't enough.

Tommy

I can't believe she fucking whacked me on the head. I was practically seeing stars. I saw three of her in front of me. As I shook it off, she took off toward the patio door. I caught her by the leg and we both crashed to the rug.

I knew I had gone too far with the way I was handling this, but today had been a bad fucking day so far and I'd seen red imagining her being taken from me, and now I was letting her know how fucking pissed I was.

She raked her fingernails down my cheek and it instantly burned. I gave her an incredulous look and then I quickly pinned her to the rug and held her wrists tight.

"Athena!" I hollered at her.

It obviously scared her as she stilled long enough for me to lay directly on top of her. Pinned, I parted her legs with my knee. I needed to be inside of her right now; needed her to submit. I dipped a finger into her pussy and it let me in a little. She wasn't soaked, but there was something. She bucked, trying to get me off her, her fists flying, then she head-butted me right on the eye.

She was so fucking sexy with rage in her green eyes and her little fists flying at me. I was seeing waves of blinding light combined with the flurry of her fists and her long hair whipping around, with flashes of hatred on her face. I growled and then reached for her.

"It's time to submit to your Master." I laughed while I told her this. My vision returned to normal just in time to see her pale under me.

I laughed again and then licked her from the base of her throat up her cheek and up to her temple. "You're mine, Athena. All mine. You're either gonna be my dirty little whore or you're gonna be nothing to me. The way you behave in the next little while will determine which one. It's time to let me in." I growled, tasting blood from the cut on my lip. "Open your legs."

Tia

Until that point I'd been struggling, not because I thought I could win but because I had to. I couldn't just do whatever he wanted. Couldn't. I started to feel like it was stupid to fight. But, I couldn't stop. And it was like it fueled him. Every time I disobeyed or fought back he got this look in his eyes, this fire. And the fire today seemed like it was burning hotter than it had so far because I'd really fought with him with all my might. I've scratched his face, I've bashed him on the head with a lamp, I've bucked and kicked at him, I've pulled his hair, I've punched him in the mouth and wherever my fists would land but he was not stopping. I guessed I should count myself lucky he hadn't hit me back. He's got way more strength than me. Lucky? Hah! I felt pride, though, in that I'd fought back, in that I'd ignored the urge to just turtle and let him have his way.

But now, after those words and because finally he got his cock against me and started to prod and damn it but he got no resistance from my body, I gave up. The bravery in me just shriveled up and wilted.

"So perfect," he moaned. and then he had my arms pinned above my head again. I feebly tried to buck him off one last time, but it only served to help him drive deeper into me. That's when I gave up; I was spent, all the fight in me depleted. He had me pinned; I couldn't move. So, I didn't have to fight any more.

I was whimpering in my defeat and at my screwed-up thoughts, and then I whimpered harder because the sensations he was creating started to feel good. Was I crazy for not knowing if I was whimpering out of desire or defeat? It didn't matter because I had no choices here.

"Good girl; you know when it's time to submit." He passionately kissed my throat, and then he got his mouth right by my ear and whispered, "No one is ever gonna be inside of you again but me, you know that?" He rolled his hips and kept pumping into me. "No one."

I couldn't move. I was completely pinned and he held my wrists tight, too tight. He was hitting my clit and up inside that front wall of me where it felt so good. The fight had left me because I was powerless to do anything but go limp and succumb to it, so I guess I did.

At feeling me go lax, he stopped pinning me and pulled out and maneuvered me so I was on all-fours. That accomplished, he began to drill me. He pummeled from behind, and it was so deep, so fucking deep, that I thought I'd tip over and just go limp. He was fucking me like a bitch, just like a dirty little whore like he said he'd do, and I hated that it felt good. Was I just as sick and twisted as he was? He kept going and then he started to rub circles around my clit, then at an "ah" from me, he leaned in to my ear and announced, "I win."

I guess he did win. He wasn't pinning my arms any longer and yet I was obeying him. I fell on my face when he said that, and that's when his belt bit into my ass.

The feel and the sound of it hitting me made me squeal in pain even more than the sensation. "Please Tommy." I begged.

He kept pounding into me, then he grunted, "Your body was fucking made for me."

Goosebumps had popped up all over me. My captor laughed low in his throat, a knowing laugh, knowing that he owned me, reveling in the fact that my body was doing just what he wanted it to do. He leaned back, rotated his hips, and smacked me across the top of my ass again, but with his hand, as he drove in. My eyes rolled back into my head and I let out another loud whimper.

He hit again with his hand, making me cry out not only in pain, but also in pleasure because inside, he was hitting that spot. He grabbed my clit and twisted, forcing an orgasm that made my body ring.

He leaned forward and grabbed my throat, mid-climax and lifted me back up to my knees, grinding out a husky, "Perfect, baby." He kept going, hand covering my throat possessively, as he used me like a ragdoll.

He went on for what felt like forever, chasing his orgasm, grunting into me. It went on so long I wondered if it was ever going to be over. My crotch was raw, sticky, and sore. He slid in and out and in and out; making me feel the ridges of his cock as they glided over sensitive places inside of me. Goosebumps were all over me as he kissed the back of my neck and tweaked my nipple, his other hand rising and lowering over my throat in a steady rhythm.

Finally, there was a long and husky groan, and oh my God, it sounded so sexy.

How? How could that thought even occur to me?

When it was finally over, I was limp on the floor, totally spent. For a brief moment he was dead weight on top of me. I heaved in discomfort and he immediately rolled off me and disappeared into the bathroom.

I was still on the floor. I could do nothing but just lie there. Maybe I would just die there.

A moment later he gently lifted me off the floor and then he had me in bed. He was covering me up. "Nap? No way I'm making it back to the office now," he whispered, kissed my temple, and then spooned me.

He was holding me like this thing he just did to me was consensual, like I hadn't fought back with all of my might and drawn his blood. And I was too limp, spent, and emotionally paralyzed to do anything but lay there. I just lay there as he stroked my hair, dropping kisses on the back of my head, twisting to kiss my shoulder, my earlobe. I tried to not let what he was doing comfort me, but I cried softly into the pillow until I started to feel myself drifting off. I kept fighting it. A few minutes later, I guess I ran out of tears. His breathing evened out in sleep so as I was lying there staring off into space, in a wet spot from his semen that leaked out of me, eyes so dry that they ached. I shifted the blanket under myself to cover the wet spot. It felt like my guts had been yanked out underneath his hand, which was resting on my stomach.

I was tuned into him, into his breathing, which was tickling my shoulder, into the feel of his hard body against me, his hand possessively over my tummy. My ass hurt from the belt and I needed to pee. I held it for as long as I could, alternately worrying about waking him and also thinking I should really bash his head in right now while he slept.

Finally, what might've been twenty minutes, maybe even an hour passed, and I couldn't wait anymore, so I slowly pulled away. His eyes opened and he watched me pull the top sheet out from the mess of tangled bedding and wrap it around myself.

His eyes met mine and while I couldn't read his hard expression, I felt shame and pain wash over me at the same time. I looked away and went into the bathroom. When I sat down to pee, I almost hit the ceiling as it stung deep inside. It felt like I was torn inside. When I was done, I moved slowly back to the bed and climbed in, staying as close to the edge as I could.

He rolled over, his arm covering me, and half his body covered me, too. His lips softly touched the center of my back and kissed upwards to the back of my neck where he stopped and fell back asleep. His lips just stayed there, on the back of my neck. I just wanted to cry because it felt so loving and tender and yet twisted me up inside like a pretzel. The guy was some sort of master of the mind fuck.

I woke up to a darkened room and an empty bed. He was getting clothes on. He left the room. I stayed in the bed. I didn't want to get up. Ever.

Tommy

I got up, while flicking the lamp on. As I pulled the blankets back, I caught sight of the belt mark across her ass and lower back. I winced. I got dressed, turned the light back out, then left, shrugging my jacket on. When I grabbed my phone and keys at the bottom of the stairs, I ran into Sarah. As I walked past, ignoring her dirty looks, I caught a flash of shock in her eyes. I passed the mirror on the wall by the front door and saw that my eye was bruised and that there were claw marks on my face. Looked like I'd have a fat lip, too.

I decided to head to the gym to punch the rest of this out. I held back with Tia this afternoon. Yeah, I've been holding back all along but today I let the beast out more than ever and if I was honest with myself I knew I could've really gone another round, could've blackened her eye and bloodied her lip, like she'd done to me. The difference was I deserved it; she didn't.

I hadn't hit her back, other than her ass; I had zero desire to hit her anywhere else. In fact, I hated how I felt when I'd hit her ass with the belt. I didn't think I wanted to do that to her again. Right now, I wanted to hit something or someone else to work these frustrations out. I had all this rage in me that I couldn't put a label on. I still tasted my blood on my lip as I drove away.

I knew where at least part of the frustration came from. I was so fucking mad about that woman tracking her down and getting her aside. That could've been anyone. It could've been someone who wanted to take her from me that had the ability to do it.

Pop and I both got identical anonymous letters today. They were cryptic, done in cut up newsprint, saying something about fresh new Ferrano acquisitions being redistributed. It might not be about her, but I suspected it was. And in case it was, I've already arranged to double security for her, but before I could pull the trigger to get that done this happened.

I felt a pang of regret at the things I said to her, at the way I took her, but I'm split in two as I fucking loved the rush of it at the same time. I especially loved it when the fight turned to submission. She was beautiful, showing fear, fighting with me and then showing more fear, and then submitting to me and coming so hard like that for me. And fuck, when she melted into me afterwards, letting me hold her and comfort her? It was what I needed; she gave that to me. The next step for me was to get her to want to give it to me. Would she get there easily or would I break her? And would I always feel guilt like this after the fact?

It was like my chest weighed five hundred pounds right now. Everything I thought I wanted was in my bed, but it felt like I was fucking it up. Royally fucking it up.

The heavy bag would take the rest of this and then I'd go back, slip in beside her and get a good night's sleep so I could think clearly tomorrow about what to do about this foster parent problem and hope that I found some clarity somewhere on the whole situation.

* * *

When I climbed back in bed at almost one in the morning after a workout, a run, and three shots of scotch during an urgent meeting about a problem down in Mexico I found her asleep in my bed and fuck me, but she was wearing the shirt I wore earlier today.

I climbed in on the opposite side, deciding to test out my theory of whether she was just moving to the other side of the bed out of habit or not. She rolled toward me. I felt a pang of something, something that made me pull her to me and bury my nose in her hair. She let out a sound that was almost a purr and then nuzzled into my collar bone and wrapped her arms around me. It made my heart constrict when my eyes adjusted in the dark and I saw a peaceful little smile on her sleeping face.

I fell asleep wondering if she was dreaming about the guy from the ice cream shop, the guy that she wished I was. I knew she couldn't be dreaming about the real me with that smile on her face and it left an empty, raw feeling deep in my gut. It was like I was consumed by guilt. This was foreign. I don't think I'd ever felt guilty about anything in my life before meeting this girl.

5

Tia

He was still asleep when I woke up. His face was badly scored with long nail marks and his eye looked bruised. It was early, 5:20 am. I was tangled up with him, legs, arms, and for some reason, we were both on the opposite end of the bed, heads down at the foot and I was on the side he usually slept on. I rolled away, went to the bathroom, put his bathrobe on and went downstairs.

Sarah wasn't up yet. I looked out the stained glass window panes that flanked the front door on both sides and saw a guy out there, sitting by the gate with a tall Starbucks cup in his hand, doing something on his phone. I also saw another guy out back when I looked out the kitchen window.

I filled the single cup brewer with water, made a coffee the way I liked it, and then explored some of the rooms whose doors were open on the main floor. An office with a big cherry wood desk, bookshelves, billiards table, and a good-sized conference table with a dozen chairs. A dining room with a table for twelve, humungous family room with big couches, a fireplace, the biggest TV I'd ever seen, also a laundry room with 2 stacked sets of metallic blue laundry machines. There was also a big, stocked pantry, two bathrooms, and a long hallway with a few closed doors. I had a feeling one was Sarah's room, so I didn't open any of them. At the end of that hallway I spotted the basement stairs. I decided to go down and see if I could find my belongings so I wouldn't have to keep wearing Sarah's clothes.

Tommy

When my eyes opened, I could smell her. I smelled her on the pillow beside me, but she wasn't here. After I'd gotten in bed on the wrong side and she curled into me, I further experimented. I woke up sometime in the night and got up to use the john, so when I got back in I climbed in at the bottom. She rolled down and curled into me down there, too. I'd wrapped my arms around her and held her tight to me. She burrowed in, letting out a little moan that gave me goosebumps and got me hard. I didn't act on it, just held her.

Now I was awake, it was bright, and she wasn't here. I got out of bed, pulled on a pair of track pants, went to the bathroom, then headed down to the kitchen. It was 7:45 and Sarah was frying something on the stove, something that didn't smell like breakfast.

"What's going on?" I asked.

"I'm making some freezer meals," she said without looking up. Then she did look up and looked at me with shock.

"What?"

"Your face! It looks worse than last night."

I felt the tenderness on my eye and lip and knew Tia'd given me a doozy of a shiner. I grabbed a silver pan off the counter, turned it over and caught my reflection on the back and sure enough, it looked worse. In addition to a black eye and a slightly fat lip I had nail marks streaked down my cheek, too. Great. We were expected at Pop's for dinner today. Sarah's face changed and I didn't need to be a mind-reader to know she was thinking I deserved it.

"Where is she?" I asked, leaning out to see by the pool.

Sarah shook her head blankly. "She's not up yet."

"She's what?" The look on my face made her blanch.

I practically flew to the front door and hollered for Marco and Nino and we soon figured out they hadn't seen her. My blood was about to boil. "Where the fuck is she?"

Tia

In the basement, I found a huge man-cave room with another pool table, ping pong table, two old school arcade games, foosball, a pinball game, plus a home theater room with a sectional and those cool recliners with the cup holders and speakers in them. There was also a big poker table with the green felt, and a long fully-stocked bar, as well as a home gym with every piece of workout equipment I'd ever heard of plus a sauna and bathroom. There was also a big storage room lined with shelves. The storage room was empty except for my few boxes and garbage bags of clothes right inside the doorway. I opened the boxes and started going down memory lane.

Report cards, post cards, boxes of clothes, books, CDs. I slipped through a photo album that belonged to my mom. I felt an overwhelming surge of emotion for her.

I didn't know who some of the people in the photos were. In the back there were a few loose photos that I'd seen before. I leafed through them and stopped at a Polaroid photo of my mother when she was younger, sitting with a young guy, both dressed up. They were holding hands. His face looked familiar.

I turned it over and saw Carlita + Tom Ferrano in blue ink. There was a heart drawn in red pen under the ink as well as dotting the i in Mom's name.

Tommy's father. What on Earth? Is that why he seemed familiar? Because I've seen this picture and his name on it over the years? It felt like something else was familiar, beyond the picture about him. I couldn't put my finger on it.

I heard someone coming down the stairs. A man, maybe in his early to mid-30's, rushed into the room, the man from the driveway this morning. He was a giant, had to be almost 7 feet tall, had a reddish goatee, a shaved head, had tattooed hands, and pretty much looked like a badass biker dressed in a suit. His facial expression was filled with relief.

He leaned on the door frame, as if catching his breath, pulled out his phone and dialed, then said, "She's in the basement! Storage room. Yeah."

I was sitting on the floor cross-legged in Tommy's shirt, Tommy's robe, with papers and piles of folded clothing around me. After what felt like a too-long awkward moment with the giant biker guy Tommy was behind him with eyes that were crazy-scary. Tommy was dressed in just a pair of track pants that sat low on his hips. He wore nothing else, but his crucifix necklace.

"Okay," Tommy said, and the guy left.

I felt the overwhelming urge to turtle, to totally cower and that's not me. He's got me turned into a nervous wreck.

I was sure I was staring at him like a timid rabbit. I felt my chin start quivering. The anger seemed to drain from Tommy's beat-up looking face (Fuck, I did that. Me!) and then he fell to his knees in front of me and let out a deep breath, looking me right in the eyes with tenderness.

Tenderness? Was I reading that right? I felt my face crinkle, confused. He grabbed me and pulled me against him. His heart hammered against me. I stiffened.

"I thought you were gone," he said softly into my ear and squeezed tighter.

I didn't know how to respond.

"I'm sorry about yesterday, baby," he said into my ear so low it was barely audible.

Then he leaned back and his hand curled around the back of my neck. He looked at my face and his eyes travelled from my eyes to my mouth and then my eyes again. Then his mouth was on mine and he was kissing me like he'd kissed me at the beach.

I didn't want to respond. He didn't deserve having me respond after all he'd done so far. But for some reason, I did.

His tongue darted into my mouth and his other hand was on my rear. He was hard; I felt it. He was hard whenever he was against me. He gently took me down so my back was on the floor and his hand travelled underneath the bathrobe, underneath the shirt of his I was wearing He was rubbing a nipple with one hand while the other hand travelled up my body from my hip to my shoulder, resting to cup my head.

I looked up at him and chewed my lower lip. He didn't have anger on his face at all. He was looking at me with some other expression; I didn't know what it was.

And then he was grinding into me and kissing me, running his hands through my hair. I wanted to be afraid, but I was so relieved that he wasn't freaking out that I just let him. It made no sense in the world, but I was letting him. His cross necklace was dangling over me, touching my throat.

Right now, he wasn't the criminal, he was the guy on the date, and I kissed him back. His fingers were inside of me and rubbing me and before my actions registered in my brain I rubbed both of my palms up and down his arms to his shoulders and then one of my hands reached down into his track pants and I wrapped my hand around his cock and squeezed.

He moaned into my mouth and said, "Let's take this upstairs." I let go of him and he helped me to my feet and walked, holding my hand, out of the storage room, up the stairs, through the hall, past the kitchen, and back up the stairs to the master bedroom. The whole way I was staring at the muscular detail of his naked back, feeling so turned on. So inexplicably turned on.

Once the bedroom door was shut, he lifted me up gently under my arms and I wrapped my legs around his waist. He kissed my throat while walking the few paces to the bed and then put me down on it and climbed on top of me, kissing my mouth so passionately I was melting. Before I knew it I was out of his robe, out of his shirt and my panties, and he was deep inside me, making love to me. Yes, making love to me.

His lips trailed up and down my neck and shoulders, his hands up and down my body, and he was pumping into me slowly, looking at me like he was savoring it, repeatedly gazing with a smoldering look into my eyes. It was beautiful. It was probably what making love was supposed to be like. I'd fucked before but this was my first time being made love to.

But when the making love thought occurred to me, suddenly I felt like something inside of me was dying. Something inside me was crumbling because he was fucking with my head and because I knew this wasn't the only side of him.

This was just one half of who he was. I think he knew I was dying inside, too, because I started to tremble and as a single tear rolled down my cheek, his thumb stroked my lower lip, then he kissed the tear away and hugged me tight, being even slower, even gentler, and he whispered, "Tia, baby, please. Please."

I didn't know what he was pleading with me for exactly, but it felt like he wanted me to just forget everything else except for what was happening right now. Could I? Could I let this happen, let this beautiful, fucked up man have me without any tears? I guess I couldn't.

I had a huge orgasm and crying episode at the same time, so I held him tight, muffling my moans with his shoulder. He finished, too, moaning my name, and then he rolled to his side, sank his head into the pillow, blowing out a long breath, then he pulled my back against his front, spooning me.

I glanced back at his face and he looked like he'd been in a bar fight. His eye was rimmed with a deep purple bruise and there were four angry red and scabbed lines down one cheek and another scratch across his nose and part way across the other cheek. His bottom lip was a bit puffy and had a tiny cut that extended about half an inch below his lip. He was looking on the outside like I was feeling on the inside. I put my head back on the pillow. He nuzzled in and kissed me between the shoulder blades, wrapping his arms tighter around me.

I was surprised that all that had ended the way it did. I thought, if anything, him thinking I'd run away – which I'd never thought would be the assumption when I headed to the basement or I wouldn't have done it – would've meant his anger again.

Until I could get out of here, I needed to think before acting; I needed to make that part of my routine now because life wasn't the same as it was before. I needed to think about what he'd think about things I'd do before I did them. He could've been angry right now because he couldn't find me. But that's not what I was getting from him. He was unpredictable and to me, that meant he was even more dangerous than I'd even realized because I didn't know what to expect next from him.

How, till I got out of here, did I stay on his good side? This side? How bad was he screwing with my head that I'd just allowed him to have sex with me, that I'd just participated?

After a long time, he said, "Hi." His voice was breathy... maybe emotional?

"Hi." I think my voice probably sounded empty or unsure. I didn't know.

There was a long pause. Then he cleared his throat. "We have dinner at my pop's today. I'd like you to dress like you're going to church, okay?" He was tracing my ear with his finger and kissing the back of my head.

"Kay," I said.

"You've got clothes like that or should I have something sent over?"

"I went to church nearly every Sunday for the past nine years. I'm good."

"Okay. My sisters will make you their friend. Just because they're my sisters doesn't mean the rules don't apply. Okay?"

"Kay."

"I mean it." There was an edge to his voice.

"I know you do." My heart sank and my body stiffened. Kay, bye bye Ice Cream Parlor Hottie. So much for that.

He snuggled me closer, maybe in response to my tensing up. "I'm very pleased that you didn't run away from me. Or that someone hadn't taken you." He sighed and played with my hair.

"I woke up early and I was just tired of wearing Sarah's clothes and you said my clothes were down there. You said I could go down and–"

"I know. You're welcome to wear your own clothes anytime but in bed. In bed you need to be naked or in something of mine. I want you to smell like me." He nuzzled into my throat and then twisted me so that my face was buried in his chest. "But you need to know that running away, had you done it, would be bad, Tia. Real bad."

Taken me? Who'd take me? The police? Was he worried Rose and Cal were trying to rescue me? And how would I get away, anyway? This place was locked down like a prison.

"I didn't," I reminded him.

"I know." He cuddled me closer. "I'm glad."

I started to cry, like ugly cry right into his chest. I couldn't hold the tears back. He tilted my chin up toward his face.

"Talk to me." His expression was soft.

I grimaced. "One minute you're being sweet and the next minute you're threatening me. One minute you're rough, the next minute you're not. Is messing with my head a sport for you?" I couldn't even believe I was having this conversation with him. I couldn't believe how weak I was, letting him fuck me and then crying like a baby again. Yet again.

He sighed, was silent for a minute, then whispered, "I need control."

He was searching my face for something with roving eyes. "I need you to keep being exactly who you have been so far, okay? You've been perfect."

I didn't know what that meant. Most times he was one guy and sometimes he was another. Gangster Tommy and what? Ice cream Parlor Tommy? How could he say I was being perfect? I was a mess. Last night I'd hit him with a lamp and messed up his face. How was that perfect? And today I had to have dinner with his family and pretend that I was happy to be engaged to him. How would I pull that off?

He twisted in the direction of his nightstand and reached for the heart-shaped box. He looked at me with a stone-cold serious face. "I want you to wear this. My family doesn't need to feel any awkwardness between us. I don't want them worrying the way you've got Sarah worrying."

I frowned.

He continued, "So you'll wear this and it'll be reality to them. Okay? Like our dinner date the other night. Alone with me, always be real, always be you. But when it's not just us, no one can think things aren't perfect, that you're not ecstatically happy to be mine."

I was speechless. He was teetering between the two personalities, it seemed. Hadn't I just been responsive while we were alone? That hadn't been enough to keep him sweet, though. I didn't understand. And now my reaction would probably tip him one way or the other. I sat up, pulling up the blankets to cover my nakedness and chewed the inside of my cheek. Me being real was fucked up. I didn't know what to be right now.

He opened the box. Inside was a gorgeous diamond ring. It was cushion-cut with a big stone and then surrounding round diamonds. More round diamonds took up two thirds of the band. I'd never seen something so sparkly, so beautiful. I wanted nothing to do with it. I wanted nothing to do with a proposal that I'd had no choice but to accept from a man who threatened me every time he looked at me, either with this mouth or with his eyes.

But, what could I do? If I showed him an emotion other than what he wanted to see, would he hurt me again? I opened my mouth to speak, but nothing came out.

Tommy

"Shh, don't say anything. Just wear it. When my sisters ask questions about setting a date or anything like that, say we haven't discussed it yet."

She nodded, but I could see she was trying but failing to guard how she was feeling – freaked. I put the ring on her finger and then I leaned over and touched my lips to hers. She stayed still. I leaned up and kissed her forehead.

"I've got stuff to do but I'll be back here to pick you up at 4:30 and then we'll head over to Pop's. Best behavior there, yeah?"

She nodded, but her eyes were filled with confusion. I couldn't exactly blame her. I was confused, too. I knew I was acting like a psychopath. I left to get a shower and get dressed.

In the shower, I tried to get my head straight. This girl, she was doing something to me. I didn't feel like me. Yeah, I felt the desire to dominate her, but I also had the strange desire to be the ice cream shop guy she'd told me she'd fantasized about. Could I be that guy?

Did I want to be? I hated the sadness on her face, hated the way she seemed to be beating herself up for enjoying it when I fucked her. So far, she was everything I wanted. But I was me.

One minute I found myself being sweet to her but inevitably I'd become me again. The way she'd responded to me downstairs? That was fucking amazing. I loved that she reached for me, that she kissed me back, and it felt real. I wanted her to keep feeling bold enough to reach into my pants for my cock because she was showing me she wanted me. But I wanted her afraid, too, and eventually I wanted her to want to please me, to do whatever I wanted, even if was out of her comfort zone, because she wanted to please me that badly. I wanted her to want me so badly that she ached for me, ached to submit for me.

A lot of girls want to be submissive, give in to belonging to a lover. I'm not saying every woman wants it but there are a lot of women who enjoy it, who crave it and embrace it. I had no problems finding women who did, but I needed the fear first and most couldn't pull off convincing me of it unless I went over the edge with them and made them truly afraid. And none of them made me want them like she did. I didn't want a submissive with safe words putting limits on what she'd give me. I wanted a willing slave, someone willing to give me whatever I needed.

If I let her go tomorrow and she went on to live a normal life I knew I'd already ruined her for vanilla. She'd always think about sex with me. No one would measure up because after me she'd think she had to pick some accountant in a sweater vest, the polar opposite of me. As she laid there staring at the ceiling waiting for sweater vest to finally go limp inside her, she'd be thinking about getting her hair pulled, her ass smacked, and having my hand caress her throat, while feeling my breath against her ear as I whispered in her ear how I owned her and what I wanted to do to her.

How did I walk the line of taking what I wanted to ensure I kept wanting her without breaking her? In the beginning I'd been thrilled by the notion of breaking her spirit and bending her to my will, but now... I still wanted her to be mine, but didn't want to extinguish that fire in her. Because unlike the women I had to take over the edge to make them feel real fear temporarily, I wanted Tia. The other women were a one off. I couldn't break her or she wouldn't be Tia anymore and I'd be married to this empty shell of a person who did what I wanted but in a way I wouldn't crave it anymore.

She was getting to me in a way I hadn't expected and I wanted something else from her, too, but I didn't know what name to give what I wanted. I wanted her to see the real me, to want me, even if I wasn't perfect, even if I could be a cold-hearted prick sometimes. Did I want her to love me? Love was something I never had before. I got praise and respect through accomplishments. I had to earn everything I got.

Right now, before work, I needed another session with the heavy bag. When I got out of the shower I got dressed to head out, but first I took off my silver chain. It was a curious thing, the way my mindset shifted when I wore it. It belonged to my mother and when I had to make tough decisions, tap into my inner beast and handle the dirty shit in my life and my line of work I couldn't do those things as well if I was wearing it.

On the other side of the coin, if I was filled with rage that I didn't want to feel and I put it on it usually helped me find my center, like this morning when Nino said she was in the basement I put it on before I went down.

I knew it was just an object, that it was all in my head, but it somehow helped to ground me. Right now, I had a tough job to take care of before dinner at Pop's so I left the chain on the counter in the bathroom.

Tia

I had a light breakfast alone and then spent the rest of the morning sorting through the rest of my things, watching the beautiful ring sparkle every time my hand moved. I wasn't generally a materialistic girl at all but this ring! It was just so sparkly. I kept staring at it. My French manicure was still intact, astonishingly, despite the fact that I'd brawled with him, and I couldn't get over how my hand looked just so grown up, just so *not* my hand.

Sarah had offered to help me sort things out, but I wanted to do it alone. I knew it was her day off, but more than that, I didn't want interference. These were my personal things. There had been nothing I wanted to throw out; I'd already done my weeding and sorting thinking I was taking that apartment at the Carusos'. But looking through my things I felt like I was looking at them again with different eyes than I had a week ago when I'd packed everything.

I brought my clothes upstairs in several armloads and I found that there were a few empty drawers in the bureau in the closet, plus some shelving and rod space were cleared out for me, by the looks of things.

I left my box of mementoes in the basement and only brought up my summer clothes. I certainly wasn't planning to stay here and make it home, so all my personal stuff that I normally liked around me, photos, stuffed animals, frilly throw cushions, they could all stay boxed. All I needed were my basics upstairs. The only other thing beyond clothing I took was my jewelry box. It had been my mother's and I wanted it, no needed it, close.

I tucked the picture of my Mom and Tommy's father behind

another picture in the album to hide it. I didn't know whether Tommy knew there was a connection between my mom and his dad or not but I felt like I needed to hide this information for the moment without any explanation. Of course I knew Mr. Ferrano seemed to want me to know he knew who she was after his comment about me looking like her.

After I got everything away, I got ready, but I wasn't looking forward to this dinner at all. I didn't know if I'd act the wrong way or say the wrong thing. I didn't know how to pull off the ruse of acting like I was a blushing bride-to-be.

Sarah was to be out the rest of the day, so I was alone in the house with a security guard that I'd seen before and another outside that I hadn't seen before.

From what I could tell they worked in twelve-hour shifts on the property. At one point I looked out the window and the one guy had been in the driveway talking to three other guys, one of which had been the Lou Ferrigno-looking burly guy from that first day. I looked back out the window later and it was another guy, one I didn't recognize.

I was ready at 4:20 and impatiently paced around the front door area until 4:48 when I heard the house phone ring. There weren't any security guys nearby, so I picked it up, preparing to just take a message.

"Hello?"

"Oh... Tia?" It was a female.

"Yes..." Who would be calling me here?

"Hi! This is Tessa, Tommy's sister. Tommy's running late so I'm gonna swing by and get you. I'm pulling up to the gate in like two seconds. Can you meet me outside?"

"I, uh, okay."

"Cool. See you in two."

Weird. And uncomfortable. I'd have to be alone with this girl and would I get a total inquisition? I stepped outside and the guard looked up at me and smiled. This was the first of the Ferrano security guys, besides Earl, to smile at me. Then the gate opened and a red SUV pulled in. The guard talked to her. They conversed for a few minutes so I eventually walked down the steps toward them. A pretty blonde unlocked the door and I got into the passenger seat.

There were two boys strapped in the back in car seats, one a toddler, the other a baby. The bigger of the two was playing on a little toddler game system and the smaller was asleep. She was very attractive, a petite blonde with a few chunky dark highlights. Lots of jewelry. Expensive-looking clothes and purse. I couldn't believe the baby was sleeping through the racket that was the dance music on her car sound system.

"Hey!" She shook my hand and started talking a mile a minute as she pulled out, talking over the loud music.

"I'm glad to meet you. Tommy said you guys were running late and that he hadn't picked you up yet, so I decided to pick you up on the way and save him the trouble. This way, too, he can't cancel because we've got you already. Back there are Lucas and Antonio."

"Uh, nice to meet you. Thanks." I waved at the older of the two boys in the backseat.

"Everyone can't wait to meet the girl that has finally stolen my brother's heart. You're nineteen? You look older than that! How did you meet? Oh my God!" She grabbed my hand again and started checking out my ring, "It's beautiful! My brother has always had great taste."

I felt the car swerve and then someone honked at us. She laughed and grabbed the steering wheel. "Sorry. Saw something shiny! Hahaha"

She was funny; I liked her instantly.

"I just gotta stop at the bakery to grab dessert. My father's wife Lisa is useless in the kitchen and Sundays his housekeeper is off, so Luc is bringing dinner and I'm bringing dessert. We do dinner almost every Sunday and we rotate who does what. You cook?" She turned down the radio a bit.

I nodded. "I do. I –"

Her phone cut me off. It was a really loud dubstep ring and it startled me.

She answered it. "Tommy, what? Driving!" She listened for a second, frowned, and then said, "Yeah. What's the prob?" She glanced over at me. Then she really scrunched up her face. "Yeah, I'll be there in like five. Whatever. Here." She passed me the phone and turned her music down some more. I almost fumbled, getting the phone to my ear.

"Hello?"

"Tia, what the fuck!" he growled.

My scalp prickled, "What's wrong?"

"Where's your fucking phone?"

"In my purse."

"I've been calling you!"

"I must not have heard it. The music was loud."

Tessa pulled into a parking space in a strip plaza, jumped out, and dashed into a bakery.

"My sister picking you up was not authorized, Tia. The guy on duty was a fucking bonehead for letting her drive out of there with you. It's not safe."

My heart was pumping directly in my ears, it seemed. Time stood still for a beat.

Oh my God. OH MY GOD! I have a chance to get away. There was no one else in the parking lot. There were no bodyguards with us! I looked around me. I was in a suburban strip mall and there were no goons with guns watching me.

"Hello?" he called out impatiently.

"I'm here." I slowly looped my purse strap over my shoulder, stepped out of the SUV and closed the door. I looked around, surveying the area. Should I run? This might be the perfect opportunity. This might be the only opportunity.

Someone had let me off the property with the wrong person, a sister who clearly didn't know I was Tommy's prisoner. I looked in the van and saw the sleeping baby and the game-playing tot. I chewed my cheek.

"Where's Tess? It's quiet," he asked.

"She's uh--- driving."

"I'll be there as soon as possible. Remember my rules. Yeah? Remind her not to stop anywhere. Go directly to my father's house. It's not safe for you to be out there unguarded."

"Kay." I frowned.

"You're still wearing the ring?"

I looked down at it. "Uh huh."

I could see his sister at the cash register, talking animatedly with the cashier.

"Okay, baby. I'll see you soon. Be good. Text me when you're inside Pop's house so I know you're safe."

"Kay. Goodbye, Tommy." I hung up.

I stood still, feeling like my pounding heart was inside of my ears. I pulled the ring off my finger.

Goodbye Tommy.

Tessa came out of the store holding three white bakery boxes. She passed them to me, so I opened the door and put them on my seat with the ring.

"Oh, just a sec. Let me get the trunk open. You can't hold those on your lap."

I passed her the phone. "Listen, it was nice to meet you, but I've actually gotta go. I wanted to leave the second you were in there, but I wouldn't have left your babies alone."

She looked at me weirdly. I started to walk away.

"Wait a second," she called after me. "What's going on? Did you and my brother have a fight?"

"You could say that," I called back. "Sorry. He's a psychopath, Tessa, he really is. I can't do this, can't be his prisoner. I am outta here." I started walking faster. She was standing there looking confused.

After a few paces I glanced back and saw her dialing on her

phone. That's when I knew I couldn't walk away. I had to fucking run.

Tommy

I couldn't believe the fucking screw-up. First, my meeting runs late because I have to watch a couple guys rough up someone who owes us money, like I have time for this piddly shit, but then I find out that my sister fucking took Tia. The gate guard that relieved Nino had some fucking stomach bug and was in the pool house taking a shit, so Marco hadn't left yet despite being on since last night. Tino was at the front gate but then there was an emergency with a shipment that was coming and a few guys dropped by and swapped out Nino's brother Tino with a newbie who just had to man the fucking gate waiting for the other guy to come back. I called Earl and told him to get over there and straighten this shit out.

My sister heard I've told Pop I'm running late and I'm not sure if we can make it and she conspires with my other sister to make sure they get their claws into Tia. So, Tess swings by my house and it's miraculously during the period the inexperienced guy is there and the experienced guy is in the john and my five foot two 100 pound sister proceeds to bully the guy into letting her take Tia to my Pop's.

He works for us but isn't in the inner circle so doesn't know the rules for handling Tia. All he knows is he's watching the gate for a minute and my sister wants to give my fiancée a ride. The guy's phone is dead so he tells her he's gotta confirm it's okay, but she starts getting pissy about running late and name dropping that she's Tom Ferrano Senior's daughter and does he really think she shouldn't take her own future sister-in-law to me? She's like a midget Doberman or something, both of my sisters are.

He lets her take Tia. The other guy comes back out and finds out. After I get off a phone call, I see I missed a text from Luc telling me not to worry about Tia; that Tessa has gone to get her. I piece everything together as my guy at the house is phoning. Tia's not answering her phone and then I finally get ahold of my sister.

Two minutes after I get off the phone with her my sister is calling me back and telling me that Tia took off on her, ran like her hair was on fire, and left her engagement ring in the fucking car. I heard her voice in my head, how she ended that call with me saying, "Goodbye, Tommy."

Fuck! Not only has she taken off without the ring that has the damn GPS in it but the anonymous note we got is nagging at me. Heads are gonna damn well roll!

Tia

I got to a mall two blocks from that strip plaza and finally found one of the few remaining pay phones in the world. I was debating between calling Susie and calling Rose. I was freaking out. I turned the stupid iPhone off and dropped it in a garbage bin a block from the mall.

I decided to call my Aunt Carol to ask where my father was. I called directory assistance and they connected me, but after the operator laughed at my asking for Carol O'Connor. "Archie Bunker?" She giggled, like I'd been prank calling.

"No, Carol a female, not the actor."

It rang twice, then there was a scratchy sounding "Hello?"

"Aunt Carol, it's me, Tia. Athena." I felt shaky but tried to keep my voice steady.

Dead air.

"Aunt Carol, I'm really sorry to bother you. I know you don't talk to him much, but it's imperative that I find my father. Like... life or death kind of thing. Do you have any idea where I might reach him?"

She sighed. "I have nothing to do with your father, Athena. He's a loser. I'm sorry to say that, but he is."

"Please; do you have any idea how I can reach him? It's really important."

She sighed, "He works at the car parts place on Dufferin Street. Last I heard, anyway. I don't know if he's working today. It's Sunday. I don't have a home number. His girlfriend is Sadie Lewicki. She's probably listed."

"Thank you."

"Athena?"

"Yeah?"

"Don't call me again."

Click.

What a royal bitch.

I called directory assistance again. I didn't have that much change left in my purse but when I fished around the bottom, looking for more, I found a folded up ten that I could break, if needed.

I got through to my dad's work and typed his last name into the keypad via the auto attendant. I got transferred to him and he answered.

"Dad!"

"Tia? Is that you, sweet pea?"

"Dad, I took off. You need to hide. I'm sorry, I don't know why you did this to me and it doesn't even matter now but you need to hide because they could hurt you and I had no choice but to run so I have and I wanted to warn you about it." Tears were streaming down my face.

"Shit, Tia. Breathe, sweet pea. Where are you?'

"It doesn't matter. I'm gonna get out of Dodge and you need to as well."

"Meet me. We need to talk."

"No Dad. I-I don't trust you. You have no idea what I've been through the last few days. I can't trust you after you did this to me."

"I have things to tell you. We need to talk." He sounded like he was choking up.

"You're at work. You're not trying to find a way to pay off the debt because it's apparently an unpayable debt, unless you count putting your daughter on the table to become Ferrano property. You're not coming to my rescue; you never planned to rescue me. For whatever reason, you sold me out. Your own daughter. I don't know what I did to deserve this but I just wanted to extend the courtesy of letting you know I took off and I'm getting out of here before he catches me. I hope he doesn't have you killed."

"Sweet pea, I just need five minutes of your time, I just want to give you my side of the story, okay?" He sounded desperate.

I held the phone and squeezed my eyes shut.

"I have a bit of cash. I can give it to you, help you get out of town," he said. "Where are you? I'll meet you after work. I'm just here today doing inventory."

I had $248 in my account and that wouldn't get me far. I knew I'd have money deposited in about a week for my allowance from social services, if they hadn't cut it off already at my disappearance. I didn't care so much about Dad giving me money, although it'd be nice to have a little bit of help, but I did want answers. I'd been losing sleep over the fact that he'd sold me out. I wanted to know why he did this.

"Fine, West End shopping center but I can't wait. I'll be in the food court. Unless I think it's dangerous, then I'll be in the family washroom near the lockers by the food court. You can have five minutes to talk and then I'm out of here. I'll wait twenty minutes. If you're not here, I'm not waiting."

"I'll be there in ten or fifteen minutes. Thanks, sweet pea."

I was parched. I went and bought a cold drink from one of the food vendors and sat at the table closest to the public washrooms so that if I saw anyone suspicious, it was a good vantage point; I'd be able to take off from here quickly.

Tommy

The first thing I did after finding out that she'd taken off was call Greg O'Connor's cell phone. I told him to not say a fucking word but to just listen. I didn't want to even hear the douchebag's voice. I told him that she'd taken off and that if he heard from her it was in his best interests to notify me immediately. He answered with a "Yes, Sir."

I initiated a manhunt with fifteen of our guys, two cops, and called my PI. I had cars parked on the streets of Rose and Cal Crenshaw and the office and home of Susan DeLong as well as in front of that punk Nick's apartment building.

Ten minutes later O'Connor called and told me where to find her. I hung up without saying goodbye. Thanks a fucking bunch, Asshole.

I didn't call in help, I got in my car and drove there alone, texting Dare to call off the manhunt that I'd started. I called Pop's house and told Lisa to hold dinner; that my fiancée and I would be there in an hour. She passed the phone to Pop, insisting he needed to speak with me. I rolled my eyes.

He knew she'd taken off from Tessa's car and he thought it was hilarious. Him laughing at me pissed me off, big time. I knew he'd find it even more hilarious when he saw me with the injuries his little gift had bestowed on me yesterday. My brother had already seen me last night after the gym and I knew I wouldn't live it down any time soon. Asshole was enjoying getting digs in at every available fucking opportunity.

I listened to Pop's ribbing for all of ten seconds and hung up on him, got outta my car, walked into this mall and as soon as I neared the food court I spotted her sitting in the back corner by a frozen yogurt kiosk, looking timid, looking pretty in a black and white checked dress with a red collar. She saw me almost immediately and the look on her face was pure terror. She stood, pushing the chair back with her legs and it fell over. People were staring.

I shook my head at her, narrowing my eyes and warning her with my expression as I picked up my pace. She didn't heed my non-verbal warning. She took off, knocking some guy's tray filled with fast food garbage, out of his hands. She apologized and kept going, running in a pair of red high heels, clutching a red purse.

I didn't want a scene, but I couldn't help it, I ran after her. She wasn't fast in those heels and I caught up to her about four stores away, catching her elbow and giving a squeeze. She let out a sound of despair and we were coming up to a hall, where there were utility rooms, so I shoved her down the hall and up against the wall. I took a deep breath in an effort to rein in my fury.

"We're gonna casually walk out of here and get into my car and we are going to my father's house for dinner. As planned. I'll deal with you when we get home. Understand?"

Her eyes were feral. She wanted away from me in the worst way. She looked around like she was gonna bolt again.

"No, Athena. You aren't gonna make a scene, you aren't gonna do anything but what I've said. Understand?" I took her hand and put it under my arm and around the waistband of my pants so she could feel the butt of the gun I had back there.

She choked on a sob. I took her hand into mine and walked, fast. She struggled to keep up with me. She had tears in her eyes but she held it together as we headed to my car.

When we got in and the doors were closed, she let out a big

breath.

"I don't want to go to your parents' house. Just take me back to your house and get the beating over with."

I laughed. "The beating? You think that's all that's gonna happen?"

She stared at me wide-eyed.

I leaned toward her. "How 'bout I burn the Crenshaw house down, put your douchebag of a father in the ground, castrate that punk you used to date, and pick one of your little girlfriends to be shipped off to a whorehouse in Mexico? How's that for a start?"

She cowered against the door. I grabbed her chin and made her look at me, "You've really fucked up. Not only did you take off, but your actions have my sister thinking that things aren't cool with you and me, and what's with you and me is nobody's fucking business. You broke two rules. Now I've had a good chunk of busy people involved in trying to find you and that means a lot of people know that my fiancée took off from me. Talk about an absolute cluster fuck!"

I squealed out of the parking lot, white-knuckled. "We're going to my father's house and you'll behave yourself or you'll be sorry. Very fucking sorry. So much for this morning, huh? Conniving little bitch."

Tia

I couldn't catch my breath; I was hyperventilating. I couldn't settle down. I was gasping and I was going to throw up. Until now I knew Tommy Ferrano was scary, crazy scary, but I had no idea he was this horrifying.

"Pull over; I'm gonna puke." I always threw up when I got super stressed.

He pushed his foot down and the car started moving even faster. I put my head in my hands, leaned forward and took a succession of slow and deep breaths, but it was no use, whatever was in my stomach was coming up,

"Pull over!" I hollered, and started to wretch, the puke came up into my throat and I managed to stop it from going projectile all over the windshield. I yanked off my seatbelt. He slammed on the brakes, jerking me forward, making me bump my head on the dashboard. I shoved open the door and he reached for my arm, but I shrugged him off and got my head out and threw up all over the road.

After a minute, once I was sure there was nothing else coming up, I sat back in the seat and closed my eyes. I wish I'd had the nerve and the strength to run. But, he had a gun. A gun.

Fuck my life.

He sat for a minute and in my peripheral vision I could see his chest was heaving. Finally, he let go of the hem of my dress, which I hadn't realized he had in his grasp. Then he picked up his phone and dialed a number, then put it to his ear, opening the glove box with his free hand and flinging a stack of napkins in my direction.

"Dare? Yeah. Tell Pop I can't make dinner. No. Yeah. Yup. Right, bye."

Then he dialed again. "Earl? You there yet? Yeah, I've got her. We're on our way there. See you in fifteen. You have back-up? Still? Whatever, just keep a watchful eye. I'll see you soon."

He started the car and then leaned over me. I flinched but he just fastened my seatbelt and then we were back on the road. I was relieved to not have to meet his family and sit at a table with them, pretending nothing was wrong.

What I was not relieved about was getting to the master bedroom, the place that had become my torture chamber. Because even when he wasn't torturing my body, he was torturing my brain.

The ride was quiet, but the air was thick with tension. Tommy's face was stone cold and he was white-knuckled all the way back to his house. I was petrified and wished I could either just disappear into thin air, or that we'd get pulled over and get a speeding ticket so that I could beg the cop to rescue me from this maniac.

The gate at his place opened and the car squealed to a halt. I saw Earl with a frown on his face. He looked at Tommy, then me, and I swear I saw what looked like pity. Tommy and I both got out of the car and just as I was about to round the front of the car, Earl approached me from the side. His hand came up over my mouth and I was being pulled backwards. I caught Tommy's expression and the look on his face was utterly murderous.

I heard a loud bang. Oh God, that was Earl shooting at Tommy! Tommy hit the ground, halfway behind his car, produced his gun, and fired it in our direction. Earl fired back at Tommy and Tommy's gun hit the ground. I saw a man come up from around the back of the house and Earl shot him. A dark red hole formed on that guy's forehead and the man fell face-first onto the ground.

I was dragged backwards past the gate and tossed into the back seat of a big, older car out on the street. I heard a few more shots.

There were two men in the car with Earl and me. What on Earth? Earl had a gunshot wound in his shoulder. Were they rescuing me? I looked at Earl, confused. He leaned over in the back seat of the car, wincing. There was another man on my left side, a slim Black man with a mustache, and there was a man in the front seat driving who sort of looked like the Machete movie actor, Danny something or another. Tall, Mexican, long ponytail. But younger.

"Are you rescuing me?" I asked.

The driver spoke. "Be quiet, miss. All will be revealed."

* * *

They drove to the airport. The airport? Then we drove into a hangar and there was a lot going on: people rushing everywhere, forklifts; it was mayhem. I was ushered into a big white plane with no lettering.

There were only a few seats in the back; the rest of it was wide open with just a few skids that were shrink-wrapped on it.

"Are you rescuing me, Earl?" I asked again.

The slim Black guy ripped Earl's shirt sleeve off and was inspecting the wound on his shoulder.

"Good, there's an exit wound." He reported and pulled out a first-aid kit.

Earl closed his eyes and shook his head as the door to the plane was closed. "Afraid not, Miss O'Connor."

The Mexican guy pulled a gun and put it on his lap, giving me a look that shook me to my core. Oh no.

"What?" All the air left my lungs.

"Ferranos have enemies," the guy working on Earl's arm said, glancing up at me. "A lot of enemies. The fiancée of Tommy Ferrano is an extremely valuable commodity."

"Earl?"

Why did I keep looking to him? I thought we'd sort of bonded over tea. There wasn't much of any conversation or anything like that, but he'd had kind eyes. He'd been sort of nice to me. He was working for Tommy's enemies? Was Tommy dead after those gunshots? He glanced in my direction, pain on his face.

"Where are you taking me?" I asked.

"Mexico," he answered.

Oh no. I'd heard stories about Mexico. Heck, Tommy had warned me about human slavery in Mexico. I closed my eyes, dread filling my veins.

"No more questions. Buckle up!" said the Mexican man. "Behave and you can sit there in the comfy seat. Act up and you'll be tossed in a sack with tape over your mouth."

I was handed a bottle of water, which I accepted with trembling hands. The guy with the first-aid kit continued to clean up Earl's arm and the other guy disappeared into the cockpit. I was petrified of what could be coming next.

6

Tommy

Earl's first shot missed me by miles, and I knew that was just a warning shot, because he was an ace with that gun and if he wanted me dead I'd be cold by now. The second shot knocked my gun right out of my hand. I wasn't hit. I was fine but Marco was dead. I shook my head. Marco was a good guy, wife and three kids. Fuck! He was supposed to be at home with his family, not here over five hours after his shift had ended!

I'm a pretty good shot, too. When Earl had Tia against him the only safe place for me to shoot for was his head, since he was more than a foot taller than her. I aimed for it but caught his shoulder instead. The guy's built like a refrigerator and had Tia on his left side so I had enough clearance to aim for his right side. It wasn't enough to take him down. Then I tried to shoot out the tires on the getaway car, but I missed and hit the hubcaps instead. I was off my game with all the rage and didn't take another chance at hitting her by mistake.

He's worked for us for fourteen years and he was one of the ones who actually taught me to shoot, for fuck's sake. He's been solid enough that he made it to the inner circle. The inner, inner circle. He was trusted. I trusted him with her, for fuck's sake. I don't understand what's happened, why it happened, don't know who he's working for, and where he's taken her. But, I'll find out.

We only bring men into the inner circle who have families. It's a collateral thing. It increases the chances they'll stay loyal because they have a family at stake and their families are brought into the fold. But Earl's wife died of Cancer last year and his son died in a motorcycle accident three months ago. He's a man with nothing to lose. If he hadn't been solid all the way he'd have been put somewhere else, but I had no reason to doubt him. I've known the man since I was practically a kid.

I floored it over to Pop's. When I walked in, the family was around the table and they all looked up at me, shocked. I know it's because my face was fucked up from Tia and in addition to that I was disheveled and dirty. I ran my fingers through my hair, "Pop, Dare, need a minute."

My sisters, their husbands, and Lisa went back to eating, but there was awkwardness in the air.

"Uncle Tommy!" One of the girls bellowed from the table. I gave my little niece a forced smile and headed out of the room.

As much as Tessa and Luciana have big personalities, they know when to keep their mouths shut. My attitude must've shown this wasn't the time to start on me with questions.

We stepped into Pop's office. "Your brother told me she beat you up. I didn't realize just how much."

I shook my head and shot my brother a dirty look. "Earl took Tia in a black 74 to 76 Grand Prix. I got a picture of the plate with my phone. I shot him in the shoulder. He shot Marco. Dead. We need to move. Now."

Smirks evaporated. As I was swiping the screen to get to the photo I'd snapped, my phone started ringing. It was a blocked number.

I answered, "Ferrano."

"Your girl is on a plane. South. Three hours we'll call with demands."

Mexican accent.

"You fucking touch her you'd might as well kill her because I won't want her. You hear me?"

Dial tone. They couldn't know she meant anything to me because they'd definitely rape her.

"Mexico," I said to them and now we could at least narrow it down. Dare brought the girls' husbands in. Both guys, Jimmy who was Tessa's husband and Eddy, Luciana's husband, worked for us. Jimmy was on our security team. Eddy ran a restaurant for us but he was solid and could double as security, if needed. He filled them in.

Three hours later I was out of my mind, sick about it, but I knew who had her and I knew what they wanted. Juan Carlos Castillo. They wanted us to relinquish an ongoing arrangement where we were being paid a kickback for every drug deal through a certain drug shipping lane in a small Mexican town near Morelia. We didn't dabble much with drugs and I didn't even know about this deal, but Pop said it was recent and that we were barely involved but were getting a decent kickback for almost no involvement. We had other non-drug business down there, so he said we had people and we had a safe house to work from in order to deal with this. I was a little put off by this news but didn't have time to process that. I just needed to get her the fuck out of there.

The only thing that made sense was that she would be held in one of two places there. The cartel's leader's compound was huge and pretty near impenetrable. He also had a vacation house in a mini compound near Chacala. Luckily, we had men who spied for us in both compounds so we'd soon know where she was. If she was in one of those two locations, we would know about it soon enough, through our contacts.

By the time night fell, I was on a plane heading toward Morelia.

Tia

We left the plane; we weren't at a typical airport. It was a warehouse with a landing strip, surrounded by prison-like fences, barbed wire around the top.

Before we got off the plane, I was told that if I misbehaved, I would be shot in the head. It was made crystal clear that I was expendable. They also said they could easily get to one of Tommy's sisters. He had a pregnant sister who would be an easy mark. I believed them and I cooperated.

We travelled in an old Jeep down a long dirt road and it opened up into a palatial property. Gardens, tennis courts, pool, pond, huge home, several smaller homes. I was in some sort of compound that had its own landing strip. Nothing further had been said to me other than the threat. Earl and his two cohorts were quiet through the flight.

I felt like I had gone from the frying pan into the fire.

* * *

When they walked me into the biggest of the houses, we were greeted by an older housekeeper, and we were led to a big flower-filled solarium where an older Mexican man was tending flowers. He was short, stocky, and grey-haired, with a weather-worn face. He was at least sixty, if not seventy. He looked at me and then motioned to a small bistro table that had been set with a tea set and a plate with little triangular crustless sandwiches.

"Please sit," he said with a strong Mexican accent.

I sat. The men at my back were gone.

"You, my dear, have the misfortune of being a pawn in a game, I'm afraid. But you'll be safe here, provided the Ferrano family meets my demands. They are not known for bargaining, so I hope that you mean something to that fiancé of yours."

I would've gulped, but my throat was so dry I couldn't.

"Please have tea, something to eat." He poured tea into the cup and glanced at his wristwatch. I didn't know what else to do so I shakily spooned sugar into the teacup.

Tommy

Pop had agreed, without hesitation, that we needed to get her back. They had demanded that he, not me, come down to negotiate tomorrow. But I was already there so we were pushing back.

I still didn't know why he picked this specific girl for me, but he clearly wanted me to have her because he was on board with getting her back, no matter the cost. He didn't try to talk me out of anything.

At first, Dare ranted about the fact that we didn't play these games with our enemies and that if we negotiated not only would we appear weak but Tia would then become an ongoing liability because our enemies would know that she was a weakness. I thought I'd have a fight on my hands with Pop, that he'd wave his hand dismissively and tell me to let Castillo do whatever to her.

But Pop was on board with getting her back and gave me the green light to do whatever it took. "This is the mother of my future grandchildren," he said in retort after Dario protested. "She's already part of this family. Yes we don't usually play these games but what if this was Luciana or Contessa? You'd pay any price. This girl is your brother's so now she's your sister, too. Besides, if we don't take care of our own what will that say to people who trust us? Tommy, you're all but boss now so you have my full support, whatever you have to do to bring her back. As soon as she's back we plan the wedding and then you are in full control. Me and Monalisa are retiring to the Caymans."

I knew that if I didn't get her back fast they wouldn't kill her. No, they'd do worse. They'd use her. Then when they had sucked out her soul and left her a shell of a person she'd be sent off to a Mexican brothel where she'd get addicted to blow and where she'd eventually die, either from an overdose, from suicide, or because a John had been too rough. They couldn't have her, couldn't ruin her. She was mine. The thought of "mine to ruin" was in my head, but I pushed it away. I actually didn't want to ruin her. I hoped I hadn't already done it.

We were going to play ball to get her back and then I would systematically destroy that cartel. I would tear Castillo limb from limb with my bare hands. If he dared let anyone touch her, I would take even longer ending his life. I couldn't even begin to think about what I'd do to Earl for his betrayal. He knew how we operated. What would possess him to do this?

"We don't play these games. What are we even fucking doing talking to the fucking pedo?" said Dario, again shaking his head, when he and I were on our way inside the airport.

I'd snarled at my brother and threw him up against the wall. "Dario!"

He hadn't said a word to me since, but when I'd responded that way he looked at me and something flashed in his eyes, a knowing look. I think it must've hit him then that she meant something to me and his whole demeanor, his body language shifted. He left me to stew and plot and seethe throughout the flight. He dealt with our guys, with clean-up back home, too. Dare also confirmed arrangements with our people on the ground. He just let me be. Now he stared out the window of the car that was taking us to the meeting place, looking deep in thought. A van followed behind with eight of our men. A car followed behind that one with six more. We were going in to negotiate, but we were protecting ourselves, too.

We were established here. We had a safe house and we had people and muscle in this area on standby as well. All this was news to me, but whatever. Castillo was small-time compared to some of the other players in the game and this had been a bold move. Too bold. I didn't understand the point of this. We'd crush him.

Tia

"So," the man said, "I'm Juan Carlos. Your name is Athena, correct?"

I nodded.

"You been engaged to Ferrano not too long."

I shook my head.

"You love this man? He kind to you?"

I didn't know what the right answer was. I didn't even know if Tommy was alive. I tried not to give anything away. Before I had a chance to respond he continued,

"If he does not come for you, I'm sure we can find someone to be kind to you. Or for you to be kind to?" He gave me a smile. He had a gold eye tooth. This felt like something right out of a movie. A Spanish man with gold teeth and broken English? Was I in a freaking Tarantino movie?

Okay... so Tommy couldn't be dead.

I didn't know if I felt relief. I thought I might, but I couldn't exactly reconcile the emotions swirling around in me right now. I couldn't process much. I felt sick.

"You don't speak? I know you must be afraid. You have nothing to fear, provided you don't give me any trouble. I have had a room prepared for you. We will speak later. Either your fiancé will come for you or we will talk again about, ah, options." He stepped to me and tipped my chin up and then touched my face. I winced. Tears were threatening but I held them back.

"So beautiful." he said. "I don't know if I'd sell you or maybe keep you for myself." His hand trailed down to a breast and he cupped it.

I felt bile rise up in my throat and remained stiff.

He sighed and let go.

"Flora!" he shouted.

A different older woman in a standard black and white maid's uniform came in. She motioned for me to follow and took me to the basement of the house. It was an unfinished basement and it was dingy and dirty, unlike the main floor of the house. When she opened a door and led me in, I felt sick at the sight. This room was decorated. Finished. It was decorated for a little kid. A little girl, more accurately. Pink single canopy bed, rocking chair filled with dolls and stuffed animals, and a tiny adjoining bathroom. She said nothing to me, just led me in and closed the door and locked it. I noticed a mounted camera pointed at the bed in the corner where the wall met the ceiling.

I sat on the bed, feeling numb for a while, until my bladder nudged so I went into the bathroom and saw that there was a camera in this room, too. Oh man, how could I use the bathroom with a camera pointed at me? The bathroom had baby shampoo, child's Disney character toothpaste and soap. It was weird. No, sickening.

I walked back to the bedroom deciding to hold it as long as I had to. It didn't last long before I had no choice but to go. At least I'd been wearing a dress so I could try to keep myself covered. I tried not to look at the camera. I tried not to think about what this room might be for. But, I knew. I swallowed back the bile that rose in my throat.

I looked down at my dress. This was one of my favorite dresses, a black and white checkered dress with a red collar and belt. It was filthy and ripped at the hem.

Funny that I was upset about a dress right now. Maybe that's all I could let myself focus on. If I focused on what was really going on here, I might not be able to handle it.

What felt like several hours later, the door opened and Flora had a tray that she left on the floor. She backed out and the lock twisted. I sat on the bed and ate a little bit of too-spicy rice, beans, and fish and drank the bottled water she'd left. There were two other bottles there for me so I supposed that might be it until tomorrow. I wasn't wearing a watch, and this room had no windows. I guessed it was nighttime by now, but I wasn't sure. I made myself eat so I could keep my strength, then I decided to try to sleep.

I prayed and prayed hard asking God to deliver me from the nightmare that was my life. I prayed that He would also keep the ones I cared about safe.

Later, much later, I didn't know how long I'd been here, I started to hope that Tommy would rescue me. Better the evil you know than the evil you don't. Even if I had to be his wife, even if I had to be his sex slave, it was back home and if I played my cards right maybe I could maybe have somewhat of a normal life some of the time. Maybe I could see my friends sometimes. Maybe I could figure out how to keep him sweet or at least not piss him off.

But, it was probably too late for that. He'd known me for just a little while and I'd pissed him off repeatedly. He'd find someone else to marry. He'd just leave me here and move on with his life. Juan Carlos had said the Ferranos didn't usually bargain. This was probably hopeless.

7

Tommy

Two Days Later...

Negotiations were done, and if I'd really meant the things I'd agreed to, I'd be feeling like I'd been fucked up the ass right now.

Of course, there had been a lot of back and forth as I had to make it look genuine. Now all was done and I had to wait for Castillo's men to come back to the table to tell us if Juan Carlos would accept our latest counteroffer, which was so close to his last offer that he couldn't possibly refuse it.

We'd tried to make our negotiations sound more like a reason to move forward due to mutually beneficial business ventures that could benefit both sides much more than it being about getting my girl back.

I was like a caged predator on the edge and if it weren't for Dare, I'd have lost my shit by now. He dealt with our translator who dealt with the Castillo translator and they showed me a live feed of her in a kid's bedroom on the bed looking at the ceiling with a lost and distraught look on her face. The feed was open, so I kept checking it on my phone. I was assured she hadn't been touched.

I speak a bit of Spanish, enough, but I just don't have the fucking patience right now, not when I want to rip anyone associated with Castillo apart.

There were ten of us in the room and countless outside all with guns and I want blood. I want it to fucking rain blood on this shithole. And as soon as I get her out of here, there will be a storm coming. Why the hell were we even involved in this business down here? Pop and I needed to have a talk about this.

Tia

I bolted awake. I wasn't alone. The bedroom lights were still on as they had been the whole time I'd been here. A man was standing over me, the Mexican man with the ponytail who'd been driving the car that took me.

I didn't know how long I'd been here. There were no windows and the lights were always on, but I guessed it'd been at least three days judging by how many times food had been brought in. Too much time alone with my thoughts, with my fears, with my regrets. All that'd happened was that a few times that Flora lady brought food and water. She didn't talk to me, just came and left.

I don't think I could ever survive a lengthy stay in solitary confinement. Being locked in this room with nothing to do was awful. But I'd tolerated it as best as I could because I didn't know what would happen once I left this room.

"On your knees," he growled at me.

I stared at him, frozen. He grabbed my hair and pulled me off the bed with it until I was on my knees on the floor.

"Ferrano says no one fucks you or the deal's off but he didn't say you couldn't suck me off." He unzipped his jeans. Oh fuck no.

He was forcing his thing into my mouth, hanging onto a handful of material at the back of my dress. I choked and sputtered so he slapped me across the head and when he hit, he hit so hard I saw a kaleidoscope of colors. He pushed his dick into my mouth again and I just gagged and then tears were streaming out of my eyes. It was disgusting, he stank like old cheese and sweat and tasted nasty. I couldn't stop gagging. He didn't care; he just kept pumping in over and over around my gagging.

"Bite me, Puta, I'll knock your teeth out," he grunted, and then I heard a scuffle behind him and hollering as his grip loosened on me. I heard a bang, a gunshot.

He fell beside me. Earl had shot him in the back of the head. Earl had a look of ferocity on his face. He helped me up and put me on the bed and then disappeared into the bathroom. I stared at the man on the floor in the puddle of almost black blood and his vacant eyes. His penis was still hanging out of his pants. Earl came back with a wet cloth and started wiping my face.

"That should never have happened, honey, I'm sorry," he said, then walked me to the bathroom and turned the tap on. I splashed water on my face and scooped a handful of water and spit it out and then repeated it two or three times. The taste in my mouth was vile, beyond vile. I couldn't stop shaking.

I looked at him with a hurt and betrayed look on my face. This guy had been assigned by Tommy to keep me safe. It was a joke, of course, because I hadn't been safe since I'd been given to Tommy, but this whole thing had just been so ugly and so, so confusing.

From the other morning when Tommy had been tender with me to the incident with his sister and seeing her babies in the car, to running, calling my father, Tommy finding me and being so angry, and then all of this.

I wanted...I didn't know what I wanted. I felt like I was on the verge of a complete breakdown.

"Let's go," Earl said.

I looked at him beseechingly.

"You're going home."

Relief flooded through me. Home?

"To Tommy," he clarified.

He must've seen the look of hope on my face. I knew my expression dropped. Was home with him? I hated what he'd put me through so far, but I hated myself, too, because my actions, my running away had probably made it easy for Earl to kidnap me.

As we headed for the front door, I saw Juan Carlos again. He was in a robe, smoking a cigar. He walked up to us and nodded at Earl. "You hand her off to Ricky and his crew and stay. We don't want the Ferrano boys to see you. Athena, your fiancé has been told if he ever gets tired of you to send you back to me." He winked. I just stared at him blankly.

Earl walked me outside and put me in the back of an old cargo van. I sat on the dirty, carpeted floor and a different, tall Mexican guy tied my hands and feet and put duct tape over my mouth.

"I'm sorry. Good luck," Earl said softly to me and then shut the van doors.

This bad guy had a guilty conscience. I was grateful that he'd at least stopped that filthy pig from finishing with me but he'd been the one who helped bring me here.

Two guys sat in the back with me with gun holsters on them and there were two in the front. The only one I recognized was the slim Black guy who'd done the first aid on Earl's shoulder. I sat and trembled. I couldn't make my body stop.

One of the guys answered a phone, spoke in Spanish, then looked back and said, "Change of plans. You been sold, bitch!" Then he said something else in Spanish and they all started laughing hysterically.

Oh no, oh no, oh no, oh no!

Was Earl lying, or had someone double-crossed someone? Where was I going? What would happen to me?

***

The van drove for what felt like a long time, maybe an hour, but I don't know if I had a realistic concept of time, only the concept of horror. I felt like I was rapidly falling apart at the seams, stitch by stitch, and there may not be much thread left.

Abruptly, the van screeched to a halt and the two in the front got out. The two in the back sat and kept their gazes focused on me. A long time seemed to pass when finally, the back door opened and I was yanked out, dropped carelessly on the road, and then the men jumped back into the van and squealed away.

For at least a minute or two I just lay there in the dust, in the dark, totally freaking out, immobile because I was still bound and gagged. Then I saw headlights coming at me, heard brakes squeal, and heard multiple sets of feet running. I squinted at the high beams in my face.

Oh no, what next? Who had I gotten sold to?

I was scooped up into the air in strong arms. I knew that scent. It was leather, it was musk, a bit of sweat, some stale coffee, but it was Tommy. When it hit me, at that second it was the best scent I'd ever smelled in my life.

My heart leapt forward with jubilation but then at the same instant I felt fear prickle like spikes through my scalp. How mad was he going to be at me for this?

And then I was in the back seat of a car; I was on his lap and he was breathing hard, getting my hands untied, getting my feet untied, and then he got the tape off my mouth. It was dark and we weren't alone in the car, which was now speeding away. There were three heads in the front bench seat and just us in the back.

I felt barely more than catatonic. I had my bottom lip in my mouth, reeling from the sting of the tape being pulled off. My feet and hands were numb from having been tied too long and too tight.

"Are you hurt?" he breathed, examining me in the near darkness of the car with just the tiny interior light on. I shook my head *no* but at the sight of his eyes, the concern on his face, the reality of where I was and what I was in the middle of, a giant sob tore out of me.

He pulled me tight against his chest and rocked back and forth, one hand on my head, the other flat against the center of my back. I put my arms around his torso and held tight, feeling him pull me tighter, feeling his mouth on my head. He said nothing but he kept rocking back and forth with me, kissing my head over and over, squeezing me reassuringly. He said nothing, I said nothing. I had a feeling that there would be plenty to say when we were alone.

A while later, I don't know how much later, the car stopped and I jolted awake. I had fallen asleep against him, feeling like his scent and his arms were a warm blanket around me. He carried me, cradled in his arms in through a gate, and then up a walkway to a large light-colored house with all the outside lights on. Once inside, the interior's light was blinding. I squinted and shielded my eyes. He said something softly to his brother who'd been in the car with us, shut the door and then he climbed a narrow staircase with me. A moment later he kicked a slightly ajar dark stained wooden door open and then swept his foot backwards once we were in to shut it. He turned around and locked a deadbolt and put me down on a bed. He was standing over me, looking down at me for a moment, his expression unreadable to me.

My dam burst and the tears fell like Niagara Falls. He flicked the light switch off, sat, grabbed me, pulled me up onto his lap, and rocked me some more in the dark. He held me tight, almost too tight. After a few minutes or an hour, I wasn't sure, he let go. He got up to his feet. I clambered up to my knees on the bed and threw my arms around him and held on tight, not wanting him to leave me alone, not wanting someone to swoop in and take me, not wanting his sweetness to change to anger.

He kissed the top of my head and whispered, "I'm gonna run a bath. Just a minute, okay?"

I let go of him and just sat on the edge of the bed.

He went to an adjoining bathroom and turned the water on. He was back a moment later and reaching for my hand. I stood up and followed him into the bathroom. I saw my reflection in the mirror. My hair was a tangled mess, my eyes were bloodshot, and my black and white checkered dress with the red collar and red belt was filthy and ruined. I had no shoes on my dirty feet. Tommy looked rough, too. He was wearing a pair of khaki cargo pants and a white button up shirt, but he was filthy dirty. He looked exhausted. His face was prickly and unshaven. He looked down at me and started to undo the zipper on the back of my dress. I let the material fall to my feet, got out of my underthings, and got into the big antique-looking claw foot tub and wrapped my arms around my legs, putting my cheek on my knee.

He shed his clothing, including two guns plus a knife and leg holster and piled it all on the floor beside the tub. He got in behind me and started to massage my shoulders. I started ugly-crying big time. He soaped my back up with a giant sudsy sponge and then passed the sponge to me and I resumed the rest of the soaping up in the front, still crying.

He reached around and tenderly cupped my chin, then tilted my chin up to pour a cup of water over my hair and massaged my scalp, lathering my hair. He lathered it up with a strawberry-scented shampoo and it felt so good I thought I might just fall asleep. Then he rinsed my hair several times with the cup and then lathered himself up hair to toes, rinsed, leaned forward, pulled the plug out and let it drain.

I went to get up but he pulled my back against his front and kissed my temple and kept me there while it drained. Then he leaned over and turned the taps back on to refill it with clean water. He reached over to a shelf beside the tub and poured some lavender scented foam bath in. He pulled me back against his chest and leaned back in the water against the back of the tub. By this time, I had stopped with the tears, but still had the shudders.

He let the tub fill and then we soaked for a while, not talking; I was just listening to the sizzle of the bubbles on our skin and the sound of crickets and frogs outside.

I started to feel like I was sinking into sleep against him but then he nudged me to let him out. I leaned forward. "We're both washed clean, okay?" he said.

I looked back over my shoulder at him. By the look on his face I think he saw this as monumental, almost like a baptism, for both of us. I nodded slowly. He looked like he hadn't slept in days. My heart ached, thinking about him coming to get me, about him saving me.

I pulled the plug and watched the bubbles and water go down the drain while he dried himself off and then put a fluffy white towel around his waist.

"Hungry, thirsty?" he asked.

I shook my head.

He left the room and I got out, dried off, and then went to the sink. I found a box of new toothbrushes under the sink, along with toothpaste and mouthwash. The tears came back and I cried softly as I washed my mouth out. I wondered if I'd ever forget that horrible man's taste for the rest of my life. Just thinking about it made bile rise and I started retching and then vomiting in the sink. I knew it was loud, so loud that if Tommy was in the bedroom still, he'd be listening to this. It was like my stomach was trying to turn itself inside out.

When it finally stopped, I brushed my teeth and rinsed with mouthwash again and again and again, until my mouth was burning from all of it. I spent...I don't know how long... rinsing, gagging, coughing, rinsing, spitting, gagging and choking some more. I towel dried my hair for a few minutes before my arms started to ache and then I stepped out into the bedroom. It was dark but I could see that Tommy was in the bed on his usual side, facing my direction. I sat on the edge, dropped the towel and climbed in beside him. He sat up and pulled a clean-smelling t-shirt over my head, then once my arms were in the holes, he passed me an opened bottle of water and said, "Drink."

I drank about half of it and then put the bottle down on the table beside the bed. He immediately pulled me to his chest and held me tight. I felt his hands in my hair and his lips on my forehead. I touched his cheek and it felt wet. Was it from the bath? I felt a drip hit my finger. Oh my God...he was shedding tears for me.

I started to cry again and he held me tighter, "What did they do to you, baby? Tell me. Then you'll never have to talk about it again." His voice sounded a bit strangled.

There were no tears left in my burning eyes and my throat hurt from all the sobbing and throwing up. He waited, rubbing his hand up and down my back and then he squeezed my shoulder reassuringly.

After what felt like forever, I finally gained enough composure to speak. "The guy who drove the car from your house, he forced himself into my... my...m-mouth. Earl shot him for it before the guy could f-finish." I felt him tense up but he didn't say anything. He just squeezed me tighter. "It happened just before they drove me to you. That's the only...the only thing," I finished off.

"No one, no one will ever, ever again..." he started and it sounded like he was saying it through gritted teeth. But he didn't finish; he just pulled me even tighter against him.

I fell asleep on top of him, our bodies pressed together, and for the first time he wasn't hard, wasn't plotting one of his games to get inside of me. Rescuing me, cradling me, washing the filth off me, holding me while I cried, and shedding tears for me – that got him inside of me in a different way.

* * *

When I woke, I jackknifed up, out of breath. Then I realized where I was.

Well, I didn't know where I was, exactly, but he was still beside me, so I settled down.

He was lying there looking at me. He pulled me to him and his mouth touched the top of my head. He looked exhausted, like he still hadn't even slept. He still looked rough, too, with the shiner I'd given him, bruised lip, and the scratches still on his face.

I settled my head against his chest and closed my eyes, trying to tell my heart to settle down. The sun was up and the room was filled with light. I looked around. It was a pretty bedroom with a white ruffled lace bedspread on the white wicker framed double bed. The white room kind of went with last night's whole baptismal theme. The only splash of color was a vase of fresh pink, yellow, and orange daisy-like flowers on the wicker dresser and a big green empty rucksack beside a black suitcase opened and sitting on a big, wicker rocking chair. I could see it was filled with my clothes and his clothes. I closed my eyes and focused on the steadiness of his heartbeat, feeling strange, feeling cared for.

"You should sleep a bit longer. We got in really late," he said, smoothing my hair behind my ear.

I nodded, thinking he was right, because those days in that basement I think I only slept twenty winks at a time, but a few minutes later it was probably obvious that I wasn't falling back to sleep.

I was lying on him, staring off into space. He pulled away, but took my hand in his and pulled it toward him and kissed each knuckle. Then he leaned over a little and took a phone off the nightstand and dialed a number.

"Hey," he greeted. "Need breakfast. Can you have her put it outside the door? Tell her to knock when she brings it, but no disturbing us. Ask my brother what time the flight is." He held the phone for a minute and then said, "Right" before hanging up.

I went to move away, thinking he was getting up, but his grip tightened and he didn't let me go. He buried his nose into my hair and squeezed me. We stayed there for another few minutes just holding one another until a noise outside the door and then a brief knocking on the door startled me. I think I must've jumped two feet at the noise.

He got up, walked to the suitcase in his underwear, got into a clean pair of army green cargos, and then stepped into the hall. I got up with the duvet wrapped around me and leaned over the suitcase and pulled out some underwear, a bra, a pair of jean shorts, and a t-shirt that had been packed for me. I glanced in the top flap of the suitcase and there was a toiletry bag with some of my makeup, hairbrush, deodorant, razor, manicure tool kit, and my own toothbrush. There were two other changes of clothes and two pairs of shoes --- a pair of my sneakers and my leather flip flops packed in the suitcase.

I took an armful of things into the bathroom to get dressed and try to make myself presentable. As I passed the door, my eyes landed on his guns and knife on the nightstand.

He came back in with a covered breakfast-in-bed tray.

I got dressed, brushed my hair, brushed my teeth, and washed my face.

When I got back out, he was sitting on the bed tapping away at his phone screen. I sat down. He wandered into the bathroom and came back out wearing the khaki t-shirt I'd slept in. He looked at me warmly. "Eat something, baby."

I smiled a little and nodded. I lifted the tray's lid and there was an assortment of fruit, muffins, pastries, bagels, with little butter, cream cheese, and jam pots. There was also a carafe of coffee, milk, sugar, and a jug of orange juice. My stomach rumbled loudly.

"Coffee?" I asked him.

"Yeah, please."

I remembered he took cream, no sugar, due to Sarah's sugar weaning. Me? I was having 3 sugars today. There were things in life that were far more evil than sugar.

I passed him a cup, my hand trembling a little. I moved the suitcase onto the floor, sat on the wicker chair and looked out the window. We were in a woodsy area, so really, the only thing to look at was the trees.

"I'm putting you on a plane in a few hours with Dare," he said, not looking up at me. "I'll be taking care of a few things and then I'll be home later tonight or maybe tomorrow."

"Okay," I said.

Then he looked up and while I was still looking out the window, I could feel that he was watching me. He watched me for a long time. I didn't look in his eyes because I was afraid of what I'd see. I knew in my gut that he was sticking around for revenge reasons.

He cleared his throat. "I need to go downstairs and organize a few things. You okay for a bit?"

I nodded, glancing in his direction and then back at the floor. I felt scrutinized, uncomfortable. There was this intensity coming off him that was making my heart race.

"You'll eat?"

I nodded again.

He leaned over and kissed me softly on the lips and then he leaned down and got into his boots, rolled up his pant leg, and then grabbed the holster and fastened it and I turned away so I didn't have to watch him arming himself. When I looked back in his direction, he was putting a gun into the back of his waistband and then he left the room. I felt like I was going to cry again, but I didn't. I was sort of surprised he'd kissed me like that, maybe feeling like my mouth was an unclean place because of what I'd told him last night. I felt my heart tug at the idea that I was wrong.

Why did he rescue me? Why didn't he just leave me here? And why was the fact that he'd kissed me so touching to me?

Tommy

Anger didn't begin to describe what was inside me pacing and biding time until I could unleash it.

Wrath, rage, fury? They might come close if they were each multiplied a hundred thousand times.

Things were in motion that would bring the Castillo cartel to their knees. Juan Carlos Castillo would be torn limb from limb, and I would personally piss on the bones of Earl Johnson. My heart felt coal black right now and if it hadn't been for the fact that she needed me more last night, I'd have already gone off to take care of it.

Listening to her in that bathroom throwing up, brushing her teeth, throwing up again, sobbing, it went on for so long and listening to her fall apart like that, it broke me like I couldn't ever remember being broken before. I felt so fucking helpless then. I never wanted to feel that way again. Ever.

Now I needed to get her home and I needed to get this done so that I could get the rage out of my head. That rage had never felt so strong in my life, and I hoped I could channel it into ridding this earth of the scum that were responsible for taking her from me and for putting her through that. And then I could go home and start my life with her and take advantage of the clean slate it felt like she was giving me.

What had happened to her here had upgraded me from villain to hero in her eyes and when I got home, I was making her my wife and taking this opportunity, fucked up as it was, to build a real relationship with her.

That t-shirt smelled like her. I'd given it to her last night and then worn it deliberately today. It was comforting to me to have her scent on my body, knowing what I was going to do next.

I was having Dare bring her home because I needed her the fuck out of Mexico and right now, he was the only one I trusted to keep her safe. He and I had shared a few glances that told me he now knew how important protecting her was to me. When I got home, I'd re-vet employees to determine who would be in the inner circle for keeping her safe. I'd also find out the truth about why Pop had given her to me and I'd make that lowlife father of hers pay whatever penance I deemed necessary.

Yeah, I knew it was fucked up that I'd punish him for the very reason I was lucky enough to own her but that's just how I felt about it.

I wasn't kidding myself, thinking that the darkness inside of me that wanted her submission, her fear, was gone. But right now, I had a different place to channel that need, that hunger. I'd figure the rest out later.

Tia

I ate a surprisingly decent amount of food and then I waited for him to come back. I fell asleep and a while later woke up to his lips on my forehead. My hands came up and rested on his chest.

"Hi," I said.

His eyes crinkled and he smiled a little.

"Time to go," he said and then kissed me on the mouth quickly and began digging through the suitcase. He looked angry and stressed. I felt the desire to do something about it, so I could see warmth in his eyes again. I just didn't know what to do to bring it back.

I got up off the bed, grabbed my toiletries from the bathroom and put them in the suitcase, and then proceed to get into my sneakers. He was doing something on his phone one-handed while pulling some of his things out of the suitcase and into a big barrel rucksack, then he tied it up.

I gave him a sad look.

"Just one more day, then I'll be home," he muttered.

I picked up his silver cross necklace, which was lying beside the vase on the dresser, "Do you want me to fasten this?"

He winced at it. "No, take that home."

I put it in my toiletries bag, then I tied my hair up in the elastic that was on my wrist, thankful that there was one in my things that had been packed for me, probably by Sarah Martinez.

He put his hands on my shoulders and his touch almost brought me to tears again. I didn't know why. I held the tears back.

"My brother is taking you home," he said, "I trust him 100% to keep you safe. You need to let him protect you."

The intense way he looked at me was his way of asking me not to try to run again. I nodded, eyes on his.

"Come back safely," I said and his eyes warmed.

He kissed me slow, soft, and sweet, taking my hips into his hands. He gave them a little squeeze and then wrapped his arms around me tight, holding me for a few minutes against him, lifting me a few inches off the floor. I melted into him, not wanting him to let me go.

When he finally did, he caressed my cheek with the ridge of his thumb and looked deep into my eyes for a beat, heat and intensity and some emotion I couldn't name lighting them, before backing up and picking up the suitcase and the rucksack.

I followed him out of the room, down the stairs, and out the front door to where Dario was waiting in a car with two local-looking men standing outside with machine guns slung over their shoulders. Two more men sat inside the car. They looked more Italian than Mexican. Maybe they were from home.

One stepped out of the back seat and Tommy ushered me in and stepped back. The man got back in beside me. I buckled my seatbelt. I saw Tommy's brother standing beside him and they said a few words I didn't hear and exchanged glances that I'd imagine had something to do with Tommy telling Dario to get home safely with me and Dario telling Tommy to clean house but carefully. They hugged briefly and I heard the trunk slam, then Dario opened the back door and signaled for the guy to get into the front so he could sit beside me.

As the car drove away, I looked back and Tommy wore a hard, angry, steely look as he watched us leave. But then he caught me looking and gave me a thin smile. I smiled back, hoping that he'd make it home and hoping that what I'd seen from him in the past twelve hours had not been a mirage. I didn't want to hope that he got his revenge, but I did. I didn't dwell on it for long, but the idea of him fighting back was a little bit satisfying. I knew it wasn't going to be all about me, probably more about holding a position of power and proving that he was stronger than those who took me to get to him, but it was still a little bit satisfying and I suspected from the way he'd handled me in the past twelve or so hours that revenge would be at least a little bit about what was done to me.

The ride was thankfully uneventful, and it wasn't long before we were boarding a small jet on a private-looking airfield. Dario offered me a drink and a blanket and pillow. He told me I could lay down on one of the sofas and sleep if I was tired.

For the next while, I just sort of stared off into space, going over the past few days' events in my head. I caught him looking at me a few times. I didn't know if it was curiosity, compassion, or what it was that was in his eyes, but I didn't feel uncomfortable around him today. I felt safe and it was a welcome feeling.

There were other men on the plane with us, but they stayed to the opposite end of the sitting area, talking amongst themselves quietly. At one point I looked up and saw that they were watching a zombie slasher type movie and that Mexican actor was in it. He looked so much like that horrible man and I felt the tears well up again and I turned over and faced the back of the sofa so I couldn't see the TV.

"You okay?" Dario leaned over me. "What's wrong?"

"It's okay, I'm okay."

"You sure?"

"It's stupid."

"What's stupid?"

"There's an actor on that movie they're watching that looks like one of the guys and the guy... hurt me."

Dario's face went ice cold. "Turn that fuckin' shit off!" he hollered at the guys, making me jump.

He touched my shoulder, "Sorry, it's okay."

He backed away to his seat and then stared out the window with his mouth in a tight line.

"I'm acting like a baby," I said and wiped the tears away.

He reminded me a bit of Tommy right then. He wasn't as tall and had fair hair and bluish gray eyes, but his facial features were quite similar, at least the angry ones as I was now noticing. His jaw tightened and he stared out the window.

I closed my eyes, deciding to try to nap until we landed.

I woke up to him tapping my arm gently.

"We're here," he said, then he grabbed my suitcase and ushered me off the plane and into a waiting SUV. He signaled to the driver to get out.

The driver got out and got into a black SUV parked behind it. It was just me and Dario in this vehicle.

After we left the airport he said, "I wanted a minute to talk to you."

I looked at him expectantly, but a little frightened because I had a feeling he was about to berate me for taking off on Tommy, for starting the chain of events that led to Mexico. I decided to cut him off at the pass.

"Thank you for being so nice to me under the circumstances."

"The circumstances?" He looked at me strangely.

"You know, since all this happened because I took off. You might not believe this, but I hope and pray nothing happens to your brother because of it, because of me. I also wanted to tell you both, I didn't get a chance to mention it to Tommy, but they told me that if I didn't cooperate, they could easily take your pregnant sister. Maybe she needs someone to watch, needs some security."

His jaw clenched. Then he furrowed his brows and shook his head. "Don't do that. This isn't your fault. Our family is under threat of some sort almost all the time. We go on living as normal because we need to in order to stay sane but believe this: this would've happened anyway, even if you hadn't taken off from my sister. Earl was part of the plan and Tommy trusted him. He was Tommy's number one for security for you, so was the perfect person for the enemy to get to flip. Either he was planning this for a long time or that plan went into motion because he was allowed to be so close to you and it would've been pulled off sooner or later. The minute word got around that Tommy was getting married, that trigger got pulled. We've got extra security, don't you worry. And I didn't plan to talk to you about this part, but don't worry about my brother getting hurt; my brother is indestructible. Trust me, he'll be back tonight or tomorrow at the latest. He'll hurry back for you. I wanted to talk to you about his feelings for you."

I looked down at my hands.

"I know you were forced into the engagement. I also know that for some reason my brother fell head over heels almost instantly. I'm not saying 'for some reason' because I don't think you're a catch, you're a beautiful girl, but this isn't Tommy. He has access to an unlimited supply of beautiful girls who want him, who'd give their eye teeth to be engaged to him, knowing full well who he is and wanting the lifestyle that comes with it. I'm telling you he's different with you. I know my brother might not seem like the relationship type, and looking at the damage you did to his face I don't think you took too well to your situation." He laughed. "He will never live that down by the way, thank you."

I grimaced.

"Sorry, very inappropriate. My point is that I know my brother can be a hard ass, but I hope you'll give things a chance with him because I think you could be good for him. Real good."

We were pulling into the driveway of Tommy's house already.

The gate opened to let us in and when we stopped, I saw the SUV behind us. There were four guards stationed at the gates.

"Thank you," I said. "I'm, uh, hopeful. Things feel different."

"Good. He is different. I've never seen him that affected by something. All he wanted was to get you out of there. We wouldn't normally negotiate in a situation like that," he added and looked at me with seriousness in his eyes.

I nodded, the gravity sinking in even deeper as he confirmed what I already suspected, that Tommy normally wouldn't have negotiated with kidnappers. If Tommy had just seen me as 'property' maybe I wouldn't have been deemed worthy enough to have made it out of there. He could've replaced me easily. I'd been thinking a lot about that.

"He did not stop until he got you out of there. He barely ate or slept and was hell on wheels until he got you back. Tommy has a short fuse; he needs to work on that. I hope...I hope he does. For you. Try to be patient. You should know he'll kill for you. I wouldn't normally say this to anybody but given the situation I think I can tell you this and maybe it'll give you some insight into who my brother is. He's killing for you right now, Tia; I'm sure of it. If this were my father instead of Tommy, Pop would've sent someone to do it for him. But my brother? Tommy will do it himself."

I shook my head. "I know it was probably a direct hit to his pride to have his so-called fiancée—"

Dario cut me off. "Uh uh. Nope. This was more about you than about pride. I'm telling you, you're not so-called. He's all in."

One of the guys who'd been in Mexico with us was at the car door, trying to get Dario's attention.

"One sec," he said, and got out and spoke to the guy. Then he rolled his eyes and motioned for me to get out, an amused look on his face. "The Calvary has come," he said.

I didn't know what he meant.

"My sisters and Pop's wife. They're here. Before we go in, Tommy doesn't want you discussing things with them. They know a little, that you and Tommy had a fight, that you messed up his face, that you took off, and that you were kidnapped, but they don't know other details. Okay? He also doesn't want you to attempt to contact anyone by phone or to leave the safety of the house until he's home and he's had a chance to prep you. All right?"

My eyes widened. Sisters, rules, craziness. I wished I could just go up and hide out in the bedroom and watch some brainless TV and decompress.

"Come, you'll be fine. They just want to dote on you."

* * *

The four women were in the family room, but spilled out into the hallway to greet me. There was Sarah, Tessa, and two others. One looked a lot like Tessa but about six or more months pregnant, and the other looked around their age, too and she had long dark hair, was model tall and very beautiful. They were all very attractive. The pregnant one pulled me into an embrace.

"I'm Luciana. They call me Luc, I'm glad you're safe."

"Nice to meet you," I said.

The dark-haired one leaned over and air kissed both of my cheeks. "I'm Lisa, I guess I'll be your mother-in-law soon?"

They all cackled like it was the funniest thing they'd ever heard.

"Monster-in-law more like!" said Tessa, who was approaching me warily. She'd stepped out of the embrace of one of the guys that'd been in Mexico with us. Clearly, he was her husband. I eyed her apologetically and was about to speak. She shh'd me and pulled me into a hug and whispered, "Forget about it. Glad you're okay."

"Let the poor girl in, guys," Dario told them. "Give her some space."

"Get outta here, you!" Luciana shoved at him. "Go home. We've got this."

"Nope, got orders to stay here until Tommy is back. James, you can head out."

James was Tessa's husband. He was dressed in a dark suit, a tall, dark, good-looking guy. He kissed Tessa on the lips briefly and whispered something in her ear. She nodded and he left.

The girls bodily pulled me into the kitchen where Sarah was putting a plate of sandwiches on the table. She put the plate down and then took me into her arms like I was her long-lost child. "Look at you, Chiquita! Are you okay? We're so glad you're safe."

I gave her a little smile. "I'm okay."

Luciana sat down on a chair and picked up a sandwich, "So you were kidnapped and taken to Mexico? That must've been awful."

"Shh," Lisa said. "Leave it."

"Yes, leave it," Tessa added. "She's been through enough in the past few days. Let the girl relax."

Dario reached over and took a sandwich and then got a drink out of the fridge. "Drink, Tia?"

"Thanks, just water," I answered.

They all started to babble about things like food, about the size of Luc's stomach, about the weather, about the latest episode of the Bachelorette on TV. It was noisy, it was hectic, it was nice. It reminded me of Rose and Cal's.

I wondered how they were. I wondered about my dad, too. Had Tommy followed him to the mall and then had someone hold him back? Had Tommy found me before my dad even got there? I still wanted to hear that explanation from my father about all of this. I'd talk to Tommy about contacting my dad when he was back.

For the next few hours I listened to the girls giggle and watched them eat the plate of sandwiches, then devour a fruit tray, and then eat a giant bag of pretzels. Sarah was right in there laughing and hooting and howling and Dario sat on the counter and shook his head mostly.

I realized that no one had asked where Tommy was. Did they know he was taking care of business? Were they here to keep me company and pass the time so I wouldn't be pacing the floors wondering if he was okay?

Was he okay? What would happen to me if he wasn't?

Tessa leaned over and patted my shoulder and illustrated some mind-reading skills.

"He'll be fine. That brother of ours is tougher than nails. Trust me! He's tougher than Pop, even, and Pop is one tough motherfucker."

The others were all nodding. This is exactly what they were doing. They were rallying together during a crisis. All of a sudden, Sarah held her cell phone in front of Lisa and Lisa squirmed. "That's disgusting!"

Sarah almost tipped her chair over, laughing so hard. I glanced over and realized she was still fixated on the picture of all the old men in the Speedo bathing suits.

"Ah c'mon Lisa, we all know that's what you're into," Dario said and everyone including Lisa started to laugh uncontrollably.

I laughed too because it was pretty funny that they were all here laughing at the expense of Lisa's husband, the girls' and Dario's father, a powerful mobster.

My back was to the entrance to the kitchen at this point and suddenly the room hushed. I saw everyone looking stone-faced past me. I looked back and Mr. Ferrano was in the doorway. He was in a black suit and looked solemn.

They all had a horrified look on their faces, like he was here with bad news.

Oh no. My belly dipped and not in a good way.

"What's so fuckin' funny?" he broke the tension. "Share. I like jokes."

Everyone except me howled with laughter. Sarah fell off her chair this time and Lisa fell, too, trying to help Sarah up. Dario was sitting on the counter but doubled over holding his gut, and when Luc piped up with, "I think I just peed a little" the fits of laughter roared louder.

Mr. Ferrano walked over to the coffee maker and stared at it, then looked down at Sarah who was still on the floor tangled up with Lisa.

"Guess I'll get myself a coffee. Would you like a coffee, Sarah?" His eyebrows perked up at her. He didn't look like those old guys, but math said he had to have about twenty plus years on Lisa.

"Everyone wants coffee! Except Luciana. You can make her a hot chocolate." Sarah beamed at him.

"What's up, Pop?" Dario asked.

"I'll make the espresso and then we'll chat for a minute, son. I just came to pick up Lisa, mostly, and to check on Athena. You okay?"

He looked at me and his face was kind, seemed genuine. He seemed different from how he was when I met him that first day. My thoughts flickered to him and my mother. I nodded, chewing my cheek.

"Good," he said. "When that boy gets home you do me a favor, okay?"

"What's that?" I asked.

"You give his right eye a pop for me too, ah? I think it needs to match!" He punched the air with a mean hook.

Everyone started to laugh, except me again. I didn't know what the heck to make of this bunch and their quirky sense of humor. Everyone clearly thinks it's pretty awesome that I gave Tommy a black eye. Everyone here wants me to feel welcome, too, it seems. Now I understand what Tommy meant by the whole "Ferrano family experience" comment. I can't imagine how nuts it is with all the kids and the spouses together with all these guys during something celebratory rather than a stressful situation like this.

Mr. Ferrano brewed espresso for everyone except me and Luc. He made her a hot chocolate with whipped cream on it and then he made me a cappuccino with a heart pattern on it and smiled at me as he put the cup down. It looked like it came from a fancy café.

"Thank you, Mr. Ferrano," I said.

"Call me Pop." He winked, then signaled Dario to follow him into the other room.

I looked down at the cup and got lost in thought. I noticed the room was quiet, so I looked up from the heart shaped foam in my cup to see all eyes on me. I felt uncomfortable for a beat and then the girls all started chatting again and suddenly Luc grabbed my hand and placed it on her belly and I felt her baby kicking.

"This better be the boy!" she said. "I have twin girls in the terrible twos and my first wish is there's just one in here." She pointed to her big round belly. "My second wish is that it be a boy so that I can say I've done my wifely duty and then the doctor can tie my tubes."

Tessa piped up, "I guarantee it's another girl. I can feel it."

"Oh, shut up!" Luc answered and pretended to smack at her sister, "If this is another girl, I'll do this one more time, just one. If it's another girl then I'm done, heirs or no heirs."

All three of them look alike, a bit like Tommy but blonde and a little different. They must take after their mother a bit because I can see that Tommy definitely takes after his father. Lisa is a pretty girl and a little older than me, but I can see how she's attracted to him. He's handsome and holds his age well. She fits with these girls perfectly. They seem like they're all best friends. I idly hope that I can one day feel carefree again. Right now that feels a little far from possible.

***

An hour later I was yawning, and Tessa took it as a cue to get everyone out. Dario and Mr. Ferrano were still somewhere else in the house. Tessa told them I needed my rest and that it was after midnight. Sarah went off to find the guys.

A few minutes later they came back in and Mr. Ferrano hugged each girl, including Sarah and then stood in front of my spot on a kitchen chair and held his arms open. It was weird and uncomfortable, but I stood and let him embrace me. I'm sure I looked shell-shocked.

Tessa hugged me and told me that in a few weeks they were having a baby shower for Luc and that she'd get me the details. Lisa hugged me and told me that dinner is always at their house on Sundays and that we're expected every week. Luc hugged me and told me it was nice to meet me and said she'd get my digits from Tommy and text me about getting together in a few days after I'm rested. They all marched out of the place in single file and that left me, Sarah, and Dario in the kitchen.

I headed to the doorway. "I think I'm going to head to bed," I said and Dario nodded at me.

"I'll be close by if you need anything."

"Thank you," I said, then added, "Goodnight, Sarah."

She smiled at me. "Sleep well, Chiquita. Welcome home."

I'm sure I frowned at her in response. Home?

* * *

I fell asleep on the bed without even changing my clothes, but only slept an hour or two and then I was wide awake. I got a drink of whiskey from the bar, thinking it might settle my nerves and make me sleepy, but it did just what it did last time – gross me out and burn my throat.

I washed up for bed and changed into a pair of pajamas, then I stared at the ceiling for what felt like hours, pondering my situation, the recent course of events, my life in general. When I finally closed my eyes again, I knew one thing for sure, I was a survivor and determined to survive all of this.

I was kidnapped and men got shot at and died. I didn't know if I'd ever get out of that situation. Hah. My kidnapper saved me from other kidnappers. But he got me out and he took care of me that night the way I could only imagine in my wildest fantasies that a knight in shining armor would. I decided that if I'm stuck here paying a debt for someone else and if I have no choice in the matter, I'm at least going to try to find a way to be happy.

Last night I didn't know if I was going to make it out of that basement in Mexico, and then I didn't know what'd happen to me when that driver told me I'd been sold, but now I was back near home, safe and warm, and I'd seen potential in Tommy Ferrano. I decided that I didn't want to just let life flutter away because I'm a victim of a parent's mistake.

Tommy Ferrano has issues, it's obvious. He's dominating and angry and he can be cruel. He wasn't nice to me the first week. He played some seriously messed up head games and he violated me repeatedly. He's about to be promoted to be the head of a crime family – the same crime family that threatened my father and that took me prisoner.

But he's also shown that he has potential. I like his family and they seem close. I could see myself becoming good friends with the girls and Dario doesn't scare me so much anymore. He'd been really nice to me today. Maybe I'm just a naïve nineteen-year-old girl, but Tommy seems to care about me and maybe I can nurture that potential so that with me he's always the guy from the beach, the guy who rescued me. Maybe in time I can forgive him for what he's done, overlook who he is. Maybe I can stay on his good side, make him always be more of the ice cream parlor guy when he's with me.

Yeah, and maybe I'm an idiot. I don't know how dark it'll get. I don't know what he's doing down there. I only know that the threats he made in the car just before I was kidnapped scared me beyond any fear I'd ever had in my whole life. I fell back to sleep feeling very conflicted.

I jolted awake again before night was over, but this time it was because I'd had a horrible nightmare. I was back in the pink canopy bed and the man forcing me to give him the blowjob was Tommy. He'd been mean and horrible, manhandling me like that other guy did.

But, then I saw my dad, thinking he came to rescue me. He had a gun. But Dad didn't shoot him, Tommy said, 'Take her, I'm done with her,' then Dad shot *me* and told me, while I watched my blood leaking everywhere, that I was too much trouble, that I'd weighed him down after Mom died and that's why he'd tried to get rid of me.

After several unsuccessful attempts he was going to get rid of me for good.

When I woke, it was four o'clock in the morning. Would this night ever end?

I got up to get a drink and the bar fridge had no water in it, so I put on a robe and decided to head to the kitchen. When I got to the bottom of the stairs, I heard a loud voice in the kitchen. I stopped on the bottom step. It was Dario's voice.

"We need to just wait. No, damn it! Don't! Just circle and keep coming back."

I stepped off the stairs and walked into the kitchen. He looked up at me and then said, "Call me in 30 minutes with an update. Or sooner if there's any change." He ended the call. "You all right?"

I nodded. "I'm just thirsty." I got a bottle of water from the fridge. "Is Tommy okay?"

Dario waved his hand at me, saying, "Of course," but I could see the stress on his face.

"I'm going to try to go back to sleep," I said.

He nodded, not looking me in the eyes.

* * *

Surprisingly, I did fall back asleep, but was awake around 9:15. I got up and took a shower and when I came back into the bedroom just in a towel I froze because I noticed Dario was asleep on the couch here in this room. He was asleep in a t-shirt and track pants, the first time I'd seen him not in a suit. He was quite built, a lot like Tommy. I didn't let my eyes linger on him for long, not wanting to look like a creep watching him while he slept. Clearly, he took his job of protecting me seriously if he was sleeping here instead of one of the bazillion guest rooms.

I rushed into the closet to find some clothes and got dressed in there. When I came out, he wasn't on the couch any longer. I went downstairs and looked out the window and I saw three men mulling about outside. I got a coffee and sat at the kitchen table with yesterday's newspaper to kill time.

Sarah came in from the back hallway, a laundry basket filled with folded towels on her hip and ear buds in her ears. She was singing a pop song. She smiled when she spotted me and pulled a bud out.

"Breakfast?"

I shook my head, "Not yet. Thanks. I'll just get myself something when I'm ready."

She smiled and wagged her finger at me. "Don't put me out of a job, Chiquita!" She headed out of the kitchen and upstairs, I presumed.

I decided to wander around. I saw it lacked a homey feeling. It was decorated sort of man cave'ish like the master bedroom with leather and dark wood and drab-colored or neutral walls without family pictures or art on the walls. There weren't any mementoes; it was sort of sterile. I opened a door in the hall off the kitchen and found two other bedrooms. One was sort of utilitarian with a single bed, nightstand with a lamp and then a table with four chairs and a coffee maker, fridge, sink, and stove so I assumed it was for the guards. There was a patio door in that room that led to the backyard. The other room I didn't venture into as it was obviously Sarah's room.

It was large and had a warm vibe, decorated with cream and burgundy furnishings and dark cherry wood. The dresser was filled with framed photos and she also had a sitting area with a coffee table fanned with books and magazines.

I found my way outside, deciding to get some fresh air. I spotted a guard in the yard, but he left the area when I went out. Good that they were trying to be as inconspicuous as possible, but it was so obvious that the place was under lockdown and that everyone was on edge. I sat at the pool's edge and dangled my feet in, staring out at the forest beyond the pool.

I heard a voice in the kitchen, so I strained to listen. Dario was on the phone again.

"I don't give a fucking shit!" he yelled. "Find him!"

He stormed out onto the patio, an unlit cigarette in his mouth, putting his phone into his pocket (he was already dressed in a fresh suit) and then he lit it as he spotted me. His expression dropped and he inhaled deeply, as if the smoke was cleansing him.

"Mornin'," he finally said, gruffly. He looked like he hadn't slept much either.

"Morning," I replied and then looked back out to the forest. I didn't want to ask as it was obvious that Tommy was missing.

* * *

That day felt like a long one; my gut was raw all day. I'd sat outside a while and then went into the kitchen and forced myself to swallow down a piece of buttered toast. I wandered back upstairs and looked around at the bedrooms, which all looked sort of the same, like hotel rooms. I found my way back to the master bedroom and tried to take a nap, but I didn't sleep. I felt that sick almost over-caffeinated feeling you feel when your body is tired but your brain is in overdrive.

I wondered how Rose was doing, how everyone was faring while wondering if I was okay. I wanted to reach out to them but there wasn't a phone in this bedroom. The cordless phone base still sat empty. Dario's words about not making calls rang in my ears, but as it got later in the day, I decided that I just had to make that call and at least tell her not to stress, that I was fine. I found a cordless in the family room and tucked it into the back of my shorts and pulled my sweater over it and then went back up to the master bedroom. I'd managed this feat without drawing any attention as Dario wasn't in sight, Tommy's office door was closed, and all the guards seemed to be outside. Sarah was busy cooking something in the kitchen.

I dialed Rose's cell phone and got her voicemail. I was relieved to get her voicemail on one hand because that'd mean that I wouldn't have to answer questions, but on the other hand it made me sad because it wouldn't tell me if she was okay or not.

I left a message. "Rose, it's Tia. I just want you to know I'm fine. Everything is okay. I hope everyone is okay there. Please know I love all of you and I'll be in touch again soon. Please don't worry and please just leave things be – I don't want anyone at risk. Don't worry about me, okay? Things are actually somewhat better so don't stress. Love you guys. Bye."

I hung up and then I hit the redial button and then the erase key. I then went down to return the smuggled phone to the family room. I got caught red-handed by Dario who walked into the family room just as I deposited the phone into the cradle.

"Tia, what the hell?"

I felt the color drain from my face. "I just left a voicemail for my foster mom to tell her I was fine. I don't want them meddling and putting themselves in danger and thought if I just left a message to tell her I'm fine she would back off."

He pinched the bridge of his nose, looking so much like his brother that I felt a stab of fear in my gut.

He shook his head. "No more, okay? I can't deal right now." He left the room. I followed him into Tommy's office.

"What's going on?"

He shook his head and reached for a phone charger plugged into a power bar under Tommy's desk and plugged his cell in. "Don't worry about anything. It's all good."

"I call bullshit," I said, folding my arms across my chest.

He rolled his eyes. "All right, we can't find him. We're looking. I'm torn between going myself and staying. He wants you safe so I'm staying like he wants and trying to organize things from here is frustrating."

"What about Earl and Juan Carlos?"

"He dealt with both of them; we know that for a fact," Dario said.

I tried to ignore the cold pit in my gut. "Then where could he be?"

"Exactly."

I sat down behind the big desk. I saw a photo in a frame of him, his father, and his siblings, their kids, and spouses, all around a Christmas tree. There was a small wedding photo of who must've been his Mom with his father, by the looks of it, and beside that photo was the engagement ring he'd given me. I'd left it in Tessa's car, so she must've returned it to him.

I leaned over and picked it up and looked at it sparkling in the light.

Dario was in the doorway now. "I've gotta go outside and talk to someone. Stay out of trouble, please?"

"I will," I told him as I put the ring back down. I stared at the picture of Tommy and his family around the Christmas tree. They were all smiling and looking happy, except him. He looked like he was forcing a smile for the camera, his eyes dark and broody. He looked like Gangster Tommy in the photo, not Ice Cream Parlor Tommy.

I stared at the wedding photo of the young and pretty dark-haired woman in the white dress and veil standing beside the happy-looking youthful Thomas Ferrano, Sr. I wondered if he was a criminal back then or if something changed him to become that way. I wondered what might've happened to Tommy to make him swing back and forth like a pendulum between good guy and bad guy. If he made it back could I find a way to keep it swinging in one direction versus the other or would that be totally out of my control?

* * *

Sarah couldn't talk me into more than a few bites of food for dinner. I just wasn't hungry. I knew I hadn't eaten much the past few days but, how could I? I went to bed early, zoning out in front of the television and feeling myself drift before it was even completely dark outside.

* * *

The next day dragged, too. Dario was miserable. I heard him snapping at Sarah and at one of the guards. I hid out in the bedroom almost all day, trying to watch TV, read a book Sarah loaned me. I helped Sarah cook dinner. I tried to keep busy, but I didn't know what to think.

If Tommy was gone, what'd happen to me? If he was gone, how would I feel? I didn't know how I felt about him. I felt numb about him, confused about him. I cried myself to sleep that night because I couldn't cope. I couldn't cope with the worry, the stress, the fear of the unknown, the flashes in my mind of him being sweet to me.

* * *

"What's this?" I heard in the dark. "Unauthorized sleepwear?"

I jackknifed straight up to sitting. Tommy was on his knees on the bed leaning over me, partly illuminated by the fact that the bathroom light was on.

"You're here," I breathed and his lips were on my jaw and then my lips. He took my face in his hands and kissed me long and deep. I put my arms around his neck and he kissed me again and then backed up and then off the bed,

"I need a shower badly, baby. I'll be back in five. Get naked."

He backed up and threw his t-shirt over his head onto the floor and was undoing his pants as he headed to the bathroom and closed the door.

I sat there in the dark, heart thumping loudly, and a moment later, without putting any thought into it, I padded to the bathroom, which was already filled with steam.

I took off my pajamas and opened the shower door, stepping in behind him. I guess I had an inkling of how I was feeling after all.

Tommy

She was here, in the shower with me, voluntarily, happy to see me, her arms around me. I flinched at first as she'd come in so quietly it startled me when I felt her reach around and put both of her arms around my waist. She put her cheek on my back and squeezed.

Seeing her sleeping in my bed when I got home gave me the oddest, most possessive, but yet happy feeling, like the first time I'd come in and found her sleeping in my shirt, but multiple-fold after all that had happened.

Now she'd come to me in the shower. She gave my back a soft kiss. I put my hands on the wall to brace myself because I was a little overwhelmed at that. Then I felt her soaping up my back. I closed my eyes and absorbed it, all of it.

I was never so tired in my life, but I just had to be inside of her, so I turned her around, got her front up against the wet shower wall and drove inside of her so fast and so hard that I saw a flash of shock in her eyes as I spun her and heard her gasp in surprise as I entered her. The sharp intake of breath was just enough to give me a little tiny bit of that rush I wanted, that I needed.

Tia

I wanted to take care of him the way he'd taken care of me the other night, because I could see he was exhausted and filthy and I didn't know if he was traumatized, too.

But now he was trying to consume me; it really felt like that. He was driving into me hard and kissing the back of my neck, holding my hair off to the side. The harder he pushed and grunted, the tighter he pulled at my hair and it wasn't easy to stay upright in the wet shower. I almost lost my footing and then he caught me and gently took me down to kneeling on the floor of the shower and he got back inside of me from behind and held onto a breast with one hand as he drove in over and over and then reached around and rubbed his middle two fingers around and around my clit.

It was hard on the knees and all I could do was brace my hands against the slippery wall, reaching up to hang onto the built-in soap dish. But, I still went off quickly, feeling that awesome ripple throughout my body.

Barely a moment later, he finished. For a moment we were both on the floor of the shower. He turned me around and then pulled me onto his lap and just held onto me. He was trembling.

I wrapped my arms around him and put my cheek on his head and we stayed sitting on the shower floor like that for a long time before he stopped shaking and pulled us both to standing. He reached up and soaped up his body and I shampooed his hair, up on my tiptoes watching him with his eyes closed and his lips parted as my fingers massaged his scalp. Then, after he got under the water and rinsed off, he grabbed me by the hips and pulled me against him and held me for another few minutes under the shower stream. After what felt like forever, he turned the tap off. We left the shower stall and wrapped ourselves in towels and then he took me by the hand and led me to bed.

I felt like I was too wet to be in bed, but had no choice, really, because he pulled me tight against himself, and I think he fell asleep three seconds after his head hit the pillow. We slept under the blankets still wrapped in wet towels, with sopping wet hair, wrapped around one another.

8

Tommy

When I'd gotten home at 4:40 AM, my brother was still up, looking like shit and a bit flipped out since I walked into my own house with my gun drawn.

I'd gotten smuggled across the border, taken a multi-leg commercial flight home, and then hopped a cab to my storage unit, grabbed a gun, then cabbed it home and greeted Nino at the front gate with my gun drawn. I had to make sure all was okay at home. He'd let me in and tried to convince me that all was well to get me to put the gun away, but I didn't until I saw Dario. When I saw my brother sitting at the island in the kitchen, I knew all was okay. For the moment, at least.

I'd wanted no one to know when I'd arrive, what flight I was on, when I was on my way. No one got to know anything until I got there. I wasn't just being paranoid; I was being smart. Who knew who else in our organization had flipped to the enemy's side and who would seek retribution for what I'd done at Castillo's? I'd done the job I needed to do, and it was done so now I could come home to her and to my empire.

If I hadn't felt like I'd earned this before, which I knew I'd already done, I certainly felt it'd be uncontested now. I saluted him; he put his phone down with a look of relief. I put my gun back into my waistband and I said, "Gotta go to bed, man. Tomorrow, okay?"

He nodded, and smiled. "Welcome home, bro. She's been anxious for you to get back."

I'd smiled back and climbed the stairs.

Now it was morning, no hang on, afternoon – I'd slept eleven hours, and I had to brief and debrief some people, including Dare, my father, and then get to work to ensure that our own housekeeping was in order, that there weren't any other traitors around, and that Tia would be safe. Then there was some business to organize based on new developments down south. I also needed to talk to my PI about Earl.

But, I wasn't ready to get outta bed – not yet. Not until I felt her body wrapped around me again, her beautiful green eyes looking at me without fear or contempt. I rolled over and surprisingly found her still here beside me, still asleep. I kissed from her collarbone downwards. She opened her legs for me before her eyes even opened, making my groin and my chest ache. She was so fucking perfect and there was no way I'd allow anyone to take her from me again.

Tia

What a reunion. And what a morning after. Ho boy; he was all over me, waking me up with his tongue just like that first morning. What a way to wake up! I had a fleeting thought about the fact that he'd eventually want me to reciprocate.

I'd never had a problem doing that with Nick or with the few other guys I'd been with. But now? After what had happened with that guy in Mexico? I didn't even know his name. I didn't want to know. I wanted to forget. There was so much I wanted to forget, but so much I didn't think I could ever put out of my mind completely.

"Baby?" He was looking up at me.

I hadn't realized it, but I was crying while he was doing that to me. He settled beside me and pulled me to his chest. "What's wrong?" he asked.

"Sorry," I said softly and wiped my eyes with my fingertips.

"What?" He gave me a squeeze.

"So much," I whispered into his chest.

"Tell me." He kissed my forehead.

I was surprised that he had stopped. I was surprised that he was looking at me with so much tenderness.

"It's a lot to get into five seconds after waking up." And I don't know if I can even say these things to you.

"Talk. Start somewhere."

"I'm still a bit shell shocked, I guess, after what happened. After everything." I swept my hand back and forth in front of me.

"Understandable," he said.

"I'm overwhelmed and I want... need... answers. Answers about this debt and how it originated and I need to know what'll happen next. With my dad, with my life. With... you."

"Uh huh."

"And you. I want to ask you what happened in Mexico, but I don't. I don't know if you want to talk about it or if I even want to know. It feels like you went to hell and back."

"I did."

"My head is just full." And I didn't know how I felt about him, about us... but I didn't know how to articulate that.

He nodded again. "I'm gonna go get us some coffee, okay? But first I need to do something?"

"What?"

"Need to fuck you, baby." His words sounded harsh but then his mouth turned up in the beginnings of a smile.

I laughed. "Romance is officially dead."

He smiled at me and then raised his brows. "Yeah, isn't it? For instance, I'll try not to let it ding my ego too much that my going down on you just drove you to tears. Just let me, like super-fast, if you don't mind? I promise not to be super-fast too often but this time, I think I just need to..." He pushed his fist forward in the air.

I laughed harder. He was being so playful. His eyes were filled with light. He looked totally adorable. He was beautiful. Before I knew what I was doing, I reached to put my palm on his cheek. He needed a shave.

He pounced on top of me, his eyes full of amusement.

"Feel free," I said, "Since you're here anyway." I scrubbed my fingers along the stubble at his jaw.

"Are you giving me permission?" he asked, his eyes darkening and face turning serious. Very serious. I took a deep breath. "I don't need permission to take what's mine, do I?" He kissed the palm of my hand and then ran a finger from my elbow up to my throat and then he put his hand over my throat. I swallowed against the space between his thumb and index finger.

"I'm all about control but baby, I don't just want it. I need it," he said, and then waited, hand looser on my throat.

I nodded slightly, not sure how to process how I felt.

"I feel out of control right now," he said, studying me. He had pain in his eyes.

I swallowed hard and then the silence between us was almost deafening.

"Then take it," I finally whispered, and he studied my face for a minute, then he let go of my throat and kissed me hard, whispering, "You're perfect."

Then he was inside of me.

A few thrusts in and he started to pound harder and faster and I just closed my eyes and absorbed the feel of him. It was exquisite. I let go, let go of emotions, inhibitions, I just opened up and let him take what he wanted, and it felt so...so freeing.

He pulled out, flipped me onto my side and pounded into me from behind while then he grabbed my throat again and held it. He didn't hurt my throat, he didn't squeeze, but it was possessive. I started to feel that quickening and then he slowed, culling it. I grabbed the headboard with both hands and held on.

"Do you want to come?" he whispered in my ear softly, tickling me.

"Mm." I felt goose bumps rise all over my back.

"Do you?" His voice got huskier and his rhythm slowed.

"Yeah."

"Who do you belong to, Athena?" He drove in deep, grazing my nipple with his thumbnail, making it feel like it sparked. And then his hand slid up to hold my throat again in a softer hold. His other hand snaked over my hip, then his fingers were circling between my legs.

"Who do you belong to? Do you belong to that punk, Nick?"

"No," I breathed.

He rotated his hips while he was inside me, eliciting a groan from me, then twisted my nipple ever so slightly. "Then who?"

Shivers ran up my body. He had the ridge of my ear in between his teeth.

"Who?"

I rocked against him with an, "Ah!"

He pulled out most of the way and then pushed back in hard and I gasped again.

"Tell me who you belong to," he demanded with my hair in his hand again. He tugged, just a smidgeon past gently.

"I don't," I whispered.

He let out a little growl, his mouth at my ear again. "You don't?" There was warning in his voice.

"I don't belong to anyone," I answered softly, feeling a little rush at the idea of this game. Then I bit my lip, swallowed, then added, "Do I?" as innocently as I could muster, though I was feeling far from innocent right now. If I played the game right along with him, maybe it wouldn't be so scary.

He took a deep breath and tightened his hold on me. "You're mine. You belong to me, and you were made for me," he said, low in his throat, then was pushing deep and slow and deliberately, kissing me all over the back of my neck, my shoulders. "Let me show you."

I felt that quickening again and I started circling my hips back against him, loving how deep he was. One of his hands now gripped my hip and his other hand moved in a pattern that caressed up and down my chest, then up to my throat and each time he got to my throat he gave a little squeeze, not painful, possessive, I guess. I tipped my head back and soaked in the symphony of his fingers, his cock, his lips, even the way one of his legs had locked around me. I was melting into a puddle of sensation, goosebumps on every square inch of my body. When he started to circle around and around my clit, I started to come.

He growled, "Who, Athena, who do you belong to?"

"Ah!" I held my breath and then let out a long "Ohh" and then slowly floated back to earth.

He slapped my ass, making me jolt.

"You're a naughty girl," he murmured into my ear, still driving in deep. "You're lucky I let you come when you're so fucking naughty."

It felt as if goosebumps rose on top of goosebumps, if that was even possible. He took me from my side to my stomach and I felt him rise up. He grabbed my hip with one hand and my two wrists into his other palm, which was used to pin me while also bracing himself.

"Ooh, let me wipe that smirk off your face," he grunted through gritted teeth. I gasped as he slammed hard into me. His free hand moved up and down my back sweetly while he rotated his hips, pushing hard. He pushed in, then slapped my ass, making me jolt, which I could tell he liked a lot because of the way he grunted. Then it was a succession of caresses, slams and slaps with grunts from him and for me, jolts, and moans.

Super quick? This wasn't quick at all. It had been going on for a long time and I was getting super-exhausted. My legs were still shaky from the orgasm, and I was breathless and sweaty, my hair plastered to my cheek. My ass felt like it was on fire.

"You like this?" he whispered, still pounding into me and tightened his grip around my wrists.

"Mm," I moaned into the pillow.

"You feel so good," he told me. "I'm going to fuck your sweet pussy over and over, as much as I want to, and you know why?"

I groaned.

"Because you're mine," he whispered, then he turned me and we were doing it missionary style.

He let go of a wrist and wiped my hair from my face and held it back then found my lips with his and kissed me tenderly for a second before it turned rough.

He was grunting with every thrust, pulling tighter on my hair. It went on and on and on. I wanted, no needed, to be done. I was sore and exhausted, and thirsty. My ass was on fire. Finally, I whispered, "Tommy."

"Baby," he hummed against my mouth.

"Come inside me," I whispered into his mouth.

He let go of my lips and then his mouth opened and he slowed his pace and then I heard him gasp, I started to tongue and nibble on his throat, digging my nails into his back. He had a full-body shudder as he came inside me.

He collapsed on top of me and stayed like that for the longest time. I could feel his heartbeat pounding against me, his breath tickling my shoulder. I twisted, feeling a bit crushed, and he rolled off me onto his side so I rolled into him, wrapped my arms around him, and gently trailed my nails up and down his back, just enjoying this closeness, this intimacy. I'd never had anything like this with anyone else. No basking in the afterglow, no dirty talk, nothing even close to this and here I was lying against an insanely beautiful and dangerous man who had killed to avenge my abduction. It was crazy of me but it was an insane turn-on.

I felt guilt underneath desire, but there was something so hot about that little game. He liked games, as I could tell from the start, and I was figuring out that maybe if I played along, they weren't so scary; they were just games.

"You little vixen," he murmured against my ear and then bit my earlobe, "You don't tell me when to come."

"Really? Then how come I just did?" I whispered against his pectoral, and he slapped my ass hard.

For a split-second I thought I was in big trouble, but then caught the smile on his face and the twinkle in his eyes. I had a face-splitting grin on my face that I couldn't hide. I looked up at him and he rubbed my bottom where he'd just spanked me. He was looking at me so tenderly I thought my heart might burst.

After what felt like forever, locked in one another's gaze, he rolled onto his back a few inches away from me, still looking at me, though now his expression was unreadable. I flushed under his scrutiny.

He looked up at the ceiling, finally, and I studied the black tribal tattoo pattern that worked its way from his wrist up to his shoulder. Points, curls, swirls. I looked back at his face. His eyes were still fixed on the ceiling.

"What's on your mind?" I asked.

"They tried to take you from me and I had to make them pay. They paid. Anyone who tries to take you from me will pay." He was silent for a moment. I snuggled into him, chewing my cheek, and started to trace the patterns on his shoulder with my finger.

Then he continued. "You need to know that life with me won't be all ice cream with a cherry on top and walks on the beach at sunset. It can't be. You need to know that sometimes you're gonna hate my guts because of my need to control everything and because I might take my frustrations out on you in here."

I let out a long slow breath.

He went on, "I'm depraved, Tia, and I have a bad temper. I want to own you and control you and I wanted that the minute I was told it was mine, but now that you are, you surprised me; I surprised me. I want to make you feel good, too, make you feel safe with me, safe enough to give yourself to me, to wanna be mine. I've never wanted that. I want it so much."

"I feel safe right now and you just made me feel very good," I whispered, my admission sending chills across my whole body.

He gave me a squeeze.

"I know you didn't choose this, but I can't give you up. I won't. Don't ever, ever ask me to. After things settle down, I'll give you everything, give you a life you'll want, but with me. But baby, you have to take all of me and there are parts of me you won't want. Know that other than that, I'll give you everything you want, everything. Everything except freedom from me."

Wow. It was beautiful and awful and fucked up all at the same time. Kind of like him. I was speechless.

He leaned over me, looking at my face, seeing that I was absorbing what he was saying to me. He looked like he wanted me to say something, or like he wanted to say more, I wasn't sure.

Finally, he said, "I have to go. I have to deal with the fall out of Mexico and everything else. Please be a good girl; don't give me any extra stress today. I need to deal with this and then tomorrow I'll take the day for us and we'll go do something together, okay? I have a special place I wanna take you." He tucked hair behind my ear.

I poked the tip of his nose. "You don't have to worry about me getting into any trouble. I don't think I can even walk after that, super-fast..." I thrust my fist into the air the way that he'd done before we had sex "thing that took at least an hour there."

He laughed a hearty big-smiled laugh that made him so beautiful to behold I felt it in my stomach like a little pang of something between butterflies and pain. I gently tapped his cheek with my palm and closed my eyes and yawned.

"Hmm, now I know what I've gotta do daily to keep my girl in line. Good to know. I'll bring you some coffee and food since I've rendered you crippled and then I've gotta go. Take a long bath and soak those muscles, sweet baby girl. I'll be back for more later and I can guarantee I won't be as quick as this time." He winked again, squeezed my rear end lightly, and got out of bed.

I smiled as he left and then my heart sank. It sank painfully, like a weighed down cloud that wanted to float but couldn't. I felt pretty darn conflicted right now.

He took a shower and left the room dressed in a charcoal gray suit. He was clean shaven. Damn, he was beautiful. Beautiful and complicated and scary-intense.

He returned a few minutes later with a mug of coffee and a toasted bagel with cream cheese plus an orange cut into wedges. "Have a good day," he said into my hair after he kissed me.

"You, too," I said and smiled shyly at him as he left.

* * *

I think I stared off into space for what might've been hours. Thinking about my family, about Mexico, about the terrifying car ride with him before I was kidnapped, about the many layers of Tommy Ferrano. And... about my participation in the little sex games this morning. My coffee and bagel were both tepid by the time I snapped back to the here and now.

Tommy

Not only was everyone in the Castillo cartel compound dead, thanks to me and my guys, but the compound was also burnt to the ground, the fire started by me striking the match after pouring gasoline on that bed in that room in the sick fuck's basement after I'd taken my time with vengeance against Castillo as well as Earl.

If I'd found the corpse of the motherfucker who'd laid his hands on my girl, I'd have fed Earl that corpse's cock before I shot him.

Beyond that, I'd secured a deal with another cartel who helped me orchestrate the downfall, handing them the Castillo business and fortifying a deal that would nearly triple our profits from Mexico.

Part of that deal included an exit strategy in a year's time, which the cartel was more than happy to agree to because it meant 100% of the profits for them from that point on and it meant a lot to me because I didn't want to be in the drug business. A smooth transition was important, though. I couldn't just make an instant break.

Earl had said some things, made some accusations that I was troubled about. And a few comments from Castillo in the minutes before he died were either enlightening or designed to plant the seeds of doubt about some of what I knew about Pop. I had some legwork to do to see if it held any truth. At the moment I was taking all that'd been said with a grain of salt. He was gone now, they both were, so I couldn't go back to either of them for more information.

My Pop didn't even ask what made Earl defect, which made me think that maybe Earl spoke the truth. Why wouldn't he at least wonder why a trusted employee would suddenly steal his future daughter-in-law and shoot a colleague in the head in cold blood?

It was pretty telling to me that Pop was impressed, however, with the way things turned out. He didn't know about the exit strategy, but then again he didn't need to know. I'd be in charge long before that would take place.

Thankfully he didn't commend me on my lemonade-making skills. He'd taught me a long time ago to take opportunities wherever you could get them, even in the face of tragedy. But I think he knew better. The lemons I'd just been served had a pretty profound effect on me. I was pushing away thoughts that this shit was all Pop's fault. I needed more info first.

But damn, the way she wrapped herself around me in the shower when I got home and tried to take care of me and then handed me control this morning...it did something to me, fortified me. Today I felt like I could rule the fucking world. But I didn't really want to, for once. I just wanted to go back and climb in bed with her, smell her, feel her, touch her. Make up for lost time. Try to make up for the tears I'd caused her.

When I walked into the office, my father handed me a brass skeleton key that was about a foot long.

"What's this?" I jerked my chin up.

"Key to the city. Symbolic, my boy. When is the wedding?"

I laid it on his desk and smiled a little. "I'll keep you posted."

"A month? Do it at my house. I'll tell Lisa. She and your sisters can help. We'll call that planner that put my and Lisa's wedding together."

I shrugged. "That could work. Let me talk to her before you get the girls involved."

He clapped his hands together. "Good. Now that that's settled, on to other business."

"One sec," I told him and reached into the inside pocket of my suit jacket and slapped an envelope on the desk.

Pop raised his chin. "What's that?"

"$35K. I'm clearing O'Connor's debt. Twenty-five for the debt, ten for the juice."

"Huh?"

"You heard; payment with interest."

"I gave her to you as a gift, my boy, and even if I didn't, the vig didn't run that high."

I shook my head. "I'd rather clear it."

"I'm not taking the gift back, son."

I nodded and shoved the envelope closer to him and looked him in the eye. "Now you can't."

"And you're marrying her. That makes her even more yours."

"Take the money."

Pop stroked his chin and looked at me, perplexed.

"The business between you and O'Connor, whatever it was, is done now. If anything further needs to be done about him, I do it," I told him.

He sighed, looking a bit defeated. "Fine," he agreed and put the envelope of money into the inside pocket of his blazer.

"You gonna fill me in?" I asked.

"Why? You're already digging around. I know you; you'll find all the answers eventually. Why spoil your moment of triumph?"

"That's what I thought."

Yeah, we both knew where I got my tendency for mind fucking from.

Tia

I lounged in bed for the biggest part of what was left of the day, despite sleeping at least fourteen hours the night he came home. He really had worn me out. The last week and a half had worn me out emotionally and I guessed it had manifested itself physically despite the fact I'd done not much other than lie around.

At around dusk, I decided to get some proper exercise and do some laps in the pool and then I spent a few hours reading the novel that Sarah had lent me. I had trouble losing myself in it. Why did I need escape into another world when my own world felt like another world? While it was a pretty stress-free evening, all things considered, my wheels just wouldn't stop turning. I thought about possible scenarios regarding my father and this whole debt thing. I thought about Tommy's words after we woke up that day, about the fact that I could look at this thing two ways.

1: He'd taken ownership of me and given me a life sentence to be with him, regardless of what I'd be put through and regardless of how I felt. I had no choice, no out.

2: He was making a lifelong commitment *to* me and I'd have to take him for better or for worse. There could be a lot worse than being with him, as I'd seen down in Mexico. He promised to protect me. No one had ever offered me that before. Not my father, not anyone.

If I chose to look at it positively, it sounded like all he was doing was articulating some marriage vows. Promising to provide for me and protect me but with an underlying threat that I couldn't leave even if I wanted to despite the fact that it'd be rough at times. And that freaked me out. A lot.

How much would be *for better* and how much would be *for worse*? Ice cream parlor guy vs. gangster guy with the dark hunger for control – the dominator. 'Till death do us part was something people promised all the time, but I had no choice but to honor and obey. I was going to be taken literally in promising to obey him and to spend my life with him, only I hadn't promised that. I'd been told that this was the deal; like it or lump it.

What was next for me, for us? Did I try to find a way to accept this, or did I keep looking for a way out? The way he looked at me made me feel wanted. He was gorgeous, he was protective, he knew how to light my body on fire. He could be charming. He also scared the crap out of me.

Tommy wasn't here for dinner. I ate a late meal with Sarah. We cooked together and had barbequed chicken burgers and salads on the patio and we both floated around on tubes in the pool after dinner. Then I went up to bed early, exhausted physically and exhausted emotionally although I'd certainly slept a lot the night before.

I woke up to him climbing in bed with me in the dark. I didn't know what time it was, but he didn't initiate sex. He just curled up against me, wrapped his arms around me protectively, and kissed under my earlobe, and was snoring softly into my hair a few breaths later.

Tommy

I crawled in bed fully prepared to yank her night clothes off her and remind her of rule number three, but the minute my nose caught a whiff of her hair and warm skin, which smelled like oats, honey, and vanilla, I nuzzled in and slept like a log beside her. The last few days had been long and painful. In the morning I'd be taking her out and trying to show her a change of scenery, maybe some romance.

* * *

She'd be spending a lot of time alone at home for the next few weeks while I took care of some business that might mean even more security because I was probably going to have to show disrespect publicly to a scumbag that didn't deserve my time. Today, I'd take her out for some fun and then broach the subject of our wedding with her. That'd keep her busy with my sisters.

I woke up first and found her with her head on my stomach. She was sleeping on her belly using my belly as a pillow, face toward my crotch. Her legs were hanging off the bed and she was flat out, sound asleep, hair fanned out across my torso.

I looked down and ran my fingers through her hair and then my thumb skimmed across her lower lip. She sucked in my thumb and actually sucked on it, still asleep. She must've been a thumb sucker as a kid. The sensation went straight to my groin, which was already awake. I then swept my hand down her back and cupped her ass.

She was wearing a tiny pair of lacy pale pink, almost flesh-toned shorts that were pretty well transparent and barely covered her cheeks. She also had on a matching lacy tank top that had ridden up. She looked edible, fuckable. If she was going to break my sleepwear rule and wear something like this I could probably overlook the infraction. She nuzzled into me and then as I reached my middle finger to stroke between her cheeks and downward, her legs magically parted. I smiled. The way she did that for me every morning so far hadn't ceased amazing me. All I had to do was get anywhere near her pussy or her ass while she slept and she would instantly spread wide for me while she was sound asleep.

I had a feeling that morning sex would become as normal for me as my morning coffee. I never had women sleep at my place or even visit so I often found a fuck somewhere in my travels, usually in the evenings in a motel, at the club (it had rooms), or their place and then went home alone. I'd always thought I'd preferred that but who knew that finding a woman in my bed when I climbed in at night and waking up to her spreading her legs for me every morning would be so fucking amazing? Time to cancel my club membership.

9

Tia

I woke up facing his massive erection, pointing up in front of my line of vision. My head was on his tummy and he was tenderly caressing my head with one hand and had his other hand between my legs. I turned my head over and looked at him. He was lying on his back and looking down at me with the biggest, sexiest smile on his half-asleep face.

I smiled and rubbed my eyes. "Um, hi."

"Mornin', baby," he said with a smirk. "All aboard?"

I blushed. He was gorgeous with a sleepy smile, a twinkle in his eyes, and a bit of bedhead. The way he looked at me made tingles work their way up my spine. He reached for me and then pulled me up by my underarms, so I was straddling him. He pulled the crotch of my shorts to the side with one hand, pulled his boxer briefs down with his other hand, connected us, and... *wow*.

He said, "Unauthorized sleepwear again. I might have to punish you."

Before I registered the words and let them scare me, I saw humor in his eyes, so I smiled and ran my hands up his gorgeous chest and then had his jaw in my hands. I leaned over, about to kiss him, but then a big bang pierced the air. I thought it was firecrackers but the second I thought that my brain autocorrected it – not firecrackers, gunfire.

In a flash I'd gone from being on top of him on the bed to being swung through the air in his strong arms and then on the floor beside the bed lying directly under him. Covering me with his body, he reached under the bed and upwards and then he had a gun in his hand.

I was about to gasp but his hand was over my mouth gently. He made a soundless *Shh* and motioned for me to get under the bed as he carefully rolled off me and then silently moved around, commando-style crawling, to the other side of the bed, closer to the door.

I stayed put under the bed and tried hard not to hyperventilate. I could see that the area under the bed had another gun strapped up as well as a big-ass knife. Holy crap.

When and how did my life become an action movie? Amid my shock and fear about the commotion and about the fact that he now had a gun in his hand was the realization that he, as an initial reaction to the gunfire, had actually turtled over me to protect me. Wow.

As that was permeating, I heard the door open and saw his feet leave the room. My heart thudded loudly in my chest. He was in nothing but underwear, holding a gun, and I was under the bed, afraid for my life!

I heard a storm of gunfire and it sounded like it was right outside the door. I plugged my ears with my index fingers and squeezed my eyes shut tight. Then there was silence. Deafening silence. Then voices. But I couldn't make out whose voices or what they said.

After what seemed like forever, I heard footsteps. I looked and they weren't Tommy's bare feet. They were a pair of black boots. My heart thudded wildly in my throat. I silently reached up for the knife strapped to the bottom of the box spring and slid it out from the strap that held it up.

"Tia?" It was a deep voice. I didn't recognize it. I had the knife in my grip.

"Tommy asked me to escort you somewhere safe. Please come out," the voice said.

I didn't believe anything I was hearing. Where was Tommy? Was he shot dead in the hallway? Was this someone else wanting to kidnap me? If they wanted me dead, they would just shoot though, right?

I heard more footsteps, then saw a pair of men's black leather dress shoes, "What's going on?"

Was that Dario's voice? I wasn't sure.

"She won't come out," the first guy said.

I saw some suit pant-clad knees, then Dario's face. I was lying under the bed with the knife pointed toward him. He looked at my face, the knife, then my face. He smiled. "You okay?"

I was frozen, I couldn't move. I just laid there pointing the knife at him.

"C'mon," he said, and he looked amused.

I slid out from under the bed and he helped me up. The knife fell. I was shaking. Dario threw a robe at me and I put it on, glad he was thinking straight because I sure wasn't. I was still in those tiny lacy sleeping clothes and they were more than revealing.

Nino, that biker-looking guy, was standing there with Dario, his eyes politely fixed on the floor.

"Quickly, come," Dario said. He and Nino ushered me out of the room.

Two men were on the carpet in the hall and one was face down, one wasn't. The one who wasn't I recognized as one of the burly guys from day one, the unibrow guy. I felt bad for thinking that thought. I wondered what his name was, if he had any family. It was not only bloody, but there were holes in the walls. Tommy was nowhere to be seen.

I breathed out a big breath as Dario ushered me forward but

leaned back, "Get her shoes and get Tommy some pants, fast," he told Nino.

"Where's Tommy. He okay?" I breathed.

"Yep, no worries. Settle down." Dario gave my shoulder a squeeze.

We got to the bottom of the stairs and I heard Tommy's voice booming like thunder. "You tell me right fucking now or I cut off your balls first!"

He sounded utterly murderous. I froze for a second.

"Dare!" Tommy shouted, "Bring her."

Dario motioned toward the slightly ajar office door.

I opened it, seeing a very bloody redheaded guy slumped in a chair and Tommy standing over him, two other men, one of them I recognized as sometimes being outside on guard standing behind him. Tommy was still just in his underwear. Nino came up behind me and passed Tommy a pair of jeans. Tommy threw them on the desk and took me into his arms and inhaled my hair. "You okay, baby?"

I sank into him, nodding but still trembling. Then I looked up at him, "You?"

"No. Not even a little bit," Tommy glared toward the guy in the chair and then yelled, "See her? She's mine. You and your fucking buddies put her in danger. See this frightened look on her face? No one makes her face look like that but me, you fucking understand? You come into my house and shoot up my bedroom door while I'm fucking my girl? You kill one of my men in my fucking house? Motherfucker!" Tommy let go of me and punched the guy right in the face.

Oh. My. Lord. I wanted to collapse. He was fricking scary. I stumbled backward and Nino prevented my fall by catching me by the elbows and holding me up.

Tommy's eyes shot to my face. "It's okay, baby. Dario's taking you to my father's house. I'll pick you up there later. Tia..."

"Yeah?"

The guy in the chair coughed into his hands and had blood on his fingers. I shivered.

Tommy reached onto his desk and then caught me by the hand and pulled me to him, slipped the engagement ring on my finger, and then traced a fingertip from the hand without blood on it, across my lips. "This doesn't leave your finger again. Ever. Say nothing to the girls."

I think I nodded. He kissed my hand and squeezed it, kissed me on the mouth quickly, then passed me back to Dario. He actually took me by the shoulders and moved me toward his brother who then took my shoulders and led me out. Tommy's mouth was set in a grim line and his nostrils flared when he looked back at the bloody redheaded guy in the chair.

As Dario led me out into the hallway, Nino put some flip flops on the floor in front of me.

"I'm going to your father's house in my pajamas?" I asked Dario while stepping into them.

"Tell Nino what you need; he'll bring it to the car."

"Umm..."

"Don't worry; I'll get you something," Nino trotted up the stairs without waiting for me to answer. I was glad I didn't have to go back up there and walk past dead bodies.

Dario and I went out to a waiting red SUV.

"What on earth?" I asked when we got into the back seat.

Dario shook his head, "Don't ask me questions. Talk to your fiancé later. He'll decide what you need to know."

Decide what I need to know? Wow. Does any one of these men know this is the 21st century? And okay, not only did I hear gunshots and see dead bodies again, what was that now, four? But my supposed fiancé had just very frankly made the fact that he liked to see fear on my face known to his brother, his employees, and a guy who maybe wasn't making it out of the office alive. I was now being ushered, in skimpy pajamas and Tommy's robe, to his father's house.

When I got there Lisa was in the doorway to receive me, literally.

She hugged me and pulled me into the house, ignoring Dario and the two muscle guys behind him. "Are you okay?"

I heard Dario, on the phone say, "Bro, we're here." He then he looked to Lisa. "Yeah, she's fine. Lisa has her." Dario and the two guys followed us in and disappeared into that office that I was ushered into on graduation day, which felt like a million years ago.

Lisa was in a robe, too, her hair pulled up into a messy bun. She walked me to her kitchen where an older grandmotherly-looking Black woman was frying bacon.

"Hello, Tia, I'm Nita!" the woman said to me cheerily with a Jamaican accent. "Coffee, right?"

I thanked her as I sat at the table with Lisa. Nino came into the kitchen with a bag in his hand. "Clothes, Miss O'Connor," he said, and I peeked in the bag and saw a jean skirt, top, matching underwear and bra, and my purse. He also handed me an iPhone box, shrink wrap half on and half off. "Mr. Ferrano wants this with you at all times," he said.

"Thank you," I said and put it on the table in front of me.

He took two steps back and stood against the counter. I looked up at him and then to Lisa.

"Nino?" Lisa asked.

"I have orders to stay within three feet of Tia at all times, Leese," he said softly.

Obviously, they were good friends by the way he spoke to her. She nodded at him, resigned-looking, then Nita passed me a cup of coffee. "Two sugars, Sarah told me?"

I shook my head and smiled. Two sugars. "I'll need one more, thanks," I said sweetly.

She smiled what looked to me like a knowing smile. She must be in the know about Sarah's sugar hatred. I wasn't going to let this happen, I had so little control over my life right now the one thing I could control was how many fucking sugars I'd get in my coffee, so I was taking that third sugar.

"So," Lisa started.

I looked at her. Nita was passing Nino a coffee and pulling another package of bacon out of the fridge.

"I hear we get to help you plan your wedding and that it'll be here!"

My face must've said, "Duh, what?" because a familiar voice chimed in, Tommy's father, coming into the kitchen.

"Ah, my little dove, that wasn't common knowledge yet."

"Oh?" Lisa blushed. "Sorry." She smiled at her husband and shrugged.

He leaned over and kissed her on the top of her head.

"Good morning, Athena," he greeted.

He was dressed in a suit, as per what seemed to be the usual. He poured himself a cup of coffee.

"Mornin'," I said and my voice came out hoarse.

He smiled at me and sat down at the large bistro style table with us.

"Everyone, leave me and Athena for a moment," he said and everyone left the room, including Nino and Nita who lifted her pan onto another burner and then abandoned the stove.

He put his hand over mine. "Are you okay, dear?"

I nodded, ignoring the urge to yank my hand back.

"Dario tells me you threatened him and Nino with a knife." He had light in his eyes, a playfulness very much like what I sometimes saw in Tommy's eyes.

I tried to crack a smile, but I don't think it looked very genuine.

"Tommy tells me you're perfect. I can see that. You seem calm and together right now despite probably wanting to run for the hills, screaming."

If only I could. I thought this, but didn't speak it.

"You're a spitfire. Beating up my son, pulling a knife on a guard. I think you'll fit in here just fine. Dario's been calling you Tia Tyson. You are a fighter." He tapped my hand gently and then stood up. "My boy has demons. I think you could be the one to exorcise them." He smiled expectantly. I didn't know what to say.

"And your father tells me you can cook like nobody's business. That's always a good quality in a wife." He winked at me.

I opened my mouth, wanting to speak but his eyes narrowed just slightly, and I decided against it. I clamped my mouth shut. He looked pleased. It was almost as if I'd just passed a test. I frowned. What a bizarre thing to say right now and what...the ...heck?

He stood. "Your husband-to-be should be here any minute. We'll all have breakfast."

He left the room.

A moment later Nino returned, saying, "If you'd like to get dressed I can escort you to a guest room."

I followed him, carrying the bag he'd brought me, mulling over the fact that my father must've had a conversation recently with Thomas Ferrano, one where he talked about me at length in a way that would result in my dad talking about my hobbies, my talents. That sort of conversation didn't typically come into play when someone was threatening you – no, that sort of conversation came with bargaining with someone, trying to sales pitch them. Did my father sales pitch me to Thomas Ferrano?

I couldn't think about this right now; I had to go back out there and try to act normal around these people. I had to try to act normal because I wasn't *allowed* to talk about what had happened this morning, to act as freaked out as I felt. It came crashing down on me, then, that I couldn't ever confide in anyone about my life without breaking his rules.

I loved my friends, I loved our sessions where we sat and shared information, gossiped, talked hopes, dreams, and uncertainties. How could I not ever share my innermost feelings and what was happening in my life with anyone else? I also thought about Dad and wondered again if he'd had any idea what'd happened to me after I didn't meet him at the food court in the mall.

It was weird that Nino stood outside the room door while I changed. I reached into my purse and found the basics. I put my hair it in a ponytail, put on some lip gloss, mascara, and eyeliner, and then put my sleeping clothes into the bag and popped the iPhone into the jean skirt pocket and followed him back to the kitchen. There was laughter from a room nearby.

Nino took my bag for me, telling me he'd put it in Tommy's car, and motioned for me to go ahead through an arched doorway into a dining room.

Tommy was sitting at a large dining room table with Lisa, his father, and Dario. They were all laughing. Platters sat in the middle of the large table filled with breakfast foods. There was enough food to feed ten, rather than five of us.

Tommy's eyes sparkled as I entered the room and he motioned for me to sit in the empty chair beside him. He looked completely composed, was dressed in a collared dark gray shirt and pair of dark distressed button fly jeans, black motorcycle boots, and he was eating a piece of bacon. I sat beside him and his lips touched my cheek. "You good, baby?" he asked me.

I nodded while shrugging at the same time. "You?"

"Peachy," he said and wiggled his eyebrows. Then he leaned over and passed me the plate of waffles. He smelled freshly showered and I felt drawn to him, I wanted to climb into his lap, tuck my head under his chin and hold on tight. Of course I didn't.

We'd just been through a shooting incident where we almost got shot, then where he'd commando-style retaliated and obviously just either killed one or two or had at least watched one or two men die. I'd just witnessed two dead men outside the bedroom and then watched him, clad in only his underwear, interrogate and sucker punch someone who was already black and blue and bloody. I glanced down as he spread jam on a piece of toast. His knuckles were bruised-looking.

Yeah, he'd probably bloodied that guy being interrogated and who knew what'd happened to the guy afterwards? And what he'd said to the guy about me, that the only person who was allowed to put fear into my eyes was him? I felt a raw sensation spread deep inside of me.

I wasn't hungry. Death tended to lower my appetite, I guess. I passed the plate of waffles along to Dario, who sat across from me, and just put a few pieces of cubed fruit on my plate.

"That all you're going to eat?" Tommy whispered in my ear.

I nodded. "Not feeling so hungry."

"Excuse us," Tommy said to the room and put his napkin on the table and reached for my hand. I took it and followed him out of the kitchen, down a hall, and out a set of sliding doors onto a deck that overlooked a swimming pool.

He took me into his arms and lifted me up a few inches off the patio, holding me tight, "You okay?" he whispered into my hair. I started shaking again.

He set me back on my feet and tipped my chin up with his thumb and index finger and then kissed my forehead softly. "Everything is fine. I dealt with that security breach and it won't happen again. You don't have to worry. By the time we get back home the house'll be 100% safe."

"It the same people as Mexico?"

"Don't worry, baby. It's dealt with. We'll have brunch with these guys and then we'll go for a drive and get out of the city for a bit, okay?"

I nodded, looked down, but melted into him feeling oddly safe.

"Tia, smile, please. Come and eat. Okay? I won't let anything happen to you. Anything. Ever."

He smelled so good. I inhaled him at the chest and nodded, then followed him back into the house. He hadn't seemed threatening with me, but that hadn't settled my nerves much, either. I saw Tommy's father in the doorway. He'd been watching us. He had a smile on his face. It was sort of a sick smile and gave me chills.

The rest of the meal was jovial. Not because of me, but because of Tom Sr. and Dario, mostly. When we got back to the table Tommy heaped scrambled eggs and bacon on my plate and then went back to eating. I picked at the food, but didn't consume much.

They were debating almost non-stop for almost two hours on a variety of subjects. Tommy was quiet other than dropping the odd wise crack in there to cut up one, the other, or both of them. I was quiet, but I tried not to be broody. He seemed deep in thought, too. Lisa sort of just sat there looking pretty, but she rolled her eyes at me a few times, too, due to the topics or the passion with which an argument was delivered.

Finally, Tommy rose from the table. "Well kids, I hate to break up the party but me and my girl need to see a man about a hog." He fist bumped his father and his brother and then gave Lisa a kiss on the cheek. Dario and Thomas both kissed me on the cheek and Lisa and I hugged. I thanked them for their hospitality and Tommy and I left hand-in-hand.

"You're off the grid, then?" Dario asked him, following us to the door.

He answered, "'Till tomorrow."

Dario saluted him and Tommy saluted him back.

Outside was a silver Jeep Wrangler. He opened the passenger door and ushered me in, moving the bag with my pjs from the passenger seat onto the back seat.

"A man about a hog?" I asked.

He smiled at me. "You'll see."

We left the city. He played the radio so we didn't chat, but he held my hand on the console between us. After about an hour, we turned into a dirt driveway toward a farmhouse and barn and I started to wonder if the 'man about a hog' thing wasn't just a figure of speech.

He parked the Jeep and motioned for me to follow him. It was a pretty place. Big barn, little stone farmhouse, a bit overgrown but wildflowers everywhere, and no visible neighbors. He unlocked and then opened a set of double barn doors on the big, powder blue barn and inside there was a path down the center and horse stalls all the way down on either side. I heard no noise and smelled nothing that resembled animals, but then he opened a stall door and revealed a very shiny-looking candy apple red and chrome Harley Davidson motorcycle. Ah, a hog.

"Care to put something exciting between your legs?" he asked, suggestively, smiling at me.

I looked down at my clothes, "I'm wearing a skirt," I said.

He shrugged, "You'll be against my back. No one'll see your cute little baby blue panties," he winked.

"Obviously you saw them." I wondered how he knew. Maybe he approved what Nino had brought me.

"But, I'm allowed to. Let's do this."

He walked the bike out and then got into the Jeep and backed into the barn, closed the doors, and locked them.

He passed me a metallic candy apple red helmet and put a black one on his head and then we got on the road and he vroomed out of the driveway.

I held him tight, loving the feel of his muscular back and enjoying the scenery. It was a beautiful day. We drove about half an hour through the countryside, up and down winding country roads, and finally stopped at a little riverside park. There were picnickers, cyclists, fisherman, and hikers. He parked the bike and took my hand, helping me off, blocking the view of my undies as I was getting off the bike and ensuring my leg didn't touch the hot exhaust pipe.

He walked me through a very picturesque area to a snack bar beside the river and asked, "What kind of ice cream?" His eyes were sparkling with mischief.

I blushed and looked up at a big whiteboard with a few dozen choices written in alternating orange and blue marker. "Blackjack Berry Thunder," I said, with conviction.

He chuckled, "Two please," he said to the older woman manning the stand and whispered into my ear. "That's got to be the polar opposite of vanilla." He kissed me behind the earlobe.

"Let's just say my palate has gotten accustomed to more, err, flavor these days." I flushed red, but stared at him challengingly.

He looked tickled pink; his eyes sparkling with mischief. "You ain't tasted nothin' yet," he told me while kissing my knuckles.

Then the lady passed us our ice cream and Tommy paid. We strolled away, hand in hand.

"And maybe if I pick non-boring ice cream, maybe my life will stop being so darn exciting," I added as we got to the riverbank.

Tommy sat on a large, smooth rock big enough to be carved into a bench and with some comfy grooves that'd serve well to sit on. I sat beside him. The ice cream was remarkably good. I stared at the water, deep in thought.

"Penny for your thoughts?" he asked.

I looked at him. He was smiling at me, licking his ice cream, looking gorgeous and carefree.

"How come you seem so calm and carefree?" I asked, then whispered, "We could've been killed this morning."

He shrugged. "My life has been one long game of chess and almost never boring, Tia. When I give myself a chance to breathe, I breathe. That's what today is about. Us taking a minute to breathe."

I frowned. It sounded awful. "Your life always been like this? Your dad never sheltered you?"

He looked thoughtful for a second before answering. "Pop's company has evolved over the years. I guess I evolved with it. I've been working for my father since I was fourteen. I've seen a lot, even before I started working for him. I've learned a lot. My sisters are a little sheltered, they know about Pop's business, they know much less, but us boys..." He shook his head. "Constant chess game. I just make one move at a time and try to be as strategic as I can be."

Clearly, it'd affected him. He had huge anger issues. He had to know this had something to do with it. I felt disdain for his father. What would Tommy be like if he'd had a normal upbringing?

"I'm sure your life experiences have taught you a lot, too," he said.

I nodded.

"You haven't had the easiest life," he added.

"Yeah, true, but nothing like yours. I don't think I'll ever get used to the constant threat, the violence."

"It's not always this amped. And I have plans so that when I take over things'll transition and eventually most of the risky stuff will be phased out."

I felt a spark of hope, but it quickly extinguished as I recalled a scene in The Godfather when Michael Corleone's wife talked about how the more legitimate he'd become, the more dangerous he'd become. I'd seen the movies so many times. What'd been apparent so far was that Tommy Ferrano did, definitely, have demons and that he had major mood swings. He was violent but he was also fiercely protective.

"You threw yourself on top of me this morning," I said, "to protect me from the gunfire."

"Of course, I did." He was staring at the river.

"You came to Mexico yourself. You rescued me and then avenged me, well avenged yourself but I think me, too."

"Yeah." He looked across the river at kids skipping stones directly across from us. "I'll always protect you. I won't let anyone hurt you ever again."

He glanced at me quickly and I saw something flash in his eyes. Pain, maybe.

"That you covered me this morning surprised me. You keep surprising me. You're not very predictable."

"I'm a bit like this ice cream," he said, twirling the cone and assessing it. "A lot going on here with the berries and the chunks of white chocolate and dark chocolate. Each bite is different from the last."

I giggled. "And I'm all vanilla, every lick exactly the same as the last?"

"No way." He tugged my ponytail playfully. "You're exactly the flavor I want. You're delicious."

I blushed.

"I'm serious," he said. "I'm new to the whole relationship thing. I never bothered with the whole dating or relationship thing and to go from not doing them to being engaged sounds huge. It is huge, but I'm ready. I never had time for that. But now I know it's because I've been biding time waiting for you, baby. I just didn't know it until I laid eyes on you."

He reached for me, about to kiss me but I stopped him and blurted, "Tommy, I need my friends. I need Rose and Cal to know I'm okay. I need..."

He cut me off. "All in time." His lips touched mine gently, sweetly.

"Really?" I felt something twist in my gut.

"I'll give you everything you need." He let that sink in for a beat, and then continued. "Let's get a few things cleared up and it'll have to be handled delicately, but you can invite them to the wedding. In fact, if you do, I'm sure it'll settle them down."

"The wedding?"

"We'd might as well start planning it. Pop offered to let us do it at his house. The girls can help you. We can have whatever you want. Sky's the limit. It'd be good to be there for security reasons. How about a month away? Tomorrow, you and I can stop by the Crenshaws' and talk to them. Together. Think about where you want to honeymoon. Sky's the limit there, too. But you won't be able to tell anyone. We'll need to keep the location quiet until we're back." He leaned over and kissed me quickly.

I gulped. "We're still there? This is fast, it's–"

He cut me off, "Your ice cream is melting."

I licked all the way around the cone quickly.

"Oh my God," he said under his breath.

I looked over at him and he was looking at me, his eyes filled with fiery lust.

I licked the ice cream off my upper lip with the tip of my tongue. "We're having a serious conversation, here, Mister." I poked his chest playfully.

He chewed his lower lip. "Lick it again."

I did. I twirled the cone slowly and lavishly licked the circumference and then slowly licked my lips.

He shook his head. "Mm."

"What were we saying?" I asked and he let out a little laugh. I felt my belly dip, but a simultaneous internal wince as I wondered if I could do that to him without remembering that horrible man.

"You were saying this was fast and then distracting me with that tongue. I know it's fast but it's right. I feel it. I'll protect you; no one will hurt you ever again. I'll give you everything. I'm a lot to take on, my family, all of that, I know, but I need you to be mine in every way. You're already mine. You know you are. Let's just make it legal."

"Legal? You care about the law? Really?"

He winked. "Selectively. Lick, baby. Your ice cream is melting."

"It's not, you perv. But..." I turned serious. "About all that. The thing with my father, I..."

He waited for me to finish but his jaw tightened.

"I don't know why all this happened and he promised me an explanation. I called him from that mall that day and he said he would give me answers. I'd like to hear what he has to say. Does he know I'm okay? Does he know all about Mexico and everything? He was supposed to meet me at that food court in the mall when I took off and then you found me first, and..."

"No." he interrupted me. He got up and tossed his ice cream into the trash bin about five feet away. I was pretty much done, too. I passed mine to him and he threw it in the bin. He came back over and crouched in front of me. He put his palms on my face and rubbed my cheeks with his thumbs, then said, "Your father told me where you were."

He stopped talking, maybe letting it sink in, and then continued. "That's how I found you. He had no intentions of coming to meet you and give you answers. None, Tia. You should have zero guilt where he's concerned. He should not be at our wedding. He doesn't deserve to be in your life. Your father is a fucking douchebag."

I winced. I hadn't even considered how Tommy had found me that day. The whole Mexico thing sort of made all of that evaporate.

He raised his hands. "Sorry, but it's true. I called him when you took off and he called me a few minutes later to tell me you'd called and then he gave me your location. He sold you out; he's done it more than once. He's already given you away. He doesn't get to hand you to me at our wedding because he already gave you away. You're already mine. I still don't know what went down with him and my pop as women as a debt payment ain't his thing, but I've got a PI on it. A good PI. That's between you and me, Tia. You and me only. My father won't tell, and I need to know."

I thrust my hands through my hair, the revelation about my dad ratting me out to Tommy sinking in. He picked up on it. I felt totally rattled.

"I didn't want your father to ruin today." He got back up and threw a rock across the river. It skipped eight or ten times and the boys across the river were jumping up and down, excited. Tommy held another flat rock up in their direction and then did a wrist flicking thing a few times to show them his technique. The boys mimicked him and then Tommy threw the rock and it skipped about a dozen times. The one boy's rock skipped 6 times and the other older boy's rock only skipped twice. The kid whose rock had done better looked thrilled. He flicked another and it skipped quite a few more times. The other kid was jumping up and down.

I turned my attention to Tommy who now had his back to the river, eyes concentrating on me.

"Tia, he's not worthy of you. He didn't fight for you. Didn't try to protect you from my family. Now it's up to me to protect you. From him, if necessary."

I was lightheaded, numb, with a sensation of tiny pins and needles rattling around inside my body. I wanted to curl up and close my eyes and hide from the world.

Tommy leaned in, taking my chin into his grasp. "Don't. Don't internalize that. This is his fault. He's the loser. You're worth way more than the $25K he sold you for. You are precious, priceless. Do you understand me? I'll find out the truth for you and then we can put this to bed once and for all."

"I'm supposed to just let you take over my whole life?" My voice was barely above a whisper.

"Yeah," he answered simply.

Twenty-five thousand? Was that all? I knew it was a lot of money, but was that all I was worth? Anger rose up in me. He saw it.

"You're mad at your father so you're going to take it out on me. Go ahead. I can take it." He waved his fingers at himself, giving me a 'give me all you've got' gesture.

"Mad at him? Sure, I'm mad at him but why shouldn't I be mad at you, too? You're mad at him for letting you have me. But yet you took me. You. Took me. Do you realize how fucked up that is?"

"Lower your voice," he warned.

I got up and stomped off down a trail. He followed me. I walked for a good five minutes until we were deep in the bush. Finally, I spun around to face him, almost colliding with him; he was so hot on my heels.

"You've played numerous mind games with me, you've been controlling, abusive, you've raped me, you have me under lock, key, and guard to keep me from escaping, you've threatened me with a gun, hit me with a belt, shall I go on? You hardly know me. You're letting your father bribe you, I don't know, into marrying someone you don't even love. Someone you hardly know. You've never even had a serious relationship and you're a sexual deviant, by your own admission, and I've got the welts to prove it and now I have to … I have to… argh!" I wanted to kick a tree but I had flimsy flip flops on and it would hurt. He folded his arms over his chest.

The lack of an outlet to take out my frustration made my rage level spike further. "I've been dragged into this with not a care for the fact that I had a life. People don't own people. That's so fucked." I started to weep. I started to weep almost uncontrollably. I leaned back against a tree and slid down to the dirty ground. There were mosquitoes swarming my face. I whacked at them haphazardly. Tommy crouched in front of me.

"My life was stolen." I pointed accusingly at him. "Stolen and given to you. You took it but you're pissed at the man who let you take it? And now you just want me to agree to marry you. Like it's the most normal thing in the world. All while following your rules, two rules that will keep me on your good side. I think. But I don't even know because you're so unpredictable. Now you tell me my father is going to be forbidden from attending our wedding, a wedding I have no choice but to be in, because he had the audacity to be afraid of your family and do what your father demanded? How are you better than him?" I dashed the tears off my cheeks with the backs of my hands.

He put his palms on my knees and leaned close to my face. "I'm not better than anyone. I'm worse than most. Life with me isn't gonna be a cake walk. Not even close. But here's the thing. I'm crazy about you. I want that feeling I get, that beautiful feeling when I crawl in bed beside you every night and the feeling I get when I wake up beside you in the morning when you're wrapped around me like you can't get close enough to me. I think about you constantly. The happiest I've been ever since I can remember has been when I'm inside you, followed closely by waking up with you wrapped around me. I wake up in fucking bliss every morning, Tia. Bliss. This is all new for me. My sleepless nights? Gone since you. I want this."

He touched my face. I flinched. He continued. "Don't pull away. I know my pop had no right to give you to me, but he did, and I know it makes me a bad guy that I agreed to it. But, I'm not giving you back. And I'm not sorry that I took you. You're the best thing in my life, baby. How can I feel bad about that? Try to forget how we got started and just…" He stopped talking for a moment and took a deep breath. "Let me take care of you. I'll protect you with my own life. You know that's the truth."

I shook my head, determined not to let his sweet little speech penetrate my suit of armor. "What choice do I have, right? I have no choice."

He stood up and reached for my hand. "How about you choose to forget how we started and just give this a chance?"

I shook my head. "Just bury my emotions and forget everything you've done? It doesn't matter as long as I obey you, right? It doesn't matter how I feel about it as long as I do it, right?"

I got up without taking his hand and started to walk past him, but he stopped me by shackling my wrist with his hand and then he pushed me back against a tree and pinned me with his hips.

"I care about how you feel, baby. We have something," he said. "Don't let your anger at him take away from what you're feeling for me. Don't feel bad for wanting to be with me because you think you're supposed to feel bad."

"When did I say I wanted to be with you?"

His eyes narrowed.

"When did I ever say that?"

"You're a damn fine actress if that's just an act. If you expect me to believe that you haven't warmed up to me since Mexico..."

"Well you already knew that though, didn't you? You told me how damn fine I was at acting that night we had that date! It's your game, man; I'm just a player," I snapped this using mock quotes in the air at the word 'date'.

He backed up and folded his arms. "You're trying to provoke me. You're trying to provoke me so that I'll do something to give you a reason to hate me. It won't work." He stared deadpan at me.

I huffed and narrowed my eyes. "I already hate you. Can we go? Master? I'm getting eaten alive."

He smiled at me with a devilish, dangerous smile, flaring nostrils, but holding out his hand. I didn't take it. I walked ahead of him.

"You're acting like a child," he mused.

"Well why don't you find someone to marry who's your own age?" I clipped.

He laughed again, but the laugh wasn't jovial or hearty. He sounded dangerously close to the edge.

I was an idiot for provoking him. An absolute dummy. Soon we'd be alone and what'd he do then? What sort of punishment would he dole out? And his declaration? Those words were trying to melt me, but I was refusing to acknowledge that, and my chest was burning because of it.

Before long, we were back at his bike and he was putting the helmet on my head, fastening the strap. He was staring directly into my eyes and the look on his face was intimidating the heck out of me, but I was trying to not crumble. My chin started to tremble, involuntarily, and I was getting mad at myself because I knew I was going to cry in front of him. Again. I cried when I was angry. I cried when I was sad, happy, frustrated. I cried too fucking much and it never did me any good.

He went from looking like he wanted to inflict pain on me to letting out a sigh and pulling me into an embrace. I tried to pull back, to struggle, but he was too strong so I eventually went limp. He let go before I fell apart again and he got on the bike. I got on behind him and fastened my hands around his waist loosely. He revved it up and then we were off so fast that I had no choice but to hold on tighter. I figured he did that on purpose.

The drive was good for my rage, I think. I settled down a bit. My mind was still plagued with thoughts of Dad's betrayal and I felt it in my gut, grappling with the fact that my father sold me out.

Riding on the back of a motorcycle with someone felt so subservient. Tommy was in control, just like he'd be if we were in the Jeep or a car or whatever, but we were out in the open and I had to give in, give him control, hold onto him, lean against his body, despite not wanting to. It felt weird, but I analyzed it all the way back. This way of driving was *so* him.

We pulled back onto the farm and he drove right up to the barn, stopped, and stepped on the kickstand. I got off the bike and he took my hand after unlocking and then opening the doors. Instead of going back to the Jeep, he led me into one of the stalls where a narrow staircase led up to the second floor of the barn.

"Where are we going?" I asked.

"We're spending the night," he answered.

Up there the hayloft had been transformed into an apartment. It wasn't fancy, but it was spacious and furnished. There was a double bed, a couch, a kitchenette, small round white Formica table with two chairs, and I spotted a bathroom. I wandered in to wash my face and scrub some soap on my mosquito bites to see if it'd help take the itch out.

When I came out of the bathroom, Tommy was climbing back up from below with a large cooler and slung over his shoulder was the strap attached to a picnic basket.

"Nita packed us a picnic for tonight," he said. "Are you hungry yet?"

I shook my head. I wanted to ask him about this place and why we were up here instead of in the farmhouse, but I was still broody. I didn't want to talk. I didn't want to be trapped here with him. I couldn't even begin to process my feelings about what he'd said about my father back there, not to mention what he'd said about how he felt about me. I knew that I'd lashed out because of that but I also knew that everything I'd said was true. He had done all those things to me. He was responsible for all of it because he'd agreed to accept me as payment and because he'd laid a claim on me from the start, playing with me like I was a toy.

But I wasn't being honest about the acting. I had started warming up to him. But I was also confused about those feelings, too. Did I have Stockholm Syndrome? Was I just a stupid little girl falling for my crush despite who he really was because of Mexico?

I wasn't sure how to walk the fine walk on eggshells with him. I wasn't sure how to proceed at living in a world where you could be shot at any moment, in your own home, in your own bed, while you were having sex with someone.

And I'd thought about the fact that if I hadn't leaned over at that exact moment to kiss him a bullet might've hit me. So did that mean embracing this relationship was the right thing? That it was what would save me from losing my life and maybe my mind?

Maybe I'd let him closer to me in the last few days because he'd rescued me from a fate worse than him and because of how I'd crushed on him when I first saw him. And because of the things he did to my body. I was so frustrated right now. I just wanted time alone to think, to process. But that wasn't an option here in a hayloft in the middle of nowhere with him. He wasn't easy to ignore.

"Why are we here, really?" I asked finally, sitting on a plush rust-colored three-seater sofa that had definitely seen better days.

He lay on the bed and crooked his finger at me, beckoning. I shook my head.

He let out a sigh. "I wanted us to get away from things for a day, have time alone. No one knows about this place. It's mine, my safe house. We've all got them. I've never brought anyone here, but I wanted to show it to you."

He got up and walked the length of the hayloft to the back doors and opened them wide. It was just a set of doors that I guess was for farm equipment to pull up to and lift hay bales inside, so it opened up to a straight drop. Straight ahead, though, was a huge field of wildflowers and a large pond, "When it gets dark, the sky is beautiful here. Amazing sunsets. Clear and starry. I thought you'd like it."

"You brought me here to seduce me," I muttered.

He chuckled. "I wanted to share this with you. I knew I'd get lucky, sure; we both know you can't resist me. After the craziness of the last few days I thought we'd spend the night, get to know one another better. Get our relationship moving in the right direction. Let my people work on the house, on erasing what happened this morning."

As if it could be erased.

I sighed. How could I keep my armor up with scenery like this and words like that? Not to mention those bedroom eyes. He lay back on the bed and he crooked his index finger at me again.

I shook my head again and looked out the opened barn doors out at the pond.

"Your temper tantrum is over, Tia. Do I have to come get you?" he asked and I looked over at him and the look on his face made my blood run cold.

He was used to getting his own way. When things didn't go the way he wanted them to go, he took matters into his own hands. He looked angry with me. Then his expression lightened and he tilted his head at me and smiled again.

I guess I was being a bitch. He'd brought me here to a place that was special to him in order to get us away from the chaos and I was, in essence, poo pooing all over it. He was trying. And he'd only been honest with me about my dad, and I took that truth out on him.

I walked over, put my knee to the bed and climbed up. I sat beside him and said, "It's nice here. Sorry I'm being bitchy."

He smiled at me and my heart lightened because I could see that the day might be salvageable by the look in his eyes.

"Come here," he mouthed and opened his arms wide. I crawled over and he pulled me down on top of him and held me close, cradling my head against his chest with his hand. "You were right about what you said. Let me make it all up to you. I'll work on making it up to you for as long as it takes."

My heart swelled. "I lied," I said softly. "I am warming up to you. I was just..." I didn't know how to finish that sentence.

"I know. Kiss me."

I kissed him quickly on the lips. "The things you said were really sweet. I like it when you're sweet." I put my head back on his chest, closed my eyes, and concentrated on the sound of his heartbeat.

"That's all I get?" he asked.

"Mm." I nuzzled in.

"Looks like I'll have to take more, if I want it, huh?"

I shrugged. "Guess you're not feeling sweet right now, huh? Well, if you think you can..." I looked up at his face and caught my bottom lip with my teeth.

His eyes lit up and he raised his brows. "Do you think I can't?" His grip around me tightened.

I shrugged, "Dunno. You'd have to be pretty bold..." Goosebumps rose on my skin, but I managed to hold my gaze steady.

He growled and flipped me over so that I was on my back and he was on top of me, pinning my arms over my head. He kissed me roughly.

"You wanna see how bold I am?" He looked like he could barely restrain himself.

"Yeah," I said, looking him straight in the eyes. I don't know what made me decide to start this dangerous game with him, but I could feel my heart rate picking up tempo.

"You like provoking me? You like to play games, little girl?"

I shrugged innocently and blinked at him a few times. "I dunno what you mean."

"You want me to take you," he said, and his words and tone made moisture trickle down below. "I was gonna get you up here, serenade you with a picnic and be Mr. Romance. You might like sweet, but you don't want sweet today, do you?"

I sucked in my bottom lip and shrugged, then said, "No."

He gave me a knowing smile. "You're perfect, Athena, you know that? You were made for me. Hide and seek. I'll give you to the count of twenty. You'd better hide good because when I find you, I'm gonna fuck you so hard you won't have any doubt in your mind about how bold I am."

I gaped at him.

"1, 2, 3... better get moving. 4, 5, today sometime? 6..."

I gasped at the quickening pace of his counting, jumped up, and took off down the stairs. The barn door was closed. I knew it'd make noise when I opened it... so I swung it wide, but then ducked back in and climbed through the already opened back hatch of the jeep and got into the back seat as quietly as possible. A few seconds later I heard him leave the barn and I let out the breath I'd been holding.

Wow. This was a rush. And at the end I'd get sweet release. I could see how this could get addicting, especially with how intense I suspected he'd play. A few minutes passed and I hadn't heard anything anywhere around me. In fact it was eerily quiet. I sat up and almost had heart failure when I realized he was standing outside the driver's side door, staring down at me with a smile on his face. I shrieked and scampered out the passenger side and ran out of the barn.

"I'll give you an extra 5," he called, "1, 2..."

I bolted toward the back of the barn and when I rounded the rear I saw the field of flowers and the pond up ahead. I thought about taking a run into the field, but the grass was deep and I was more than a little afraid of snakes. I didn't know where to go, though, so I ran around the back of the barn and then up the other side thinking I'd head toward the house that was also on the property. He wasn't behind me. My heart thudded rapidly against my chest wall. So much adrenaline!

Tommy

That she'd gone from angry to wanting to play got my heart pumping. Maybe she had more in common with me than she realized.

I allowed her to have her moment, her hissy fit, because although I wanted her obedience and her submission, I also didn't want to extinguish that fire in her that I liked so much.

I'd always been one-sided in sating my desires. Sure, I'd get the woman I was with off, too, I got off on that, but I'd never gone out of my way to make sure that beyond getting an orgasm that I cared what she felt like afterwards. Playing with Tia, playing a game that got us both going? She was showing me that this got her juices flowing. This was different. I liked it. Thrill of the chase? Fuck yeah; it was a thrill.

She'd gone counterclockwise around the barn, so I stayed out front, crouched low against the barn. As she ran past me, I watched her pass and counted to three in my head before I was hot on her heels.

She squealed at the sight of me and ran faster toward the house. She looked gorgeous. As she ran, her already loose ponytail came completely undone and now her hair was flowing freely in the breeze. She kicked off her flip flops so she could gain more speed and then as she took off faster, I quickened my own pace. She passed the house, which was on the front of about eighty-three untended acres. I knew she'd come upon stone ruins and tear up her bare feet within a minute or two of running, so I decided to catch her before she got to the rocky area of the property.

Tia

He was gaining on me and the thrill of it was making my heart race, my face flush, and my body tingle all over. As I rounded the house and got to the back, I could see it was a little overgrown with grass and some more wildflowers. I was facing a combination of open fields, stone paths, and treed areas beyond the farmhouse. I could head toward the trees if I went right, or if I went straight ahead it looked mostly clear but hilly. To my left was the barn, the pond, and the huge field of flowers.

I decided to run toward the trees. Not many paces in that direction he caught me by the waist and tackled me to the ground but yet he did it sort of gently, breaking my fall so I landed on him instead of on the ground. As soon as we landed, he flipped and was on top of me, pinning my wrists over my head. We were both heaving but I'd say I was breathing a lot heavier than he was.

"Gotcha," he said in a low and husky voice.

The sun's rays were right behind his head, and it was as if they were bursting from him. He looked almost angelic to me. His whiskey-colored eyes sparkled, the corners of his mouth were turned up in a smile. His slightly stubbly jaw looked rugged, and his muscles looked particularly defined.

I tried to catch my breath. I wasn't struggling, just lying limp in the tall grass with my arms pinned above my head gazing up at his male beauty. My nose itched, so I reached to move my arm and his grip tightened and his eyes, though still sparkling, had a sudden shift, like they'd tinted with a bit of a challenge. I tilted my head to my shoulder and used my shoulder to try to eradicate the itch on my nose.

"Whenever you run," he said with a hint of darkness, "I'll catch you."

I felt my heart constrict for a beat and he must've seen my expression shift because then he smiled and nuzzled my throat, I think, trying to salvage the moment. Would it always be like this with him? Seesawing between light and dark? How could I keep up?

Tommy

She'd stiffened under me, and I knew that she had gone into the darker recesses of her mind. She'd gone to that place that said she was my prisoner.

I needed her to know she was mine completely, but I wanted her to want it. She wasn't there yet. I was pushing, probably too hard. She'd been shot at, kidnapped, and had her entire world turned upside down because of being mine. It'd take some getting used to. She was doing so good so far, all things considered, and I didn't want a setback. I had to be patient. We'd get there. And the journey would be fan-fucking-tastic.

"Rough or sweet?" I said into her ear, wanting, for some inexplicable reason, for her to feel in control right now. I looked into her eyes and tried to show her the tenderness I felt for her.

"Rough," she answered very softly, and it made my heart soar. Her giving me control and wanting rough when she could keep it sweet, when she could keep control of me was such a gift. She was made for me.

I gave her a little smile and she must've read my mind because she swallowed hard and looked like she might've wanted to backpedal. That hesitation, the fear in her eyes, it got me hard. So hard.

Tia

I didn't understand why I was opting for Dominating Tommy when he was offering to be Ice Cream Parlor Tommy, but I craved rough right now. I wanted him to pound me hard, to pull my hair, to spank me. What on Earth was wrong with me?

Maybe I felt like I'd wanted to beat myself up after finding out Dad sold me down the river... again. Maybe having Tommy pull the pain out of me would help me find the release I needed, would pull it out from where it was, sitting in the middle of my gut, clawing at my stomach. I wanted to feel it fully so I could then let it go.

Was it screwed up to want the pain to be real and tangible instead of inside me? Maybe. Probably. But then I could feel it and let it out. I wanted release. And I hoped that like other times that afterwards he'd hold me and caress me. And he'd get something out of it, too. I tingled at the idea of pleasing him.

His grip on my wrists tightened and he started grinding his hard cock against me. Then he let go of my wrists but grunted, "Don't move" into my ear.

He unzipped my denim skirt and shimmied it off my hips. He then grabbed the waistband of my baby blue cotton panties and ripped them clean off of me, tearing them somewhere. The tearing sound startled me, making this morph from hot to sordid, dirty. I reached quickly in modesty, but he warned, "I said don't move".

His eyes changed, got even more intense. He pinned my wrists above my head with one hand and I felt so exposed out here in the open air. He undid his pants, freeing his cock and in one move, rammed it into me to the hilt. I gasped. He gathered the length of my hair into his fist and used it to pull my face to his cheek and started hammering into me. His other hand went under my rear end and he held me by it, digging his fingers into my flesh. It hurt. Plus the ground wasn't exactly soft, and he was pulling my hair. But the sensation inside of me, the sensation of him plunging in over and over, was good. Really good. He got my earlobe between his teeth, and he wasn't biting hard, but his hot breath in my ear sent tingles over my body in waves. I willed the tension to leave my body and when I felt that moment of surrender, that moment of just giving myself over to what he was doing, it felt like a release. Even if it was sordid and dirty it was what I needed right now.

He let go of my bottom and then his fingers were between us, rubbing my clit. I opened my eyes and saw the clouds moving over us in the sky, saw birds in flight, and my nostrils were filled with scents of grass, of loam, of my arousal, of Tommy's spicy warm scent. I was ready to climax, my breathing getting shallow and faster, but then he stopped. Just stopped. He pulled out. His fingers left me and he looked down at me with a wicked look in his eyes. "Do you want to come?"

I must've stared blankly at him due to my shock.

"Do you?" he repeated.

I nodded a little. It felt like my heart rate was moving to a dangerously high tempo. How fast was it going? Double, triple? He arched an eyebrow and leaned back, breaking contact completely.

"Tommy," I croaked out, my voice hoarse. Tears stung my eyes. I wanted release. I didn't want to be teased right now. It was like he knew how badly I needed it and was reveling in this moment where I was ready to beg for it. He grabbed my rear end and then slammed into me once and then pulled out. A tear slid down my cheek. He kissed it away.

"What do you say?" he asked.

I tried to look past him, up at the clouds.

"Look at me," he demanded.

I met his eyes and saw a flash of tenderness but then the hardness returned. "I'll ask you again. Do you want to come?"

I wanted to burst into tears and say no. Because suddenly I didn't want to be here. I wanted to be somewhere else, anywhere else, somewhere alone. But I didn't say no. I searched my brain for the right answer.

He moved his mouth closer, our noses nearly touching. "Tia," he whispered and as much as I knew he could see the need in my eyes I could hear that same need in his voice.

"Yeah?"

"Say please." He waited.

"Please, Tommy," I finally whispered and then he let out a breath and his lips touched mine tenderly, sweetly. He dipped his tongue in, his lips touched mine again, and then he let go of my hair and gently caressed my cheek. But then he grabbed my chin roughly and I could see his jaw go tense as his eyes narrowed. "What do you want?"

I was frozen.

"What?" he urged.

"You," I whispered.

"You want me?" he asked, intensity emanating from his eyes.

I nodded.

"Say it," he growled.

"I want you," I said. And I meant it.

He seemed to absorb my words and savor them for a moment, then added, "Want me to do what?"

I sobbed and got my hands over my eyes. I couldn't look at him. I was suddenly overwhelmed with something... I didn't know what.

"Athena," he asked, voice laced with warning.

"Just ... whatever you want to give me or take from me."

He gently took my hands away from my eyes and kissed my eyelids. Then he lifted me up into his arms, grabbing my skirt and torn undies from the ground and carried me back to the barn. I buried my face into his shoulder.

He carried me up the staircase and gently put me on the brass four poster bed. I curled into the fetal position and buried my face into a pillow. He got undressed and climbed beside me and then gently pushed me onto my back and got on top of me. He lined up, then entered slowly and sweetly brushed my hair out of my face, looking at me with tenderness. He kissed me softly. I waited for it to change to rough but it didn't.

"You okay?" he asked, already inside me, and the concern on his face, it gutted me. This wasn't dominating Tommy, not the Tommy I needed right now.

"No," I whimpered, "not sweet."

"No," he said. "Not this time, baby girl." He kissed me on the forehead.

He lifted my legs up so that my ankles were resting on his shoulders, kissing an ankle and then pushing deep into me again. His hand stroked my leg while he scraped his teeth along his bottom lip and then he set about a rhythm – slow but deep, penetrating, almost but not quite punishing. This wasn't exactly sweet, but it wasn't rough either.

What was he trying to do to me? He gave me a choice, but then he chose sweet when I asked for rough. Maybe he was just reminding me that he was in charge.

He pulled my ankles down so my legs could wrap around his waist and then he rained soft kisses from my throat to my earlobe, over to my chin, then his lips landed on my lips and his tongue darted in, angling with mine.

"You're mine," he said, leaning back an inch.

I let out a little sob.

"Do you understand me?" He took my throat into a soft but possessive grip. His eyes were suddenly fierce. His eyes searched mine as he plunged into me over and over, not breaking eye contact and I gulped in air, giving a fractional nod. When he came inside of me, I let out a huge breath, and then he collapsed on top of me.

I could feel his heart hammering against me. I let out another rush of air as if I'd been holding my breath. He rolled off me and then his hands were between my legs and he started working his fingers, working to get me off. In a matter of no more than thirty seconds, he accomplished his goal. I arched my back and let out a loud "Ah!"

Then I curled into him. I was spent. Totally and utterly spent. He stroked my hair, rubbed my back, and rained soft kisses on me until I fell asleep.

* * *

I woke up hearing music playing. Tommy was sitting at the back of the loft, denim-clad legs dangling out the opened doors, a guitar in his arms. The sun was setting over the pond and the sky was a brilliant orange. The view was dazzling. Seeing his strong naked back and hearing the strumming made for an even more beautiful view.

I got up and took my t-shirt off, dropping it with my skirt that was on the floor beside my flip flops, which he must have gone and fetched for me. I put his discarded dove gray dress shirt on, did up the buttons, then padded to him. I sat on the floor behind him, putting my legs on either side of his hips so that my calves were over the edge, and I rested my cheek on his bare back. He continued to play and I recognized the tune. *Wild Horses* by the Rolling Stones.

He played beautifully, soulfully. The sky, the sounds, the smell of the warm air, the smell of him, feeling his warm and smooth skin under my cheek, I was inexplicably glad that I was here with him. I actually felt free for a moment.

When he finished playing it, I recognized the next song as *Iris*, from the Goo Goo Dolls. It was one of my favorites.

Tommy

I knew it'd been brewing since before Mexico, but today sealed it for me. I wanted her to want to be mine so bad I was willing to do just about anything to get her there. I wanted to take all the things that were fucked up in her life and erase them. I wanted to reboot our relationship.

I wanted to make the sun set and rise for her. I wanted to protect her. I wanted her to love me. I'd never felt this way before. It created fear and a fierce protective instinct in me that I'd never before experienced, but right now her body against me, watching the setting sun and inhaling the summer night air we were breathing...this was it. This was all I needed.

She'd come to me on her own and put her arms around me again, just like she'd done in the shower the other night. This was what I wanted. This. Not more money, not more power, just this. It was like

I'd been missing something in my life that I didn't know I was missing until her.

I wanted to dole out fear, pain, and punishment all the time. *All the fucking time.* But today she wanted pain from me. It was beautiful to me to see that, but it meant I didn't want to give it to her. I made her want something from me, something only I could give her. She didn't even name what she wanted from me, and I didn't want to give it a name, either. I just knew it was so satisfying, even more than I'd expected.

I wanted this time away to be different, but I knew soon we'd go back to exploring her willingness to travel down darker corridors with me. Right now, I just wanted her to relax and forget everything she'd been upset about. I wanted her to feel safe, not trapped, to enjoy being with me.

I put my guitar down and looked ahead. She was still behind me, her legs on either side of mine, and her cheek on my back. A breeze picked up a little and her silky hair blew up around my face. I inhaled and caught the scent of oats and vanilla. Cookies. Her arms came around my waist and she flattened her palms against me, the right one across my abdomen, and the left across my chest. I looked down and saw her engagement ring on her finger and something welled up inside me. I held my breath to hold back the overwhelming emotion surging through me.

We sat and watched the sun go down the rest of the way in silence. It was like the whole world was silent for a moment.

Finally, it was dark. I twisted my body around. She let go of me and backed up. I think she thought I meant to get up but instead I climbed on top of her on the floor. I gave her a long, sensual, deep kiss, running my fingers through her hair, cupping her chin. I wanted to devour her. I held that desire back.

Tia

After he kissed me, hovering over me on the floor, he got to his feet and helped me up. Then he pulled a screen roller blind down over the opened barn door area and fastened it to the floor with snaps. The little table with two chairs was not far from the back doors and on top of it sat the cooler and picnic basket. He lifted the basket down to the floor and opened the cooler and took out a few plastic lidded food containers and then a bottle of wine and motioned to the basket with his chin, giving me a little smile. He was smiling more often since we'd arrived here. That smile was so beautiful it made me feel almost giddy inside.

I found a square blue and white checked tablecloth in there so shook it out and let it fall over little round table. I pulled two wine glasses from the leather straps holding them to the lid and set them on the table and then set out the two plates and two sets of cutlery as well as cloth napkins that matched the tablecloth.

Tommy reached in, pulled out a candle stick and candle holder, then fetched a barbecue lighter from a tall and weathered-looking armoire against the wall. I watched him light the candle and as he poured wine while I layered cold breaded chicken, garden and potato salads from their containers onto the plates. There was also a lidded container full of fruit salad and a mason jar filled with a fragrant balsamic salad dressing.

Tommy put his phone on the table and *Holding Back the Years* by Simply Red played. We sat at the table, and he lifted his wineglass up. I lifted mine.

"To beautiful sunsets," he said.

"To beautiful sunsets," I parroted.

"And winning at hide and seek or tag or whatever that was," he added, watching me closely.

"Congratulations, champ, but I'd say there were no losers in that game." I dipped my glass in his direction and then took a sip.

He winked at me and had the biggest smile on his face. We dug in to the delicious food.

After a few minutes of serious chowing down of Nita's gorgeous food, I came up for air.

"So, no one knows about this place?"

He nodded, swallowed a mouthful of wine, and said, "Nope. Every guy needs a retreat. Every guy in my line of work needs a safe house. So, this is both for me."

"But you brought me here," I said. "Isn't that against man cave rules?"

"Rules schmules." He reached across the table and took my hand. "We needed to get away. I think maybe we should stay tomorrow night, too. Totally detox. But I'll have to call in tomorrow and see what's up before I'll know if I can do an extra day. Would you wanna do that?"

"Sure," I answered.

"Cool. We'll stop by and see the Crenshaws tomorrow. Then if everything's kosher, we'll come back. If not, we'll go back to the house."

"Okay."

After a few minutes of silence where I felt an odd and intense vibe coming from him, I piped up again, wanting things light and airy. "How long have you had this place and your house?"

He swallowed, wiped his mouth with a napkin, took a sip of wine, then answered. "Pop bought me the house a few months back. I've had this place a year and a half. Before the house, I lived in a condo down near our office. I started renting that out to my brother when Pop bought me the house."

"He bought you a house?"

"For my 29th birthday, yep. Should've known that was the prelude to getting married."

I frowned at him. "You don't have to get married if you don't want to."

"I want to," he said and reached for my hand.

Awkwardness crackled in the air.

"Do you like the house?" he asked after the awkward moment didn't pass.

"It's a bit sterile. But it has potential. It's the exact sort of house my mother would've picked from the outside."

"Feel free to inject some personality," he said.

I raised my brows at him.

"I'm serious. After the wedding or now, whatever. A few projects to keep you busy, right? And if you don't love it, we'll buy something else."

I must have made a face of distaste because he looked a little like he'd deflated.

"Listen," he said, "I know things are different from what you planned but instead of mourning those plans, why not get excited about possibilities?"

"I wanted to get my degree. I..."

"Get it. Do online school."

Not exactly the same as the college experience.

"Then I wanted to work in social work."

"You won't need to work. We have money."

"We?"

"You and me," he answered.

We?

"I wanted to," I said softly.

"Nothing's really off the table, babe. Once things are settled you can take on charity projects. Start your own charity. Hell, I don't know, start your own business. As soon as things are settled and safe we can talk about what you want. Nothing is off the table right now, just be open to this, to us. Please?"

Asking *please* touched something in me. I stared at the flickering candlelight for a few minutes. Then he squeezed my hand and got up from the table, taking me with him. He leaned over and fiddled with his phone, pulled me to him, music started, and he twirled me a little, then started to slow dance, pulling me against his chest and kissing me. I felt shivers climb up my spine. Just a bar in... the song registered in my brain.

At Last by Etta James. I felt my knees almost buckle because... wow. *Wow.*

I knew, back to when I was a little girl, that if I ever found my dream man, if I ever got married, this song would be it. *The* song. This song would be the wedding song, the first song I'd have my very first dance with my new husband to. I'd never told anyone that. Nobody.

He tucked my head under his chin and he moved us around so gracefully that it was almost as if I could dance, too. It was as if we'd practiced. Tears stung, unshed, in my eyes and emotion tried to claw its way up my throat. I fought to hold it together.

I'd thought, when I saw him that first time at the ice cream parlor, that he had the looks and the swagger of my absolute dream man, but I thought he was totally unattainable. Older than me, more sophisticated, above my station. Then I met him the day I graduated and thought he was my worst nightmare. Now where was I?

I didn't know. I'd hated him, I'd surrendered to him sexually, I'd tried to escape him, then it all went horribly wrong when I was kidnapped and then he'd rescued me from a fate worse than him and I'd clung to him like he was my hero. I'd warmed up to him a bit. Maybe more than a bit.

Tommy Ferrano was the man of my dreams, but he was also the man of my nightmares.

What if I hadn't been taken that day; what would he have done once he got me back in the house? What sort of punishment would I have faced for taking off from his sister? Did my kidnapping change him? Was he capable of change? Was he capable of being loving and giving and sweet all the time or was I only getting a temporary reprieve from the angry, punishing control freak who wanted to play scary sex games and mind fuck games?

Just how dark and evil was he? How many people had he killed? What kind of illegal stuff did his family participate in? Was he involved in profiting from the sex slave rings he'd threatened me with?

This morning when we were shot at and when he turtled over me... it did something to me. It did something I couldn't quite name. Like the night he rescued me in Mexico, he'd sliced me open and then when he climbed onto me this morning to protect me, that open wound still there, he climbed right inside of it, of me. But because of the way he'd seesaw between dark and light I felt like I was always on eggshells.

The light was nice; it almost verged on puppies and rainbows in my heart sometimes. The dark was scary. But, then the dark could also be exciting. I'd even invited it, with volunteering to play sex games, with provoking him. What was my problem? Was I just a stupid little girl playing games out of my depth? Yes, way out of my depth. Way.

He sang into my ear the very last line of the song.

"For you are mine, at last." He looked into my eyes in the silent loft. The only light was the little glimmer of candlelight from the table and the stars outside the opened doors, or no... wait, those were fireflies twinkling out there. Fireflies. *Oh, man!* How could I keep my guard up at this rate?

It was a magical moment, dancing in candlelight and firefly light, wearing only his shirt, him half naked and gorgeous, up where there was no one but us, in his special place that he'd only ever shared with me. And he was full of light right now, not darkness. For someone who didn't do relationships, he sure knew how to set a romantic scene. The music stopped and we were still dancing, dancing to the sound of nature outside.

If it could often be just like this, would it be enough for me?

Would I be able to live under his regime, under his rules, in a world of crime and danger? Did I have a choice in the matter? How dangerous was his life? What sorts of illegal things did he do? I still didn't even really know.

So many questions.

He was still looking into my eyes; I was looking into his. It was like we were both stripped bare. He lifted my hand and kissed my knuckle just above where the engagement ring sat. Then he looked at the ring for a beat and dropped to one knee, making my heart skip a beat.

"Tia, I want you. I want you to be mine forever. Not because you clear a debt, not because I have to get married to take over for my father. I want to marry you because..." He stopped and looked away for a second. Then he looked up at me again and took a slow breath and said, "I'm about to say something to you that I've never said to another woman, so know that when you hear this."

I gave him a little, almost imperceptible nod, suspecting I knew what was about to come out of his mouth but not sure that it was at all possible he was about to say what I suspected was about to come out of his mouth. But then he said it.

"I'm in love with you."

I think my mouth dropped open.

His eyes took on fierceness. "Right here, right now, decide to give me a chance. Forget, for a second, everything on the bad side of the scales you've been weighing out and think only about the possibilities. Will you wear this ring voluntarily? Will you marry me?"

"Yes," I said without even pausing first.

This beautiful, powerful, rich man who could have almost any girl in the world wanted me.

Me. The foster kid with the fucked-up life, the lowlife father, no money, nothing all that special about me. He wanted me. How could I say no? I didn't even factor in the consequences of saying no because right then, I wanted him, too.

I wanted this beautiful moment to be real. I wanted my life to be a life, not a life sentence. I wanted this man who would not hesitate to be a human shield to keep me safe from gunfire. I wanted this big, strong, beautiful man who would fight scary dudes with big guns because they tried to hurt me. I wanted to feel the safety of his arms, the insane pleasure his body was capable of giving me. I wanted to dance in the moonlight with fireflies; I wanted him to be mine.

I fell down into his arms and wrapped my limbs around him. He pulled me close to him, so close it felt like he was trying to absorb me.

His hands went under the shirt and gripped my bare back as he buried his head into my chest and just held me and let me hold him for what felt like a really long time. I rested my cheek on the top of his head and melted into him. After a while just staying like that, he lifted me up as he stood, like I weighed nothing, and I was about to wrap my legs tighter around his waist but he hoisted me over his shoulder, making me squeal in surprise. He tossed me onto the bed and then playfully pounced on me.

Then, he made love to me, tenderly, sweetly, his eyes liquid with unshed tears. When Tommy brought me to climax, I held onto him for dear life, wanting to freeze the beauty of that moment in time. I cried afterwards, a different kind of crying. A big cathartic release and he held me tight, caressing me. We were both shaking. It felt so real and so, so right.

Flickering light danced through the dim loft amid the sounds of crickets and frogs. And wow, the way he looked at me? He looked at me and touched me like I was the most precious thing to him. It was beautiful. I fell asleep wrapped around him, ready for possibilities, because feeling like this felt like a priceless gift.

* * *

I woke up alone. I sat up and looked around.

Birds chirped and there were other noises coming in via the still-opened doors. The sky seemed alive with noisy birds, butterflies, and the sun was beating through the screen with intensity. The bathroom door was closed. I knocked and there was no answer so I opened it, finding it empty, but with a steamed up mirror, meaning he'd very recently showered. I got out of his shirt and got into the shower, washing and shampooing with his all-in-one hair and body wash. I used his damp towel as it was all there was, then I put yesterday's clothes back on, minus the underwear, which had a large rip straight up the back of them, rendering them an ass-less piece of scrap material.

I dashed down to get my pajama bag out of the Jeep from yesterday, figuring I could hand-wash my sleeping shorts and let them dry so I could use them as undies for now, but when I got down the stairs and out into the middle of the barn, no Jeep. The door was closed, but I wasn't locked in. I frowned, but then remembered that the iPhone was in my jean skirt pocket.

I lifted it out and saw it was 9:25 am. I swiped over to contacts and there were just Tommy and his brother listed there. I dialed Tommy and it rang once but then went to voicemail, so I went back upstairs and sat down on the sofa, which was facing the doors, and watched out the back. The phone only had 19% power remaining and I didn't have a charger, so it wouldn't last for long.

I needed caffeine. And underwear! There was a fridge here and a sink and microwave but no stove, no coffee maker. No coffee supplies. I looked in the armoire and fridge. The fridge had the remnants of last night's dinner, our untouched fruit salad, and some bottles of beer, bottles of water, a sports drink, and a vitamin water. The cupboard had some odds and ends, mostly. Some tools, a flashlight, lantern, lamp oil, bug repellant, guitar strings and picks, and a box of bullets. No coffee or tea or sugar). There were a few t-shirts of Tommy's and a pair of jeans. There was also a half-eaten, but not closed properly box of Sugar Crisp. The clothes were all folded and clean-looking but no underwear. I'd have even settled for a pair of his right now.

I opened the vitamin water and then made the bed and then lay down, deciding to wait for him. What else could I do?

Two hours later he still hadn't come back, and I'd spent enough time in my own head. I was about to wander outside just out of boredom but then I heard a car pull. I heard voices, so I walked down the stairs and peeked outside through a window in one of the stalls and saw that an older couple were standing in the gravel driveway right beside the barn (despite it being a few hundred feet from the road) looking at a map, and loudly discussing the right way to get to some town I hadn't heard of.

I listened for a minute and then saw the woman wave at me. How she'd spotted me in the shadows peeking out the window I hadn't a clue, but she had seen me. She moved closer and the man with her followed.

Shit.

I stepped out of the barn.

"Hello," I greeted.

The lady looked to be in her late sixties or even her seventies, maybe. "I'm sorry to disturb you dear, but we're trying to get to highway ten. It's a big confusing on the map."

I looked at the map. "I'm sorry, I'm just visiting, and I don't know the area very well."

"Well, if you'll just look–" she pointed, but the husband interrupted.

"Millie, she obviously doesn't know where highway ten is so let's not waste her time."

"We're here," She ignored the crotchety old guy and put a bright pink pointy fingernail on the map and I saw that it said Line 10.

"Oh," I said. "If this is where we are, this is Line 10. That's not the same as highway ten. That's over there." I pointed a few inches over to the left.

"It looks like if you take this road twenty-four over, you can then get to highway nine and that'll easily get you to highway 10. It looks pretty straightforward. I don't know the area, though, so not sure I'm the best judge."

"Line 10," the husband said with a eureka look on his face, "That's the last time I let you navigate, Mill!"

Something about his demeanor wasn't sitting right with me. I frowned.

She waved her hand, looking mildly embarrassed. "Well thank you so much, dear. You've been a huge help." She looked me in the eye, smiling big.

I backed away, expecting them to head off. The old woman stared for a moment.

"Are you alright, dear?" she asked.

"I'm fine," I said. "Have a nice day."

She looked at me for another beat and the husband just stood there, looking out at the fields in a way that made it seem phony.

My spidey senses were suddenly on even higher alert. Tommy said no one knew about this place. Surely these old people weren't here to kidnap me or kill me or something, right? Why wouldn't the husband have looked at the map himself? It was pretty obvious that they were on line ten and not highway ten.

"If you're sure..." she nudged in a way that seemed like she was urging me to say I wasn't fine.

"Yes, Ma'am. I need to get back to my, uh, chores. Have a safe drive."

She nodded, looking a little frazzled suddenly, and then they headed back to the car and started pulling out of the end of the driveway. I walked back to the barn, but as I did I felt an eerie feeling, so I glanced over my shoulder and there was Millie, on her cell phone looking right at me and with a very serious look on her face as the car pulled away.

I got back into the barn and went to a different stall and looked out the window, watching to ensure they were actually gone. I decided to wait and make sure nothing was *off*. The whole time I waited, I was plotting, thinking of ways to defend myself. There was a big cop-sized flashlight upstairs that would be good for knocking someone over the head. Above the door in the barn was a horseshoe that I could bash someone with. Beyond that, I didn't know what I'd do other than run or hide. Maybe there were tools or something in another stall. Tommy had bullets upstairs. Did that mean there was a gun somewhere? Maybe there was one strapped under the bed like back at his house.

I pondered dashing up to look, but kept watch out the window instead. I must've stayed there twenty or thirty minutes before I felt like I was safe. When I was half way up the stairs I heard a vehicle pull in. My heart started racing.

I peered out the window carefully and saw the silver Jeep. I was so relieved I must've sounded like a tire that'd sprung a leak with the long breath I let out.

A moment later, he opened the doors and then I heard him get back in and pull into the barn and then get out and shut the doors. I emerged from the stall to see him getting out of the vehicle with a tall paper coffee cup in one hand, another coffee cup held by his teeth at the rim, and in his other hand he had a bouquet of flowers and two big paper bags with rope handles. He looked good in tight jeans with a tight black t-shirt, his hair pushed away from his face with sunglasses. He gave me a little smile and a sexy wink as I walked up to him and then he handed me the cup in his hand and took the cup from his teeth into that now free hand. He leaned forward and kissed me quickly on the lips and then motioned, with his chin, for me to follow him upstairs. His eyes were sparkling. He looked happy.

I followed him to the little table where he put everything down and gathered me tight against him.

"Hi," he whispered softly into my hair. "What were you doing in there?"

"Hi, I, uh...I'll explain. You should've left me a note or something."

He made a face that I couldn't get a read on. "Oh. Never thought of that. Needed coffee." He handed me the bouquet. "For you."

"Thank you," I looked at the bundle and realized they were from the fields. He must've picked them and brought them with him when he left. They were tied into a bouquet with a long yellow ribbon.

I took a sip of coffee.

"Liquid gold..." I murmured, then said, "These are gorgeous. Uh, there was this older couple that were just here that wanted directions, but then when they left I got this sort of weird spidey sense and thought I'd tell you in case they were, uh...I mean at first they didn't seem like anything but an older couple who were lost, but the more I think about it the more–"

"Don't worry, baby. No one knows about this place." He cut me off and nonchalantly rummaged through the bags, lifting out a take-out bag. "Breakfast sandwiches," he announced and put them on the table, then he passed another bag from inside the large bag.

"I picked you up something else to wear. I hope it's all right. I should've gotten a bag packed for us yesterday, but with everything yesterday morning..." He shook his head, then he reached in the other bag and pulled out new clothes for himself, stacking them on the table. I saw jeans, a blue t-shirt, a black zippered hoodie, a package of socks, a black wife beater, and three-pack of boxer briefs. I also spotted a pink toothbrush. I glanced in the bag he'd handed me and found a short yellow sundress, a long, pink maxi dress, white lacy bra, white thong, pink thong, pink bra, black boy short panties, black bra, and a pair of simple black flat t-strap sandals along with a pair of baby blue & white Converse high tops. Sizes all checked out and he evidently knew my taste, in addition to my size as well as the fact that I always wore matching bras and panties.

"I borrowed the ribbon from your new dress," he said, motioning with his chin at the bouquet.

I put the bag down and took another sip of my coffee, eyeing him with scrutiny. He was acting a little sketchy.

"You were gone quite a while," I said. "And you've been busy."

He turned around and faced me with his brows raised, face looking carefully wiped blank.

"What's going on, Tommy?"

He shook his head and shrugged. "The dresses okay?"

I nodded. "Perfect."

Something wasn't right. "Tommy?"

He pulled me close to him and murmured, "Did you miss me?" His voice was husky. He kissed the top of my head, hands trailing down to cup my backside.

"Yeah; I wondered where you went. I called, but your phone went to voicemail. Maybe next time you could leave a note or a text."

"Sure, babe. And I'm officially off the radar today," he said tucked my hair behind my ear with his fingertips.

"And you were gone a long time. I felt a bit stuck, a bit trapped here."

"But you didn't run away," he said softly into my hair and then started walking me backwards toward the bed while nibbling on my ear.

I opened my mouth to speak, but nothing came out. I was processing the course of events as he unbuttoned my skirt and then pulled to pull it down but before it was over my hips I stumbled as the backs of my legs hit the bed and fell backwards. He was right on top of me.

I stiffened. "Was that...was that a test?"

He made an *Mm* sound and then was kissing my neck.

"Tommy?"

"Mm, you taste so good, baby. Even if you do smell like a man." He laughed.

"Tommy!" My hands landed on his chest and I tried to push him back. He reared back onto his knees at the end of the bed, so I sat up and scooted backwards.

He gave me a grin. "I'm very pleased with you right now. Let me show you." He reached forward and ran his hand up my leg. I swatted his hand away and blazed a dirty look at him. He reached for me again and when I went to swat him away again, he caught my wrist in his hand and his expression darkened.

"I said I'd like to show you how pleased I am with you. You want me this pleased, trust me." His facial expression made a chill crawl up my spine.

He laid me back down and started kissing from my throat down my arm and then his mouth was between my breasts. He looked up while kissing me and gave me a little smile. I lay there stiffly, a scowl on my face.

He stopped and looked up at me and sighed. "Okay, yes. You passed. Can you forget about it so we can move on with our day? I have so many things planned. So many things..." He tongued my earlobe.

I winced, feeling a little sick. He'd left me alone here for hours wondering where he was and then I'd been afraid that those people were part of something sketchy. And they were; they were here to scam me, to see if I'd try to, to what, escape with them? Would they have driven me right to him? Then I'd have been in big trouble. What would he have done?

I shook my head. He rewards obedience. He punishes defiance.

"Don't be mad at me," he whispered. "I'm *so* not mad at you."

I squirmed out from under him and went over to the table to take another mouthful of coffee and then wandered over to the screen and looked out at the pond. He came up behind me and put his arms around my waist and his chin on my head.

He softly said, "I wanted to believe that you're being real with me, about what we discussed last night. I guess I just had doubts and I wanted to put it to rest. Either you'd pass and I'd know you're really giving me a chance, or you'd fail and then I'd know."

I spun around. "Know what? That I was capable of Oscar-worthy performances? And then what would you have done?"

"I..." He started, took a deep breath, then said, "I don't know what I would've done. But I'd have been devastated. Devastated. I'm glad you passed. Now I can breathe easier, baby. Please don't be upset. I want us to have a good day today. We can go fishing, I bought us fishing rods. We can go to dinner later. I booked a table at this little place not far from here."

I shook my head, giving him a disapproving look.

He continued, caressing my face as he talked to me. "I'll cut wood and we can have a bonfire with some marshmallow-roasting tonight, then tomorrow morning we'll head back to the city. I called the Crenshaws, and they were busy today but we're meeting them at their house tomorrow for brunch and then we'll head home. I have to jet away for a business trip, and I'll be gone for a couple days so this is time for us before I go."

He was looking at me with puppy dog eyes. I wanted to stay mad. But I didn't, at the same time. I wanted today to be the first day since the day before grad of not hating my existence, I wanted today to be the first day of my engagement, the engagement I'd agreed to be in last night. I meant it last night. But the reality was that this wasn't a typical engagement. He wasn't a typical man.

"You didn't trust me. Last night meant so much to me and you thought I was playing you. I thought we decided on a new beginning." I looked down at my feet away from those puppy dog eyes. They were totally adorable and cracking my armor.

"I want that so much. I wanted it to be real. I fell asleep believing it was real. I was so happy last night, baby. It meant a lot to me, too. It meant everything. But when I woke up this morning, I had this little voice telling me it was too good to be true. You probably wanted me dead a few days ago. When Earl shot at me, all I could think of was that you'd be relieved if he killed me, relieved thinking you had your life back. You've been through a lot. I started to doubt that I deserved this about-face and then I started to think maybe you were just placating me until you got a chance to run. I couldn't think straight, so I went for a walk and picked those flowers. Then I went for a drive. I decided to set up a little test, that's all. You passed. I feel better. Please just…"

He looked a little bit lost. He ran a hand through his hair and looked at me, eyebrows raised, lips a little pouty.

I felt my anger soften a little. I guess he picked up on it, because he started jerking his head to and fro, searching my face, looking like he was searching for a sign I wasn't angry. He smiled but it was punctuated by a question mark. Then he raised his eyebrows again and I smiled back.

"S'mores," I said, "For the bonfire and you've got a deal."

He scooped me up in his arms and kissed me hard. Then he popped me onto the bed and rolled me onto my belly and lay on top of my back, pinning me to the bed, holding my hands above my head while he nuzzled the back of my neck. He then lifted my top and rained kisses over my bare back. It tickled a little, so I squirmed. He must've liked that because I then felt his erection poking me in the backside. That was when he started to really tickle me, and that made me begin to struggle. He flipped me onto my side and I caught his expression and the struggling seemed to wake something up in him.

He let out a growl while flipping me onto my back, pinning my arms above my head. His hands and eyes travelled up and down my body as he undid his jeans, holding my eyes captive in his gaze. I swallowed hard.

"Don't move," he warned, his expression looking deadly serious.

My heart hammered against my chest.

He pulled my already undone skirt the rest of the way down, smirking, seeing I was commando. He kissed my hip and worked his way over to between my legs.

His tongue certainly knew what it was doing, so I went off like a cannon in what felt like about ninety seconds. Bang, boom; holy shit! As soon as I came, he rammed hard into me and grabbed me by the hair. I winced at the bite of pain as he then he twirled me, moving so his legs dangled off the bed, me straddled, riding him.

He grabbed my shoulders and looked me right in the eye. "Never leave me. Ever."

I blinked hard and shivered.

"Because. You. Are. Mine." He hammered into me with every word. I closed my eyes, and I think I winced again because he got my chin into his grasp and pulled my face forward and his nose was an inch from mine and he demanded, "Right?"

I swallowed hard. His eyes softened.

"Say it," he said softly but there was still an edge to his voice.

It was all too fresh. I wasn't ready for this declaration. Nowhere near ready. I wasn't remotely interested in playing this game. But judging by the look on his face, I needed to play it. I needed to play it and then move on from it otherwise the lovely day he'd organized for us would be gone to pot.

"I didn't leave," I whispered, chin trembling.

"Why?" His narrow eyes were filled with warning.

"Because I didn't want to. I told you I'd give you a chance. I meant it, Tommy."

"You'll marry me?" he asked, eyes hard.

"Yes," I answered.

His jaw clenched, he huffed, then he pushed my shoulders slightly back so that I was sort of suspended in midair. He used my legs to keep a firm hold on me, pulling me tighter to him while driving so deep into me that it felt like he was hitting parts he shouldn't be hitting.

"You can't leave me, Tia."

Now it was more like a plea instead of a demand. Was that pain in his eyes now?

I had nothing to hold onto, my abs were killing me. I grabbed at my stomach and he spun me around so that I had the bed to lie on and now he was standing up, pummeling me from standing, pulling my legs up, driving in so deep that I cried out. This was sweet, sweet pain and with the look on his face, the sexy expression... I became lightheaded. He was so sexy I would've swooned if I wasn't already horizontal.

As he plunged into me, he tweaked my clit with his thumb,

almost in a strumming motion and the heated stare, the sensation, and the feeling of him sliding in and out at that rapid pace all culminated in a loud moan from me as I hit another peak. But he wasn't done.

I was flipped to my belly, my ass in the air as he drove into me from behind. Ramming hard, fingers gripping my hips, and then out of nowhere he made a low growling sound and a stinging slap rang across on my ass.

I jolted, dislodged him, but he grabbed my hips and rammed back in, eliciting a squeaking protest from me. He gripped my rear hard with his hand and I didn't know if I loved it or hated it. His breathing pace changed and then he groaned my name as he came. I collapsed face first on the bed under the weight of him pinning me. He stayed half on top of me for a few minutes and the feel of his breath on my neck, of his heart pounding through his chest against my back, it gave me a weird feeling, a peaceful feeling.

He gathered my hair to one side and ran his fingers through it.

"I'm sorry," he whispered against my ear. "It'll take time for us to trust one another. I want us to have a good day together. Still upset?"

"Not really," I answered, but in truth I wasn't sure how to feel.

"Did I fuck you into submission?" I felt him smile against my shoulder and then he planted a soft kiss there.

"I think you might've." I smiled, too.

He rolled me onto my side and spooned me. "I may do that often, you know?" He kissed my ear and gave me a squeeze. "But you didn't submit 100%, did you?"

I knew he wanted that, "yes, I'm yours" from me, and I hadn't given it. But, he didn't seem angry right now.

"Mm, maybe ninety-ish," I said.

He let out a little laugh.

"Progress," he murmured. "Huge progress."

I heard a flock of birds overhead and as they flew over the barn and the expanse of the property and I sighed with relief and euphoria blended together. "It's lovely here."

"I love it here," he said. "I needed to feel like you were safe. Home wasn't safe. Here feels better."

I turned over and put my arms around him, nuzzling into his chest. His bruises were fading. I felt safe there, then, in his arms, which was the strangest thing because I'd probably never known actual true danger before I'd met him. I traced his tattoo with my finger and enjoyed the feel of a gentle breeze that swooped through the loft.

Tommy

I hadn't earned it yet. I hadn't earned a "Yes, I'm yours." I hadn't earned, "I love you, Tommy" yet. But I would.

After making love, we just stayed in bed, her in my arms, for the longest time. It was funny to think of it as "making love" instead of fucking, like it'd always been, but I guess my mindset had started to shift. Did it qualify as making love if it was a little rough? To me it did. I loved her and I wanted her. I was expressing that love and that hunger with my body.

She cuddled into me and drew circles on my arm and then my back with her fingertips and then I did it back and she squirmed. She made me feel like a teenager. A horny teenager who couldn't get enough of her and who, in that moment at least, didn't care if it was vanilla, chocolate, or blackjack berry thunder as long as it was with her.

"You're very ticklish," I told her. "I like how you squirm against me when I tickle you."

She blushed and batted her eyelashes at me.

"Why don't we warm up those sandwiches and eat and then we'll go fishing?" I suggested and tapped her on the ass. She smiled and stretched.

I got out of bed and popped the bag into the microwave. She got up and put a new pair of panties on, a sexy silky pair that I'd bought her, put a matching bra on, and then pulled the yellow cotton dress over her head and started hunting for something to put her flowers into. I found her a mason jar that was down in one of the stalls and she cleaned it, put the bouquet in, and then put the yellow strap back around the waist of her dress.

We ate and then I walked her downstairs and pulled out the new fishing rods I'd bought that morning. I bought her a pink one and she thought it was hilarious that it was pink like her new toothbrush. We made our way down to the pond where I put the worm on for her and taught her how to cast. She was a natural; she caught twice as many fish as I did, but wouldn't touch the worm or the fish. I finally grabbed her as she muttered "one more cast" for the fifth time and carried her back to the barn over my shoulder.

"We've been fishing all day. We have reservations, no more casts."

She giggled as I put her down near the bed and reached for my keys. She wanted five minutes to freshen up and grab her purse, so I waited in the Jeep for her, thinking about the fact that I had to go to Vegas for some business and that I didn't want to leave her at the house.

I didn't want to leave her because, a) I still wasn't content the security issues that plagued me after Earl and then after the shooting yesterday were totally resolved. I knew that there'd very likely be blowback from what I did in Mexico because Castillo had a nephew who was semi-local. He was a small-time drug dealer and thug and it was him and his guys that'd breached security and gotten in by scaling up and in from behind the swimming pool. A taller fence was being put in today to make sure no one could get in that way.

Still, I needed to see that nothing would go wrong before trusting anything. And besides, b) I hated the thought of her not being beside me at night. What a one-eighty from congratulating myself so frequently that I had my king size bed all to myself to now aching for her when she wasn't in my sights. The night I'd taken her to dinner and the beach when I'd left her alone for the night had been a long cold and sleepless night in a guest room without her warmth wrapped around me. The nights in Mexico without her had been torment, not feeling her, not hearing her breathing.

The Japanese restaurant I took her to was almost empty. The hostess I'd talked to that morning wasn't in sight. The rest of the staff welcomed us and pointed to a table. She didn't know what to order so I told her I'd order for us.

She examined everything carefully and skeptically but tried every dish that the server put in front of her after having first asked the waiter about shellfish. The waiter had waved her concerns off because of what we'd ordered but he didn't speak very clear English. She was good-natured about it despite telling me she hadn't been a very adventurous eater in life so far.

"No shit, Miss Vanilla Ice Cream is my Favorite," I teased.

She blushed bright pink. "Until I found you, Mr. Blackjack Berry Thunder. Or should I say, until I was betrothed to you."

She didn't look unhappy when she said that. I smiled at her. "I'm expanding your palate, and your horizons." I wiggled my eyebrows at her.

She wiggled hers back at me. "Mm hm. So you're off on a business trip?" she added.

I scrunched up my face. "Yeah."

"Unpleasant business?" she asked, then she added, "Or should I not ask?"

I shook my head. "I'm just not looking forward to leaving you at home. I'm thinking I should take you with me."

"Really? Why? Where?" She looked excited and the idea of her being happy to come with me instead of having time without me felt good. Real good.

"Yeah, it's too soon for me since the security breaches at home to feel comfortable, so I don't know that I'd be all that productive unless you were with Dare. But he's too wrapped up with work shit to be your bodyguard 24/7. I'm vetting a few of my senior guys and will make a decision soon about rotations for security for the house. And I'm not sure I want to be without you."

She blushed and smiled at me.

"So, tomorrow maybe after we see your foster parents we can go home and pack for Vegas."

Her face lit up, "Vegas?"

I nodded. She clapped her hands and then was suddenly downtrodden.

"What?" I asked.

"I'm nineteen. Vegas isn't fun unless you're twenty-one." She pouted.

"Unless you're a high roller," I said. "No one will card you when you're with me, baby girl."

Her smile returned. She took a sip of her Japanese green tea and then started to scratch at her chest. I leaned forward because I could see big blotchy hives across her neck and cleavage. She was a little pale.

"What's wrong?"

"I don't know. I hope nothing we ate had any shellfish."

She didn't look good at all.

"You'd better go make yourself puke, Tia. Now!" I waved the waiter over as she dashed to the bathroom. I tried to talk to the waiter, but he kept telling me *no* to the shellfish question. Clearly, she was having a reaction to the fucking food. Bonehead.

I burst into the bathroom, finding her sitting on the floor beside the toilet in a cold sweat and she looked like death warmed over. Fuck!

I pulled out my phone and called 9-1-1. They were too slow, so I called back from the Jeep and told them never mind. I'd carried her to it then sped down the highway to the hospital five minutes away, carrying her in myself, losing my shit until they rushed out and got her on a gurney. She'd still been conscious, but she was covered in hives and she told me her heart was racing.

By the time she was stuck with a needle, stable, and admitted in the little country hospital I'd found out the restaurant's miso soup's secret family ingredient was clams. The hostess had originally had no idea because it was a secret recipe, and the waiter was a fucking bonehead for not alerting the kitchen.

She was going to be fine. They'd given her epinephrine and wanted to watch her overnight. I spent the night in the chair in her room.

In the morning, I called her foster parents and told Cal Crenshaw we couldn't make brunch and I explained what had happened.

Two hours later they turned up in the waiting room, despite my telling them on the phone that she'd be fine and that they didn't need to come. I never should've told them what hospital we were at.

I wasn't pleased about it because I wasn't on the ball after barely sleeping. They approached me all judgmental-looking in the hall while I was on the phone with my brother, dealing with some business stuff and giving him an update, telling him to keep everyone there, that I'd bring Tia home the following day rather than come straight home. I wasn't ready to step back into my regular life quite yet.

"Mr. Ferrano? Cal Crenshaw. My wife Rose," the tall, fair, thin professor-looking guy greeted, then shook my hand quickly. His wife, a short Italian woman, held her hands together firmly in front of herself while shooting daggers at me with her eyes.

"Glad to meet you," I said. And then I almost lost my shit totally because coming up the corridor directly behind the Crenshaws was Gregory *fucking* O'Connor. I recognized him from the photo I'd been given. He was looking at me, looking like he wanted to shit his pants.

"We called Tia's father," Rose Crenshaw said, shooting more eye daggers at me.

Great.

Tia

Hoh, boy...did I ever feel like shit. Tommy was like a scary, psychotic madman trying to get me help when we got here. And he'd been here since last night doting on me, holding my hand while I slept, yelling at nurses to make sure I had more pillows, more blankets, etcetera. He was like the worst den mother I'd ever seen.

I was getting out of here today. The doctor told me I needed to carry an epi pen with me all the time. I'd always found it easy to keep my allergy under control because I never ate in fancy places where they didn't understand you when you asked them about their ingredients. Now things were obviously different.

Tommy told me we'd go back and relax for the day at the farm if I wanted, and then we'd go home tomorrow and pack for the trip to Vegas. The quiet of the loft sounded good to me, and then seeing the bright lights and Sin City would be fun. The only place I'd ever been was Florida that once, and the idea of travel really appealed to me.

My hospital room door opened, and in walked Rose and Cal. Shocked, I felt my heart constrict. Did Tommy know they were here? Where was he? Rose quickly hugged me and Cal stood behind her.

"How are you, Tia?" Cal asked as Rose dabbed her eyes with a tissue.

"I'm fine, don't worry. Good as new."

"I know you're fine from the allergic reaction but what about everything else?" she asked. Her eyes landed on my hand and widened at the sight of the engagement ring.

"Actually, I'm really good," I tried to reassure her. I had to oversell it so that they'd just back off. Plus I was pretty good, all things considered. "Things are working out after all."

She opened her mouth to speak, but I stopped her. "Seriously. I'm good. I think we're getting married in a few weeks and I'd like you to both be there." I smiled at her.

Her mouth dropped open and she looked at me like I was a puzzle to her.

I looked to Cal and as I said, "I hope you'll consider doing the favor of giving me away? If it's not too much to ask..." The door opened and Tommy walked in with his hands in his pockets. He didn't look surprised to see them. I let out the breath I'd been half-holding.

Cal looked back at Tommy and then to his wife. He looked a little perplexed. Rose was giving Tommy the evil eye.

"Maybe before then we could get a rain check on that lunch or brunch idea, so you can get to know Tommy?" I said quickly.

"I'd be honored to walk you down the aisle, Tia. Thank you but wouldn't you rather your own dad? He's –"

"You've been a dad to me. He's only biologically my father, Cal. You've been there for me, helping me with my homework, being stable and reliable..."

(Not selling me to the mafia...)

Lines crinkled around his eyes and he nodded. "Thank you. I'd be happy to." Then his gaze swept over to Tommy. I bet he was thinking that he'd rather me not be marrying at this age and not be marrying this guy.

I looked at Tommy patted the side of the bed that was opposite where everyone stood. Tommy rounded the bed and sat on the edge and put his hand on mine.

Rose and Cal both looked confused. Rose's face was red.

"You have another visitor, baby," Tommy said as he leaned over and kissed my temple.

"Who?"

"Your father," he said and my expression dropped.

"If you don't want to see him..." he started.

"I don't," I stated.

"Okay." Tommy rose and left the room.

Rose winced as she watched him leave. "He's intense."

She had no idea.

"Did you guys call my father?" I asked.

Rose turned her attention to me and nodded. "He came up with us. We wanted to talk to him about your... situation on the way here."

"And what did he say?"

"Very little," Cal said and lowered his voice. "First, he tried to brush things off when we described the visits from the police, what Susan had told us. Then he admitted that he'd gotten involved with some unsavory mafia types some years ago. They had demanded that you be handed over to marry the mobster's son to settle an old vendetta. He was cryptic, but said he hadn't given up on finding a way to get you out but was still working on it. We asked him to work together with us to help get you out of this safely and he told us he'd rather continue on his own, not involve us with the unsavory people he was talking to. Said that he'd already tried to barter, negotiate, but said this family was sort of above the law. We thought we'd come here and make sure you were okay and then see what this Tommy was like and go from here. We're very worried about you."

"You can't believe a word out of Greg's mouth," I said stiffly. "He lies. I don't know yet what happened with him and Tommy's father, but you don't have to worry about me. Tommy and I...we are fine."

"You have a lovesick look about you," Rose said, "And it's very different from the way you were at the store last week."

I smiled. "I'm fine. I'm happy. A lot has happened since then, Rose. My father is hiding something, I don't know what yet, but please don't work with him, don't trust him. You don't have to get me out of this. I am fine."

"You hardly know him. What sorts of illegal activities is he into?"

"I think it's probably not all that Hollywood hype, Rose." I rolled my eyes. Inside, I saw flashes of that cargo plane, that pink canopy bed in that dank basement in Mexico, and then the bullet holes on the bedroom door back at Tommy's house with the dead men in the hallway, and my blood ran icy cold.

A man in scrubs entered the room and brought me a tray of food. I thanked him and cautiously lifted the lid and then stuck my tongue out, "Eww."

"We should go," Cal looked at his wristwatch. "We will go have a word with your fiancé about getting together. In the meantime, we're just a phone call away if you need us, day or night, okay?" He leaned over and kissed my forehead. "No surf and turf for you!" He smiled.

I smiled. "Thank you so much for driving all the way up here."

He left the room. Rose leaned over and kissed my cheek. "I suspect you're not telling me everything but what can I do? You tell me to back off and I trust you. You're really okay?"

My heart flared with emotion. "I am," I said. "Tommy can't control who his father is any more than I can control who my father is. It doesn't mean that Tommy's a bad guy."

"But your father said—"

"Don't trust my father. He is a lying liar who lies out of his lying liar hole."

"And those people who visited us and tried to get us to stop talking to the police – and them stopping you from talking to me at the supermarket."

"Rose, I'm fine. A lot is going on. It's too much to explain right now. Please trust me."

"Why not move home? If he wants to see you, date you, go from there? My parents were so looking forward to having you."

Tommy walked in as she said this and he obviously heard her.

I shook my head. "I'm fine. Please tell Nono and Nona I'm so sorry. I will try to visit soon."

"I am happy to reimburse them the rent Tia would have paid until they find a suitable tenant," Tommy offered softly.

"That won't be necessary," Rose bit off without looking in his direction. She looked at me skeptically. "I've been keeping Ruby and the girls in the dark a little. Ruby is getting impatient. I'll have a talk with her."

"I'll call her as soon as I can."

"She won't understand and..."

I saw the alarm on Rose's face, but then as she glanced in Tommy's direction her stare hardened.

"I'm not going to tell her anything that will upset her."

She gave me a sharp look. "You're a good girl. Don't be a martyr, though. Okay? No one is above the law. If you need help, we will find a way to help you. And carry an epi-pen, okay?"

I nodded.

"Call in a few days?"

I nodded again. "Tommy has a business trip and I'm going with him. When we get back, I'll call."

She squeezed my hand and left, giving Tommy a dirty look as she passed him.

I hadn't sold them very well, I knew they were doubtful and worried, but I guessed it was enough. For now.

As she left, Tommy looked like he was trying to soften his hard expression. "What is that?" He looked down at my bowl.

"Cream of something soup. But of what, I don't know, and I highly doubt this is even cream." I lifted the spoon in the bowl and let some soup fall off the spoon and it was runny, gloopy, and filmy at the same time.

"Don't eat that slop. I'll get food for us on the way back. The doctor's releasing you. You can get dressed."

"My father?"

"Escorted him out. I need to make a call while you're getting dressed. I'll be back in ten."

I watched him leave. He looked super-pissed. Dread worked its way through me.

* * *

After directions and a filled prescription for the epi pen, I was on my way out the door with Tommy.

He clicked the button to unlock the door to his Jeep and we got in and he let out a big breath. "How are you feeling?"

"Fine," I told him, "Can you stop at the store?"

"Yeah, I was already planning to get something for us to eat. You want something in particular?" He pulled out of the hospital parking lot and onto the main road.

"Graham crackers and chocolate bars and marshmallows," I told him. "Since you got me poisoned, you at least owe me some s'mores."

He caressed my cheek and looked like he visibly relaxed.

"And worms," I added with a big smile. "For more fishing."

He rolled his eyes. "I've created a monster."

"So..." I said after a moment of silence.

His jaw tightened. "Your father said a few things about his history with my father. And he's got an ulterior motive giving me the information. I'll give my PI the info."

"And that information is..." I asked.

He shook his head. "No point bringing it up until I know if he's bullshitting or not."

He had a point. "Tommy, there's something I didn't tell you. You may know about this, but you may not."

He pulled over to the soft shoulder with a squeal of the brakes, startling me.

"What?" he spat.

I grabbed my chest and I must've blanched because his hardened expression softened, marginally, and he motioned with his hands for me to speak.

"When I sorted through my things in your basement, I found a photograph of my mother with your father from when they were like teenagers in one of my albums. They looked like they might've been together."

His expression was unreadable to me for a moment, then he said,

"Anything else?"

I shook my head.

"Why didn't you tell me this?"

"I didn't know what the connection was, what the truth was, and I... didn't trust you."

"No more secrets," he said and then he put the SUV into drive and merged back in with traffic.

"But you get to have secrets," I mumbled.

He didn't answer me. I didn't push it. I didn't feel strong enough to argue with him. He didn't say anything until we stopped at a grocery store.

He grabbed a shopping cart. "Whatever you want for later and tomorrow morning before we head back," he motioned to the empty cart and I nodded and he followed me up and down the aisles while I grabbed tea bags, instant coffee, sugar, milk, marshmallows, graham crackers, Hershey bars. Then I asked, "What'll we do for dinner? Microwave food?" I made a face.

"I have a grill in the barn. I'll bring it out," he mumbled, clearly still in a foul mood.

"What's with the farmhouse? Is there a usable kitchen?" I asked, thinking there may be appliances in it.

"Gutted," he answered and picked up a bag of charcoal, putting it in the space under the basket of the shopping cart.

"Steak? Chicken?" I asked him when we got to the meat section.

He shrugged, "Whatever."

I shook my head in frustration at these one-word answers I'd been getting, and tossed one of each in the cart and then stormed off to the vegetable section and left him behind.

When we got back to the Jeep and loaded the bags into the trunk I said, "Listen, you're obviously not in the mood for this so if you'd rather just go back to the city, why don't we just do that?"

He didn't answer me. He got into the driver's seat and turned the ignition. I got into the passenger seat and folded my arms across my chest. He leaned over and blazed a dirty look at me and fastened my seatbelt for me.

Tommy

I didn't want to be pissy with her. I was so relieved she was okay after that allergic reaction, and I felt like garbage because I let that happen to her. I brought her up here for safety and this shit happens. I wanted to pamper her, spoil her, make love to her non-stop for the next twenty-four hours before we had to go back to real life.

Everything was just getting on top of me right now. Seeing the Crenshaws and getting attitude from them, seeing O'Connor, and then talking to him and listening to the shit that came out of his mouth just pissed me off. I was tired and stiff from a long night trying to sleep in a chair. I wanted her away from all of them, all to myself. So, why couldn't I let everything go so I could just enjoy the next twenty-four hours with her?

When we got back to the farm, she put the groceries away, so I got some grass cut out back with the old manual push mower to make an area for the barbeque and campfire. I looked up at the second story doors and decided it might be a good idea to build a deck up there. Maybe we'd come back before summer was over and spend a few days so I could work on that. Because I'd started off at fourteen working for my father's construction company, I could build just about anything.

In a year or two maybe I'd start working on building a cradle. I couldn't believe where my mind was going, imagining having babies with her when we'd only been together not even a few weeks and when she'd only agreed to try with me not forty-eight hours ago.

I took my frustrations out with my axe as I chopped enough firewood for more than a few campfires.

Tia

I put all the groceries away and then made a marinade for the steak and another one for the chicken. Then I chopped potatoes, mushrooms and onions and put them in a tin foil packet along with some butter and spices. I also spiced and wrapped corn cobs in foil. I made the bed and tidied up and then watched him out at the back busying himself. His muscled skin glistened in the sunlight as he chopped wood wearing just his jeans and his motorcycle boots was quite a sight.

After a little while of watching him chop wood, lost in thought – thoughts about him, about my life, about my dad, about my future, about the muscles on his body flexing (who knew how sexy a guy chopping wood could be to watch?), I decided to take my container of worms and my pink fishing pole and head down there. As I passed him, I put a bottle of beer on the log beside him, he looked sweaty, dirty, and thirsty. He mumbled thanks to me, but kept chopping wood.

I sat down on a huge, flattened rock to fish from, but when I opened the lid of the worms and saw them squirm in dirt ...ugh. I couldn't imagine touching one let alone poking it with a hook, so I put the lid back on and just sat and stared out at the pond.

When I glanced in his direction, I thought he still looked pretty pissed off, broody, grouchy, and then I caught him stealing glances at me here and there, his expression softening. Finally, he stared at me as he drank from the bottle of beer and then he walked over and without saying anything to me he put the worm on my hook and passed the rod to me.

"Thank you," I said and then cast out.

He walked back to the now massive wood pile, grabbed the neck of the beer bottle, downed the rest while watching me, then resumed chopping until the sun started to set when he started fiddling with the barbeque, so I headed back to the loft and washed my hands, tossed the salad, set the table, and started grabbing the steaks and the vegetables to bring down.

"That needs to heat a little still," he said, "I'm grabbing a shower. Join me?" He pulled me against him and even though he was sweaty, he still gave me the tingles.

I squirmed against him, "You're all sweaty and manly." I guess his foul mood was over?

He let out a barbaric little growl against my throat, making me giggle, and then nibbled on my earlobe. We walked back up to the loft hand in hand and after I put the food back in the fridge, I turned to face him but he crouched, put a shoulder to my belly, and hauled me up over his shoulder.

"Rawr! This manly man want woman in shower!"

I giggled all the way there. Then when he put me down, my dress came right up over my head in a fluid motion. But there was hardness in his eyes, so my giggle faded to a hard gulp.

After shower time, which included some pretty spectacular getting-slammed-up-against-the-shower-wall sex, he promptly passed out cold on the bed, towel around his waist, still soaking wet, lying on his stomach. Evidently when Tommy Ferrano was pooped, shower sex put him over the edge.

In the shower, though, he'd looked me in the eyes while holding my face in his hands and said, "Any secrets I keep from you, baby, are so that you can sleep at night. You don't need to lie there like I do wishing you didn't know shit. Okay?"

I'd nodded.

I took a rest beside him for a bit but didn't fall asleep. He was snoring. After a while I decided to check on the barbecue. I added more charcoal and got it going again and got dinner cooked for us, using his flashlight to aid me.

When all was done and the table was all set, I woke him up by tugging his towel away. He hadn't moved at all and it'd been a few hours. His eyes stayed closed, but a smile spread across his face. Then I climbed onto his back and sat on his naked and very fantastic rear end and started massaging his shoulders and his arms. He had a hard, muscular body. It was gorgeous. I kissed his muscled back in between his shoulder blades,

"Dinner's ready," I murmured against his skin.

He twisted around onto his back and rubbed his eyes with the heels of his hands and then caught my face between his hands and pulled me close to kiss him.

"Somebody's awake," I mused, feeling his erection hardening underneath me.

He groaned and tried to gyrate, grabbing my hips.

"Dinner will get cold and I worked hard. Let's go, Mr. Sleepy." I ruffled his hair, scooted off him, and he smiled lazily at me.

Tommy

And she could cook. Fuck me. It was sweet that she'd done that while I slept, taking care of me like that, especially considering she'd spent last night in the hospital.

After dinner was finished, we cleaned up together, talking casually about things couples who were getting to know one another talked about: movies, music, video games. We didn't have the same taste in most of it (her taste in music generally sucked) but she seemed open-minded enough and promised to watch old Bruce Lee movies with me if I promised to watch some Notebook movie with her. I had a feeling it was a chick flick. She shook her head when I muttered that but didn't verbalize a *no*.

I built a campfire and once it was roaring, she proceeded to prepare and then demolish a bunch, maybe six, of her s'mores. I barely got one into me, trying to refuse it because I was stuffed from dinner, but relented and only because she insisted I eat "the best thing ever." Talk about toothache on a graham cracker!

She was drowsy, yawning and staring sleepily at the fire, so I scooped her up and carried her back up to bed with thoughts of making love to her again. She acted all shy when I lifted her up but then the yawns and the moans as she held her belly from all the chocolate, crackers, and marshmallow led to me simply tucking her in and holding her until she fell asleep against me, her head on my chest, her leg hooked around me, and her fingertips slowly scrubbing the stubble on my chin. When her hand dropped as she finally dropped off, I kissed the top of her head and pulled her tighter to me.

I lay awake half the night holding her and thinking that I didn't want to take her back to the house. I wanted to stay here with her, away from gunfire, seedy business dealings, and people who hated me enough to want to take out someone I loved. Being here, living a simple life where she cooked me dinner and I chopped wood and baited her hook... just us two... it had appeal.

Fuck the big house and the servants. Fuck the business. Fuck the truth. I just wanted to keep her here and forget everyone else existed. Keep her here and protect her, spend every minute making up for the shitty hand she got dealt when she ended up with O'Connor as a father and then wound up with me in her life.

Funny how I initially thought getting married was a means to getting more power, more autonomy, but now the idea of getting married got me thinking more about life with a wife than anything else, about the things and people I'd have to protect her from, about keeping my own demons at bay. I felt sick for a second when I imagined the fear I'd have one day when she carried my baby, the fear of someone taking her, hurting her, and my child.

A child. Shit. I also thought about the shit her father had told me, the shit Earl'd told me, and it all went round and round all fucking night long.

10

Tia

We woke up bright and early and Tommy grumpily told me that he hated tea, that it tasted like dishwater, that instant coffee was sacrilege, and that it was even worse that I was trying to offer either to him when it was to be made by microwaving water, that we needed to get a move-on quick because he needed real coffee 'like now'. So we packed up and off we went, deciding that the next time we came we would bring a coffee maker and a few other staples to leave up here.

* * *

The drive back to the city was quiet; he seemed broody, even after he got a coffee. As we strolled in through the front door of the house and he turned his phone on, it made a long succession of text and voicemail alert noises. He scowled at the phone and if it weren't an inanimate object it probably would've run and hid at that scary scowl.

He headed into the office without saying anything to me. A bodyguard I didn't recognize carried the few bags we had upstairs and I wandered into the kitchen for a glass of juice before heading upstairs. My heart tripped as I walked through the hall, remembering the dead bodies of a few days ago. Now it looked like nothing had happened. The guard smiled at me and gave a business-like nod as we passed one another in the hall. The carpeting was gone and instead there were gleaming hardwood floors. The bedroom doors were open. One of the doors looked the same but was bullet-free, so a replacement door that was just the same must've been put in. Our bags had been dropped on the sofa. I got down onto my knees and looked under the bed. Sure enough, there were two guns and a knife up there. I got back to my feet and walked out onto the deck off the bedroom and now the backyard had a glass-like fence that was at least 20 feet higher. You could still see the forest beyond the infinity pool but through glass. My heart sank at that. I wandered into the bathroom to run a bath, wondering where the bodies had gone. I'd never been asked to make a statement to the police about how we were interrupted in bed by gunfire. Clearly, the police hadn't been involved in the clean-up and there'd been no investigation. I sank into bubbles, trying to put it out of my mind.

Tommy

You'd think I'd been gone a month instead of two days with all the shit that had piled up. Holy fuck! I got two quick calls taken care of and decided to handle the rest later. I headed upstairs and heard the bath running so my clothes were quickly off and when I opened the door in the buff she looked up from the tub and gave me a sexy smile. I climbed into the tub with her, and we made what she called a "soapy, splashy mess".

While I was about to get dressed afterwards, my phone went off. I needed to meet with my private eye to discuss the additional information I'd found out from O'Connor as well as follow up on the Earl stuff. I asked Tia to give me the photo of her mom and my pop and she found it for me in the basement. I kissed her goodbye and told her not to wait up, but to talk to Sarah in the morning for help packing for us for Vegas.

I made her promise to be no more than two feet away from her phone at any given time, and then I had a quick chat with the four guys on the house, including my brother-in-law Jimmy who was gonna be my main house security guy, replacing Earl. Until I really knew all was good, I wasn't taking any chances. Maybe when we got back, I'd take her to the range and teach her how to shoot, too.

Tia

The rest of the evening was, thankfully, uneventful, except that Tommy didn't come home. He texted me at midnight to ask if I was okay. Then he texted me again at 3:30 am, waking me, to say he'd be home in the morning. It sort of nagged at me and I didn't sleep much after that.

I couldn't help my mind from wandering to wondering if he was seeing another woman. Was he out somewhere giving someone else the 'rough' so that he could give me the 'sweet'? I knew I'd have to swallow a lot being with him, but if infidelity was one of those things, I wouldn't be able to handle it. It'd revert to being a prison sentence for me and one I'd never stop trying to find my escape from.

At 7:30 in the morning, I got up because there was no point continuing to lie here and torment myself. Sarah was up so she and I packed. I would've done it myself if I had a clue of how to pack for him. She clearly knew what she was doing, what sorts of clothes we'd need, etc. She was being sweet and chatty and tried to broach the topic of my and Tommy's relationship.

"So, you two? Things better?"

I smiled and changed the subject. "Do I really need all these pairs of shoes for a short trip?"

She smirked. "You can talk to me. I'm like Fort Knox. You tell me somethin' and it won't go nowhere. I sat under interrogation for six hours once. I was in a hundred-degree room, and I had to pee. Still not a word."

I found that hard to believe since she never shut the heck up – like... ever. I didn't even want to ask her why she was interrogated for six hours.

Tommy strode into the bedroom and saved me from The Sarah Inquisition. He came right to me and folded me into an embrace. Sarah left the room and shut the door.

He ran his hands up and down my back and his nose traveled from the nape of my neck up to my temple, then he kissed it.

"Miss me?"

I stiffened.

He looked down at me. "Something wrong?"

I shrugged.

"Tia?" He had alarm in his voice.

"Where did you stay last night?" I asked. My face felt hot.

He frowned. "I didn't stay anywhere. I haven't slept yet."

I looked down at my feet. "Oh."

"Tia?"

He let go of me, then backed up and sat on the bed beside the opened suitcase and crossed his arms and stared.

"What time do we have to go?" I tried to change the subject. My face still felt hot.

"In half an hour. Look at me."

My eyes met his.

"Did you think I spent the night with someone else?" He had his eyebrows raised and he looked on the verge of pissed.

I shrugged my shoulders once, slowly.

"Athena."

I chewed the inside of my cheek and stared at the ceiling. Weird how in a few short weeks he felt like he could use my given name like this to show he was serious. But it worked.

"Answer me," he demanded and his voice wasn't friendly. I looked at him. His eyes weren't friendly either. He jerked his chin up at me.

"I just didn't know where you were."

"So you assumed I was off fucking someone?" His voice was calm but menacing.

"We never talked about fidelity, Tommy, and I dunno; you've been really nice to me the last few days and I know you need..." I stopped.

He gave me an incredulous look but was silent for a moment before asking, "We engaged?"

I nodded, chewing my cheek.

"We don't need to talk about fidelity. It's a given. I have no desire to be with anyone else. You won't be with anyone else. Got me?"

"Okay," I said and looked back down at the floor.

"Whatever it is I 'need' I can get from you. I *will* get it from you."

"Okay." A chill crawled up my spine.

"Baby?"

I looked at him and his expression had softened.

"It was three weeks between the day I first saw your picture and the day you came to me. I was with no one during that time. The minute I knew you were mine I wanted no one else."

My eyes must've been like saucers.

"I won't want anyone else."

"Okay."

"Ever."

I nodded.

"I told you if you played your cards right no cock but mine would be in you."

He got another nod.

"You played your cards right."

I gulped.

"It won't be in anyone else, either."

"Okay."

"C'mere."

I stepped closer to him and he pulled me onto his lap. He inhaled my hair and then kissed me on the neck, saying, "I'm yours. Okay?"

I smiled, "Kay."

"Is that what you want? For me to be only yours?" His voice was husky.

Goosebumps rose on my body and chills ran up my spine. "Yeah."

He gave me a squeeze. "Already done. I was working on something, working on figuring things out about our fathers. I had to do a bit of a stakeout."

"Any joy?

"Nope."

"You must be tired."

"I am. I'm running on empty, two nights with almost no sleep and zero sleep last night. I'll snooze on the flight."

He lay down onto the bed, taking me with him, and held me close. "It's kinda hot that you were jealous," he whispered into my ear.

That surprised me.

"Really?" I asked.

"Mm hm. Maybe more cute than hot, actually. But more than that, it gives me hope. Hope that you're really being open about this. If you didn't want me you wouldn't care."

I smiled. That was sweet. Then he added in a warning. "But now that I've put your mind at ease don't accuse me of that again."

Fear spiked. Why did he have to do that? Go from sweet to like that? I let out a little sigh.

"Hey?" He tipped my chin up and held my gaze. His face looked pissed.

"I understand," I told him quietly. Then he bolted up and hauled me over his knee. I shrieked in surprise.

"Maybe I need to spank you, so you'll remember."

Now his voice was very husky. He ran his palm down my back and onto my bottom. He squeezed. Then someone knocked on the door. He let me go and tapped my bum playfully and winked at me.

Phew.

He got up to answer it. James, Tessa's husband, was at the door. Tommy stepped into the hall and closed the door. I took a deep breath, smoothed out my clothes, and zipped up the suitcase and heaved it onto the floor.

About twenty minutes later he was back and got the suitcases. His whole demeanor seemed way off. He seemed intimidating, fierce. Was it lack of sleep, was he pissed at me, or had something else happened? I got my purse and my train case and followed him out.

When I stepped into the hall, James was still there. He took my case from me and signaled for me to head down the stairs ahead of him. I smiled at him and he returned the smile. We hadn't really been introduced but I thought it was odd that he was a member of the family by marriage but yet was carrying luggage to a car for me. I wondered if Luc's husband was a guard, too.

Tommy

I nodded off and on throughout the flight. I had a lot on my mind, and though I was exhausted, I couldn't get my brain to completely rest on a plane, when falling into a deep sleep could mean I wasn't able to react to something going wrong. I've flown a lot but always hated it. She got the window seat and was thrilled about looking out.

* * *

"Slot machines in an airport?"

"You ain't seen nothin' yet," I told her.

We stepped out into the hot Nevada sun and got into the limo the hotel had sent.

"The city comes alive when the sun goes down. Wait till tonight. I'll show you why they call it Sin City."

* * *

We settled into our hotel suite, which had an adjoining room with my two security guys, Jimmy and Nino. I could handle myself so with the exception of Mexico I didn't typically use personal security. These guys were here for her. I'd leave them with her when I did what I had to do.

Nino was the son of Pop's former right-hand man and he was married to my Pop's former partner's daughter who was like a cousin to me.

I'd filled him and his wife in on who Tia was and I'd filled him in on info I'd just discovered, telling me who her mother was to my family, so I figured he'd be extra vigilant about her. He was eager and had been trustworthy for the past six years he'd worked with us.

And Jimmy, though still working up the ranks, had proven to be a good guy. He'd been a good friend of Dare's all through school and was good to my sister. These two were the best I could do for the moment from a peace of mind perspective. I had to hope it'd be good enough.

It was like having my eyes off of her for more than a second wasn't good enough. I had to slow my anxiety. It could be I still wasn't over the whole Mexico thing. Or maybe it was my gut telling me something else wasn't right. I was sifting through information from Earl about Pop that I wasn't okay with, and there was all the shit Greg O'Connor had fed me, too, to contend with. That, coupled with anxiety about Tia's safety had me off kilter. What I probably needed more than anything was a solid eight hours of sleep.

11

Tia

Our suite was luxurious, with three bathrooms (a his, a hers, and another one), separate bedroom and dining slash sitting room, and we had a great view of the Bellagio fountains as well as the Vegas version of the Eiffel Tower.

Tommy left shortly after we arrived, telling me to stay in the room, to order room service if I wanted anything, and just relax for a few hours, but that he'd be back for dinner.

He had Nino and James staying in an attached room that was accessible from the sitting room, to be close in case I needed them. I was given strict orders to not answer the door, only to inform James or Nino if someone knocked on my door who they hadn't already noticed. Tommy handed me a wad of cash to put in my wallet and told me to simply sign for everything and give out 25% for tips for room service and for if I have someone from the spa come up to give me a massage or manicure.

So, the three of us stayed in our rooms while everyone else in Las Vegas had fun and while Tommy was off doing whatever he was doing.

At 10:00 James knocked, then poked his head in, and asked me if

I wanted some pizza. Evidently, they'd given up on having a break to have dinner, too. I accepted a few slices and watched a pay-per-view romantic comedy by myself. I gazed out the floor to ceiling windows and saw that it looked pretty awesome down below. The city looked alive and bustling with activity.

Eventually, I crawled into bed and turned the TV off hoping that tomorrow I'd get to see more of Vegas.

* * *

Tommy was gone until 3:07am. I'd been fast asleep in what might've been the most comfortable bed in the world when he came in. I spotted the time on the digital clock when woken up because he tripped and almost fell. He staggered a little, getting out of his clothes, and I could smell the alcohol coming off him from the bed. He'd been gone for about ten hours, never texted or called me, and was now staggering into bed, clearly drunk.

He got in beside me and his hand swept up my side from my hip to my ear and then his fingers were in my hair. He murmured something unintelligible against my ear, something about me being lucky, then something about the smell of my hair, and then he was softly snoring.

* * *

I woke up early in the morning, and when I lifted his clothes off the floor, I noticed red lipstick on his collar. My heart thundered in my chest. I lay them on the chair before slipping the 'do not disturb' sign on the door handle so that housekeeping wouldn't come in while he was still asleep.

At 11:00 I knocked on and then entered the adjoining room. The guys were dressed in suits but had their shoes off, both of them on their respective beds and watching a sports event on TV. I asked them what the plan was today and they'd both shrugged, telling me they were awaiting direction from Tommy and informing me the Do Not Disturb sign was useless; no one would be barging into the suite without their go-ahead.

James said he'd already ordered breakfast up to their room and asked if I wanted him to order for me. I told them I'd do it. Apparently, they had CCTV of the hall outside of our suite.

The room service didn't take long. As I pushed the cart into the sitting and dining area, I heard noise in the bedroom so peeked in and Tommy stirred in bed and opened his eyes.

"I ordered breakfast for us," I told him. "Not sure if you're hungry."

"Call down and ask them to send up some Tylenol, baby?"

"Already thought of that," I said stiffly and passed him a glass of orange juice and the bottle of pills. He looked strangely at me, took two and downed some juice and then got out of bed and headed to the bathroom.

I'd left his clothes purposely in a position near where I was now sitting, on the sofa that would make his lipstick-covered collar obvious, very obvious.

I poured coffee for both of us and when he came back out a few minutes later, he was showered and in a fresh pair of tight black boxer briefs. He reached onto the chair and fished his cell phone out of his pants pocket and was fiddling with it. I saw his eyes land on his dirty collar. He grabbed a bottle of orange juice from the minibar and downed it.

I stared at him over the rim of my cup, looking at his gorgeous body, his broad shoulders, sculpted chest, six pack, his muscular legs, and wondered if he'd let some other woman touch his body last night.

He glanced at me a few times while thumbing away on his phone and then said, "Got something to say?"

"Nope," I answered, making direct eye contact.

"I've got a meeting soon. I think I'll grab another hour of sleep first."

"Okie dokie." I had trouble hiding the snark from my reply.

He let out a sigh and pinched the bridge of his nose, "Nothing happened. A business associate had entertainment for a post-meeting party, but nothing happened. A chick tried to get frisky with me and I pushed her off. All right?"

I'd been chewing the inside of my cheek. "Alrighty. You were pretty smashed."

"Yeah, well I'd had about 5 hours of sleep in three days so the alcohol hit me hard. Nothing happened. Didn't we just go over this yesterday? Do you really think I'd promise to be faithful and then break that promise the very same day?"

I shook my head. "I didn't accuse you of anything."

"No, but your attitude says different. Believe me, if I wanted to fuck someone else, I'd just go ahead and fuck someone. I'd have no qualms telling you the score. Alrighty?"

Each 'fuck' was delivered with so much venom it churned like acid in my stomach.

I raised my hands defensively. Really nice. His eyes were bulging at me; he looked furious. And rough. I kept my mouth shut for a minute while he continued doing something on his phone.

"So, do I have to stay here all day waiting for you?" I finally asked.

His eyes narrowed. "Yeah. Yeah, you do."

Then he stormed into James and Nino's room, slamming the door. I sat and seethed. Some fun Vegas would be. I turned the television on and flopped on the sofa.

A while later the adjoining door was thrust open and Tommy came back in and when he caught my expression, which I imagine probably looked pissed off still, his lip curled and he slammed the door shut and locked it and then stalked in my direction and the look on his face and the way he walked had me suddenly holding my breath. He lifted me up by grabbing fists full of my bathrobe just below my shoulders.

Once we were almost nose to nose, my feet not touching the floor, he growled, "Lose the fucking attitude!"

My eyes must've been bulging out of my head. He let go of me and I landed on the floor right on my ass.

He stood there over me. I could hear him huffing. I was afraid to look up, so I buried my face in my hands and just stayed there on the floor.

A moment passed with me just sitting there and him just standing over me radiating anger.

Tommy

Damn it. She was on the floor looking so small and afraid. Her beautiful, silky hair all messed up and hiding her face, her hands over her eyes, and just this white pool of terrycloth fabric surrounding her. I felt like the biggest asshole in the world right now. I was the biggest asshole in the world. I kept fucking this up. Why did I keep fucking this up?

Her shoulders started to shake a little and I knew she was crying. I got down in front of her on my knees and reached for her. She flinched.

"I'm sorry, Tia." I pulled her to me.

She kept her arms around herself instead of putting them around me and I could hear that she was trying to mask crying. I sat down on the carpet and pulled her onto my lap and held her tight. "I'm a dick when I'm hung over. I'm sorry, baby."

She stopped shaking and wiped her eyes with the sleeves of her bathrobe. She looked up at me for a second and then looked away, pain on her face, her eyes red. I felt like I'd been punched in the gut. I tipped her chin up so she'd have no choice but to look at me and then I kissed her lips softly. "I have to go out for just a while today and then we'll go do something, okay?" I tucked a lock of hair behind her ear.

She shook her head, and her voice was timid, small. "I know you're here on business, not to entertain me. Maybe you should've left me back at your place." She still wasn't looking me in the eye.

"Our place. And no, I want you here." I let out a sigh and tucked her head under my chin and rocked her for a minute. Then I got up, taking her hand to lead her back to the sofa. I pulled her on top of me so that she was lying on me with her head on my chest. I wrapped my arms around her. She was so warm. My head was fucking pounding so hard.

"I need to close my eyes for a few minutes, Tia. Stay with me?"

She didn't answer but she didn't try to move away. I closed my eyes.

Tia

I could reach the remote on the coffee table, thankfully, and found something else to watch on TV once I heard his breathing even out. He had me on top of him and he was snoring. His arms were tight around me and I wasn't going anywhere without waking him, so I just made myself comfortable and watched TV with my head on his chest until he woke up a little over two hours later to the sound of his cell phone ringing.

So much for breakfast. I tried not to think about what'd happened. I didn't want to think about that temper and what it might mean for my life going forward. I didn't want to think about it, so I just let it feel good to be in his arms. I let him comfort me with his arms around me, which was beyond bizarre because those same arms had lifted me up by my bathrobe a little while ago and were attached to a man who was hollering right in my face. I closed my eyes and focused on the sound of his heartbeat while I let myself get caught up in The Wizard of Oz. I'd never get sick of this movie. Ever.

He didn't reach for the ringing phone, though. He ran his hands up and down under my robe, then gripping my rear end. Bile rose in my throat. Sex was the last thing on my mind right now. His phone started to ring again and at that same moment there was knocking on the adjoining door. We got to our feet. He grabbed his phone and I decided to go into the bathroom, get a shower, and get dressed.

I didn't know what was on the menu for plans today, so I wore a pair of dressy cream-colored walking shorts, a frilly tan peasant blouse, and sandals. I put make-up on.

I couldn't find my tweezers to clean up my eyebrows, which were looking a wee bit unruly, in my train case so I started to go through my purse, seeking the small make-up bag that Sarah had put together for me when we were in Mexico. I'd used it at the farm, too, and I knew there was a manicure kit in there with tweezers. I rifled through it until I found the kit and my eye caught something shimmery. It was Tommy's silver chain with the crucifix. I lifted it out and looked at it. Then I remembered Tommy said I could call to have the spa people come up. Maybe I'd do that today while he was out and get my eyebrows and girlie bits done.

He came into the Hers bathroom, just walked right in. He grabbed his toothbrush from my train case and then his eyes landed on the necklace in my hand. He made a face I couldn't quite read.

"Um, I could've been doing something embarrassing in here," I said.

He rolled his eyes at me, but he didn't answer as he squeezed toothpaste onto his brush and started on his teeth.

"Next time I guess I'll lock it," I mumbled.

His eyes narrowed and he spat toothpaste in the sink. "Don't ever try to fucking lock me out of anywhere."

This made me jolt back. Loaded silence filled the space as he looked at my reflection in the mirror, then he put the toothbrush back in his mouth and resumed. His eyes were on the chain in my hand.

"I, uh, Mexico," I said, motioning to the case it had been in.

He gave me a swift nod. "Put it on for me."

I fumbled and fastened it around his neck as he finished brushing his teeth. He was looking at me weirdly in the mirror. After it was finally fastened, I plugged in my curling iron and flicked it on and left the bathroom.

As he came out, I started, "Breakfast got cold. Should I –"

He shook his head, "I gotta run. Boys are next door if you need them. Stay here. I'll be a couple hours and then we'll go do something."

I nodded.

He took my face in both hands and caressed it, looking deeply into my eyes. I chewed my cheek.

"I'm sorry," he said.

I nodded, but wondered if he was referring to being sorry about earlier or just now. He was still being a dick.

He kissed me on the forehead and then on the lips. His lips lingered, looking for mine to respond, I guess. I tried, but probably failed at being convincing. He backed up and stared at me for a minute and then he shook his head slowly.

"Fuck, Tia. What are you doing to me?"

I frowned. How was his hangover and / or his temper tantrum my fault?

He pulled me against him and held me tight, almost too tight. Then he backed up, shook his head with dismay, grabbed his phone and then left through the adjoining room. I was relieved to be alone. When I woke up today, I had no desire to sit in this hotel room all day while it seemed like the whole city was having fun. But now? I hoped he stayed busy.

He'd been off, mood wise, with me frequently since we got back from the farm. He was broody, temperamental. Actually, it'd started at the hospital, I think. I hated it. I hated that I had to walk on eggshells. Was this going to be my life from now on?

* * *

He picked me up about two and a half hours later. His eyes were sparkling and he seemed like he was in a good mood.

"The rest of the day is ours," he told me and took me by the hand into the adjoining room where the two guys played cards with poker playing on the TV.

"Free time, boys. I'm going to show my girl Sin City. Just have your cells on. I'll have an errand for you in a few hours, so I'll text about it."

They both looked elated. I guess they were both itching for a real card game and some time out of their hotel room.

Tommy

When I picked her up, she was timid with me. I couldn't blame her for that after the way I'd been that morning, but right now I didn't want timid, I wanted to show her some fun and erase what'd happened that morning.

It'd been a few hours since we left the room. We got lunch at an outdoor café and then I asked her what she wanted to do. She wanted to walk the strip. So we let the Bentley that the hotel had given us go and we walked, and walked. I took her to a jewelry store and told her to pick out a new pair of earrings. She didn't want to. I insisted. She chose a simple pair of princess-cut diamond studs.

They looked beautiful on her. I suggested we look at wedding bands, too.

The jeweler suggested an eternity band that would complement her engagement ring nicely and she liked it, so I bought it and told Tia to pick something for me. She was really wary about it, so much so that it made me feel like she was having second thoughts. I guess I was probably doing this to make her forget about the way I'd acted this morning as well as to move forward with the wedding plans, too.

After a long time, she chose for me. She made a really nice choice, actually. It was a twisted gold and black band, the two colors woven together in a Celtic knot pattern. It made me think of her and I. Light and dark, wrapped around one another.

"I love it," I whispered in her ear. "It's perfect. It makes me think of us." She nuzzled into me and smiled shyly, her expression showing me that she and I had similar opinions about the design.

I arranged for the rings to be sent home, but Tia put the earrings on before we left the store. She was still quiet and a little timid, though, and it was getting to me. I needed to snap her out of it.

Tia

I guess he was trying to make up for that morning. I wasn't trying to not let him off the hook or anything, but I just felt... I don't know... sad. I didn't know if he was being honest about the lipstick on his collar and I didn't know what else was on his mind that'd made him so awful earlier. I didn't know how to fake it. And he told me he didn't want me to be fake when it was just him and I, anyways. But him buying me jewelry and acting the way he was acting felt fake to me. I wished we were back at the hay loft.

Tommy Ferrano was light and dark, like the colors in the wedding band I'd chosen for him. He thought the light and dark represented us but to me, it represented him. Woven together, the light and dark was who he was. I wondered if I'd be able to take the dark, though; I wanted the light to win out over it. But it looked like it'd be both I'd have to live with. Unless I found a way out. Did I still want a way out?

I needed a restroom. As we were walking through a mall-like area in between two hotels, I told him so and he said he did as well. Once we found bathrooms, he said he would meet me right outside the door afterwards.

But, he wasn't there when I got out. It felt strange to find myself totally alone and with no eyes on me, no security guards around. I had the urge to run, to disappear into the crowd. My heart pounded with adrenaline as I looked around myself.

If I did take off, what would happen? My father clearly hadn't been honest with me and so did that mean they wouldn't have killed him if I hadn't cooperated? I knew, for a fact, that they didn't hesitate to kill their enemies, so Dad probably would be in danger. But did he even deserve my consideration after selling me out when I had escaped from Tommy? I didn't know. But, where would I go?

No. I wasn't going to do it. I had to give him the benefit of the doubt. He'd promised to be faithful, he'd said he was sorry about this morning, and he was trying to make his miserable mood up to me. I'd been weighing the good and the bad and right now the scales were still tipping in his favor. And if he was starting to trust me to be alone, without security, maybe it meant that it'd evolve to where I'd have enough freedom that if I ever did need to run, I could do it then. I didn't want to run. I just wanted him to always be who he'd been in many of the moments when he'd been sweet to me. I could handle the hotness in the games we played, too, I liked the hotness, but this morning? Not hot at all.

I didn't know what was keeping him. It'd been at least ten or fifteen minutes. I pulled my phone out of my pocket and texted him with:

"Did you fall in? LOL"

Five more minutes. Ten more minutes. No reply to my text and no sign of Tommy.

A man went in and then came back out of the bathroom, an older grandfatherly-looking man.

"Excuse me?" I called out. "My I'm wondering if my fiancé is all right. He went in kind of a long time ago, and hasn't come out. He's quite tall, brown hair, wearing a green t-shirt and dark shorts."

"Bathroom's empty," the man said, shrugging.

I'm sure I must've looked shocked. "Thank you," I said. I leaned against the wall and dialed Tommy's phone number. It just rang.

I looked back at the text message. It was iMessage and it now said the earlier message had been read, just a moment before.

Where are you? I texted.

It was read immediately.

I waited to see the little dots showing me he was typing. It showed nothing after the read notification.

I looked around me. There were people everywhere. I sat there for another few minutes and finally, I felt like I had to do something. So I called him again. It rang and rang. Then I called Dario. His was the only other number in my contacts.

"Yeah?" he answered on the first ring.

"Dario, it's Tia."

"Hey-ya Tia Tyson!" he answered enthusiastically, and it sounded like he was smiling through the phone, which was weird because he'd gone from being the angry brother to this other person, still pretty intense, but now nice to me.

"Um, hi, uh... sorry to bug you but I don't know what to make of this."

"What's that?" He sounded like he was in a restaurant. There was a lot of background noise.

"Um, I can't find your brother. I went to the ladies' room, he went to the men's room, and I've been waiting outside the door for a long time, like almost half an hour. Someone told me the washroom is empty, he's not there. I don't know what to do."

"Where's security?"

"Tommy let them go have time to themselves."

"Shit," Dario said.

"Yeah," I agreed.

"Okay, someone said the washroom was empty?"

"Yep."

"Go in the washroom and check every stall, make sure he's not passed out or something," he told me. "Keep me on the line." Then I heard him shout in the background to someone, "Gimme your phone."

I walked into the mens' room and followed his directions. I pushed every door open and there was no one there. I could hear Dario's was voice muffled as he probably had his hand over his phone while, I imagined, calling Nino and James on someone else's phone.

"Tia, where are you?" he asked.

"The Mandalay, in the shopping part between hotels. The bathroom's definitely empty."

"Go to the concierge's desk in the Luxor and tell them you need security immediately and then put me on the phone with the concierge. Get out of that fucking bathroom in case someone's behind this. Now. Keep me on the phone as you make your way to the front. Tell me if anything looks suspicious. The guys'll be on their way."

What now? I couldn't wrap my head around this. Was this life, *my life,* going to entail one drama after another? Had Tommy been kidnapped or something? I prayed there was a logical explanation for this.

* * *

The fact that the concierge didn't even make a weird face when I told him I needed immediate security and then passed my phone to him was beyond wonky to me. I guess in Vegas they are accustomed to weird requests.

My phone got passed back to me and Dario said, "I've got people on it. Don't stress. I'm sending Jimmy to pick you up."

I thanked him. I was taken to an office and offered refreshments and then I sat there, fidgeting with the water bottle I'd been given, until Tommy walked in. Not Jimmy. Tommy. I was shocked and relieved to see him. I jumped up and threw my arms around him.

"Thank God. Are you okay? What happened?"

He gave me a little smile and a big squeeze, momentarily lifting me off my feet. "We'll talk after. Let's go."

Tommy

Flying colors. She'd passed again. The way she'd handled that was just about perfect. She could've hocked the engagement ring and the earrings to get out of here, get away from me. She had at least $250 in her bag, too, as I'd given her pocket money for tips. The jewelry would've given her enough money to get gone and possibly even stay gone if she was smart about it. She could also have handled things the wrong way, called the cops and reported me missing, and involved them or something stupid like that.

But she didn't. I saw her mind working from a security booth; I knew it'd crossed her mind to run. It was almost like I could see the thought bubbles above her head. I could see it in her body language as she chewed her lip, chewed her cheek, looked around herself, blew her hair out of her eyes like she was faced with a dilemma. But she did the right thing. The exact right thing. She called someone she knew I trusted and got advice.

There was only one problem. I needed her to misbehave. I needed her to misbehave so I had a reason to punish her. I was about to crack. Yeah, it was good to see she could handle an emergency, but why I probably really ran this test today was because I knew there would be fall out. I needed fall out.

When she'd put my necklace on me that morning it had floored me, made the reason for my mood swings and my needs so clear to me, and it hadn't even done much good to wear it. I was tired, yeah, hadn't had a lot of sleep in the past few nights, but I was craving confirmation and release. Confirmation that she was really mine and fear that she really wasn't. And sexual release. I was fucking exhausted but had all this unused bottled-up sexual energy.

Last night didn't help, either, when Ben Goldberg, the real estate developer I'd met with to talk about a new club here in Vegas, lined up some girls for us. I could've taken that redhead in the red leather dress wearing the bondage collar and grabbed the collar and fucked her up against the wall roughly. But I didn't want her. I'd stared at her, thinking about that collar on my Tia.

The desire I had to be ice cream shop guy for her was overshadowing things. It was fucking with my head. That, the sheer fucking exhaustion, and the million things going through my head... overload. So, I got loaded, feeling sorry for myself instead, which was something I didn't do. I needed a release, to get back to feeling in control again.

Our limo was out front waiting for us. She got in and I told the driver to just drive for a while, so we could figure out where we were going next. I closed the privacy glass.

"What happened to you?" She was wide-eyed and had her palm against her heart, like she was filled with relief, relief that I was okay.

I ignored the piercing sensation in my chest at that and I took a big breath. "I wanted to see what'd happen if something happened to me in a place like this without my security around. You handled it beautifully. If, God forbid, there's a next time don't stand around like a sitting duck for an hour, though."

Her mouth dropped open and I started to feel guilty. I shoved it back.

"If you haven't figured it out already, being with me means you have to think on your feet and think in a certain way. I thought I'd have to coach you on all of this stuff, so you'd know how to handle things, but it's like you were made for this life. Good job, baby girl."

Her fingertips shot up to her temples and she closed her eyes and took a deep breath, holding it in for a long time before exhaling. Her mouth was still wide open. I waited. She kept her eyes closed and massaged her temples and then her mouth shut, shut tight. I could see her working her jaw muscles by clenching her teeth.

"Tia?"

"Mm."

"You alright?" I leaned over and put my hand on her knee.

She recoiled right against the car door, as far away from me as she could get.

"I'll just give you a minute, shall I?" I suggested and snickered.

Her eyes were still closed but she was shaking her head slowly and I could see she was working up toward a royal fucking fit.

Tia

"How many more times are you gonna do this?" I finally asked, eyes closed. I had a throbbing tension headache coming on, a whopper of one.

"As many as I feel I need to," he said softly, his voice laced with warning. "As many as I think I need to put my mind at ease."

"Put your mind at ease about me not running away?"

"That, and about you being equipped to deal with emergencies. This was probably more about emergencies."

I guffawed.

"You got a problem with that?"

His tone of voice grated on my nerves. I should just open the car door and walk the fuck away from him.

"Was that roughing me up this morning part of the test? Piss me off by being a total prick and then leave me alone to see if I run away?" I finally opened my eyes and looked into his.

"That was just me," he said softly with a shrug. He looked so arrogant, so unapologetic.

And that was worse because that meant that on top of everything else, every frightened and helpless emotion he'd just put me through, that he really was an abusive asshole.

The car stopped at a red light and then I did what was probably the stupidest thing I've done since meeting him. I thrust the door open and I got out of the limo and stormed off between other waiting cars and then down the street in the opposite direction.

An instant after I did, I caught the view of someone running, from the corner of my eye. It was Nino. He'd gotten out of a small smart car behind our limo and he was on his phone, talking while he was following me. Figured. The whole thing was staged; I was probably never alone at all.

I shot Nino a dirty look over my shoulder and I kept right on walking. My pocket dinged. I kept walking, but faster, more determined. Then I was through a revolving door, Nino not ten feet behind me, and inside of a casino, I didn't know which one, and I was storming down the trippy-looking butt-ugly carpet and because I'd ignored it the first time, my pocket dinged again. I ignored it again. Suddenly, I felt fingers grip my arm at my bicep. My heart hit the bottom of my stomach.

"Read your text," Nino told me. He was not smiling.

I shrugged him off and thrust my hand in my pocket and pulled the phone out to read the text from Tommy.

Fine, cool off. Nino will keep you safe. Be back at the suite in half an hour. I'll be waiting.

I responded to his text without hesitating.

FUCK YOU!

The read receipt popped instantly, and I turned the phone off and then thrust the phone back in my pocket. My heart sank, but that sensation was below the surface of my anger, which was bigger than my fear or my common sense right now, so I resumed walking and Nino followed right along behind me. After a few minutes, I was beyond annoyed with him being right behind me. I needed to lose him. I just needed five damn minutes by myself, totally by myself.

I spotted a blonde woman in a skimpy outfit carrying a tray of drinks. I saw a drunk-looking middle-aged Asian guy approaching her, so I suddenly took off running past him, sort of bumped him, and he knocked her drinks all over the place. This happened like it was carefully rehearsed choreography, right in front of Nino and I was off...half walking and half running, hoping casino security wouldn't think I was suspicious and try to stop me.

I zig- zagged through rows of slot machines and then card tables and roulette wheels. I finally got the nerve to glance back and there was no sign of him.

I found my way out into the lobby of that hotel and left. I went to a café a few doors down and sat and drank an iced cappuccino and took my time about it. The longer I sat there, the angrier I got. How dare he! What the heck was his problem?

My angry rage fog cleared and made me ask myself a better question: what the heck was my problem? My heart sank as gravity sank in. Provoking him like that? I had no idea how pissed he'd be. But I was pretty pissed, too, and the way I was feeling I'd have no problem articulating that to him.

After over an hour in the café I hailed a cab out front. I asked the driver to take me to the hotel. I had no death wish desires so, no, I wasn't running away right now. I guess I was just teaching him a lesson. How dare he do that to me and then have the audacity to 'give' me half an hour to cool down!

I paid the cabbie and strolled up to the concierge's desk and told him I was with Tommy Ferrano, gave the suite number, and said that I'd forgotten my room key.

He punched some keys into his computer and told me he remembered me from the previous day and that he'd escort me up in a moment and asked me to just have a seat.

I had to stand my ground. If we were going to have a real relationship, one that was a two-way street, I had to have a voice he paid attention to. If he really wanted me for me, he'd understand that he couldn't keep doing things like this. And he'd have to learn to rein in his temper, too, because what'd happened this morning was totally unacceptable.

The concierge came over a moment later and told me he'd escort me to my suite. Once inside, I kicked off my shoes and then I poured a glass of wine from the bottle sitting in the ice bucket in the bedroom from the night before. The ice had melted, but it was still chilly. I sat on the bed and I waited, arms crossed. I was ready for a showdown with my fiancé.

I turned the phone on and saw there were 2 missed calls and two texts.

Tia! Turn around right now and meet Nino at the front desk.
Another one.
Are you seriously stupid enough to do this? I fucking hope not

Nothing since then. It'd been over an hour ago. I answered with a text.

Cool your jets. I'm in our room.

Immediately he read it and those three dots appeared, showing he was typing. I waited.

big fucking trouble baby

I wrote back:

You know what? Bring it on. I'm so fucking pissed at you. This relationship needs to be a 2-way street. You want to test me and play games with me over & over again? Treat me like crap & like a piece of property and then expect me to have zero reaction at you playing mind games? Wrong! If you want me to be the faithful and dutiful fiancée, I SUGGEST you start treating me with respect!!

My phone rang almost immediately after he read the message.
I answered it practically spitting, "What?"
"Be ready and waiting, baby girl. When I get there, I'm gonna paint your sweet little ass black and blue."
Click.

All my bravado drained out of me and I instantly felt like throwing up. I am such a stupid naïve little girl. I thought I was so tough, so determined to stand up for myself, but here I was now quaking, wondering what sort of rage I'd be faced with when he returned. His voice was so angry, so scary, that I wished I had an undo button for that conversation.

I paced, entertaining thoughts of taking off and escaping, but before I could form a coherent thought, I heard something outside so I looked out the peep hole and saw a hotel security guard standing directly outside the door. *Holy shit.*

I went back into the bedroom, into the Hers bathroom to splash water on my face, and about fifteen minutes later I heard the door open. My heart sped up, so I took a deep breath, trying to push my fear away. I steeled myself, narrowed my eyes, and crossed my arms.

There was a knock at the bedroom door, which was already halfway open. I walked over to the doorway and both James and Nino were standing there. They both looked absolutely pissed. The sight of the pair of them in my doorway was pretty damn intimidating-looking. I swallowed and hugged myself.

James spoke. "Tommy asked that you wait in the bedroom for him to get back. He's asked us to lock the door. Since this door doesn't lock from the outside, one of us'll be right outside the door on guard till he gets back. You need anything?"

"No," I croaked out.

Then without saying anything, one of them slammed the door shut in my face.

Shit. What have I done? Even the guards were mad at me.

Almost three hours later, I was still in this room and I'd worked myself into a frenzy of scared shitless. Every time I heard voices outside the door, my heart and stomach plummeted. So far it'd only been their voices.

When I finally heard his voice, I wanted to scamper and hide under the bed. Adrenalin coursed through my veins. It was getting dark and the Vegas lights were starting to twinkle on outside, bit by bit as I sat in the darkening room on the bed with no lights on. I'd had two glasses of wine into me, and I didn't know if when he finally came in if I'd resume my pissed-off stance or if I'd cower.

The door opened and clicked closed. He was standing in front of me. He flicked the lamp on beside me.

"You say bring it? Consider it brought."

I stared down at my lap like a fricking coward.

"Look at me," he demanded softly.

I looked up and he was taking his necklace off and putting it on the nightstand.

"Not so tough when you're not hiding behind your phone? I can't believe you took off like that."

"I was making a point," I mumbled petulantly and as the last word was coming out of my mouth, he had my chin in his grasp. His eyes were fiery mad and fricking scary.

"Then I guess I need to make my point now," he told me.

He let go of my face and sat on the edge of the bed beside me. "Over my knee," he said calmly, so calmly that for a second, I thought he was going to crack a smile. It was so preposterous that he couldn't possibly be serious. But, he didn't crack a smile. He was serious. And he had a belt in his hand.

I gawked at him, then at the belt, then at him again. He raised his eyebrows and pointed to his lap, tightening his lips.

I shook my head. "When we have a problem. We need to talk about it; we–"

He grabbed me and threw me across his lap before I could finish.

"We can talk later, Tia. Right now, I need to beat your ass." I could feel a rock-hard erection under me. His hand was flat across my lower back.

I tried to get up, but he suddenly had my hair. He made a ponytail with it at the nape of my neck.

"Tommy, please don't."

"No? Why?"

"We need to talk about our problems, we need–"

"Oh, talk? You mean not take off and run away, leaving the other person in the middle of the fucking street?"

I opened my mouth, but nothing came out.

He slapped my rear, not very hard, and with his hand, but then he reached under, undid my belt, button, and zipper, then yanked my shorts and underwear down just past my butt and having them around my thighs just felt so...so tawdry or something.

Another slap, still his hand but on my bare rump. Ouch, that hurt.

"Wrong answer," he said. Then his hand was on my butt. The coolness of it felt soothing after the two slaps. I held my breath.

"What should you have said?"

I frowned. Did he think I was going to apologize?

"You're out of your mind if you think I'm apologizing to you after what you did to me today," I told him.

Slap. The sting was incredibly painful.

"Hey!" I shouted and tried to struggle out of his hold. I couldn't believe this was still, at his core, who he was. After everything we'd been through, after all that he'd said.

It was like he read my mind just then. "Do you think that because I've been sweet to you that this part of me is gone?" He spoke low and menacingly. "Do you think because I'm in love with you that you can walk all over me? Do you fucking think you can tell me what I need to do for you to be faithful to me? Really? Fucking really?"

Whoa.

"I'm in control," he said low and dug his fingers into my rear end, hard enough I knew it would leave a bruise. "Me."

"Tommy," I whimpered.

"What?"

"Don't."

"You don't want this?"

"No. If you're so in love with me—"

Smack. This time the belt bit across my ass and I bit down on my lip hard and tried to pull away. He did it again. This wasn't a sexy game, this fucking hurt. And he had to know the difference. Tears stung in my eyes.

"You don't set the rules around what I will and will not do if I love you, do you hear me? If I'm in love with you? Unfuckingbelievable."

He took me by the arms and pushed me off his lap but onto the bed on my tummy and then I heard him undo his pants. Before I could move, he pushed into me in a quick thrust. I was not wet, I was not aroused, and it fucking hurt.

He had my hair. "Not wet for me? Oh baby, this is a problem. Don't you remember that I ordered you to get wet for me whenever I spanked you?" His hot breath was against my ear and under any other circumstance I probably would've thought it was sexy, it probably would've created some moisture down there. Not now.

"Another reason to punish you."

"Tommy," I whimpered.

"What?" he spat.

"Stop," I pleaded.

"How else will I teach you that running from me is absolutely never okay? Don't tell me to stop. I fuck you how and when I want to fuck you." His hand covered my mouth.

He pulled out and tried to go in again, slower, but I just winced, still bone dry. Then he pulled out and flipped me over onto my back and ripped my blouse open and then pinned my arms with one hand and covered my mouth with the other.

"I don't want to hear another fucking word out of your mouth," he spat.

I was shaking and it felt like we were back where we started. Me afraid, him being horrible, but worse, because I knew he didn't have to be like this but he was choosing to be.

I hated this. This wasn't a game; this was something else, something hideous. This was so hideous it was going to take me back to when I first met him and would erase the moments we'd had together that had made me go from feeling like my life was over to feeling like I could fall for him, fall hard.

In Mexico when he held me and washed me clean.

In the hayloft when we danced and he told me he was in love with me and played the song I'd dreamt of dancing with my future husband to.

In the hospital when he was so worried about me and showed me that he would look after me, when he slept all awkwardly in the chair holding my hand all night long.

On the floor in the bedroom the morning we were shot at, when he'd been a human shield to keep bullets from hitting me.

Something inside of me was shriveling up and it, whatever it was, was dying. He let go of my wrists and my mouth and then let out a big exasperated-sounding sigh. Then he leaned over me.

"Stop it," he said, looking me in the eye. His eyes were so cold. I was sobbing so hard I was starting to hyperventilate.

"Stop," he repeated, angrily.

I couldn't stop. I'd probably need to breathe into a paper bag before I could stop.

"Shut up!" His hand came down over my throat and he squeezed. I think I stopped breathing out of shock as much as him cutting my airflow off. Tears froze in their tracks on my face and my mouth and eyes were wide as I gasped and then he loosened his grip.

He stared at me. He stared at me with such an angry, hateful look. He still had my throat, but he'd loosened his grip. I swallowed and felt the lump in my throat touch his palm.

He got up and opened the door. I stayed where I was. I was just lying there with my shorts down around my knees, my ripped blouse, and my tear-stained face.

He was back with a glass of whisky. He stood there, his fly undone. He drank from it and then threw his t-shirt over his head and then dropped his shorts.

I closed my eyes and held my breath. He took my shorts and underwear the rest of the way off me. I just laid there.

"Sit up," he ordered.

I sat up. He pulled my ripped blouse off and undid my bra and then took that off. He did these things almost clinically.

"Up," he muttered and I stood up. He pulled the blanket back, and said, "In."

I lay down and he got in beside me then climbed on top of me.

"Open your legs," he said.

I shook my head. "Please, Tommy." Enough. Please enough.

"Now!" he snarled.

My legs obeyed but I was whimpering.

He leaned over me, took his cock and began gliding it up and down and up and down between my folds, against my clit. I just stared at the ceiling.

"Look at me," he demanded.

My eyes met his.

"You're mine," he told me.

I felt my eyebrows furrow. I tried to relax them. I didn't want to provoke him further.

"Never run from me again."

More rubbing, especially on my clit. I was trembling.

"I'm the one in control," he advised.

He leaned down and took a nipple into his mouth and sucked. Then he took his cock and repeated the process of stroking it up and down. After several strokes he rammed into me to the hilt. He did this not taking his eyes off mine.

"I own this pussy," he declared coldly. "It's mine."

I couldn't hide my disgust and tried to look away.

"Look at me," he demanded.

"Fuck you," I whimpered.

"Oh, it's back on, is it?" he asked and he looked sickeningly pleased.

He leaned down and tried to kiss me. He actually tried to kiss me! I reached up to push his face away but he caught my arm and then pinned both arms. He started to pound into me, fuck me and use me like I was a piece of meat. Then he abruptly kissed me hard, painfully, grunting out, "Try to slap my face again and I'll slap your face. In fact, I think I still owe you a black eye and a fat lip, don't I?"

My whole body went lax, I didn't try to fight. That threat was his winning move. He threatened to hit me while his cock was inside of me and at that I was just done, the fight drained out of me. I just stayed there, letting him push into me over and over until he leaned back over and started to kiss me, hungrily, roughly, his hand back around my throat.

I tried to float away in my mind. I saw the sky over the field back at his farm and imagined his beautiful face looking at me with love and I tried to feel that love. But I couldn't. I just wanted to float all the way away.

He finally came, but not inside me; he pulled out and came all over my stomach, marking me like I was his property. He reached over and wiped my stomach with something, I didn't see what. Then he went lax and breathless on top of me.

He stayed there for a second, breathing hard. I don't know if I even breathed or if I was just frozen in horror. Finally, he leaned, reached over me, and flicked the lamp back on and said, "Put it back on me." He had the silver necklace in his hand.

The necklace?

I usually fumbled with things like that. I don't know how I got it unclasped and re-clasped in the dim room in the state of mind I was in, but I did, first try, as he hovered over me watching me do it, looking at me stripped bare and vulnerable and at his mercy, his own expression stripped bare and telling me so much with his eyes. His eyes came into focus for me and they were on mine and suddenly pain-stricken, sorrowful. My throat and chest both started to burn.

After it was around his neck and my hands dropped back listlessly to the mattress, he looked at me, that pain and sorrow etched in his features intensifying. I just stared back at him, feeling empty, raw, feeling utterly broken. I bit back the emotion. He rolled off of me, reached down to the floor and grabbed the t-shirt he had on, and then he put it over my head. He took a wrist and motioned for me to get my arm into the arm hole. I did the second arm myself.

He lay back down on top of me, burying his face into my neck. "Fuck baby. I love you," he whispered into my ear and then ran his thumb over my bottom lip.

He stroked my hair, and we just stayed still while he did that with me pinned underneath him. I didn't make a sound, I didn't move a muscle. Eventually, he fell asleep right on top of me like that.

When his breathing evened out, my hand came up and covered my mouth. Realization of how dark and deep that rabbit hole actually was had just sunk in with his I love you. This was him, the rest of him.

This was what he meant when he said, "and you have to take all of me." I was in so much more trouble than I'd even imagined. I held back the tears, held back the sob that threatened to burst from deep in my gut out of my throat and just swallowed it.

Tommy

One of the many great things about Vegas is that it never sleeps and because of that you can get anything at any hour. I woke up at 2:40 am and I was starving. She was underneath me, still, and she was awake.

I leaned up onto my elbows and looked down at her and assessed her face for a few minutes. She was looking me right in the eyes; she was looking straight into my soul. But I couldn't read her.

"Hungry?" I asked. We'd skipped dinner.

She kept staring at me for a moment, blinking at me like she was stunned or something. Then she gave me a little bit of a nod.

"Let's go find some food," I said and kissed her on the mouth. I rolled off and got into my boxers, then headed to the closet for clothes. She got up, wrapped in a sheet and hurried into the bathroom.

I touched the crucifix that sat against my chest and then pulled it back and forth on the chain, deep in thought, waiting for her.

She came out a moment later with her hair tied in a ponytail. She'd put some makeup on but she looked rough. Her eyes were puffy from all the crying and her lips looked a bit swollen and bruised. I knew I'd kissed her hard. Her eyes landed briefly on my necklace and then she averted them quickly.

I watched her go to the closet and get out a pair of white jeans, a pink collared shirt, and a pair of ballerina type shoes and then she grabbed a bra and underwear and went back into the bathroom and got dressed. I headed to the other bathroom. I was done before she was. When she came out, she put her phone in her purse and then zipped it up and wore it diagonally across her body. She stood there, staring at the carpet, staring anywhere but at me.

I texted Jimmy to tell them that we were going out, but that we were good for the night and then I took her hand and we headed out in search of sustenance.

* * *

We found a deli where I ordered corned beef on rye with fries and a Coke.

She softly told the waitress "Same for me."

We'd walked in silence, and then ate in silence, people-watching out the window. I caught a glimpse of her throat and it was red from when I'd grabbed her. It would probably be bruised tomorrow. My gut twisted when I saw that. I looked away and as I did, I caught a young college-aged guy in a varsity jacket checking her out from across the restaurant. I glared at him, and he went red in the face before he looked the other way. She saw it happen. She looked back down at her food, which she'd barely touched.

Then on our way back, as we made our way past the Bellagio's fountains, I saw her stare at it in what looked like appreciation, so I stopped, and we stood there so she could watch.

She watched the fountains, and I watched her. Her eyes were sad. I felt my heart constrict.

Fuck, Tia. I'm sorry, baby. These words stayed in the middle of my throat.

I turned her to face me and caressed her face while I stared at her for a minute, trying to say things with my eyes that I couldn't find the words for.

She stared back, and the look on her face... it wasn't anger. It wasn't cold. It was as if she was devastated.

It fucking hurt. After a minute I pulled her in close for a kiss. Her lips parted and she let me kiss her, but she didn't really kiss me back. She winced. I think her lips were sore from earlier.

Anyone walking by would've thought we looked like a happy couple in love with the backdrop of the Bellagio water fountains. It'd make a winning postcard. Good thing we weren't standing there holding one another with thought bubbles dangling over our heads.

My thought bubble: I'm so sorry, baby. Sorry for what I am, for what I need to do to you. I went too far. I wish I could take it back.

Hers: I fucking hate you. I hope you die, you rotten to the core animal.

Tia

At the restaurant and walking to and from, he kept stealing glances at me.

I think he was looking to see if I hated him. He probably wanted to know if I'd stopped caring about him, if he'd killed that. He'd shown me many sides of him since we'd been thrown together and after seeing this side, after seeing him snap like that with me and then find it within himself to use me like that... he was probably trying to determine whether or not I could handle this.

The truth was that I didn't know. I didn't know what I felt. I knew I had to handle it from the perspective of being trapped with him right now, but what I didn't know was if I could handle it in the way that... would it break me?

In the moments when he was being horribly cruel, I thought my feelings had shriveled up and died. I would've guessed that now in the public I would take my chances by screaming bloody murder, hoping someone would rescue me.

But then with the reveal of the necklace being some sort of anchor for him, then the way he held me and said he loved me and fell asleep against me like he was completely exhausted, like he'd been through the ringer, just like after Mexico, it just hit, twisted a knife in me somewhere deep. I had fallen asleep, but just for a little while.

I think my brain made me sleep to protect me because I couldn't process it at the time. After I'd woken, most of me underneath him, unable to move without waking him, I just stayed still and tried processing it. I was still processing it. All of it.

That necklace had come off and on him. He'd been broody for the past few days and then there it was and he settled down. He took it off to be horrible to me when I'd pissed him off and then when I put it back on he told me he loved me and passed out like he'd exhausted himself.

It was on him at the beach after our first date when he'd been so passionate. It was on him in the basement when he wasn't upset after I'd gone downstairs before he woke up.

I'd seen him take it off a few times when he was about to be particularly horrible. He didn't want to wear it in Mexico when he went off to enact revenge against my kidnappers. He took it off when he wanted to punish me, twice from what I could remember.

What was it with that necklace and more importantly, how could I keep it on his neck? And how would I convince him that he needed therapy? He'd been really stressed out since the hospital. He'd hardly slept the past few days. That stress on his mind and his body…did it build up to this and then erupt like a volcano, spilling molten lava all over me?

Tommy

After I kissed her, I wouldn't say she responded, but she didn't pull away either, she looked at me like she was trying to de-code me.

Good luck with that, baby.

I pulled her tight against me and kissed her on the top of her head and we stood for a long time just watching the lightshow. I ran my hands up and down her back and her arms, just holding her close to me. I wanted her to relax against me, but she was stiff, holding her arms at her sides.

"Ready?" I finally asked after it was obvious she wasn't going to relax.

We walked back toward the hotel, hand in hand. Then two beat cops passed us on the sidewalk just before we hit the entrance. My gaze darted to her face. She glanced at the cops and then straight ahead, the way she'd glance at anyone we passed. I squeezed her hand real quick and then let out a long breath of relief. I wasn't sure if she noticed or not.

We got up to our suite in silence and then when we got into the bedroom she disappeared into the bathroom. I heard the shower turn on.

I debated whether or not to get in with her or go to the other bathroom, but finally decided I had no choice. I had to look after her. I had to make sure we were okay.

I walked into the bathroom, took off my clothes, climbed into the shower, and found her sitting on the tiles inside the shower stall, huddled in the corner, bawling her eyes out under the running water, her face buried in her knees.

She gasped when she saw me step in and then it was like transparent shutters came down and her expression went cold.

No. Fuck no! I had to fix this.

"Tia, come here," I said as gently as I could, despite the emotion twisting in my gut, and motioned for her to get up.

She did, but robotically. I took her face into my hands and I kissed her and pulled her tight to me.

She stood there, trembling, despite the fact that the shower was scalding hot.

"Put your arms around me, baby, please?" I pleaded with her.

She did, but it felt robotic, too. I soaped up my hands and started on her back, rubbing my hands up and down. I massaged her shoulders and then took a step back and started on her beautiful breasts, moving my soapy hands up and down and then massaging her throat while softly kissing her face.

She reached over and took the shampoo and squeezed some onto her palm and then started to rub it into her hair, squeezing her eyes shut tight and focusing on her shampooing as if I wasn't even touching her. I let go of her and started to scrub myself instead. She turned her back on me and got further under the stream. When she was rinsed off, she said, "Excuse me," not looking at me, and then she squeezed by me and left the shower. I leaned against the wall and contemplated what to do next.

I could hear her blow-drying her hair outside the shower stall.

I got cleaned up and tried to let the hot water wash something, I didn't know what, that was part of me, away. Yes, I'd wanted her pissed, I wanted her provoked so I could bring her to heel and satisfy my urges and work off my frustration, but it had gone off the rails. I never knew she'd run from me. The time between her taking off and her telling me she was back in the room put me over the edge. I knew she wasn't far, I had a GPS in her ring and had seen she wasn't far, but the fact that she'd pushed back that hard made me lose my shit like I'd never before lost it with a woman.

I never knew that it'd get me so filled with rage and that at the same time it'd light a fire in me that way. I knew, when I'd been berating her, spanking her, fucking her, that I was doing damage to her, to us, but I couldn't get a lock on it. I'd let it bubble over. I'd gone over the edge with her to a point that might've been the point of no return. That's why I guess I had her put the necklace on me, I needed her to know I was past it, that I could still be sweet, maybe even be the ice cream shop guy she dreamt of sometimes, not all the time, but sometimes.

I needed her to know I had that other side of me, but that I was done. For the time being, anyway. I didn't know what would happen now.

The look on her face, how distraught she was, it wasn't just about what I'd done, it was about who I was. It was about how crushed her hopes and dreams for our relationship now were. I'd fucked up huge, probably irreparably.

I found her in bed. She was wearing a white tank top and white underwear that looked like short shorts when I pulled the blankets back. Her back was turned to me.

I curled into her back, ignoring the sting of her tightening, and nuzzled in and kissed the back of her neck. Her hair was still a little bit damp and it smelled different, like the hotel shampoo. I wanted it to smell like vanilla, oats, and honey, like cookies, like it had the night I played guitar while we watched the sunset over the pond at my safe house when all felt right in the world. Everything right now felt wrong. I was wrong. So fucking wrong.

I whispered in her ear, "I'm so sorry, baby. I'll fix it."

She stiffened even further, so I knew she heard me, but she said nothing. I leaned over and turned her so that she faced me and her cheek was against my chest. I stroked her throat where I'd marked her and fell asleep with my nose buried in her hair.

* * *

In the morning I woke up fifteen minutes before my phone alarm went off and for a split second, I panicked that she wasn't beside me. But, then I saw her. For the first time, she wasn't draped over me. She was huddled into a ball on the bottom of the bed, no blankets on her, and she was asleep, but she was shivering. Pretty poignant to me that in her deep sleep she was that repelled by me that she wasn't even seeking warmth. If someone had just ripped my heart out of my chest, I doubt it'd hurt as much as seeing her like that. I had to figure out how to fucking fix this.

I climbed down to the bottom of the bed and curled into her back and wrapped my arms around her. She didn't nuzzle in to my warmth; she continued shivering. I reached in between her legs and started to circle her clit with my fingers. She stilled. She wasn't wet. She wasn't opening up for me like she usually did. If I had any decency, I'd leave her alone and let her recover from what I'd put her through. I had no decency. None.

I wasn't giving up until I made her shatter and willingly wrap her arms around me. I needed that right now. I needed it more than my next breath. I needed to know we were gonna survive this, that I hadn't lost her.

I kept going, but she wasn't giving me anything. She was trembling with fear now, instead of just the cold, and I knew she was awake and afraid. I decided to pull out the moves and kissed her from her shoulder all the way down to her hip. I turned her onto her back and pulled down her panties and started lapping at and prodding her clit with my tongue. Her eyes were squeezed shut tight and her bottom lip was sucked in, a deep V between her eyes.

After a long time and a fuck of a lot of effort, it didn't seem like it'd get me anywhere. I worked two fingers in and finger-fucked her hard and fast while working her clit with alternating between sucking and tongue action and fuck me but I felt elation when I finally tasted some of her moisture. Her breathing went shallow and then she let out a little moan and then a little gasp. About fucking time.

Then she was clawing at my arms and pulling on my hair and then she tried to pull away and I knew she didn't really want away. She was only reacting to the intensity of it. Then she squirted. The way she jumped, almost five feet in the air, and said, "The fuck?" made me laugh.

I tackled her to the bed and kissed her all over her face, a succession of powerful smooches all over her gorgeous face. I expected she'd be all loose and covered in an awesome sex glow, but instead she was crimson and shaking her head and her hand was over her mouth. Tears filled her eyes but, didn't spill over. They looked so green. So shiny. So fucking sad.

"You squirted," I told her matter-of-factly, looking down at my wet chest. She looked at me like I was speaking Greek. "Women can ejaculate, too, you know," I added.

She shook her head. She had no idea what I was talking about.

"Baby, it takes a very skilled lover to pull that off. Many try and fail. Many women never get to experience it. Congratulations."

My cockiness did nothing to help my cause. She hid her face, mortified. I got up and grabbed her wrist and tugged to get her to follow me to the shower. She wouldn't look me in the eyes. I knew that other than getting to watch her come apart sexually, that my efforts hadn't given me a damn thing.

Tia

When I'd woken up at the wrong end of the bed with him all over me, I wanted to die. I'd climbed down there when I couldn't get to sleep in his arms. I needed space. I had contemplated sleeping on the sofa but suspected he'd be pissed and be more than happy to dole out another punishment if I dared sleep somewhere else. After he washed and shampooed me, trying to be all sweet and attentive again in the shower, he got washed and shampooed and then he left me in there. I stayed in there for a very long time, until I was pruny. When I finally got out he was gone. He wasn't in the sitting room or the bathrooms either. I checked the stupid iPhone and there was a text from him.

. . .

Baby, gone to a meeting. See you in a few hours. Order breakfast. Go down to the spa too (take Nino & Jimmy) and I'll text you in a bit with the name of who to see at a boutique for you to pick a dress, shoes, and whatever for tonight. We have a dinner and show thing with my associates. I left a credit card for you. Pin 5683. Get whatever you want! Text me when you get this. Xo.

I replied.

Ok.

I knocked on the adjoining room's door. Nino opened it. He eyed me warily. I was surprised neither of them was stationed in here with me after yesterday.

"I'm about to order room service. Do you two want anything?"

"No," he grunted.

"I'm sorry," I said, looking him in the eye. "I'm sure I put you in a bad position yesterday and I'm sorry about that. I let my, uh, emotions get the better of me. I hope you didn't catch too much slack."

His mouth turned up into a smile. "It's okay, doll. And no, we're good." He winked.

I think I garnered some respect by speaking up and apologizing. Then I saw his eyes land on my throat.

"You all right?" His expression darkened.

I nodded and pulled my robe tighter. "I'll be booking a spa appointment and–" I heard my phone ding, "some visit to a dress shop or something. I'll let you know about that?"

"I've already got the details. Get breakfast. Then let us know when you're ready to go."

I nodded.

It was already 11:45 and I wasn't surprised since I saw the sun rise before I finally fell asleep. I looked at the phone.

Tommy had messaged with a boutique name and address and the name Suzette and wrote that I should call down to the hotel spa, that they had an appointment for me.

I replied with:

Thanks.

He replied back with three x's.

I headed to the bathroom to examine my throat. It had a purply and fairly distinct handprint on it. There would be no hiding that I'd been choked. Nino hadn't looked pleased when he saw it. But what would he do about it, right? Nothing, likely, except pity the boss's poor stupid girlfriend who'd gotten herself in trouble.

I ate some oatmeal and fruit while watching the news on TV and tried to get my mind straight. I pondered things, wondering if I'd kept his dominance cravings at bay after Mexico with the games we'd played at the farm. In the past few days since then there hadn't been any games but there had been stress. Oodles of stress.

He'd warned me after Mexico that he might take his frustrations out on me in the bedroom. I had no idea what that meant at that time. Did he need me to be stress relief? Maybe if I played the kinds of sex games with him that we'd played at the farm that'd help. That'd give him the thrill of the chase and so forth. Maybe if I made sure I did that, it'd be enough and he'd keep the necklace on. And maybe if he didn't have the necklace on, I'd know to be extra careful.

I'd do my best to make him not want to take it off and if it was off, I'd make sure not to provoke him.

Right now, I wasn't thinking like a girl happy to be with her fiancé on a trip; I was thinking like someone who had to find a way to survive. I resisted the urge to crawl back into bed and cry some more over the lost love of my life that I now knew was just a mirage and decided that I just needed to get through the rest of this trip and when we got back I'd try to figure out what to do next.

But when we got back home, he wanted me to start planning our wedding. At that thought, it felt like ice pierced my veins. I looked down at the engagement ring on my finger. It was beautiful alright, and right now it felt like it weighed a thousand pounds.

* * *

By 7:00 I was ready for him, as ready as I could possibly be to go on a date and pretend that I was okay with it.

I was in a knee-length sleeveless and fitted short-sleeved gold dress with a high lace neck. I had stammered to the dress shop lady about wanting something with a turtleneck and she laughed asking how I could think of wearing such a thing in the desert in June, but then I pulled my hair back and showed her my throat and she didn't even flinch, just strolled over to the rack that had this beautiful dress.

I kept on my new diamond earrings and wore a pair of gold strappy heels that had been paired with the dress. Thanks to the spa I had freshly done fingernails and toenails with perfectly shaped brows and I was ready to go. I'd foregone the bikini wax today. My girlie parts had seen enough action in the last twenty-four hours, thank you very much. My trip to the dress shop in a cab with my two bodyguards had been uneventful, but they seemed to be very alert, probably figuring their balls were on the line if I managed to give them the slip.

When I got back to the suite, I was surprised when he came out of the *His* bathroom ready, dressed, looking dapper, in a tuxedo.

Dapper wasn't an adequate word, actually. He looked like a movie star heading to the red carpet. He was freshly shaven, his hair had been trimmed just a touch, and when he opened the bedroom door he smiled and his whiskey-colored eyes twinkled.

"You're gorgeous," he breathed, opening his arms. "Come here, please."

I went into his arms and said, "Not so bad yourself" but I couldn't look him in the face.

He inhaled my hair. "Orange blossoms?" he asked.

I shrugged. "I guess?"

"Nice, but I love what your hair smells like best at home," he whispered.

"When are we going back?" I asked in a returned whisper.

"Tomorrow," he answered and passed me the little gold clutch purse that I'd packed with the iPhone, a lipstick, a handkerchief, and the remaining cash from the wad of tip money he'd given me. I noticed this morning that he'd topped it up.

"Ready?" he asked.

"You were going to, ah, brief me?"

"Ah." He sat on the sofa and patted his knee. I leaned to sit beside him instead, but he caught me by the waist and pulled me onto his lap. Figures; control freak. I sat and stared at my hands in my lap.

"Ben Goldberg is a real estate developer who looks like a CPA but throw in a heavy dose of kink. He's getting in with some grey area and wise guy types to finance a project. He's a little out of his element, so he's trying too hard, trying to show everyone a real good time, hence the hookers the other night. Earlier he met with me, an associate and friend of mine John Lewis, and a local Vegas guy, Leo Denarda, who's a real sleaze ball. Leo has similar interests to Juan Carlos Castillo, suspected pedophile. The only reason no one has taken him out is because a) no concrete proof yet and b) he's very well connected in these parts. The reason I tell you this is so you know he's not a friend, be polite, of course, but know he's not a friend. We'll be doing a dinner and a show thing with them and a few other couples. A little bit of business will be discussed, but very little. The project is to take a legal brothel just outside of town, and expand. He wants to make it into an adult theme park and fetish club and we've all gotten the pitch and seen the financials and business plan. Tonight's his last kick at the can through schmoozing all the potential investors with their wives or girlfriends. He's doing this dinner and then we're all going to a show and then we've been invited to his club to check out a show. I suspect you and I will be done after the show, the Blue Man Group."

"Okay," I said softly.

"I'm here representing the Ferrano family and this is an area my father wants explored. It's probably the last major project he's delegating to me before retirement. I won't bore you with any other details and in general you don't need details as I do not plan to bring you into the fold with business but for this, appearances are important and I wanted you to know the backstory so you're not unprepared. Okay?"

I nodded, absorbing all he was talking about. Brothels? Pedophiles? Real nice. And what he'd said about Juan Carlos? That pink basement prison bedroom? Tommy's comments told me what I'd refused to acknowledge while I was down there. I cringed. I wanted to cry imagining a child being locked in that bedroom with those cameras and that vile man.

"I know what you're thinkin'. Ben tried that the other night, brought escorts in for all the potential investors. I told you I didn't partake and I was honest. Tonight, it's wives and girlfriends. The only way it's anything less than wholesome is if we opt to go to the club and the after party. I don't think we're doing the club and we're definitely not touching that after party. Okay?"

"Kay." I hadn't been thinking what he'd thought I'd been thinking but I already wanted this evening over and done with.

"Tia?"

"Hm?" I didn't look him in the eyes. I just...I couldn't.

"I know things aren't ideal with you and me after last night. I'll work on that and believe me, baby, it's a priority. I know I fucked up. I fucked up huge. But we need to put it aside tonight. We're an engaged couple getting married in a few weeks, happily engaged. That needs to be the tone this evening. Got me?"

I rolled my eyes and then my filter obviously malfunctioned as I said, "Yeah, gotcha. Don't worry, damn fine actress over here, remember?"

He chewed the inside of his cheek and murmured, "Baby."

He said it like I'd wounded him. He looked at me for a minute with pain in his eyes. I tried to soften my features so I wasn't frowning or grimacing at him, so I wouldn't provoke him. He reached up toward my face and I flinched. Pain on his face intensified with my flinch.

His hand landed softly on my cheek in a caress. He let out a slow breath. "Fuck, baby, you're killin' me here." And then his hands were on my hips as he eased me off his lap and then took my hand and headed toward the door.

I don't know what he expected. Did he expect me to act like nothing had happened last night? He certainly wasn't acting like nothing had happened. He'd been giving me long stares, seemed like he was thinking about things he said before he said them, had been sort of acting like he was treading in uncharted territory with me.

We were both lost.

I didn't know how to behave tonight. I wasn't feeling like myself and this was uncharted territory. I guessed I'd just try to blend in and observe and if he was sweet to me in public, I guess I'd try to behave like I was receptive.

* * *

We took a limo a short ride to a restaurant, riding in silence, and we were met by five other couples. I held his arm and was introduced to all of them including Ben and his wife Olive, they were probably late 30s or early 40s. They both looked like accountants and I found it confounding that they were looking for help from 'wise guys' to fund a brothel expansion into a sex fetish club.

Leo Denarda was probably in his early 30s (wearing a cheap-looking ill-fitting suit and too much jewelry) and his date, Heather, most definitely looked like a hooker. She probably was one.

I was glad Tommy had me see Suzette today as she'd professionally styled me. If I'd gotten ready myself maybe I'd have been mistaken for an escort. Among the other couples were a good-looking couple just a little older than Tommy and the others were anywhere from a bit older to quite a bit older.

The dinner consisted of pretentious food and plenty of small talk among the women at the table and talk of politics, current events, and sports among the men. Tommy seemed knowledgeable in all of those areas and it was interesting to see him in this element, a business type of thing. I could see that it'd be very possible for him to be a traditional businessman as men he met with could definitely see him that way. This was in stark contrast to Leo Denarda, who was pretty clearly a thug in a not-so-nice suit, but by the way the guy handled himself I didn't think even Armani would make an iota of a difference.

After the meal, we were all taken together in a stretch SUV limo to see Blue Man Group. We had great seats and the show was unique. Comedic elements, great music. I'd seen them on late night talk shows before and wasn't sure what to make of them, but I enjoyed the show a lot. My mind was never too far from my troubles, but I think I was handling myself okay outwardly.

When it was all over, Tommy was about to hail us a cab but Ben and another of the men, a good-looking guy in probably his early to mid-30s, John, I couldn't recall if his wife's name was Kathy or maybe Katie, I think, but her husband John just kept referring to her as Cupcake so I was thinking of her as Katie Cupcake.

They reminded me a little of Posh Spice and David Beckham. She showed me pictures of their cute kids, six of them, toddlers to tweens, and did a lot of fashion name-dropping in conversation. John nudged him and tried to talk him into attending the club.

As John spoke to him, Tommy looked at me quizzically for a beat and then changed his mind and the next thing I knew we were back in the SUV limo and headed with them: Ben and Olive, John and his wife Katie Cupcake (or whatever), and Leo and Heather. The other couples that had been at dinner and the show had made their way back to their hotels or homes.

I was a little queasy at the idea of attending a strip joint and was very surprised that Katie Cupcake wasn't being ushered back to her hotel instead of being here with us, but I tried to not let my anxiety show. Tommy was rubbing his thumb across my knuckle rhythmically, maybe reassuringly.

In the limo, the energy started to shift and suddenly Katie Cupcake took her wavy blonde hair down from her updo and licked her lips and then leaned into John and whispered something that was obviously very seductive. A look passed between them that made me feel like a voyeur. It was actually arousing to see them look at one another that way. Tommy leaned into me and whispered into my ear, "You good?"

I nodded.

He let go of my hand, kissed my earlobe, put his arm around me, and then his fingertips skated down my shoulder.

I noticed Olive's eyes on us. I smiled at her and trained my eyes on the window, watching the lights of Sin City pass by.

The club was dim with strobe lights and had a lot of thrumming bass that I felt in my chest. It looked pretty standard as far as I knew from what I knew about strip joints, which was limited to what I'd seen on TV and in the movies, but it was smoky and packed. We were ushered by a giant of a doorman dressed in a suit through the crowd, past the stage that was littered with poles and cages that all had scantily dressed females on, in, or attached, and down a back hallway and into a theater-like small arena with a stage that had a big screen on the back and heavy black curtains on either side.

Tables filled the floor via several levels pointed at the stage area. The theater was full, except for several small tables, in the center floor area that had been saved with small, 'reserved' tabletop signs. Tommy and me, John and Katie Cupcake sat at one table. Olive and Ben sat with Leo and Heather at the adjacent table.

Drinks were brought. Katie Cupcake and I were drinking cosmos, Olive had a Chardonnay, and the guys plus Heather ordered beers. Tommy and John were discussing something about construction, I didn't really pay attention, they seemed like good friends, very comfortable with one another. I was feeling very uncomfortable about being there. Then again, I'd been feeling uncomfortable in my own skin since we've been in Vegas.

The lights went down and then a beautiful sparkle-covered long-haired redheaded woman dressed in a top hat and glittery bodysuit tuxedo, announced it was the end of an intermission. Then there was a couple on the stage dancing this awesomely choreographed number that was a tribute to Dirty Dancing, the big number "Time of my Life." But then things got odd, because it became glaringly obvious that she, the *Baby* in the act was actually a she-male and the Patrick Swayze stand-in went down onto his knees and pulled a penis out from under the dress and gave a blowjob. The Patrick Swayze got his pants undone and had no penis and 'she' was finger fucking him. So, the Patrick Swayze/ Johnny Castle character had a vagina and the Baby character had a penis., but also with real boobs.

I looked to Tommy, wide-eyed, and he gave me a little shrug with a half a smirk. I couldn't see the reactions of John or his Katie Cupcake because they were sort of sitting closer to the stage and had turned so we saw their backs, mostly.

I glanced over to the next table to see Leo Denarda was grimacing at Ben. Olive was amused. Leo's date was watching with rapt attention, chewing gum with her mouth open. The audience evidently approved judging by show of their applause.

The next act consisted of two nude women doing acrobatics from long ribbons that came down from the ceiling. It was beautiful and artistic and dirty. *Way* dirty. Their boobs defied gravity, were so obviously fake. I spotted Mrs. Katie Cupcake reach and grab her husband's bulge and then she leaned in and whispered something into his ear. Oh. Okay, then... Mrs. Katie Cupcake *Soccer Mom* was clearly pretty kinky.

And I was feeling a little bit tipsy. I'd had a few glasses of wine with dinner, wine in the limo, and now had almost a whole Cosmo into me. I was about to break the seal and needed the restroom. As the curtain opened and an upbeat song I didn't recognize started, I leaned over and whispered to Tommy that I needed the ladies' room.

Katie Cupcake heard me and piped up with, "Me too!" and she linked arms with me and led me away before Tommy could do more than purse his lips.

"Your fiancé is so tall, dark, and hunky, Tia. I've met him several times. I bet he's a handful in the bedroom," Katie Cupcake said to me while washing her hands.

She was definitely tipsy, or more than tipsy.

I smirked. "Oh you have no idea..." I almost flashed my throat at her, but changed my mind, logic winning out over my own slight tipsiness.

"I'd like to." She fluffed up her hair while looking in the mirror and then puckered her lips and put lip gloss on. "You two into group play?" Her eyes darted in my direction.

"Uh, no," I said flatly, my eyes wide as I tried to de-clump some of my eyelashes with my fingernail.

She shrugged, reached into her purse, and pulled out a little marijuana box-shaped pipe.

"Pity. My Johnny doesn't mind sharing as long as he can watch. I feel the same. If you change your mind, I bet Olive would be interested, too. She's had her eye on you all night." Katie Cupcake took a haul off the pipe and then motioned to offer it to me and I waved my hand. I didn't need to be high right now. I was having enough trouble holding my alcohol.

I winced at the swap / group sex bit. Olive wasn't unattractive, if you liked the curvy pin-up shaped accountant type, which many would, but I wasn't in the least bit bi-curious. What was with this group? Clearly Ben put it together well. Tommy was into kink, too; he'd introduced me to it. Were his dark sexual tendencies common knowledge?

* * *

We walked back to the table amid heavy bass that thumped in my chest, it seemed, and there were fresh drinks there for me and Katie Cupcake. The curtain closed on whatever act was ending, and a moment later rose again.

I recognized the beginning of the song Wicked Game. I knew the Chris Isaak version, but this was arranged a bit differently. This guitar-playing singer sat in the corner in the dark on a stool while he sang and played his acoustic guitar. This acoustic arrangement seemed much more powerful than the version I knew, the singer so very soulful.

A second set of curtains opened and revealed a spotlight-drenched four poster bed that was artfully unmade. A screen behind it played images of a bi-racial couple in a collage that flashed through a slideshow of their life together, living a happy-looking life, walking a Border Collie, eating dinner together, staring into one another's eyes, and another, snuggled with a bowl of popcorn.

Then another light shone down on the couple themselves. He was a tall and muscular attractive bald Black man with a chin strap beard. He stood on the stage in just a black G-string and towered over her, a petite woman with a blonde pixie haircut dressed in leather pants and a black corset with platform boots. She was the woman in the images, but she looked almost nothing like her. She looked like she'd transformed from kindergarten teacher to Dominatrix.

He had a long braided black leather whip in his hand. I felt sick for a second and then confusion set in as he handed it to her and got down to his knees and bowed into a stretchy yoga-looking pose, his gaze directed at the floor.

She circled him and then lifted his chin with the toe of her boot. He looked up at her lovingly. Then she lifted her chin toward the bed and he climbed on and laid flat on his stomach, spread eagled. She cuffed him to all four posts with handcuffs that were already attached and then proceeded to sweep the whip up and down his body gently. The screen went from pictures of them licking ice cream cones, feeding baby ducks at a pond, riding on a Ferris wheel smiling together, and then zoomed in to a live stream of his face and he was still looking at her lovingly.

Then she pulled the whip back and lashed out, whipping him. I jolted at the sound of the first crack of the whip. And my insides tingled with awareness at the visual. His face was suffused pain. At the sound of the second whip crack, I started to tremble.

But as the soulful-sounding song played on and lamented about love and dreams and feelings and wickedness, his face read like he was lost in it, and enjoying it. Her eyes continued to focus on his face and behind the hardness and Domme persona the love on her face was unmistakable.

My heart was crumbling, watching the scene and listening to those lyrics. It was like tears were sitting right in the middle of my throat. My hand came up to cover my mouth, but then I felt Tommy's fingers gently around my wrist. He pulled my hand down away from my face and onto his lap and gently rubbed his thumb across the back of my hand. I knew without looking at him that his eyes were not on the stage; they were on me.

As the song hit a series of high notes at the end, the man was untied and they wrapped their arms around one another and lay in the bed and held each other and the screen zoomed in to both of their faces on the bed, both totally at peace, totally in love.

They both got what they needed from that scene.

Then she straddled him and fucked him slow and sweet and as

they both cried out their orgasm together, eyes locked with one another, the curtains closed and the applause roared.

The show continued with other acts, but for me that was it, show over; game over. I stared ahead for the next three acts, but I saw nothing. I was just in my own head.

When people clapped, lights came on, and there was no more music I was numb getting to my feet. My legs felt like they were boneless. I couldn't even look at Tommy. His hand held mine that entire time, squeezing, thumb skating back and forth. I knew his eyes were on me that whole time and strangely, they felt like a blanket covering me, cloaking me.

We said our goodbyes and got into a taxi outside the club as the rest of them were off to have drinks back at Ben and Olive's. Tommy declined the invite, and Olive got very pouty. Thank God he declined. I'm sure they had some party in mind!

Tommy stood outside the cab while I was in it talking to the other men for a minute and then shook their hands and got in with me. He took my hand in his and kissed it and we rode in total quiet back to the hotel.

After I washed my makeup off, brushed my teeth, and stepped back into the bedroom he immediately asked, "What do you need tonight, baby?"

He'd taken his bowtie, jacket, and shirt off. The shirt was on the bed. I kicked my shoes off and then took my earrings out. My eyes were fixed on the silver chain around his throat. His eyes were fixed on me.

The way he said it made sense. What do you need? Because he got what he needed last night. At least he was trying to reciprocate. I guess.

I thought about it for a minute while he undid his pants, took them off, setting them on the chair beside the bed with his tux jacket. He straightened the waistband of his black boxer briefs.

"I'd like to be alone," I said softly and met his eyes.

I could see by the shift, the shock on his face, that it probably felt like a slap in the face to him.

He looked down at the floor for a moment, then skimmed his bottom lip with his teeth, and I was sure for a second, he was going to turn on his heel and give me what I wanted, but instead he shook his head.

"No. Not that. I won't ever sleep somewhere away from you if I can be beside you. I don't care if I'm mad at you, if you're mad at me, we sleep beside one another. What can I do to make this better? I know I fucked up last night, I fucked up huge. Tell me how to fix it. Please, baby."

He took a step toward me. I took a step back. He stopped.

I closed my eyes and sighed and then let the dress fall to the floor before I sat on the bed and pulled his white dress shirt over my head, undid my bra under the shirt and pulled it out one of the armholes, tossing it on the chair with the rest of his clothes. I got under the blankets.

He'd stood there quietly, watching me while I did all that. He got in beside me and pulled me close.

"Baby?" he called.

"What if you can't fix it?" My voice was barely a whisper.

"Please don't say that. Don't fucking say that." His voice was strangled-sounding. "I wanna make love to you. I need to make you feel good. Tell me what I can do to make you whimper for me and put your arms around me because you want to, not because I've told you to. Let me show you how much I love you."

Goosebumps rose on my skin and my throat was so dry. But, I didn't want to feel good. I didn't want to think. I didn't know if there was anything he could do to fix things. How could there be? I wanted to sleep and forget everything I'd seen tonight. Forget everything that had happened last night. Sleep it away, all of it.

His palm swept up from my shoulder to my face until his fingers weaved into my hair near my ear.

"Tia, baby?"

I reached up and fingered his dangling necklace without touching him. He kissed the tip of my nose.

We needed to talk things out and figure this out if we were going to have a future that wasn't just me pretending to be okay. But I wasn't ready to talk; I was still processing. I didn't know if talking would do anything at all, anyway. He was in control. He made the rules. I was just a participant. Willing or not. I didn't know if I could ever be okay with it. With any of it. But, he was waiting for an answer.

"Just..." My voice caught.

His eyes widened fractionally as he urged me, with his expression, to continue.

"Vanilla," I whispered, feeling totally and utterly defeated.

He kissed me slow and sweet, exploring my mouth with his tongue and letting his hands drift up and down my body, sending shivers up my spine. He started to undo the tuxedo shirt I was wearing, tonguing an exposed nipple as he exposed the other one.

"Touch me, babe. Please," he whispered against my skin.

I put my hands on his back and rubbed up and down. His back was so strong. I put my hands on his shoulders. They were big and muscular. He had a lot of muscle. Enough muscle to crush me without even really trying.

My mind drifted to that couple on the stage, about how she, the tiny little woman, wielded power to control a man who could crush her even more easily than Tommy could crush me. In a physical sense, anyway. Tommy could crush me, had crushed me, in other ways just through words and actions. But the tiny blonde had looked at that big, muscled man so lovingly because he gave her what she needed. She controlled him but he controlled her too, through giving her what she needed. And that big strong guy seemed like he wanted to be dominated by her, too; you could see it in his eyes. His face had gone to a state of bliss when she whipped him. It was a quid pro quo thing for them.

Tommy needed this from me, my submission to him. Sometimes

he needed it rough and sometimes he gave it to me sweet. I knew I'd wanted rough that day at the farm. I couldn't forget the release it gave me that day he tied me to the headboard and took my control away so I wouldn't have to fight anymore. I didn't know if I could ever crave that again. And if I did crave it, after what'd happened last night, did that mean I had gone over to the dark side, that I was irrevocably broken?

His mouth was on my breast, his tongue toying with my nipple. My hands continued to roam up and down his arms, his back. I thought back to us at the farm and how sweet he was after my playing that hide and seek game with him, because I was giving him what he needed. He'd seemed so happy and carefree that night. And I remembered how exciting it was to run and be caught and how insane it'd driven me when he talked dirty to me during the game. I also thought about when I wanted it to be rough and he wouldn't be rough with me. He was a control freak. Plain and simple.

Right now, he was trying to be sweet but we both knew my heart wasn't in it. My hands rose to his hair as he continued to kiss and tongue my breasts and I felt the chain around his neck touch my skin. I sucked my lower lip in and had a thought.

I needed to change the tone of this situation. I couldn't handle this sweet business right now. The only way I could get through this right now was if it were just a game. A game where I could get release, release from the prison I felt like my brain was in. Would it help?

I quickly bucked until he was off me enough for me to get out of the bed. He looked at me, first confused, and then his expression started to drop. I backed away from him slowly and then gave him a smile and waved my finger and tsk tsk'd at him.

"Tia?" He tilted his head at me.

"The only way you get to fuck me tonight, Tommy Ferrano, is if you can catch me."

Shock flashed on his face. I gave him a big, dazzling, maybe phony-looking smile and then I bolted into the closest bathroom, the Hers bathroom, locking the door.

My heart was racing. I could do this. I could play a game tonight. Granted, it wasn't very creative, but it seemed to distract me from the emotions whirling around in my brain, if only temporarily. If I played a game maybe the tone would stay where I could handle it. I was wet with anticipation. I pushed away my "What the fuck?" thoughts.

A few seconds later, I heard the doorknob jiggle and then it went silent. I stood there, heart racing, almost panting with anticipation. I waited. Then I heard a tinny scratchy sound. Was he picking the lock? I braced myself.

Approximately 4.5 seconds later the door swung open and he was standing there with this intense look on his face, his eyes lit with something dangerous. I'm sure I was standing there, wild-eyed, too. I had his white tuxedo shirt on, with just the bottom few buttons done up and my hair must've looked like it'd been in a windstorm.

He was naked and his erection should've been allocated its own zip code. He leaned on the door frame and folded his arms, "You're not very good at this game, are you? Where do you think you're gonna go from here?"

I summoned my inner vixen and shrugged at him. "Maybe I wanted to be easy to catch."

"Didn't I tell you not to try to lock me out?" He was trying to be serious, but failing. He gave me a smirk. I smirked back. Then he tried to look serious. So I tried to look serious, too.

I caught my bottom lip between my teeth and looked at him for a second, then shrugged and said, "Do you think you need to maybe teach me a lesson for that?"

He grinned at me. "Damn straight. But you made it too easy."

I shrugged. "Maybe I've got a surprise attack planned."

His eyes went cold. "A what?"

Whoa; a bucket of ice-cold water might as well have been dumped on my libido and my smugness right then and there. Not the right answer given the state of our relationship the past few days. I shook my head frantically, needing desperately to backpedal.

"I didn't mean anything violent... I meant..."

He closed the distance between us and was right up against me, making me gasp in surprise. His lips crashed into mine and then he said against them. "Drop the fucking act."

My heart was thudding wildly.

"Just drop it," he whispered. He then had my bottom lip between his teeth and he let out a sound of pleasure that reverberated through my whole body.

I couldn't be a player; I was going to lose. He was totally in control here right now. I sucked at this.

"Who do you belong to, Athena?" His mouth was by my ear.

Fuck. Shit. My blood ran cold.

He moved back an inch or two and looked down at me. I looked up into his eyes and he looked so sexy, red fucking hot with lust.

"Who?" he demanded.

It felt like all the air left my lungs and then like something inside of me snapped, like an elastic band pulled too far.

"You," I said and a huge weight vanished off my shoulders. Vanished.

Then it was like a bomb went off in that bathroom. He hiked me up onto the vanity and violently tore my underwear down my hips and off of me, and then he plunged his cock deep into me, one hand on my lower back and the other braced against the mirror. Bottles, hair tools, and cosmetics tumbled onto the floor and something splashed into the toilet. Something glass smashed. He didn't stop. He didn't take his eyes off mine. He was, clearly, completely thrilled with that declaration.

I wrapped my legs around him, dug my nails into his back, and he let out this primal sound, almost like a growl. He let go of the mirror and had a fistful of my hair in his hand. I squealed in both surprise and pain as desire surged through me.

He stopped and looked at me for a beat, breathless, then moved a few times in and out of me. I bit hard on my bottom lip, my chest rising and falling rapidly.

He lifted me and then we tumbled to the floor in the midst of curling and flat irons, hairbrushes, a broken glass bottle of facial cleanser, broken plastic blush case with chunks of blush powder all over the place, that he shoved aside. And then my legs were up and over his shoulders. As I pulled the prickly round hair brush out from under my lower back and tossed it out of the way, he started to pound the fuck out of me on that bathroom floor.

"Don't stop," I pleaded and that must've supremely pleased him as he didn't.

He went harder, he went faster; he pounded and pounded. And I received every single connection of our bodies with a grateful grunt and nails that dug into his backside.

Suddenly, I was up and he was carrying me toward the bed. We didn't make it. A few steps later, I was against the wall, impaled on him, my fingers in his hair. We were sweaty and grunting like wild animals and I knew I'd have crazy sex bruises and make-up smears all over my body tomorrow. So would he.

"Love you so fucking much," he grunted.

I was drunk on him; he was my oxygen. He fucked me slow but hard, with power, against that wall and then moved us and put me on my back on the bed. He kept going, speeding up his thrusts and with so much force that there were veins popping on his neck and his forehead.

"Tommy," I gasped.

He pulled out and got me on all fours on the bed. He put one hand around my throat and the fingers from the other got me by the clit. As he drove into me, he twisted his fingers around below until I was trying to crawl away to get away from the intensity of it, screaming out, and then I was hanging off the bed, my butt in the air, my nails clawing at the rug, him now holding my hip with one hand, circling my clit with his other, and fucking me hard. So hard.

I came hard, whimpering, "I love you, too." as I cried out into the bed's dust ruffle.

I told him I loved him? What the fuck?

I can't believe I said that to him. I'd never said that to Nick, not to the few guys I'd dated before, either. Did I love him?

Did I?

I loved elements of him, but could I love all of him?

Was my emotional outburst really about being relieved that my experiment had seemed to bring about the result I'd hoped for, sort of, that even though it kind of backfired a little, that I'd pulled a reaction out of him that told me that maybe I could get and keep this under control? Me, in control, controlling the control freak by knowing how to handle him, what to give him.

Or was I so relieved that I could do this because I did love him? I loved the possibilities of being in love, the moments of sweet, the fierce protection he'd shown me. I didn't know. I just didn't fucking know.

He grunted my name and came inside of me, and we were both breathless. He pulled me back up onto the bed. Me on my belly, him laying on my back and then after a minute of kissing me all over my shoulders and the back of my neck, he rolled and took me with him so my back was against his front and kissed me on the earlobe.

"I love you, baby girl. You have no fucking clue how much. You mean everything to me. Everything."

I glanced back at him and his eyes were closed, but there was this look of bliss on his face. Pure bliss. The look on his face crushed me, sent emotion through me that I'd never felt. I squirmed in tight against him, letting him comfort me and hold me. I closed my eyes and heard that poignant chorus in my mind.

I... don't wanna fall in love... with you.

But I was pretty sure it was too late. He had me. Fucked up as it was, I'd fallen. And it might very well be the demise of me.

Tommy

I woke up to see Tia sitting in a chair, staring out the window. She was wrapped in the thick hotel robe, her knees up against her chest and her hands around a steaming mug. She was blowing into the cup but staring out the window, looking deep in thought.

I watched her for a long time before she glanced in my direction. When she did, there was a flash of something. Was it regret? Was it fear? It punched me right in the gut, but then it disappeared, and she got a shy little smile on her face.

Was she putting on a mask for me or was she just torn up inside with conflicting emotions just like me?

I smiled and opened my arms wide for her. She took a sip, put the cup down on the table beside her, and then climbed up onto the bottom of the bed and crawled from the end of the bed toward me slowly, the sexy little smile growing bigger the closer she got. I'd opened my arms wanting to hold her close and snuggle her tight but okay, I could deal with this, too.

She climbed up my body and pulled the blankets down past my hips with a sultry look on her face and then took my cock in her hand and made sure it was good and awake, before she guided me inside herself. She undid her robe and threw it back. She was still wearing my shirt from last night and only the bottom button was done up. I groaned and undid it and then pushed it off her shoulders.

She closed her eyes and her lips parted as she took me deeper and then when she got me in balls deep, she clasped my wrists, pinning them above my head while rotating her hips with me inside of her. I let out a little chuckle and she tightened her grip on my wrists and gave me this little warning look but then wrinkled her nose at me before she continued with eyes closed. I watched as she got lost in sensation. Her gorgeous tits were over my face, so I tongued a nipple. Seeing her like this was a beautiful thing to watch. A few moments later her breathing got shallow as I'd gotten an arm free and was toying with her clit while she continued to take my cock.

She tightened around me and began to tremble. She shuddered through her climax until she collapsed onto me, her mouth against my earlobe, her warm minty mingled with fresh coffee breath warming my face. I turned over, putting her onto her back and took myself home with slow and deep movements, letting the inside of her stroke me until I fell apart.

Right as I was groaning out an, "Oh, baby" my phone started to ring. I finished and then I flopped onto my back beside her, ignoring it, catching my breath.

Fuck, that had been beautiful.

She curled into me and put her hand and cheek on my chest. I got lost in thought for a bit, about last night, the best sex I'd had in my life, about the last few days, and about this morning, her being so bold and taking what she wanted from me like this. It was fucking sexy that she'd climb onto me and fuck me. I loved it.

I didn't know whether she was being a chameleon and just trying to blend into her reality or if she'd started out playacting but was now morphing into who she needed to be for me. Whatever it was, it felt real. Her words last night undid me. She kept undoing me. I didn't know if we were both just evolving into who we wanted to be for one another. Maybe that was the closest way to describe it. Both of us struggling through this, waiting to see where our emotions would take us, trying to figure out how to be who we were and what the other needed at the same time.

It wasn't like me to be all fucking philosophical, I just knew I loved her, I wanted her, and that when she said she loved me after everything she'd been through because of me, it was like those three words ripped a layer of darkness that'd been around my heart and soul off like a Band-Aid. How many layers were left was something that, I supposed, remained to be seen.

Another ding of the phone made me realize I had to get out of bed and get on with the reason I was here. We were heading back home this afternoon. I needed to talk to Pop and then go see Goldberg and see what his decision was.

I didn't know how he'd take the news that the Ferranos as well as John Lewis, would not get involved in his project if Leo Denarda was even remotely a part of it.

We'd talked just briefly before I got in the cab last night and the three of us were meeting for lunch at John's hotel. If Goldberg opted to work with just us and turfed Denarda out, I had a pretty good idea how Denarda would take it and it'd probably mean another step-up in security.

The smarmy goof had been leering at Tia last night instead of his skanky date and we'd already had a showdown of sorts where he puffed up his chest when I'd given him a look. If it weren't for the fact that his sick uncle is an important man down here, he'd not even be at these meetings. Goldberg fucked up by even involving that crew. The guy would've been smarter just coming to us. But it was a timing issue, too. When the uncle croaked, there'd be a power play in Vegas and it wouldn't take long for Denarda to be out. Problem was that the uncle had been on his death bed for almost a year, not getting better but not kicking the bucket, either.

I talked to Pop on the phone in the other room while she took a bath and then when I was done I got in with her. She had the jets on and had her eyes closed.

I got in and she immediately started to scrub my back. When she was done, I leaned back against her chest and tilted my head back and looked up at her. We didn't talk, but her eyes said so much. If I was reading them right they said she and I were opening a new page, starting a new chapter.

I wanted to say so much to her, but right now I didn't have the words, so I just let her scrub my chest and then I reached down and pulled her calves up so that her legs were wrapped around my stomach. I massaged her feet and we just hung out for a while in the bubbles, not talking, just touching and cuddling and looking at each other, just being.

It felt beautiful; it felt right. I never wanted to hurt her again; I felt bone-deep remorse over what I'd done the other night. I just prayed she was okay, really okay.

Tia

Tommy left for a meeting as I ordered some soup and a sandwich from room service. He said he'd be back in a few hours and would take me gambling before our flight, which was at eight o'clock. I packed up our stuff and I stared at the TV, but was lost in thought until he got back.

Vegas had been enlightening, to say the least. I was curious about whether or not having me see that specific act last night was intentional or whether it'd been a coincidence. Whatever the case was, I guess it happened for a reason. I was just taking things minute by minute, breath by breath. I had strong feelings for him. I felt love, I felt fear, I felt dread, but I also had hope.

When he walked back in, he was smiling, had a spring in his step. "Let's go show you why they call it Lost Wages."

* * *

The ringing of the slot machines and the buzz of excitement: people and glasses tinkling were overwhelming at first. But before long I probably had dollar signs in my eyes because the slot machines were fun and addicting. But I kept complaining that I sucked at it. I don't know how many twenties Tommy had fed in, probably seven or eight, maybe more. It felt bad because it felt like I was flushing his money down the toilet.

He didn't gamble, he just hung out and watched and followed me from machine to machine. When I'd cashed out of a machine and then saw it pay out right afterwards with a thousand quarters to some old lady with a blue hair rinse, I decided I wasn't moving again until I won, or until we had to leave to catch our flight, whichever came first.

"Cash out, baby. This machine is shit."

He said this after I let him feed two twenties into it and was down to nine quarters left without going up more than once or twice.

"One more pull."

"You don't have to pull, you know; you can just hit the button."

"I like to pull." I wrinkled my nose and glanced up at him and he was smirking. I smirked back.

"Tia, this is getting a little like fishing."

"I'm not catching anything, though."

"No, but remember what I had to do to get you away from that pond?"

"You'd seriously carry me out of this casino over your shoulder?"

"What do you think?"

He was serious.

"This machine is lucky. It's pink, like my fishing rod. I'm gonna win." I reached up and pulled the tall chrome lever again and stuck my tongue out at him and it started dinging and lights started flashing. I won five thousand dollars. Not five thousand quarters, dollars!

"Holy shit!" I exclaimed, "Told ya so, told ya so!"

He shook his head and laughed simultaneously while I jumped up and down. There was a guy, early twenties, beside me and he raised his hand up for a high five. I gave him a smack of my palm and looked to Tommy.

"Lost Wages my ass!" I declared and did a little twirly dance, probably looked ridiculous, but did not care. He shook his head in astonishment and then leaned over and kissed me.

"Sticking your tongue out at me is a spankable offence, Missy. Watch it." He said against my lips and then winked.

"Why do you think I did it?" I winked back and his face split into a huge grin.

* * *

He slept on the flight home, holding my hand the entire time. I watched the in-flight movie. We travelled without James and Nino as Tommy had said they had an errand to run for him locally and would be flying back tomorrow.

I tried to give him the five grand, but he looked at me like I'd lost the plot. I was actually surprised they never asked for my ID in the casino.

"But you paid for everything on the trip," I reasoned.

"So what? I'm not taking your money, Tia."

"You're too old-fashioned for your own good," I told him.

He rolled his eyes at me. "Well, a leopard can't change his spots, babe. Put it in your underwear drawer when we get home; save it for a rainy day."

"Well maybe I'll just buy you a present with it then," I challenged, thinking that he'd dropped the leopard and spots cliché for a reason far beyond the five-thousand, but I was trying to avoid focusing on that statement. Was letting me hold onto enough money to get away from him another test? Or was he trying to show me trust?

"Yeah, well, I won't stop you." He shrugged.

I gave him a big hug. It felt so light and jovial that day and I was deeply grateful for that as it was helping me cope. Denial was helping me cope, too, but I figured I'd take whatever help I could get!

12

Tia

When we got back, his convertible was waiting for us at airport parking, and he drove us home. It was nice to not have security. It felt almost normal. Almost.

When we got home there were two security guards outside, but there was no Sarah as Tommy revealed he had sent her on a surprise holiday to see her family and she'd be a few more days. I thought that was very sweet of him.

She left me a note telling me that she'd prepared some meals in advance and froze them for us to get us through the next few days, if needed. I surveyed the refrigerator, pantry, and freezer and she'd stocked everything up well and there were plenty of ingredients for if I wanted to cook from scratch instead of simply defrosting and heating food up. She'd made a few casseroles, some batches of soup, had multiple groups of marinated meats in zippered freezer bags, a few batches of pasta sauces, and a few lasagnas.

Tommy had gone to his office right after putting our luggage upstairs, telling me he'd be taking care of a few things and that he'd be a few hours. I went upstairs to unpack and found a gift box beautifully wrapped in silver paper with a big pink bow on it on the bed with my name on it. I opened it and it was a shiny new laptop. It was metallic pink, just like my fishing rod, and when I booted it up the screen wallpaper was a photo of the pond at the farm from the view of the hayloft doors at sunset. My heart swelled.

This man wanted me and said he loved me. I *so* wanted this to work. I wanted the emotion I felt at the moment to be real, not just another brief reprieve from pain.

I spent a few minutes playing with it, did a few quick personalization things, a few Google searches, and then went downstairs to his office. The door was open a few inches, so I pushed it open. He was in his office chair, but had the chair swiveled away from the desk to face the window, which had a view of the pool. He was on the phone.

"I don't care how difficult; I need you find out the truth about Carlita and Greg O'Connor and you get me answers within the next two or three days. Got me?"

I swallowed hard. I almost wanted to back out before he saw me, but he was turning around. His brows shot up and he gave me a *one second* gesture.

"Good. Yeah, bye." He ended the call and his expression softened. "Hi."

"Hey. I got my present."

"Hm?"

"The laptop?"

"Oh yeah." His eyes lightened as what I was talking about dawned. "Ordered that before we left, but it got here too late for you to bring it. Like it?"

"I love it. Love the color. And I especially love the background picture."

He gave me a big smile.

"Thank you," I said.

"Come here," he replied.

I rounded the desk to get to him, climbed up and straddled him in the office chair. He reached back to close the blinds on the window behind him. As they were closing, I saw that a tall, blond guy strolling by the pool. My thoughts momentarily flickered to Earl. If Earl weren't dead, he'd probably be the man strolling by the pool right now.

"What's wrong?" Tommy asked.

I shook my head, pushing away that thought plus the urge to ask about that phone call. No point, because it was clear he was still waiting for information.

"Forget it. I don't want to get into heavy discussions right now. I wanted to show my gratitude." I leaned in and kissed his neck, feeling a flood of relief at seeing that silver chain around it. My lips touched it as well as his neck. Maybe that wasn't an accident.

"Mm, okay. We can talk later. We need to have a chat, actually. Can't put off the heavy discussions indefinitely, but right now I'm quite happy to focus on your gratitude."

The idea of a chat freaked me out. Was it about us? Was it about my parents? Was there some shoe about to drop that would overwhelm me even more than I was overwhelmed already? I needed to push everything negative in my head away right now. I didn't want to give him any sort of negative vibe. I didn't want any stress putting a black mark on today. And if he was stressed about that phone call, I needed to try to erase it.

I was thoughtful for a second. "I'm not only grateful for my awesome pink laptop." I kissed his earlobe.

"Mm," he replied, cupping my bottom with both hands.

"I'm grateful for it and..." I said.

"And?"

My fingers threaded into his hair, "And the lovely jewelry you bought me while we were away."

"Mm hm." He squeezed my rear end, and I could feel him bulging beneath me.

"That you couldn't bear to leave me here while you were away because you'd miss me." I kissed his neck again.

"True story."

"And I'm grateful that you love me," I whispered against his collarbone and then kissed the top of his chest, where his shirt was unbuttoned.

I heard a sharp intake of breath. Now his hands were in my hair.

"Why are you grateful for that?" he whispered.

In my mind the thought flashed that if he didn't love me and was who he was with me without that emotion it'd be intolerable but there was more. So much more. So much that I couldn't even articulate to him. That this beautiful, fucked up, powerful man wanted to spend his life with me, that he wanted me to have all sides of him, that there were things he wanted from me and things he needed from me, that he had pledged to be with only me. That he'd put the huge burden of giving him everything he needed on me, that he would put himself in the path of bullets for me. That he would give me everything he could to make me happy and fulfilled because I was his. And that he was so remorseful for hurting me; it was everything.

I looked in his eyes. "Because it's you. My dream guy. And it means I get to be yours."

The heat that flickered in his eyes lit my blood on fire. Yes, he made it my job to be his, whatever that entailed. The realization that I wanted that job was more than a realization; it was a revelation. I knew in my head it was crazy, but yet it made sense for me.

Submitting to him was freeing. No more fighting, stressing, worrying about freedom. There was actual freedom in this. He'd love me, he'd protect me. And I didn't have to change who I was to be what he wanted because he kept telling me I was perfect. If I could harness that power I had to keep him sweet most of the time, and to make the rough sex a game instead of letting it get out of control, I could do this.

I'd learn how to do this, and the rewards would be the bliss I got when I let go and it'd keep him sweet enough. Not just orgasms but this peace that I'd found came over me in those moments after I gave in but before I let my mind beat myself up because I'd given in. I wouldn't have to beat myself up anymore. I'd have more bliss than pain. And when I got pain, I'd use it to release the shit in my head that was trapped there. I'd purge that crap one game at a time.

Funny how I suddenly felt like bliss could come from pain. Funny how meeting him changed my life in a heartbeat and funny that being with someone for just three weeks could change my whole outlook, my whole way of thinking.

"I feel like a very lucky girl, today. The casino, the laptop, you..."

"I'm the lucky one, baby girl."

There seemed to be so much sincerity in his voice, on his face, that I felt like I was going to burst into tears. I didn't. Instead, I climbed off his lap and got on my knees on the floor in between his legs and fumbled to undo the buttons on his jeans. I reached into his underwear and pulled his cock out. He made a hissing sound and arched a little. I looked up at his face and he was staring intensely at me, baring his teeth a little, his shoulders all tense.

I moved toward him, and the tip of my tongue touched his cock, but then there was laughter outside.

Startled, I looked up. The blinds were closed, so no one had seen us. But there was talking outside the window. A guy was talking on the phone. Tommy had been looking down at me with lust in his eyes but then that laughter made him snarl at the window. He took my hand to pull me up. "Upstairs," he said and tried to tuck himself back into this pants. Clearly, things were far too awake down there to make that comfortable.

He thundered, "Fuck off away from my window, Dex!"

"Shit, sorry, Boss!" was the alarmed reply.

"Gimme two minutes, baby," he whispered. "Get upstairs, get naked, and wait for me."

He winked and I dashed off.

Tommy

How on earth did I luck out like this? I was a diabolical, cold-hearted, sadistic prick. And this beautiful, sweet girl had been through so much shit with me in a few short weeks but yet she was declaring her love for me. Not only did she declare her love for me, but she was also making it her mission to take care of my needs, on her knees even. I had everything. Everything I wanted. I didn't deserve it, but I was gonna fuckin' take it.

I could see it in her eyes, the way she examined me, wondering if I was going to be approachable, the way she was careful and then took cues from my mood but still seemed to be the Tia I'd fallen for so far, mostly. She wasn't 100% okay yet, but I could see that maybe, if I was smart about all this, she could be. I was a lucky sonofabitch. I just hoped I didn't fuck it up by taking things too far with her.

I almost broke her the other night in the hotel room. It had to be divine intervention that the show I'd gotten talked into bringing her to was some kind of epiphany for her. I didn't really wanna go to the show and subject her to Goldberg's brand of kink, but being out in public, having her pretend we weren't entrenched in the middle of our relationship falling apart...I guess I just wanted it to last a little longer.

When I saw what unfolded on that stage and how she reacted to it I didn't know if it'd ruin her or bring her back from the cusp of breaking. It was like she understood a bit more about me, enough to help us move forward. Where we'd end up ultimately, who knew, but for now she was okay, it seemed.

When she declared herself mine, it had been the highest moment I could remember. Until she said she loved me, too. That had blown me away and made me want to make sure I never fucked up again. I knew I'd fuck up, though. The question was...how badly?

I tamed the beast momentarily by putting it away, and then went out and read Dex, who wasn't new but who was new to the house security team, the riot act and then headed upstairs to get a blowjob from the girl I loved. That was another thing; she was going to give me something I knew couldn't be easy for her after Mexico and I'd make sure she knew how much that meant to me.

* * *

Tia was on the bedroom floor naked, and not just on her knees but fucking bowed down, her elbows touching the carpet and her ass in the air. The laptop was on the bed so I strolled past her and lifted it off and put it on the nightstand.

"Baby," I said, my voice gruff.

She rose up onto her knees and looked at me with huge eyes and a whole lot of what looked like fear on her face.

I stepped in front of her and put my hands in her hair. "I love you," I told her.

"I love you, Tommy." she said softly, making every nerve in my body come alive, and then her expression softened. She undid my pants and took my cock into her hand, kissed the tip and then slowly ran her tongue from the tip to my pelvis. Then she planted a kiss on my abdomen and then did the reverse, taking her tongue slowly back to the tip. She then proceeded to take half of my cock into her mouth while gripping below that with a tight fist.

She looked so fucking sexy, alternately closing her eyes and getting into it and looking up at me, like she was looking to see if she had my approval. It was like she was worshipping my cock, and it was beautiful to watch.

I didn't want to come in her mouth, I wanted inside her and if I didn't stop her, it'd be all over. So, after absorbing the feel of her mouth for another minute I leaned down and caressed her face before pulling out, taking her by the hand and guiding her to the bed.

When I reached between her legs, she was fucking soaking wet. I got inside of her and rubbed her clit, making sweet love to her. I wanted to blow, but held back until she arched her back and cried out my name at which point, I detonated inside her. We fell asleep together afterwards, arms wrapped around one another, my cock still inside her.

Tia

I'd waited for him on the floor in that pose after remembering the man on the stage and seeing it again having checked out a BDSM website quick for information about dominants and submissives, and it'd obviously done the trick, pleased him. I bookmarked the site so I could get more information later. I found the whole thing exciting and got wet just thinking about surprising him like that, waiting in a submissive pose.

But, I almost had a panic attack waiting for him to come to me because two feet away from where I waited on the floor I knew there were two guns and a knife.

I had alternating visions playing like a movie in my head of me shooting him in the head with his gun and me plunging his knife into my own stomach. My heart had hammered in my throat and my ears had gotten hot. The sound of his footsteps when he'd come in had made me feel like I was about to commit one of those two acts and I really didn't know which one it'd be.

But, then as soon as he called me *baby* and told me he loved me, he was all I saw. The weapons under the bed were momentarily gone from existence. I was afraid I might be losing my mind.

* * *

He spent the next day in his office and as it hit late afternoon I asked if he wanted me to cook something for him. He surprised me by saying he wanted to go out for burgers and to see a movie. I was shocked he didn't want to just chill and do nothing since we'd just gotten back last night. I was also shocked that he wasn't tied up with work after being away, but he told me that his brother had everything well looked after and there was nothing too pressing.

It was near sunset, but it was still sweltering-hot outside. We'd gotten dressed in shorts, tank tops, and flip flops and Tommy looked so young and carefree compared to his polished serious suit persona. He told me he knew the perfect burger joint. We swung in, filled out burger contracts (a checklist of how we wanted our burgers prepared) and ordered milkshakes. He ordered chocolate and I ordered vanilla. Of course my face got flushed when I asked for vanilla and he laughed, then kissed me breathless while we were waiting for our order. With the food on my lap, he drove to the same beach we'd gone to after that first date. I wondered if he'd taken me there on purpose so that I'd see we *could* have sunsets on the beach sometimes.

We found a picnic table and ate. It was the perfect burger. He looked at me with this mortified look when I swiped one of his onion rings (a really crispy one) and then shoved it under the bun of my burger then gave me a big kiss and stole one of my fries, which led to me feeding him half of my fries one by one, looking at one another all googly-eyed. We got to watch the sun set, all cuddled up together. It felt like we were a normal couple.

He kept looking like he wanted to say something. But he didn't. I could've said stuff too, but I didn't. So much was exchanged in those glances, it was almost like a conversation that didn't need words. He wanted to know I was okay. I wanted to be okay. I didn't know if I was okay, but I was trying to be. Maybe if he never got like that again, I could be. Maybe I could make sure he never got like that again. I knew I was taking on a huge responsibility for something that might be completely out of my realm of control, but I wanted us to work, so I wanted to try.

After eating, we went to a drive-in and I fell asleep watching the movie. It was some fast car / gun-toting/ lots of explosions / bromance partner cops type of movie. I woke when he re-started the car to drive us back.

* * *

The next few days were amazing, playing house without a housekeeper. I'd been keeping the house tidy, cooking for him, doing laps in the pool and spending time in the basement gym, doing research on my pretty pink laptop about him and his sexual tastes, and considering options for online school.

I played Miss Pacman on the arcade machine in the basement, determined to beat Dario's #1 spot high score. In a few days I was at the #2 spot and I wasn't giving up. I put "TiaTyson" as my name on it.

I'd had two conversations on the phone. One was with Lisa about wedding plan ideas, and an upcoming baby shower for Luciana. I told her I'd come over and meet with her and the sisters and we could make plans. She told me they were all happy to help so I said I'd talk to Tommy about dinner on the upcoming Sunday and then we'd sit down and go over things. The second phone conversation was with my best friend Ruby.

I'd brought it up to Tommy after afternoon sex when we were all cuddled up afterwards. I nervously told him I needed to talk to her, to put her mind at ease because she'd just been wondering about me for all this time, and because I'd promised Rose that I'd call her. By not calling I'd be leaving them wondering and worrying about me.

He said it was fine, but that I had to remember that any call could be being recorded and that I had to be very careful of what I said. I assured him it'd be fine to talk to Ruby and that I understood. When he left the room I braced myself with a deep breath and dialed her cell.

First, she was pissed at me. I'd just disappeared for weeks and she'd only heard that I'd run off with a guy. Her parents had evidently protected her from their suspicions even in the beginning when they were involving police and my social worker.

I was easily able to sell her on this being a case of a whirlwind romance, especially with the way I'd been obsessing about 'ice cream parlor hottie' before grad. The guy from the ice cream parlor had swept me off my feet and we'd moved in together. She was a romantic at heart and so it wasn't at all hard to convince her that this was just all that'd happened. She was mad at me but said she'd seen how gorgeous he was when he picked me up from the post-grad party in that convertible. When she asked why I was all upset at the house after grad and why I'd disappeared like that I said, "Let's just say my father did something to seriously disappoint me." She'd replied with a knowing, "Enough said."

Hallelujah.

I told mostly the truth, or at least selective parts of it, about how Tommy had come in and flirted with me (which she'd already known), I stretched the truth a bit by saying he found out our parents knew one another so had my Dad arrange for us to meet. I told her he'd wined and dined me, taken me on a vacation, that we'd had sunset beach walks, made love in a hayloft when he proposed, told her that I knew when my dream wedding dance song came on and that he'd picked that moment with the fireflies and the stars in the sky to ask me to marry him that I didn't need to wait to get to know him better, that everything he was in that moment was just what I wanted in a husband.

I told her he was protective, fiercely protective, that he was strong, that he was smart and funny, and that sometimes he could be so sweet that it made my heart melt. I also told her a little about the panty-melting sex. That it was hot, not what it entailed. She practically swooned over the phone when I told her he'd repeatedly made me come hard, not once, but two and three times per sex session.

I told her I was getting married in a few weeks and that of course she needed to be my maid of honor. She was sort of awestruck and didn't ask me a lot of questions. She gave me shit about not calling a few times during the conversation, but I just kept saying it had to do with shit about my dad that I couldn't talk about and then she'd say "Enough said" and let me off the hook.

If it'd been Beth or Mia, I know I'd never have gotten away with it. Mia wanted to be a journalist and Beth wanted to go into law. They'd be tag-team interrogating me, trying to understand why I just disappeared, why all the plans were suddenly out the window for a guy I'd just met. But Ruby wasn't a skeptic; in fact, she was a lot like a Disney princess who was listening to me and envisioning the day her prince would come. I cut her short when she told me that Mia was there and wanted her to pass the phone and said I'd call back later.

When I hung up, the bedroom door slowly swung open. Tommy was standing there. By his face, I could tell he'd heard the whole thing. I wasn't surprised he'd eavesdropped at all, but couldn't be mad because he strode in like a man with a mission and ravished me until I'd had two orgasms. He told me that it was beautiful to hear the way I'd chosen to tell the story of us. He'd heard me tell Ruby how beautiful he was, what an amazing lover he'd been. I'd said something to the effect of him fucking me into oblivion multiple times a day, which was pretty much true because we'd been at it like rabbits for the past few days. Vanilla rabbits, though.

After hearing that phone call, he looked so moved, then made love to me so tenderly I wound up crying during the first of the two orgasms.

He kissed away my tears and then brought me to climax again, murmuring how much he loved me, how he wanted nothing more than to spend the rest of his life making love to me and making me happy but then he whispered in my ear that not only would he make love to me for the rest of our lives but that he'd fuck me for the rest of our lives, too, and that while he'd fucked before, he'd never made love to anyone before. He would never make love to or fuck anyone but me ever for the rest of his life.

I knew that to him sometimes he wanted to make love and sometimes he needed to fuck. Those whispers spoke to me, let me know that he would sometimes want one and sometimes need the other. I knew it would be my job to be what he needed, to feed his sexual appetite, and I was determined that I could do it.

And I was happy. I was waking up in the morning to sex, I went to bed and had sex (or was woken up by it if I fell asleep first), and the day after we were home from Vegas I'd been washing a frying pan in the kitchen sink from the breakfast I'd made him, and he'd come in and screwed me from behind. Just waltzed in, lifted up my sundress, slapped my ass super hard, and then took me with his cock and his fingers and I didn't even get the way unsexy yellow rubber gloves off.

When he finished, he washed his hands, grabbed an apple from the fridge, winked at me and then went back to his office. I was just standing there, propped up by my elbows in front of the sink with the ugly yellow gloves on, skirt up, hair all mussed up, and feeling boneless and thinking that it was fairly calm for Tommy but it'd definitely been fucking.

It'd been three days of mostly sweet, beautiful vanilla sex and cuddling and talking (but never about the serious dark stuff we eventually needed to discuss) and just enjoying one another. We did things like curl up in front of the big screen at night watching TV or movies, I cooked for him, we had a naked swim together (it must've been premeditated because he'd obviously made the bodyguards leave for a while because I never saw them). He'd just lifted me after sex, both of us naked, and carried me through the bedroom balcony doors down the stairs and then jumped into the pool with me.

I'd said, "Hey! What about security?" and he'd answered, "Do you really think I'd allow anybody to lay their eyes on your beautiful, naked body?"

We hadn't left the property since we got back from the drive-in. He'd spent time on the phone in his office a lot, but he spent a lot of time with me, too.

Sarah was due back and the next day we were having dinner at his father's. And I was starting to get a little worried because there'd been no sex games since Vegas. He didn't seem stressed; he seemed fine. But how long would it last? Would I see the sudden shift so I'd know it was something I needed to handle proactively, or would it come out of nowhere and blindside me?

Maybe I should initiate something. Or maybe we should talk. Every time he came in the room I was in, I was looking to see if his necklace was on. He'd talked about us needing to talk a few times, but it never seemed to happen. I couldn't blame him for that; I wasn't initiating it either. It was easier to be ostriches with our heads in the sand, pretending there wasn't an elephant looming in the corner.

As he held me that morning after our wake-up sex, he talked about the possibility of moving Sarah out.

"Why?" I asked, tracing the pattern of his tattoo, my head on his chest.

"She's gonna get in our way. I like that I can just bend you over anywhere I like without worrying about someone else coming in."

I laughed but then turned serious. "She already warned me not to put her out of a job. She'll be pissed at me, put a price on my head."

"She won't be surprised. She cleaned and cooked at my condo but has only been live-in since I moved here so hasn't had time to get too comfy. Nita's retiring so we can move her back there until Pop retires. He may even want her to come to the Caymans. She'd have her pick at either of my sisters' places, too, helping with the kids and their houses. And if she wants, she can come in here to clean on a schedule you set up with her. If she doesn't want to take care of multiple houses, I'll hire someone part-time. Then it's just us most of the time. You're a way better cook than she is, anyway. If you don't mind feeding your future husband, that is?"

I winced, "Oh, please, please, please don't tell her that. And no, I don't mind. I love to cook. And you have a very healthy appetite, my future husband."

He laughed and then kissed me. "We need to talk," he said.

I felt my heart constrict. His tone was serious.

"Okay," I said, hesitantly.

"I don't want to just brush shit under the rug, baby. We need to talk some things out and I need some info from you."

A talk. Finally.

He looked thoughtful for a second and then seemed to change gears. "First, I'll go get us coffee and cook you breakfast," he said. "I do a mean stack of flapjacks."

More procrastination.

"Ooh," I answered and stretched out. "Bacon, too?"

"Duh? Of course." He kissed me and left the room.

I was now on his side of the bed, and I was suddenly very aware of the weapons under the bed. Maybe him saying we needed to talk jolted me out of my self-imposed stupor. I leaned over and hung over the side and looked under the bed. I couldn't see very well so I reached my hand up and yep, still armed to the teeth.

I rolled back under the blankets and got lost in thought. I'd been so happy these past few days, but he was right, we did need to talk about stuff. It was healthy that he wanted to, wasn't it? What wasn't healthy was me wanting to keep ignoring it with the idiotic notion that anything bad or dangerous would just go away.

Tommy

The last few days had been just what I needed, a bubble with just her and I. I was finding a way to blend my work life with my relationship with her. Things with work were going well, smooth, and I was thinking about our wedding, a honeymoon, about the future.

I hated that we'd soon have to leave our bubble. Here I was, putting talking to her about her father and Pop again off with breakfast, but before I pricked the bubble with a pin, I wanted a few more moments of peace, to show her what life could sometimes be. It was like I was trying to fortify things before bursting the bubble or something.

I used to help my mother make big breakfasts on weekends before she got sick. Breakfast was the only cooking I'd done. Really, she'd only let me handle the cracking of the eggs and the putting bread in the toaster and popping the button down as I was just a kid, but it made me want to learn how to do breakfast so when I lived on my own for the first time I mastered the art of breakfast. I'd had burnt pans and smoke alarms going off at first, but I'd gotten there.

Before Tia, if I wasn't slammed with work, I'd make it for myself and sit alone and eat it as I read the paper on a Saturday or Sunday. I wanted to make making Tia's breakfast on a weekend morning part of our tradition together as a couple. Someday, kids would be part of it, too. Sundays were important in my family, always had been, and I wanted that for when me and Tia had kids. Breakfast with us, dinner with the whole family. Church, maybe, too. She'd be a good mother.

I had things to figure out, but I was confident that I'd get to where I needed to be with the business, with ensuring I'd eliminated threats. But I wasn't so sure in one area. Sex. I wasn't clear how that'd be managed. I was loving all the vanilla we'd been having, surprisingly, but that might've been because of the guilt I felt about Vegas.

How long before I wanted more flavor? How long until something tipped me over the edge of frustration and I took it out on her? How did I get what I needed without hurting my relationship with her? Better yet, how could I make myself not need it?

She loved the pancakes. She ate everything on her plate and asked if she'd be getting a repeat performance the next day, since it'd be Sunday.

I agreed and couldn't bring myself to ruin the day with talk about the dark shit in my head, the shit I was dealing with regarding her father and my father. I needed to do it soon, though. I was at a dead end with Zack, my PI, and needed answers from her. She didn't ask about what I wanted to talk about, but she broached another topic.

"Um..." she said, after she loaded the dishwasher. I'd been sitting at the kitchen island reading the paper and finishing my coffee.

I looked up from the paper and waited.

She was looking a little nervous.

'What's up?" I put the paper down and showed her she had my full attention.

"I've been doing some reading."

I waited. She looked at the ceiling and then summoned some courage.

"About dominants and submissives and I was wondering if maybe..."

This oughta be good...

I jerked my chin up to encourage her to continue.

"Maybe we should outline some things. Like they did in Fifty Shades of Grey; they had a contract of guidelines and safe words and..."

I started to laugh. Her face went red.

"I don't want a submissive, baby girl."

She frowned a little and then moistened her lips, "Okay..."

I got to my feet and closed the distance between us, backing her up against the pantry door. I took her face into my palm and rubbed my thumb along her lower lip,

"I want a cock slave. No safe words. Whatever my cock wants you give me. Whatever I want. Degradation, humiliation, I could order you to fuck someone else while I watch, fuck a girl…"

The color drained from her face.

"You good with that?" I gave her an intense glare.

She swallowed hard.

I couldn't fight it: I laughed. "Gotcha."

Her eyes narrowed. "That's not nice."

I let out a big belly laugh.

I turned around to go back to the island and she swatted my ass hard with her open hand.

"You need a spanking, Mister!" she growled at me.

She was fucking adorable. I grabbed her and threw her over my shoulder and carried her upstairs. She paddled my ass with her palms all the way up, calling me cruel, mean, a jackass.

When I got her onto our bed, I kissed her and said, "Don't try to define us, okay? All I know about our relationship is that we're on a road together and I'm trying to take us someplace good."

She nodded, emotion making her eyes all sweet and wet, and then gave me her mouth.

Tia

Tommy had to go out before we got a chance to talk about anything serious, so I had hours to myself. I wondered if it'd get to a point when I could come and go as I pleased. I wanted to talk to him about it, but he came home in a pissy mood. So, I decided that I needed to think up a game, so he and I could play. Maybe I could fix his mood.

I made a homemade lasagna for dinner (despite the three in the freezer) and it seemed to help with his mood; he told me it was the best lasagna he'd had in years.

"If I was having a cook-off to pick my wife and this was your entry, baby, you'd win. Hands down."

"If I didn't cook well would I be out of the running?" I pouted.

"Not at all; just sayin' if cooking were a qualifying category, this lasagna would buy you the race."

I beamed. His mood had lifted a little, but he seemed preoccupied.

"You seem a bit tense," I said, walking to his side of the table. I placed my hands on his shoulders and leaned down to whisper in his ear. "How about if you grab a shower and meet me in the bedroom and I give you a full body massage? Then maybe we can play."

He smirked. "I'd love to, baby, but I have a conference call in..." He glanced at his phone, "Five minutes ago. Shit. Rain check?"

"Sure." I deflated. I leaned over to clear his plate.

He pulled me down onto his lap and claimed my mouth with his. "Dinner was delish, baby. I can't wait for dessert. Half an hour, hour tops, okay? I'll try to keep Saturday nights and Sundays as free as I can going forward."

He planted another kiss on me, then lifted me off his lap and swatted my bottom playfully.

I chewed my lower lip, giving him a heated stare. He returned it.

"What flavor tonight, Tommy?" I asked, trying to look as seductive as I could muster.

"Mm," he eyed me up and down. "Neapolitan?"

I smiled and gave him a nod. A little vanilla, a little strawberry, and a little chocolate? Sounded good to me. I cleared the table as he strode off toward his office.

Tommy

"Okay," I told her, "You're gonna put me to sleep."

She was sitting on my rear, massaging my back with sweet smelling oil. I was on the bed, a towel around my waist.

"Maybe you need to sleep," she told me, her lips against the ridge of my ear.

"But, I have plans for us."

"Neapolitan plans?" she murmured.

I laughed. "We need to talk first, baby. Switch."

She got off me and lay beside me on her belly. I climbed onto her backside and kneeled, not putting my full weight on her, lifted her t-shirt and pulled it off her, leaving her in just a pair of Daisy Duke jean shorts and her bra, a sexy, red satin one. I snapped the band and she jerked and then giggled shyly. I kissed her shoulder and then wiped oil from my own over-oiled shoulders, transferring it to her body, working it in to her back and her shoulders. She let out a little moan that went straight through my groin.

I ignored what her sexy moan made me wanna do; I needed to talk to her, not let myself get distracted again. The best way to do that was probably to stop touching her so I could stop thinking about getting inside of her and just play the recording.

I wiped my hand on the towel beside her, reached for my phone, which was on the nightstand, and put it beside her head.

"Listen," I said and planted a kiss on her shoulder. "Then we'll talk. We have to talk about this and then we have other shit to discuss. It's going to be a lot. But it's important. Okay? I didn't want to come to you with this before I had everything figured out, but I'm at a dead end and need info from you before I can go further."

She nodded softly. I brushed her hair behind her ear with my fingertips, kissed her temple, and then I pressed *play* on the recording while I continued to gently massage her shoulders and then moved down to her legs as the recording played what Greg O'Connor said to me outside the hospital when Tia had the allergic reaction. She tensed up almost immediately, upon hearing her father's voice, but I kept massaging gently.

"...known your family for years. I've wanted to be on better terms and I tried to patch things up with Tom. He just didn't wanna know me because Lita chose me over him, you see. And he always had this grudge about that. He told me one night out of the blue in a dark alley when he turned up after a poker game I was in that he'd have her back and that if he couldn't have her, he'd make sure I didn't either. He was in love with her, had been since they were kids, but he was best friends and business partners with her older brother, someone even more connected than he was, so she was off limits. A few years after your ma died and Lita's brother died he tried to hook up with her but she broke up with him a few months later and when she met me, she told me her ex was a crazy possessive, psycho. She started to see me on the rebound, probably, but got pregnant so we got married before we really knew each other. I loved her, though. She was amazing. He said Tia should've been his. If we hadn't had Tia, he wouldn't have lost Lita. I was scared he was gonna hurt Tia. He was a bad motherfucker and I was afraid for my life, too. I tried to befriend him, started working on one of the crews, but when he found out about it, he canned me. All this shit kept happening to me and it was like he was out to destroy me. I know he was behind a lot of it.

Then he left us alone for a few years. But me and Lita had a huge blow-up about my gambling and partying, and she took my daughter and left. But she came back a few days later and wouldn't say why. I think she'd gone to him, but changed her mind. Or maybe he'd kidnapped her and she got away. She wouldn't tell me. He turned up drunk and stormed into my apartment and told us if she didn't leave with him, he was taking Tia instead. Started screaming in my face telling me to pick whether I wanted to keep my wife or my daughter. Lita pleaded with him, but he pointed a gun at me and finally took Tia, put her in his car. Lita tried to change his mind, go with him, but he said it was too late. Tia got so upset that he let her come back a few hours later but he told me it wasn't over. Lita killed herself a few weeks later. Your father showed at the funeral and told me he'd be back for Tia someday. That I took from him, so he'd take from me. Hinted that he was responsible for Lita's death. I carried that shit around for years. Always watching my back, always wondering if she really killed herself. I was fucked up. I know it affected my relationship with my daughter. I just, I dunno, malfunctioned. But I want a relationship with her. I thought maybe you and I could be friends. I could work for you. See my daughter, be in her life, help you with the business. We'll be family after you get married. Maybe Tom will finally let it all go now. Think about it. Will ya do that for me?"

I turned it off and climbed off her and got into a pair of boxers. She stayed still. I gave her a minute and then asked, "Do you think your mother was depressed before she died?"

"Yeah," she said softly.

"Long before or for just a little bit."

"Long, I think."

"Do you remember my father taking you out of your apartment?" I asked her.

She was quiet for a minute. This was key.

"I do," she said eventually, climbing up onto her knees and then she twisted and planted herself down beside me and re-fastened her bra and then reached for her t-shirt.

I passed her a bottle of water from the nightstand and she took it with trembling hands.

"I knew he was familiar," she said, pointedly. "I knew when I met him that he was familiar. But I couldn't place it. Then when I found that picture I gave you, I knew he was really familiar beyond the picture but still didn't know from where. When I heard that recording, when I heard it, I saw it playing like a movie in my head. I remember him putting me in his car and I was crying and crying and he tried to settle me down and told me he'd buy me a pony, build me a dollhouse, take me to Disney World. He said he'd give me anything I wanted. I wouldn't stop crying for my Mom and finally after he drove around for a little while he took me back. Maybe I blocked it out. I don't know. If it was just before she died maybe I blocked it out."

I nodded. "Do you remember you and your mother being kidnapped or being with my father somewhere for a few days?"

"No, I only remember him taking me and driving me around in his car until he took me back." She got this horror-stricken look on her face. "Tommy we're not, oh my god, we're not siblings, are we? Is your dad—"

"No," I told her, "No way. You've got O'Connor's eyes, no doubt about it; that man is your father."

She was quiet for a few minutes, eyes looking active, like she was combing through details of her memories.

"I don't know if my father killed your mother. I'm trying to find out. There's shit to sort out about my own mother's death, about your mother, your uncle, lots of shit."

She sipped her water with her eyes on me.

"You heard my father's best friend was your mother's older brother. His daughter, your cousin, Bianca, she's married to Nino, Nino who came to Vegas with us."

She looked shocked.

"So, I grew up with your first cousin. She's my age."

Tia was flabbergasted, "I know no one from my mother's side."

"Your Uncle Joe, a man I called Uncle Joe all my life, he died in a car crash. Some say my father staged it over a business dispute. I've heard it over the years but never believed it."

She didn't say anything.

"Earl told me he flipped on our family and took you because he found out my father had his son Michael killed because Michael was about to expose him for being involved in a meth op. If that's true, Pop kept it from me and Dare. Earl said he didn't wanna hurt me but saw red and wanted back at my father. Castillo made promises, promised to deliver Pop to Earl for revenge down in Mexico and they chose you as the tool, knowing who your ma was."

I reached for her water and she passed it to me. I took a swig and continued, "I hear that my pop may have killed your mother alone and I'd never believe it. Your father, zero credibility. But that you remember him taking you and that he picked you for me, and the other shit that's unfolding," I shook my head. "I have a lot to figure out."

She blew a long breath out and put a palm over her forehead.

"You okay?" I reached for her. I half expected her to pull away, but she didn't. She climbed onto my lap and put her head on my shoulder and her arms around the middle of my back.

"Don't know. Are you?" she asked.

"If I have you, I will be," I said.

She gave me a squeeze.

Tia

"Tell me about your family," I said to him. "About your childhood, about your pop, about the business."

I suddenly wanted everything on the table.

He leaned back against the headboard and let me settle against him, putting his chin on my head.

"My mother died of Cancer. I was just a little kid. Spent a lot of time by her bedside as she was dying, and she said a lot of fucked up shit. Shit a little kid shouldn't hear. I think it went to her brain before she died. Pop was out running the business; it was around then that the business started to really flourish. He was raking in money hand over fist and my ma was in bed dying a slow and painful death. A few months later he married Dare, Tessa, and Luciana's ma. The math didn't jive so I figured out later that that she, Annette... had Dare before Ma died. They showed up and moved in just days after ma died; Dare was a toddler and she was pregnant with Tess. They divorced a couple years later but Pop kept all the kids. She lives in Italy. Comes by every year, but not much of a relationship. I get the impression that's the way Pop wants it. Pop's third wife died in a car crash. Maybe he killed her."

He shrugged and continued.

"She was a bitch and now I think about it, it wouldn't surprise me. All the fucking car crashes, huh? All my life he had such high expectations of me and my brother. We work to earn his respect on a continuous basis; it has a short shelf life. He pushes and pushes us and is always testing our loyalty. I got to a point where I wouldn't let him push me. I started to show him before he had to push. Now I have all this to figure out."

He sighed before continuing. "If this is who he really is, how do I live with that? I know we've ordered people dead. But they're enemies, not family, not innocent. I've practically run the business the last few years. I handle a lot of the legit stuff and some of the shadier shit, too, and Dare and I have plans on how to get shot of the shadier stuff because we just don't need it. We have money, we have power, and we do well. We know where to focus to boost earnings even more and without the risk, without having to pay people off, without worrying that the house of cards'll tumble down at any minute. When Pop retires, we have a plan, a good one. I know I'm not the ice cream shop guy you wanted, baby, but I'm planning for a better life for us."

"You are better than the ice cream guy," I told him. He looked so distraught right now. "You're real, Tommy. You're a man with many layers and the fact that you're looking for the truth even if it's not what you want to hear? That's huge. The ice cream guy probably wouldn't have rescued me from Mexico, probably wouldn't have done a lot of the things you've done. He was two dimensional. I'm here with you, not him."

"The shit I've done that's hurt you. That's hurt others." He looked lost.

"I'm Thomas Ferrano Jr. Maybe the apple doesn't fall far from the tree. Maybe that's what's wrong with me. I'm his son. It's so fucking fucked up, baby. He goes from being a philanthropist to doing this fucked-up shit. He's hiding behind the charity, the talk about family, about loyalty."

I threw my arms around him and squeezed. I had an ache spread through me, an aching desire to help him. His pain was palpable.

"Will you tell me about the necklace?" I whispered.

He let out a big sigh and then finished my bottle of water. "It was my mother's. One of the last lucid talks I remember with her she put it around my neck and told me that if I wore it I'd remember to be a good boy. Maybe she knew the apple wouldn't fall far, too. Some of the shit she said, warned me about, it was all riddles to me but now I think she hated Pop when she died, and knew I'd probably turn out like him. Sometimes she screamed at me like I was him, told me why she hated me. I think she was afraid for me and what I'd become without her to guide me. When I have to make hard decisions that I know she wouldn't have approved of, I can't wear it."

"You've been having a lot of epiphanies," I said softly.

"Yeah," he said. "Never told anyone this shit, baby." He shook his head, then rolled his eyes.

"You don't have to be the apple. You are your own man. You

already want to change the way that this family earns money; you can change other things, too."

"I'm not giving you up." He looked at me with ferocity.

"What?"

"I told you not to ever ask me to give you up." His jaw muscles flexed.

I shook my head. "That's not where I was going with that. I don't want you to give me up, Tommy."

He didn't believe me.

"I don't," I assured him. And it was true. There was hope in me for him, for us.

"You don't want to go home?" he asked and there was pleading in his eyes.

"I'm home. You're my home."

He shook his head like he doubted what I was saying, got up and walked to the bar and poured a drink. "Want one?" he asked.

I nodded.

He drank a shot of whiskey and then poured another shot. Then he reached into the fridge and pulled out a bottle of wine and poured me a glass.

I was surprised and a little hurt that my declaration had no apparent effect on him. "I just mean that you don't have to let the darkness engulf you. You could go to therapy. Maybe you should."

"Fuck that," he said through gritted teeth and I stopped talking and accepted the glass of wine. I took a sip and then decided to try again.

"But..."

"Fuck that!"

He downed the shot and threw the glass; it shattered against the wall, making me wince. He stormed out of the room, slamming the door.

I bit back tears and just sat and stared off into space. I thought about the recording. I thought about my parents. I thought about Thomas Ferrano Sr. I thought about who Thomas Ferrano Jr. was, why he probably was the way he was, and I knew that there was hope for him, for us.

He knew his father was wrong. If his father was guilty of all of the things that he looked to be guilty of, Tommy wouldn't just stand for it. The demands that had been put on Tommy from a young age, losing his mother, had all caused this darkness in him. That he could also be sweet and fun-loving was hopeful, wasn't it?

I wondered what would happen next, how Tommy would get to the truth. I also wondered how I'd cope with the fact that the man I was about to marry was the son of a man that might have been the reason my mother was taken from me.

When I got ready for bed I put on the blue and white checked shirt that was on the chair beside the bed. He'd worn that before I gave him the massage. I put my nose to the sleeve. It smelled like fabric softener and it smelled like his aftershave. It was comforting to smell it. I fell asleep with the sleeve against my nose, absorbing the fragrance, wishing my nose was against him.

I didn't know if he'd gone out or if he was in another part of the house, but he clearly wanted space, so I just turned out the light and climbed under the thick, fluffy duvet sniffing the sleeve and imagining he was beside me.

Just as I started to drift off, I heard him come in and then I heard the sound of the shower. When he got into bed a few minutes later he didn't touch me, didn't reach for me. I crawled over and put my head on his chest and my palm over his heart. He still didn't touch me. He just lay there. The tension in the air was so thick.

I rubbed my hand up and down his chest and touched his skin with my lips and snuggled in. He let out a sigh.

"Tommy?" I whispered.

He didn't answer me.

"I'm here for you," I said.

"Yeah?" he whispered.

"Yeah," I draped a leg over his and rubbed the sole of my foot up and down his calf.

"Tia." His voice was laced with warning.

"I'm yours, baby. Take what you need," I offered, trailing my hand down toward his waist.

He caught my wrist before I reached my goal.

"Fuck, baby. You don't know what you're offering." He shifted me off of him and put his hands over his face.

"I do. I can take it," I said huskily. "Be your cock slave..." I moved back over and started to tongue his nipple.

"Athena, I'm good. Go to sleep."

"Tommy, I can take it. If you don't release it now it'll get worse and it could be more than I can handle, I'm here for you, let's play a game, I–"

He put his hand over my mouth. "I just spent two hours beating a punching bag to a pulp so that you don't have to deal with it instead. I am fine. Go to sleep."

He took his hand off my mouth.

"Tommy–"

His hand came back over my mouth and stayed there.

After a few minutes, he lifted it.

I didn't say anything. He pulled me against him and I kissed his chest and eventually fell asleep with my nose against his skin.

Tommy

What has she become? Some armchair psychiatrist who thinks she knows how to keep me from going overboard?

I could've shown her that she hasn't a fucking clue how bad it could get, that it could get even worse than it did in Vegas, but I didn't wanna hurt her, don't want her to think she's in over her head with me – especially after I'd already almost broken her. I had my head together enough that I wasn't looking to inflict anything on anyone. What I was craving was finding out the answers I needed. Even if her offer did make me as hard as a fucking rock.

Did my father kill Carlita O'Connor? Did he kill Joe Trulia? What about Earl's son Michael? What else was going on here? And what the fuck should I do about it?

13

Tia

I was alone when I woke up. There was a text on the iPhone.

Gone out for a bit to take care of some things. I'll meet you at Pop's for dinner. Jimmy will pick you up and drive you. Be ready @5. Say nothing about what we discussed last night to anyone.

Well duh.
I wrote back:
Okay. <3 You. Xoxo

Pop's for Sunday dinner? Oh boy. I couldn't believe he wasn't getting us out of it with what was going on.

I stayed busy getting things done around the house. Sarah would be back either tonight or tomorrow and I didn't want her to have to come back to dusting, vacuuming, and laundry.

Nino was on the grounds with the blond guy, Dex. I looked at the big biker-looking Nino and wondered about this cousin of mine, his wife. I wondered if they had kids. I wondered if I had other family. I wondered if they all knew about me or not. I pondered the things my father had said, about how losing my mom hurt our connection. I knew it did. He was so broken after her. And did he blame me? Maybe he did.

He was always so fascinated with the mafia, though. Surely that was odd under the circumstances. And he was still trying to get a job with Tommy. Clearly, he wasn't against the idea of living in that 'life'. It was perplexing. He sold me out instead of trying to protect me. He was saving his own ass. And now he was trying to profit from my misery. Well, I guess it wasn't misery anymore, but it had been and he didn't know if I was happy or if I was in my own personal hell and yet he was trying to get a job with Tommy.

I baked a glazed lemon Bundt cake to bring to dinner and had it ready when James knocked on the front door. No one had been wandering around inside the house since we'd been back from Vegas and I knew they used the staff quarters but the hall door off the kitchen was left locked. Tommy had said they had keys for emergencies but had been instructed to give us our privacy. Earlier that day I'd gotten James to get me the ingredients at the store per Tommy's instructions if I needed anything.

He carried the cake to the car and drove me the short drive to Tom and Lisa's. I was thankful that it was a short drive because our awkward efforts at small talk didn't have to last too long.

I plastered a smile on my face as I went inside because the first person I laid eyes on was Tommy's father. He was standing in the doorway ready to greet us.

"What's this?" He smiled at me but his smile twitched almost nervously as he eyed the cake in my hands.

"Lemon Bundt cake," I said with a sweet smile.

His expression dropped. This was my mother's cake. Clearly by his reaction he'd had it before. It was the only thing she cooked that didn't make the person eating it look for the nearest dog or potted plant (some dogs had even looked for potted plants!) and she'd made it for every occasion. It was a just a store-bought lemon cake mix with lemon Jell-O added into the box recipe. Then it was glazed with icing sugar mixed with lemon juice.

"You don't like lemon cake?" I asked innocently, a mask firmly in place.

He appeared thrown for a split second and then seemed to recover. "Can't wait to try it. Sounds great. Take it to the kitchen; girls are in there." He kissed my cheek as I passed him.

The girls were in fine form, laughing, talkative. Luc was the size of a ranch style bungalow and eating cheese as Tessa shredded it on top of garlic bread. Lisa was chopping cucumbers.

"How can I help?" I asked as I stepped in.

They all looked genuinely pleased to see me and bombarded me with questions about Vegas, about where we'd been hiding out, and asking about planning the wedding.

I helped Lisa with the salad and then helped Tessa set the table. We (except Luc) drank a bottle and a half of wine together before Tommy and Dario arrived, which I was thinking was a good idea since I was in need of some liquid courage being around Tommy's father. The men sat in the family room with all four kids. There was a debate over what they'd all watch. Disney movie or some rugby game.

Luc's girls were adorable, Katrina and Serena (Luc joked that when she wanted them to come, she'd just holler "Rina!") and they were dressed exactly the same in little white with red polka dot sundresses with their dark curly ringlets up in pigtails. They sat on the floor playing with the boys' toy cars.

Tessa's boys, Antonio and Lucas, sat on James' lap like angels. Finally, Tom settled the "big kids" down by putting the Disney video on the big screen and giving the dads a tablet to watch together for their game.

Tommy and Dario turned up together, just as the food was being put out. Tommy swept me into his arms and gave me a very amorous hello with an old Hollywood style dip and a long kiss in front of his whole family. They all looked a bit surprised, so I guessed they hadn't seen this type of behavior from him before. Truthfully, I was surprised, too. Last night he didn't want to even touch me as we went to sleep.

He was sweet, attentive, and affectionate with me during the meal, which felt light and happy. Tommy didn't seem at all awkward with his father. I felt awkward, but tried to push it away.

When dessert was served, Tessa, Lisa, and Luc's hubby Eddy were all going on and on about my cake. When Tommy's father was served a piece, he stared at it for a long time before taking a bite. I tried not to look at him while he tasted it. I tried, but I couldn't help it. His eyes, as he chewed, went far away for a second. Then he caught me looking and our eyes locked . I think he knew. I think he knew right then and there that I'd made that cake knowing something about their past. I saw something dark and sinister pass over his expression, and I knew I had to switch gears pretty darn quick to make sure I didn't give myself away.

"Do you like it?" I asked, giving him a big smile.

He licked his lips. "It's very good." He said this softly, assessing me, trying to see through my act. I wasn't about to let him; I couldn't mess this up. I nonchalantly leaned over and put a forkful up to Tommy's mouth. Tommy had been talking to Eddy across the table about a restaurant Eddy managed for the family. He stopped mid-sentence and made eye contact with me and then accepted the bite. I kissed him on the mouth and totally ignored his father. My heart hammered in my chest; I prayed he bought it. I didn't look back at him for a good minute, just fixed my eyes on Tommy's eyes and Tommy seemed to totally get that I needed to keep eyes locked with him for as long as possible. When I did glance back in Tom's direction, he was talking to Lisa animatedly with his hands and paying no attention to me.

I settled down and Tommy must've read me. His lips brushed mine and then he whispered in my ear, "What is it?"

I whispered, "Can we go soon? I can't get into it now but I'm having trouble keeping it together."

"We'll finish the coffee and then I'll get us out of here," he whispered back. "That okay?" I nodded. He kissed me on the lips again and pulled me closer.

"Fuck, you two; get a room!" That was Luc.

"Oh, jealous bitch," Tessa told her, then explained, "She's got Placenta Praevia so orders of no sex from her doc. She's getting a bit bitchy."

Eddy started to laugh. "Yeah, and she's like a big horny cat in heat walking around clawing at everyone who's getting any. The only thing I can do to calm her down is keep feeding her."

Everyone started to laugh, including Luciana, and then Luc swatted her husband. "Watch out or this cat'll act like a praying mantis and gnaw your head off after the next time you get lucky, especially if this isn't a boy!"

"Notice she said 'after' the next time I get lucky? Hey, at least she wants it one more time before she whacks me," Eddy laughed some more and that got the room roaring with laugher.

A few minutes later, Tommy looked at his phone and then put his napkin on the table and took my hand, pulling us up to stand. "Sorry kids, but something's come up. We gotta fly."

"Oh, I wanted to help clean up," I said innocently. Tommy winked at me. "Sorry, baby girl. Duty calls."

Lisa waved her hand. "Don't even worry. It's covered. You were a great help setting up. But when can we talk about your wedding?"

"We're postponing it a bit," Tommy said nonchalantly, swiping his phone as he pulled me along. "Plenty of time for that."

He made his way around the table, kissing all the girls on their cheeks and shaking hands with back slaps or fist bumping with each of the guys.

I tried not to show my surprise. Everyone else seemed surprised, too, especially Tommy's father.

"Thank you guys so much for dinner and the great company," I said cheerily.

One by one I got kisses and hugs as we made our way out of

there. Tommy's father whispered to Tommy for a second before letting go of him. Tommy seemed like he was trying to wave whatever the discussion was off as if it was no big deal. I accepted an awkward hug from him and then when Tommy grabbed my hand, I was happy to be getting out of there.

When we got in his car, I tried to explain the Bundt cake snafu. Tommy was a little pissed, told me I had to be careful not to tip our hand while he figured things out, but seemed like he understood.

"Why are we postponing the wedding?" I asked.

He smiled at me. "I'd have thought you'd be relieved at that."

"What do you mean?"

"Tia, you've made no secret of the fact you thought we were moving too fast. I don't want that all in the midst of everything I'm trying to sort out. We'll figure that out after. When I get married, I want to be focused a hundred per cent on my bride and nothing else."

I don't know if my heart sank or soared right there. It sounded sweet, but maybe he was having second thoughts about us amid everything he was figuring out. It sounded silly of me because of all the worries I had, but the idea he might be unsure about us was unsettling.

"And for you. I want our wedding day to be the happiest day of your life," he added softly.

His expression said it all. I got a little choked up. I looked at him with tears in my eyes. He squeezed my hand and then kissed each knuckle. Soaring. My heart was definitely soaring.

"Have you found out anything else?" I asked after recovering.

He shook his head. "No. But I think we should talk to your father. Get more info. Have him over. How do you feel about that?"

I didn't know. I finally shrugged.

"We'll talk more later," he finally said as we were pulling up to the front gate. "When we get inside, I have to make a quick phone call. When I'm done, I'm coming up and we're going to play. In the mood to play?"

I was surprised. I smiled at him. "Play what?"

He smiled wickedly at me as we got on the other side of the gates. "Play cock slave?" He brought my hand to his mouth again and took my index finger in between his teeth, raising an eyebrow.

I smirked. "Hmmm. You missed out on that offer, Sir. How about ping pong?"

"Uh uh." He let go of my hand and reversed into the garage.

"Monopoly?"

"Nope." He put it in park.

"Strip poker?"

"Hm. By George, I think you've got something there."

As we got out, I was laughing.

"I have a deck of cards in the game room downstairs. You get down there and shuffle them and wait for me," he said and then he unlocked the front door. "Be prepared to lose the shirt off your back." He winked.

When we got inside, he went to his office and I headed down to the basement. The games room was awesome and I'd been spending considerable time down there the last few days. Ping pong and pool tables, big home theatre, foosball, the arcade games (I still hadn't beat Dario's Ms. Pacman high score, but I was close). The poker table had a storage drawer underneath it and it contained several brand-new decks of cards.

I set them on the felt had a thought, so ran upstairs to the bedroom and stripped out of my yellow sun dress Tommy had bought when we were at the farm. I put on a sexy pair of black underwear with matching bra and a pair of black stay-up fishnet stockings. Then I layered on a t-shirt, a hoodie, a vest, a pair of tights, track pants, and then a pair of his jeans (mine wouldn't fit over all those layers. I had to roll his up at the bottom about half a dozen times as they were just way too long). Then I put on two pairs of socks and booted it back downstairs.

He was sitting on the poker table with no shirt on, looking sexy with his muscled arms folded across his chest. He stared at me,

"Wondered where you got to." His face lit up with humor. "Hitting the ski slopes?"

"I'm just not sure how good you are at poker. I thought I might need an advantage."

The fact that he was already half undressed either spoke to him giving me an advantage or to him being anxious for the payout.

He wiggled his eyebrows at me and then took the deck of cards out of the box and did this fancy card shuffling in mid-air thing. Yikes. He laughed at my horror-stricken face.

Not long later, he had only taken off one sock and I was down to the bra, panties, and stockings. My gigantic heap of clothing was on the floor between us and he was very pleased at the surprise lingerie under all those layers.

"Fuck, you're sexy," he told me as he lifted me up and my stocking-clad legs wrapped around his waist.

"We never got our Neapolitan last night," he advised as he carried me up the basement stairs and into the kitchen. I held on tight, tonguing his earlobe until he put me on the kitchen counter and then opened the freezer. Sure enough there was a carton of Neapolitan ice cream.

"Hey, lookie lookie," he said.

He opened a drawer and got a spoon and spooned a bit of vanilla up and got between my legs and put it in my mouth.

"Mm," I said. "Not a thing wrong with vanilla."

I hadn't seen that there earlier. When had he gone to the store?

"Nothing at all," he replied and licked the empty spoon. Then he dipped his tongue into my mouth and added an "Mm" before dipping the spoon back into the carton.

"Tonight, I feel like some chocolate, though." He scooped up a big scoop of chocolate and put it in his mouth, then his lips were on mine and he shared what was in his mouth with me.

It was so sexy, so intimate. I wrapped my legs tighter around his waist and threaded my fingers into his hair.

"I see what type of ice cream to get next time I go shopping," came a familiar female voice.

Oh shit!

Sarah was in the doorway between the kitchen and the back hallway with her suitcase, eyeing us. I was on the kitchen counter in underwear and a bra with my stocking-clad legs wrapped around his waist, bra straps hanging down off my shoulders and him in just a pair of jeans that were halfway undone plus him wearing just one sock. Yikes!

"Goodnight," she chuckled.

I couldn't look her in the eyes, but her smile could've lit up the neighborhood.

"Goodnight, Sarah," Tommy re-shut the hallway pocket door and locked it, effectively blocking the staff quarters from the kitchen.

"Ohmigod!" I was mortified.

Tommy dropped the spoon on the counter and plunked the ice cream back into the freezer and then picked me back up, legs wrapped around him like before, and he kissed between my breasts over and over as he carried me up the stairs. It was as if we hadn't just gotten caught almost *doing it* on the kitchen counter.

When we were back in the bedroom, he turned off all the lights but one dim lamp, then he laid me on the bed on my back and lavished my breasts with affection as I pushed his jeans the rest of the way off with my feet. My panties weren't coming off; they were shoved to the side instead and then he was inside of me.

He thrust in and out two or three times, then breathed, "You here for me, baby?"

I frantically nodded.

"You gonna give me what I need?"

I nodded some more, running my fingers through his hair and thrusting my pelvis at him,

"You my little cock slave?"

"Mm hm." I thrust my tongue into his mouth.

"Mm. Bend over my lap." He pulled out and sat.

I blinked for a second or two and then directed my mind to forget about Vegas. We weren't there and there was no anger on his face. I crawled over him eagerly.

His hand began a journey up and down my ass for a moment before he hauled back and a slap rang out, sending my pelvis down, flat across his lap. He ended the slap with fingers digging in, not painfully, possessively. This didn't feel like punishment, this was fuck-hot.

It filled me with lust, made me so wet down below I was almost seeing stars in the dim room. His fingertips slid under the lace of the panties and teased me for a few strokes before he took his hand away.

I was so into this right now. I lifted my rear end into the air and he slapped it again and murmured, "Greedy girl."

I moaned.

Yes, I could be what he wanted; all his. I could make sure he had what he needed. I could give him me, let him have me, it'd be what he wanted and exactly what he needed. This idea had me so wet, so ready for more.

He slapped my ass again, "You like that?"

"Yes, baby," I answered, feeling so wanton, so his.

He slapped me again and this time grabbed my ass harder. It hurt, but I let myself feel it. I gave in to it and the feeling – it was so freeing. He leaned over and bit my butt cheek, which made me squeal in both surprise and pain.

He let out a deep throaty laugh and then said, "Mm, you're so fucking mine, you know that?"

"Yes," I answered breathily, feeling emotional.

"Beg for it," he whispered.

"Please, Tommy."

"You want me to spank you?"

"Yes, please."

Oh fuck; oh please.

"You want me to fuck you?"

"Oh, yeah, Tommy."

"Yeah what?"

"Please, Tommy."

He put me on the bed on my knees and then took me from behind, holding my hair in a ponytail at the nape of my neck.

"Please what?"

"Please fuck me, Tommy."

"I'm gonna fuck you so hard."

"Yeah, baby."

"Tell me you're mine."

"I'm yours, Tommy."

"Forever."

"Forever, baby."

"Tell me you love me."

"Love you so much, Tommy."

"Good girl."

Goosebumps rose all over me. I melted at that.

"Say it again," he grunted against my ear.

"It again."

Slap.

"Ouch!" I laughed.

"Naughty girl."

I laughed again.

"I like it when you're a little bit naughty, you know that?"

"Mm."

"Why do I like it when you're naughty?" He squeezed my ass really hard.

"You get to punish me for being naughty," I answered hoarsely.

He moaned.

"That's right. I get to spank this sexy ass. I want to fuck this sexy ass, too."

My throat went instantly dry. He flipped me over and kissed me hard. I kissed him hard right back. My ass cheeks were on fire, my girlie parts: practically begging for it. He gave it to me hard and fast, thankfully not in the ass (I was flipped out by that idea) and it didn't last very long, but we both came hard.

I drifted off pretty quickly afterward, but jarred awake to him whispering to me, "Athena."

"Mm?"

"I love you."

"I love you, too, Tommy." I put my palm to his cheek.

"Do you really? Or have I just fucked you up so much that you think you have to love me so you can survive me?"

I opened my mouth, but for a second but nothing came out, then, "I don't know" spilled out as sorrow lanced through me.

Tommy

I pulled her tight to me and just fucking broke.

"Thank you, baby girl. Thank you for being honest. I know I'm a fucking asshole and I've hurt you so bad and messed with your head. I don't deserve you, but please hang in there with me. I'll try. I'll try to be what you need, try so fucking hard. Keep being honest, okay? You are everything to me, do you understand me? You're more important than the family, the money, the power, the control, any of it. Be strong for me, baby. I need you to be strong. Don't let me break you. Please don't let me break you."

She clutched me what must've been as tight as she could.

"I won't. You're worth loving, Tommy. You are worthy of real love and that's what you are going to get from me, okay? And I'll be everything you need, too, okay? I will love you and be yours forever. I won't break."

She wiped the wet from my cheeks with her fingers and put her lips to my chin.

"I'll hold you to that," I said, kissed her nose, and then we fell asleep locked together.

Tia

I meant it. I wanted him to know unconditional love. I think that's what he needed.

Why did I fall in love with this man who had fucked with my head so much? It was a combination of things, maybe. Maybe it was partly because of what he'd been through that I thought my love could cure him. It must be unconditional if I was still willing to be in this at this point, right? I told myself I was strong enough, that I could endure, for him, for myself.

I think feeling unconditional love, the love a mother can give, was a missing ingredient from his childhood, maybe because his mom died so young and his father was so driven, but such a dirty dog having all those different women around and no one to really raise Tommy properly, teach him the right morals. Sure, Sarah was sweet, but obviously he lacked the maternal figure he needed. I lacked it too, in the years between Mom and Rose, but Rose had *so* made up for it. Susie had been amazing, too, going far beyond what I saw some of the other girls in care got.

Was I fucked up as a result of what I'd been through with him? Maybe. No, probably. But with the glimpses he'd shown me of who he was underneath what his father had made him become, I wanted him. I wanted to help him see he could be who he was meant to be. I'd been pushing away my dark thoughts, reaching for the light.

The last few honeymoonish days had helped. It felt like we were gearing up for something big. It was like it was fortifying me for what was to come because I knew how things could be. Yeah, there was dark. This was a man who didn't hesitate to kill his enemies. This was a man who had been rough with me, too rough with me. But this was also a man who had also shown me that he loved me, that he'd keep me safe, that he'd risk his life for me. I wanted him to feel loved. I wanted my love to be what made him want to stay in the light.

If giving him justification meant I was fucked up, so be it. There were a lot of fucked up people in the world who had evolved because of what they'd been through. I wanted my happily ever after. Would I get it with Tommy? I sure hoped so.

He'd told me when he first got me here that he looked forward to breaking my spirit. Now he was begging me to never let him break it. I sure hoped I could honor that wish of his. When I woke up, he was holding me close, but he was staring at the ceiling, looking like a tortured soul.

Sadness swept through me at his facial expression. I was no stranger to coming to terms with having a fucked-up father who put his own needs before his kids. The two situations weren't the same, but I still got it. I was still coming to terms, myself, with what I'd heard on that recording, admission that my dad's relationship with me was broken because of my mother's death, and his selfish requests. Things were already screwed with the father- daughter thing so he'd might as well get his lifelong dream of being a wise guy out of it.

When I'd seen Tom Sr. yesterday a part of me wanted to spit in his face, to demand answers. But another part of me just felt numb. I had been forced to face and feel so much in the past several weeks. I didn't know how to categorize my feelings. I just knew I had to put one foot in front of the other and move forward somehow. At least I had Tommy with me. He'd help me, he'd protect me. And I'd help him and I'd give him what he needed at the end of every hard day ahead of him.

"I'm calling Greg today. I have more questions for him," he said without looking at me, aware I was awake and watching him.

I snuggled into his side and put my lips to his shoulder and started to trace the outlines of his tattoo with my fingertip.

"I'll have him here this afternoon. You can decide if you want to talk to him or leave him to me."

"Kay," I said, not sure which option I'd choose.

Tommy kissed me on the mouth and then kissed between my breasts, then my navel, then gave me a devilish grin on the way down farther. Sex was a good distractor from our problems. A very good distractor.

Tommy

I had evidence corroborating Earl's story. Regardless of why he did what he did, he took her from me and that was unforgivable. His son Michael had stumbled upon the meth situation because Michael was using and selling and spotted Pop leaving the house of his dealer's dealer.

Earl was dead and gone; I'd shot him after I'd tracked him down, after he told me why. He knew he was a goner when he saw me. He told me that he had a feeling when she was given back to me that I'd be coming for him. He told me he didn't think, at first, I'd get involved. Never thought I was the type to be a girl's hero. My father didn't get involved in these sorts of things since Tia was just a pawn and Earl had known about her father and my Pop's quest to ruin the man's life.

While he didn't think I'd come for her, he hoped my Pop might get lured down here due to his connection to Tia's mother and he'd get his chance for revenge. He told me it wasn't personal with him and I. Obvious to me or I'd have been dead when he shot near me instead of at me. Didn't matter. It was him who took her and he had to pay.

I never figured Pop would get heavily into the drug game. Yeah, he'd said he profited from cocaine here and there back in the 70s and 80s, but didn't bother nowadays beyond weed, which we made good money from, and which I didn't classify as any worse than alcohol. It was now obvious he'd been keeping it from me.

My PI showed proof that he was moving about two million every few weeks through a few guys locally and with that, who knew what else he was into? He'd financed the start-up of a lab and was making a good chunk of change off it. But my PI also talked to Michael's girlfriend, who admitted she had told Earl after Michael died about the meth and that Michael had been worried about seeing Tom Ferrano leave his dealer's dealer's house. Earl had done some investigating of his own and put the pieces together. The girlfriend died of an overdose a few days after my PI talked to her though my PI Zack said she didn't seem like a drug user.

My father was set up for retirement. He was set up to leaving all his kids enough money to live comfortably, (although Dare and I had already set ourselves up and didn't need Pop's dough) as well as leaving money to set his young wife up for life. He had thriving businesses that were run by his people and that continually brought profit. So why was he in the meth game? It was ego, power, it was all so important to Pop. If there was a business where money could be made, he wanted in, wanted to be seen as a master of all trades.

It made me wonder how on earth he'd retire to the Cayman Islands with Lisa. If he was still in the day-to-day shit of this life when me and Dare practically ran Ferrano Enterprises and the subsidiaries for him, would he really let go for retirement? Or had I gone through all these motions for nothing? It made no sense; he was practically shoving me down the aisle so he could hand me the reins, but why was he dabbling in new business, shadier-than-fuck business, at the same time? Did he have Michael's girlfriend killed because Zack was hot on his heels?

Signs pointed to evidence that Tia's Uncle Joe's death wasn't an accident. It was brake failure on his car during a snowstorm and he'd been out on this crazy winding stretch of road that was known for being a bad accident area. He was out on an errand for Pop during that storm. Pop gained a fuck of a lot from Joe's death.

Wife number three, Stacia: she crashed into a tree and died of head injuries. Her airbag didn't go off. They found drugs in her system and figured she fell asleep at the wheel. But she wasn't a known drug user. What she was, was a shrew. She was always getting up in Pop's grill about shit. She was a former model, she was gorgeous, high maintenance. Did Pop get sick of her?

He married Lisa, friends with the girls, just months after Stacia died. Lisa was just as beautiful as Stacia but without the high maintenance. And Lisa got along great with the girls. Stacia and my sisters hated one another, so Pop wasn't getting his Sunday dinners with his family around him with Stacia. That tradition was back after he married Lisa.

Maybe I'd talk to Annette, mother to Dare and the girls. She was all right to me growing up. I wouldn't say she treated me like a son, she always seemed a little afraid of me, she never disciplined me; wasn't affectionate. But she was real affectionate with her own kids. Maybe I needed to get information from her to help put some of the puzzle pieces together.

I hadn't talked to Dare yet. I didn't know how he'd take all of this. I knew he'd believe me, I mean the evidence was right in front of us, but spilling my guts would hurt my brother. Laying out the sort of man our father might really be, the man behind the mask, it wouldn't be a fun conversation. Did I want him to feel what I felt right now? I guess I had to; it was the only way forward.

As for Lita O'Connor: I didn't know if she'd offed herself or if Pop had something to do with it. Had it been a car accident, I wouldn't have had a doubt in my mind. But slit wrists in the tub? I found out her tox screen came up clear, so it wasn't likely Pop could've drugged her and then slit her wrists. There was nothing on the coroner's report that pointed to a struggle.

I'd have a discussion with O'Connor today and then I'd go from there. I didn't know if he could tell me any more than I already knew, but I also wanted Tia to have an opportunity to put things to rest, too.

Tia

When I got downstairs that morning, Sarah was in the kitchen.

"Good morning Chiquita!"

She poured me a coffee and then I watched her put one and a half spoons of sugars in it. That was pretty bold, considering I hadn't seen her in more than a week and had been putting my three sugars in consistently. I accepted the cup, tasted it, then leaned over and fetched the sugar. She smirked at me.

"Tell me about your trip!" I said and sat down, trying not to blush too hard about what she'd walked in on last night.

I spent the next hour listening to her tell me about her relatives, about her holiday. She asked me about our trip. I told her about the Blue Man Group, I told her I won five grand on the slot machines, and then she asked me why our wedding had been postponed.

"Tommy's busy. We're just going to wait until things are less crazy," I said.

"So, you're happy with him? You see what a good man he can be?" she asked.

"I am. And I do." I answered.

Tommy was strolling into the kitchen at that point. He stopped and gave me a narrow-eyed look. I smiled hesitantly.

"How was the trip, Sarah?" he asked her and flashed me a dirty look.

My heart sank. She seemed oblivious to his mood and his features softened as she began to regale him with tales of the trip for the next few minutes while he stood leaning against the counter. Clearly, he knew some of the people she mentioned as she didn't offer explanations of who they were like she'd done with me.

Since I'd heard all these stories I excused myself and went back upstairs with my coffee and left them in the kitchen.

Ten minutes later he came into the bedroom, looking miffed.

"Rule number two?" he said accusingly.

"Huh?"

He closed the distance between us and I backed up until my back hit the closet door. I didn't like the intimidating vibe coming off him.

"Rule number two: do not discuss me with anyone. You give her even a little she'll keep at you for more."

I shook my head. "I didn't. And are we still seriously about that?"

"That's not what it looked like when I found you and Sarah in the kitchen and yeah, when did I say the rules no longer applied?"

Seriously?

I shook my head, "All she said was –"

"I heard her. I'm just reminding you."

"I didn't forget," I said softly.

"Good."

"Where's your necklace?" I asked softly, seeing it wasn't around his neck.

He rolled his eyes. "I took it off last time I worked out. This has nothing to do with the fucking necklace," he snapped.

"Doesn't it?" I asked.

He got even closer to me. "I don't want you discussing me with anyone."

"I wasn't," I defended, feeling intimidated by his body language.

"If I hadn't come in when I had, what would you have said?"

"Nothing more than what I said. She obviously saw us in the kitchen last night practically *doing it* on the counter and she was fishing to hear good things. She knows how I felt before and she's obviously just noticing the change. I wouldn't have –"

He cut me off, "I'm very private."

"She's just happy for you, Tommy."

"I don't want you discussing me with anyone."

"I won't." My heart sank. "You didn't mind what I said to Ruby."

His expression softened and he touched my face with his fingertips.

"I did nothing wrong."

"Your father will be here in half an hour. Are you coming to talk to him?" He changed the subject but kept caressing my face, his eyes warm and filled with apology.

I nodded. "I don't know what I'll say. Maybe I'll just see what he has to say. Can you put your err...necklace on, please?"

Tommy pulled me close. "I love you," he whispered into my hair.

I squeezed. "I love you, too."

He moaned deep in his throat and held me for a minute. "I could say that a thousand times a day to you just to hear you say it back."

My heart swelled. "I'll say it back every time."

He gave me another squeeze. "I'll come get you when I'm done talking to him. Don't give him any information, okay? About anything. And Tia, I've checked and he's spending about half his paycheck every week on drugs. His girlfriend, she's a kindergarten teacher and she likes to get high, too. Since being with him she's now got a lien on her car, which he drives, her credit cards are racked up with cash advances, and she's on probation at work for missing too much time. I'm not sure how much we can trust what comes out of his mouth and this might be pointless, but I at least want to hear from him, okay? And I want you to hear from him, so you can get your answers."

Drugs. *Great.*

I nodded.

He went to the dresser and put his necklace on. I followed him downstairs and as he headed to his office, I headed to the games room in the basement to play Ms. Pacman to pass the time waiting for Tommy to come get me.

Tommy

Hearing love in her voice and hearing her say those three words after having her *I hate you* etched in my brain... it did something to me. It gave me strength. I'd need that strength in the coming weeks as I kept digging through the shit about Pop; that was for sure.

Nino escorted O'Connor in. He sat down, mouth twitching nervously. I hadn't told him in advance of the meeting, just sent Nino to get him from his job. He looked freaked out. Rightly so.

"O'Connor."

"How are ya, Tommy? Good to see ya. How's my sweetpea?"

I gave him a sour look. That he would call her "My" anything made me sick.

"Not thrilled that you're here; I'll say that. Drink?" I poured myself a whiskey.

"Yeah, please. Thanks." He shifted around in the chair. He reminded me a little of Denis Leary.

He was clearly nervous. Or he was tweaking from withdrawals.

"I wanted to ask you some questions about the death of Tia's mother."

He accepted the whiskey and drank it with shaky hands. "Yeah. It's still raw. Hard to believe sometimes that she's really gone. Mind if I smoke?"

"Yeah, I do mind, actually. Tell me about that day. Tell me about before you left her at home and about when you got back that day. Be truthful. I'll check out your story. Don't lie to me."

"I don't come across well in this story, unfortunately," he said, putting his cigarette package back into his pocket with a sigh.

I lifted my chin, urging him to talk.

"Lita and I weren't getting along. She left me after a fight about my gambling and my partying. She saw me flirting at a bar when she'd come to try to drag me home. So she left, but turned back up a few days later and wouldn't say why, wouldn't say if she was giving me a chance; she was just sorta empty-eyed. She was going through the motions, y'know, cleaning the apartment, getting Tia to and from school, but she wasn't herself. The day she died she told me Tia had this school trip and I'd have to pick her up late from school since the bus'd be back after dark. I was running late. I'd been at the track all afternoon. I was in a bad way, you see, I knew my marriage was on the rocks, money was shit, your father kept getting me fired from jobs. I'd get a job and then I'd get canned for no reason. I figured it had to be him; he was out to ruin me. He'd said as much. So I was at the track with my last twenty bucks, not knowing how we were gonna pay the rent 'cuz Lita had quit her waitressing job when she'd left me and they'd hired someone else so when she got back she couldn't get it back. I won $1800. I was stoked. Then I remembered I had to pick up Tia from the school. Didn't know why Lita wanted me to do it, though. No reason why she couldn't do it, so I called home and she didn't answer. I swung by the apartment with flowers for her, ready to give them to her in the hopes she'd perk up before going to pick up my daughter and when I got home, I didn't think she was there but then found her in the tub, a tub filled with her blood." He choked up, covered his mouth, reached into his wallet and pulled out a small wallet-sized photograph and handed it to me.

I'd seen Lita's picture, the picture Tia'd given me of her and Pop and like that, this was like looking at Athena but with darker features, skin more olive, darker eyes, same but darker hair. Same mouth, same bone structure. I felt bile rise in my throat imagining my girl dead in a tub, how that must've felt to him, even if he was a shitty father and a shitty husband. I passed the photo back.

"At first I thought it was suicide. She was so depressed. And then your father hinted it had something to do with him. Tommy, if I weren't such a mess at that point, I might've tried to kill him. But I was already beaten down. And he was untouchable. He spent years destroying my life bit by bit and by the time I lost my wife, I was a shell of a man. I think he pushed drugs in my direction. I was getting offered free blow at those card games when no one else was, getting offered blow for cheap, too; I couldn't afford it, but my guy was selling it to me for dirt cheap and he ran for one of your father's guys. Tom wanted Lita and she wouldn't leave me so he destroyed me in her eyes. I think she didn't leave me out of principle, not because she loved her life with me. I know there's more, more she wouldn't tell me. But I dunno... I think he stalked her and taunted her and she dug her heels in until she couldn't take it any more or until he ended her life somehow." He shook his head.

"So why do you want to work for me?" I changed the subject, feeling a chill. The stuff he said was just my pop's style. If he couldn't have what he wanted, he'd make it so no one else had it either. That didn't mean he killed Tia's mother, but the stuff O'Connor was describing, I'd seen my father destroy men this way, twice already in my life.

Fuck, I'd seen my brother do it, too, for revenge against the bastard his ex fucked around with. Maybe it was another family trait.

He straightened up. "I know the business, I know how things work, I wanted to work for your father years ago, tried to call a truce, but he wouldn't have it. I hear you're taking over and I thought maybe I could get close to my daughter, work for you, help you..." He trailed off, shrugging.

Tia said he'd always had a mafia fascination. If my pop was such a bad fucking guy who'd ruined his life why on earth would he want anything to do with my family?

"Why didn't you take your daughter and run, get away from my father? Why the fuck did you leave her right under his nose?"

He winced and then shrugged and then started talking fast, too fast. "I didn't think I'd get away. He stopped bothering me, too. I just hoped that he'd moved on. She didn't live with me anymore. I let her stay in foster care for her protection, hoping she'd be off Tom's radar. For all these years he left me alone. But then about three- four months ago, I saw him at a poker game, but a small-time game, like he showed up 'cuz he tracked me down and he gave me this look and he winked, and I knew I hadn't seen the last of him. He and I talked for a minute, I tried to make him see I wasn't a threat. Then your brother turned up out of the blue to tell me the score; that it was time to settle my debt. I kicked myself for not protecting her better, but I asked around and found out Tom was retiring and you were taking over. I heard good things about you. I'm good friends with Marco Savarro's brother-in-law and he said Marco said good things about you. I knew Marco worked here at your house while Tia was here. I was devastated when he was killed and when I found out that those Mexicans took my daughter. Then I heard you got her back, and I knew that she was safe and it was this huge weight off my mind. The foster dad says she's wearing your ring and she acts happy. I only ever wanted her safe."

It didn't make sense, what he was saying. A Swiss cheese story. And I wasn't fucking happy about the fact that Mexico seemed to be common knowledge. Who was spreading that around?

"I may have more questions for you," I said. "I'm gonna go get Tia."

"Can I go somewhere and smoke, Tommy? This shit has been stressful," he said. "I need some nicotine before I face my baby girl."

My jaw clenched at him calling her that.

"Nino'll take you out back."

Tia

"Are you sure you want to see him? I think he's tweaking from withdrawals or something."

We were walking upstairs from the basement together.

"I'm sure. What did he say, though?"

"I'll fill you in later. I'll bring you in and then you can be alone with him?" He posed it like a question.

"Can you stay?"

"You want me to stay, I'll stay."

I nodded. "Wait. If I say things that don't sound positive, about how I felt in the beginning with us..."

He shook his head, "It's okay. I won't be offended. But I don't have to be there if you don't want me to be."

I didn't want him to think I was hiding anything, that I had any ulterior motives, so I did want him there. He'd come into the games room, looking frustrated. I'd stood when he walked in and he waited in the doorway and opened his arms and I went right to him and he held me for a minute like he needed the hug. I wanted his support facing my father, too.

We walked into the office and there sat Dad, wearing his work clothes, a blue work jumpsuit with his name embroidered at the breast pocket. He was looking shaky. All the things I'd wanted to ask or say or scream and now here he was, looking pathetically at me with regret in his eyes. It felt so fake.

Tommy shut the door behind himself and motioned for me to sit behind his desk. Dad sat in front of his desk in one of the three chairs facing the desk. Tommy sat on top of the conference table behind him, looking casually out the window.

"Sweetpea," Dad said to me, about to stand.

I raised my hand to halt him and sat in Tommy's chair.

"You look good," he said softly. "So grown up. Remind me so much of your mother."

I was dressed up a little. I wasn't sure why I dressed up for this occasion. I was wearing a white pencil skirt and matching bolero jacket with a pink frilly blouse and a pair of nude heels. I had my hair back in a sleek ponytail with the earrings Tommy had given me in Vegas. I was wearing a necklace that had been my mother's. It was a dainty gold chain with a rose and gold cameo on it. Thankfully the bruise on my throat was now mostly faded and I wasn't sure it was even noticeable, but Dad's eyes landed on my throat. I wasn't sure if it was still visible or if he might be staring at the chain.

His eyes trailed down from my throat to my hand and widened at the sight of my engagement ring.

"Nice rock," he commented, and it was said almost in a prideful way, like he was taking credit.

It made me feel a little queasy.

"I want some truth from you, Dad."

He let out a breath. "The truth is that I know I was a lousy father, but I've always loved you. You've always been the apple of my eye. Tom Ferrano set his sights on you and there wasn't a damn thing I could do about it. You don't know how it is in this world, Tia. The man had power and reach and there was nothing I could do. Your mother grew up in that world and I know she didn't want it for you, but I just prayed you'd somehow be happy and safe. It looks like you are. I wanna be in your life. I feel like I can finally be in your life now that I'm not looking over my shoulder all the time. I tried to stay away to keep you safer. It didn't work, and here we are, but maybe it'll be okay. Maybe now we can move ahead, put all that behind us."

"You left me to rot in foster homes to protect me?" I was incensed.

"Crenshaws? That big house? That was rotting?"

I didn't like the snark in his voice, like I'd had it so easy.

"You had no way of knowing where I'd end up and I wasn't there the whole time. Do you know the stories I've heard from some of the girls? Some of them that lived in group homes or who got molested or abused by other foster kids, foster dads? You had no way of knowing I'd be okay. You'd go months without checking on me. And as good as they were to me, they took me because you abandoned me. You. You abandoned your daughter after her mother died and social services paid someone else to do your job, to raise me. Everyone tells me I'm very well-adjusted considering what I've been through in my life but Dad, you get zero credit for that. Zero fucking credit."

"I've never seen you so angry." He looked down.

"This? This is nothing! Let's talk about how you tricked me on my high school graduation day to be your "marker" when you knew, you fucking knew what you were really doing! You basically sold me into slavery, Dad."

Dad winced. Tommy was still seated on the conference table, arms folded while watching me with an unreadable expression.

"I was sold like a piece of chattel," I continued, rage propelling my words. "I was treated like a piece of property to be pawned off. And then when I escaped because it was fucking unbearable..." I glanced at Tommy, but he made no moves, his expression didn't change. "What did you do? Did you help me? Did you? No, you called Tommy and told him where to find me. Do you know what I had endured up to that point? Do you have any idea? Do you even care?"

Dad shook his head. "I had no choice. And you were obviously safer here than down in Mexico. Imagine what might've happened to you if I hadn't told him where you were? If you'd gotten nabbed before he found you, maybe escaped a bit longer he wouldn't have wanted to rescue you from Mexico. Maybe you should've just did what you were told and stayed put."

"That's enough," Tommy spat.

My eyes were wide, I was shocked. What kind of twisted logic?

"Listen," Dad drawled, smiling now, trying to salvage this, his eyes darting to and fro between Tommy and me. "I did what I thought I needed to do. I always did. I just wanted you safe. I was no match for the Ferranos. I knew you'd have a good life here. Tommy is a good man; he's taking care of you. You're happy. I never understood why Mom wanted away from this life. I tried to work my way up, but Tom wouldn't let me in. I thought I was a dead man, that Tom would have me taken out after your mom. But he didn't. Then when he came for you I thought through you, I dunno, maybe I'd know we were now safe and then I'd be a part of your life. Tommy, I'm available. I'm happy to start at the bottom, I–"

"Get out," I interrupted.

Dad looked at Tommy beseechingly and stayed perfectly still. There was silence for a beat.

Finally, Tommy notched a brow and jerked his chin up. "You heard her. Nino will walk you out."

"Uh," Dad got to his feet, "Can I uh... can I get a lift back home? I don't have cab fare, I..."

"Get the fuck outta here." Tommy pointed toward the door. "Nino!" he hollered, making me jump a little.

The door flew open and Nino was in the room, looking ready to crush bones.

"Escort him out," Tommy said.

Nino hauled my dad out of the room by the scruff while Tommy followed them out into the hall and shut the door.

I don't think I was breathing.

Then Tommy was back. He shut the door and leaned against it and looked at me while I stared into space. Dad hadn't even looked back at me on his way out the door. I looked up at Tommy finally, not sure what I'd see.

"Come here, baby," Tommy said.

I stood slowly and fought the trembling that had started in my chin. No, no more tears. Not for my father. Tommy pulled me against him and kissed the top of my head and held me. The strength of his arms around me, the solidness of his chest, the smell of him, he smelled like home to me now.

He softly started to fill me in on the rest of the conversation he had with my father, and I kept dry eyes throughout the time he talked, my head just resting against his chest.

My father was a fuck up. My father was probably a rebound for my mother who was looking for a different life than what she'd grown up with, but my dad was the wrong choice. Tom Ferrano set out to ruin my dad, to show my mom what a loser he was so she'd come back to him. It didn't work. It might've driven my mom to suicide. Tom Ferrano might have killed my uncle as he had been allegedly obsessed with my mother and the power my uncle wielded. Mom's family were connected, even more than Tom Ferrano back in those days. I never knew. She told me nothing about her past.

Tommy didn't have any proof that his father did anything to my mother directly, but Tommy had concerns that a lot of what my father had said was true because he said it fit his Pop's MO. Tom Sr's MO was get to someone anyway he could and often that was by hitting them where it hurt and making their life crumble around them.

With my Uncle Joe out of the way he had more power than ever. Tommy said he got off on the power, the control over peoples' lives. Tommy said his pop loved being a puppet master and his eyes were filled with irony, apology, as he told me that.

"So, what now?" I asked, looking up at him and trying to ignore the way Tommy's voice changed as he talked about his father's love for control.

Tommy shook his head. "I'll dig for more info. I have plans to talk to Bianca's ma, she's been an aunt to me. And to talk to Dario and the girls' mother. Then I've got to decide what to do."

"What do you mean what to do? What can you do?"

Tommy shrugged. "Let's see where the truth takes us and then I'll decide."

I didn't like the darkness in his eyes at that statement.

I heard a commotion outside the door. Tommy opened it. Nino and another guy I didn't recognize were rushing toward the door.

Nino said, "T, I think you should come outside. Your father and Greg O'Connor are at it."

Tommy booked it toward the door. I followed.

Outside, the front gate was open, and Tom Sr. was beating the snot out of my father out on the street. Tommy ran, passing James, and hauled his father off my father, whose face was gushing blood.

"Tia! Back in the fucking house!" Tommy yelled.

His father tried to pull free of Tommy's grip and then the most awful thing happened. Tommy's silver crucifix necklace flew airborne during the scuffle and it fell. I ran for it, but it fell down and when my eyes landed on the ground, they didn't land on concrete or on grass. It was a sewer grate. I landed on my knees and cried out. Tommy let go of his father and reached for me.

Tom grabbed my dad again and cold-clocked him. Dad was knocked out, lying on the ground bleeding right beside the sewer that had swallowed up Tommy's necklace, Tommy's anchor to goodness.

I was inconsolable. I was on my now bloodied knees bawling, staring at the sewer. Anyone watching might've thought that I was crying for my passed-out bleeding father, but my eyes met Tommy's and I knew he saw precisely what I was weeping about.

He hollered out, "Jimmy!" and then Nino and James got my father up off the ground carried him, barely conscious, back toward the house.

Tommy yelled at his father. "Pop, inside!" And then he lifted me off the ground and cradled me to his chest, carrying me tight against himself, back to the house while I cried inconsolably into his chest, clutching his shirt.

Tommy

The guys put O'Connor into a car and had someone drive him. I knew they'd either get him looked at by a doctor or they'd bring him back to his house if he was all right. I got Tia into the family room, set her on the couch, and covered her shoulders with a blanket. I dabbed at her bleeding knees with tissue.

She'd stopped crying, but was making shuddering noises and had the hiccups. Sarah brought her a glass of water and put two glasses and a decanter of scotch on the coffee table, left the room and then came back with a first aid kit. I took it from her and waved her away. I put antiseptic and then Band-Aids on Tia's knees and then I poured a drink for Pop and for myself. He sat a few cushions away from Tia on the sofa, watching me bandage her up with a weird expression on his face. I was sitting on the coffee table, my legs between the two of them.

"Pop, it's time for the truth."

He downed his scotch and looked at her.

I said, "I know some of it, I know you know that I know some, but we need you to fill in the blanks."

"I'm sorry if that upset you," he said to Tia. "That necklace you're wearing; I gave that to your mother for her eighteenth birthday. Caused quite an uproar at the time."

She put her hand to her throat.

"We were crazy about each other but her brother, my best friend and business partner, wanted no part of it. He didn't want one of his buddies dating his little sister. Died when he was 28. Tragic loss. I was there for her and she was there for me. We started to date. It was at the end of my marriage to Annette. But Lita and I had a fight one night and split up. Stupid fight. She decided she wanted no part of the life I lead. We went our separate ways. She married your father. She married fast so I'd know we were really over. You were born. Then we reconnected again; she wasn't happy with him, talked about leaving him. She got pregnant with my baby."

Tia gasped.

"She had all this guilt. She decided to give things another go with him. Your father made her get rid of my kid. I've always hated him for that. I'm Catholic, you know; we don't believe in that. When he made her have that abortion, I believe it destroyed her. He was the reason she died." Pop poured another glass of scotch.

"I saw you a few months ago," Pop said. "Saw you all grown up one day on the street with your friends and it was like looking at her all young and happy again and I, I ... I decided to give my son what I should've had. I've been married a lot. But if I'd married Lita, that would've been forever. I won't deny I wanted to take Gregory's child the way he took my child from me, the child I never got to know." He shrugged and downed the drink. "So I hate your father. Sorry but that's how it is. Tommy cleared his debt and it's done. I've wanted to knock him out for years and saw his smug face when he left here today and so I just closed the chapter with my fists, that's all. I'm done." Pop looked at me and raised his hands defensively. "I'm done, my boy. I know what you said when you cleared the debt, but I just needed to knock the smug look off his face. I'm done now."

Tia had stopped shuddering and hiccupping. She was dabbing her eyes.

Pop got to his feet. "You wanna have him at your wedding, I'll keep my mouth shut and I'll be nice. As nice as I can be under the circumstances. You two have kids and he has to come to the baptism and so forth, I'll be on my best behavior. But don't expect me to be friends with him and unless it's important don't expect me to be under the same roof."

"C'mon Pop," I said and signaled for him to follow me. I leaned over and kissed her on the forehead and whispered, "Back in a few."

Pop and I stepped outside. His driver was standing by the gate talking to Nino and Jimmy and they halted conversation when they saw us come out. I shot a dirty look their way. They looked like a couple of gossiping old ladies.

"What brought you by today?" I asked.

"Just wanted to say hello," he answered and shrugged but he was looking me right in the eye, the way he always did when he was feeding me bullshit.

It was obvious that he knew O'Connor was here. Someone told him that my guys were picking the guy up. Who?

"Come by the office tomorrow morning, we gotta talk more about the Fete plan. Unfortunately, Denarda's back in. People flying in tomorrow. I'll fill you in later."

"Right," I said, jaw tight. Leo Denarda. Great.

"When ya getting married?" Pop asked.

I shook my head. "Not sure."

"What's the problem? You not sure about her now?"

I shook my head. "I've never been more sure about anything in my life."

He frowned at me.

"I want it to be right. We're almost there. It won't be long."

"You're keeping me from my Valhalla." He wagged a finger at me.

"Naw, Pop. You go. We'll be good. We'll get married soon."

"Maybe. The new house is still bein' built so not a major rush. We'll talk more later." He slapped me on the back and then headed down the front stairs toward his car. His driver jogged over from the gate and opened the car door for Pop. I followed the car out and stared at the sewer in front of my house. My mother's necklace was gone. No way I'd get it back. Just as well, maybe. I needed to learn to control myself without it, anyhow.

I heard Nino call out, "T?"

I looked over my shoulder to see that suddenly Tia was beside me, staring at the sewer.

I gave her a sad look. She grasped the cameo necklace around her neck and yanked hard, breaking the chain. She looked at the necklace in her hand for a second and then she dropped it over the sewer grate, it caught for a second and then slid down between the slats. She turned on her heel and walked back toward the house. I let out a slow breath and followed her.

Tia

I walked up to the bedroom and kicked off my shoes and crawled into bed, the soft gray cashmere throw Tommy had put over my shoulders still wrapped around me.

The shit my father had pulled in my life all pointed to him being a weak and broken man. But what I saw today was like an addict swindling to get his fix. He was looking for an in with this family and thought I was it. And he turned on me. Tommy had said he was still using drugs. Was he imagining working for this family and getting wealthy and having access to all the sins he wanted? Drugs, gambling? Notoriety? Was he that out of touch with reality?

Tommy came into the bedroom a few minutes after I did, looking stressed. He took the navy-blue suit jacket he was wearing off and climbed in beside me and pulled me to his chest. I was going to cry again. It couldn't be helped. So much for my tough, hardened self that I thought I was after my conversation with my Dad.

"Your necklace," I whispered, rubbing my hand up his chest.

"I know," he sighed.

"That was really fucked up," I said.

"Yeah," he replied.

"But what did he mean?" I asked.

"Hm?" he asked distractedly.

"He said you cleared my father's debt. That didn't make sense. Don't I clear it by marrying you?"

Tommy's eyes focused on me and he said, "I paid your father's debt."

"Huh?"

"Pop gave you to me as a gift. But I paid it anyway."

I shook my head and frowned, not understanding.

He continued, "I paid it. Despite the gift, I wanted the debt paid. So when we got back from Mexico I paid it, with interest. To make it done."

I started to feel spinny. "You paid for me?"

"Not for you, for the debt. To end it."

"You paid money for me." My fingers were at my temples.

"Tia, listen—"

"You really just had to 'own' me, didn't you? You had to pay money for me because I'm a piece of fucking property to you!" I pushed at his chest to get away from him.

"No, that wasn't it."

He made me look at him by grabbing my chin and staring right into my eyes. "I paid money so that the debt was settled. The debt being settled meant my father wouldn't meddle, wouldn't think he had a right to do anything to your father again. Because he's your father I did that so that you wouldn't have to deal with my father fucking with your father's life anymore. I know how Pop's brain works. If I hadn't settled the debt, he'd still think he had a right to continue to settle the score. Stealing you wasn't enough. Fucking with Greg's life wasn't enough. It might never have ended. Never. And you're not just a piece of property to me; you're every fuckin' thing to me."

I couldn't think straight, I wanted him to let go of me. I pushed at his chest again, but he pulled me tighter against him. Instead of fighting, which I knew was useless, I just went limp. He held me close and rocked me for a long time and I was just limp. No tears, no expression, no thoughts. Just limp.

"Baby?" he finally said and touched his lips to my forehead, one hand threaded into my hair.

I closed my eyes tight. "I can't," I said.

"Athena." He hauled me back a few inches and held my face in both of his hands. I opened my eyes.

"I love you," he said.

I nodded a little.

"Baby, I love you," he repeated.

I opened my mouth but nothing would come out but a little sob that I pulled back. Tommy's expression dropped. He let go of me and I dropped limply onto the pillows. He left the room, slamming the door.

I'd promised him just this morning that I'd always say it back. I failed him.

* * *

Sarah was tapping my shoulder. I jackknifed up in bed, gasping.

"Sorry, Chiquita; you been sleeping three hours. Tommy has to go away on business. I need to pack a bag for him, he asked me to tell you. He's in the office if you wanna go say bye. He says he'll be gone a few days."

I put my head back on the pillow and pulled the blanket up over my head. I didn't fall back asleep; I just sort of laid there. I heard her leave a few moments later.

I didn't know where Tommy was going and I didn't care. Whatever. Him away instead of here meant I wouldn't have to endure his mood swings, endure his wrath without the protection of his necklace.

14

Tia

Five Days Later...

For five days, I stayed in the bedroom other than to make trips to the kitchen, the Ms. Pacman machine, and back. I read, watched TV, and played games online. I'd gotten my period for four days and now it was gone. I got a big zit on my chin that was now pretty well near gone, too. My knees were almost healed, my throat no longer had a bruise (not on the outside but I suspected I was internally scarred for life from it).

I was raging for sugar or something comforting other than ice cream, anything but ice cream, but Sarah had no other junk in the house other than sugary cereal, which was bizarre because she was a sugar hater but purchased several boxes of cereal with the word "Sugar" in a huge-ass font on the box so I threw myself headfirst into said sugary boxes of cereal, using them to drown out the emotions about my life, my parents, my future, my relationship. Sarah brought me food. Sometimes I ate it, sometimes I didn't. I woke up every night several times. I think I was looking for him, but I wouldn't allow myself to acknowledge it.

I ignored Sarah and the four guards at the house. Yeah, he'd left me here but doubled the security. Twice a day, at least, Sarah asked me if I'd checked my phone and I'd always say that it was charging. It was plugged in on the nightstand but turned off. I didn't want to turn it on because I didn't want to know whether or not he'd messaged me. If he had, I didn't want to read them. If he hadn't, I didn't want to know either because that'd make me consider the fact that he hadn't bothered to message me. Stupid girl.

Yesterday, Sarah had said that Tessa and Lisa showed up to visit me, but I feigned a headache and made her get rid of them. I missed Luc's baby shower. I knew Sarah went. She came up to tell me she was going but didn't invite me. I suspected Tommy didn't want me leaving the house, anyway. And what good would it do for Tommy's family, friends and everyone related to the Ferranos that I hadn't met yet to meet Tommy's fiancée, a member of the walking dead?

After five days, he came back. The door swung open and there he was. I was in bed with my laptop playing Texas Hold 'Em poker online with fake money, a lot of fake money as apparently I was some sort of poker savant (ever since losing my shirt, literally, at strip poker to him). My hand was inside a box of Sugar Crisp. It was 11:30 at night. I was in sweats, a messy bun in my hair. I'd had a shower that morning, but I didn't even brush my hair, just shoved it up.

He dropped his suitcase on the floor and threw his jacket on the chair in the corner by the window. He folded his arms and stared at me. I glanced in his direction and looked back to my screen. I unceremoniously shoved another handful of the sticky cereal into my mouth and pressed the button to fold from the game on the screen and licked my fingers. The tension level in the room shot up to near nuclear as he spoke, no roared,

"Where the FUCK is your engagement ring?"

My blood ran cold.

Suddenly he was in my face, the cereal and the laptop swept off the bed onto the floor.

I looked at the nightstand where the ring sat and then up to him. His eyes landed on it and then he picked it up and shoved it on my sticky finger. I made a painful squeal and swallowed hard. My heart thumped painfully in my chest and in my ears. His face was distorted into a snarl.

"That never comes off your fucking finger!" He glared at me. "It has a GPS in it. If anyone tries to take you again, it's how I'll fucking find you. I see that ring off your finger for any reason that tells me you're planning to run. You planning to run?"

I shook my head *no*.

"No?" Heat and rage were all I could see in his eyes.

I shook my head again.

"Why was it off?" he demanded.

My head dropped to the pillow and I covered my face with the blanket. He ripped it right off me and tossed the blanket behind him so that it fell on the floor with the cereal and the laptop. I shrieked and pulled a pillow against myself and backed up against the headboard.

"What is your fucking problem?" he shouted. He picked up my phone and turned it on and it made a whole bunch of bleeps. Obviously, he'd been messaging me, lots.

"Done feeling sorry for yourself yet?"

"You're the one who left!" I yelled, my voice hoarse. It might've been days since I'd spoken.

"You've been fucking catatonic. Obviously, you didn't care," he retorted.

"I don't fucking care!" I retorted snottily. "I'm tired of fucking caring. Everything I care about means nothing. My father, my mother, you. Nothing."

"Why am I nothing?"

"You're not nothing. I'm nothing. I'm just…" I put my hands over my face.

He sat on the bed and leaned forward and took my hands off my face and weaved his fingers through mine. His face was seriously pissed off-looking, but his touch was gentle.

"I told you that you're everything."

"What do you want from me? You want to hit me? Go ahead and hit me. You want to fuck me? Go ahead and–"

He let go of me and got up. "Fuck," he stared at me a beat and then said, "I'm taking a shower."

I lay there for a second and then lifted the phone, which he'd tossed on the bed, and scrolled through the texts sent throughout the time he was gone.

Come down to the office, baby.

Tia?

I'm flying to Italy with my brother for a few days. Tell no one. Just that I'm away on business. I'll text when I land. Love you.

P.S Delete my texts after you read them.

I'm here. You okay?

I'm laying here wishing you were beside me, baby. I can't seem to sleep without you beside me. I should've brought you. I know you're upset. I'm sorry you've been through so much in the last month. I'm working on fixing things. I'm on that road to making things better. Promise I'll find a way. Love you.

I heard Etta James on the radio today in a restaurant and miss you so much. I didn't know I was lonely without you until I had you. Now I don't think I would want to live

without you. Can't wait to marry you and dance again with you to that song.

Then there was a link to a YouTube video link. Then another text.

I miss the smell of your hair & how you wrinkle your nose at me & the way I wake up every morning with you all wrapped around me. Love how you keep wearing pink since I bought that pink fishing rod for you. Miss you. Write back?

That was four days ago. He'd given up on messaging me. I touched the link to the video and it opened a YouTube window and started to play the Etta James song. It was playing to images from the Disney Wall-e movie. I loved that movie.

As the song filled the air, so much emotion surged through me I thought I was going to fall over. When she sang about her heart wrapped up in clover the night she looked at him I thought about us in that field on his farm with me in the grass, him over me with sunrays practically bursting from him and how much emotion I'd felt in that moment.

I thought about him dancing with me and singing this song in my ear. I pushed away thoughts of him screaming in my face with his belt in his hand and then I saw that couple on the stage in Vegas embracing one another after he gave her what she needed and she gave him what he needed. I thought about how amazing it was when I declared I was his in the bathroom in the hotel that night.

The look in his eyes, the heat, the emotion. The freedom in being his was something I wanted now. Right now.

When I gave into being his, I didn't have to feel anything but the bliss of giving myself over to him. I put the phone down and ran to the bathroom and hit the brakes when I got to the shower door.

He was still in the shower. Did I want to climb in there with him and bridge the gap between us? I was so fucking scared of what I felt for him, of what he'd made me into in such a short amount of time. I was so scared of who he could be. Did I embrace our relationship and take the good with the bad? Or did I stay in this shell, this sub-existence I was in for the past several days?

This man bought me and at first, I was so infuriated about it because it made me a thing that could be bought but thinking about him doing it to end his father's hold on my father, it was something that spoke more of him thinking of me instead of himself. But it was still me being traded among these men like property.

Was it so awful to be the property of Tommy Ferrano? He loved me. He wanted a life with me. What kind of life we'd have, I didn't really know, but I was the one he wanted to seesaw through light and dark with. He'd sent me lovely messages while he was gone. He'd missed me. I was here feeling sorry for myself while he was off trying to fix things to make our lives better and missing me while I was ignoring him. Regret lanced through me.

I pulled my sweatshirt up and over my head and unhooked my bra. I took my pants and panties down and pulled my socks off and then I opened the shower door. He turned around and looked at me and finger combed his wet hair out of his eyes and sighed. I pulled the elastic out of my hair and dropped it and then wrapped my arms around him and put my cheek against his chest.

He didn't put his arms around me, just stood there. Maybe I'd pushed him too far. My heart squeezed painfully.

"Tommy," I whispered into his chest and then touched my lips to his wet skin.

"What?" His voice was cold.

"I've been a naughty girl."

His torso stiffened.

"I've been cold and distant and living in my head and I need you to bring me back to life. Show me who I belong to, that it's not okay for me to be like this, to feel like a robot."

His hands gripped my shoulders and he stared right into my eyes, straight into my soul, even.

I needed this. We needed it.

"You're free to go," he said.

I frowned. "Huh?"

"You're free. Go."

He left me in the shower. He just left me there.

I pulled my chin off the floor and got into a bathrobe and when I came out of the bathroom, he wasn't there. I exited via the patio doors and hurried down the stairs, water still dripping off me in just the long white robe and nothing on my feet and saw that all the garage doors were shut. The gates were closed and there were guards mulling about. I didn't think he'd left that fast, so I went back into the house through the main floor patio doors.

Not in the kitchen. Not in his office. Not in the family room. The door to the back hall was open.

I went down the back hall and heard thudding downstairs. I ran back up to the bedroom and queued up the song on my phone I'd been listening to multiple times a day from the laptop during my poker playing, and quickly blotted up the water in my hair with a towel, then as I got to the bottom of the basement steps I slipped it into the pocket of the bathrobe. I could hear the thud, thud, thud very loudly. I found him in the gym. He was in just a pair of black gym shorts and he was beating the ever-loving life out of a big heavy bag, his skin still wet from the shower or maybe wet with sweat.

I stood behind him.

"Hey," I said softly.

He flinched and then started hitting the bag harder.

"Tommy."

"You have until the count of ten to get outta my sight," he said, not turning around.

"What? Why?"

"Go upstairs, pack your shit, and go. The guys'll open the gate. Go. You're free."

"Why?"

"I can't control this rage in me. You stay and I will break you. I know it, Athena. You know it. You're almost broken now. You need to go now before I finish you off. I'm that fucked. And you're that close. Take your casino money, hock the ring, and go. Leave town. Have a nice life. Don't ever let me know where you are. Don't."

I stared at the muscled details of his back as he resumed punching. I stepped to the side and caught his profile. His jaw was tight, his eyes were narrow, and he was punching the bag so hard.

"One," he said through gritted teeth and then there was a loud thud as he punched the bag.

"I don't wanna go."

"Two," he said and punched the bag harder.

"Tommy, I don't."

"Three. I don't have the necklace, Athena. It can't stop me," He snapped and punched again a bunch of times. Pow, pow, pow pow pow.

"I'm sorry I got stuck in my head the last few days. I've been through a lot. It's just been, I just need..."

"Four."

POW! I think it must've been with all of his strength.

"I need you. I want us to figure this out. Together, we can–"

"Five!" he yelled and then he turned around and faced me and whipped his gloves off and to the floor.

I stood still, staring him in the eyes, summoning courage while facing the rage emerging on his face.

"You're not fucking Dumbo the goddamn elephant who needs the feather to fly, Tommy Ferrano. You don't need the necklace. I'll be the necklace. Fuck me, take me however you need to, then hold me afterwards and tell me you love me. Do what you need to do for us both to get back to where we need to be."

I took a step forward.

"Six," he said it softly, shaking his head back and forth, his voice and his eyes stone cold, warning me.

I took a step back. "What happens if I'm still here when you get to ten? Are you gonna hurt me? Are you going to...what? Kill me?"

"Seven." He took one step forward.

"Babe," I pleaded.

"If I get to ten, Tia," he growled. "If I get there and you're here, you are getting hurt. Because it means you're never allowed to leave. This is your one chance, baby girl. One chance. Take it or accept me for the fucked up, sadistic prick I am. Take it or be prepared to be everything I need you to be for me. The love of my life. The only thing that keeps me from going postal. Be sure you're ready, ready to be there for me, to be what I need whether that means I need to hold you, spank you, whip you, fuck you, destroy you."

I gulped.

His voice was low, guttural; words came through clenched teeth. "Eight. Make your mind up right the fuck now!"

The room might as well have been devoid of oxygen.

"Nine."

He folded his arms across his chest and his brows were up. I stared at him. And then I opened my mouth and closed it. Then I opened it again and blew out a long breath, then I turned my back on him and went to leave. I got three steps away and I stopped in my tracks and stood there with my back to him.

He said nothing. I stood still. Time stood still.

Then, after an eternity, he said, "Ten." His voice sounded hoarse, pained. And that's when I started to run for the stairs.

A few paces and he tackled me to the floor. He was on top of me.

"What in the fuck?" He had my arms pinned above my head.

I went limp and looked at him.

"You wait until I get to ten and that's when you decide to run?" Rage shot out of his eyes and his voice boomed like thunder. "What's that supposed to fucking mean?"

"It means it's too late. I can't go."

"Do you or don't you want to fucking go?"

"I don't. But I wanted you to stop me, show me you couldn't let me go." I wriggled one arm free from his grasp, took the iPhone out of my robe pocket, and hit play on the video app; it played the Stone Sour version of Wicked Game. It was the closest thing I'd found to the version we'd heard in Vegas.

He grabbed me roughly and flipped me onto my belly, sending my phone sliding several feet away. The song kept playing. Then my robe was yanked off me and I was naked on the cold basement floor. My hips were lifted and I heard him fumble and then he impaled me with one slam of his hips. He had me a few inches off the floor by holding my throat and his mouth was right at my ear,

"You're mine," he growled.

"Yeah," I breathed.

"Fuck!" he grunted.

"I love you," I whimpered.

"What have you fucking done you stupid, beautiful girl?" he moaned, his voice strangled sounding. He kept pounding into me from behind.

"I know," I breathed, "I couldn't help it. I fell in love with you. I'm yours."

He let go of my throat, grabbed my hair roughly and groaned into my ear as he pushed maybe ten or fifteen times before he came inside of me as the song hit the chorus.

Then I was up, off the floor, in his arms. He grabbed my phone and stopped the song from playing, tossed the robe over me, my face buried in his neck, and he carried me up the stairs and back to our bedroom where he was ready to go immediately and where he then fucked me hard for the next hour or ten, I didn't know, not letting me come, just pounding into me, using his cock and his mouth and his fingers to repeatedly and torturously bring me right to the edge, to the brink, and then stopping and pounding into me some more, saying dirty, filthy words into my ear about how I was his to fuck, how hard he was going to fuck me, about how I didn't get to come until he allowed me to come, and that today he'd fuck me not only until I couldn't move but until he couldn't move.

He repeatedly slapped my ass, pinched my nipples hard, he bit into my shoulder, not drawing blood but definitely leaving a mark. He came again, and then he was almost immediately hard again.

He took me. Again. At the end, he drove his fingers into my sopping wetness and then he wet his cock with me and then told me, "Your ass is mine."

I tried to get away, squealing, "Wait!" but he didn't wait. He got me on my side lying down and he pushed his cock slowly into my ass, taking my anal virginity.

At first it burned, it scorched, but then he told me, "Give in to me; relax and let go, baby," and when the word 'go' left his lips, my muscles loosened and the feeling transcended, changed from pain to something else, something I wouldn't quite call pleasure at first but in my head I think it was about giving in that made the pain change.

While he was deep in my ass he grabbed my clit, tweaked it and said, "Come for me, baby." As he circled it fast, it began to build and build.

Finally, getting to the peak, my legs shook so hard I couldn't control them, and he was moaning into my ear, rotating his hips against my backside. I came harder than I'd ever come in my life. I was *done*; it was as if a thousand pieces of me had shattered all over the bed.

Tommy

She was in my bed, in my arms, we were tired and sore in all the right places and for her, some of the wrong places. Almost all was right in the world. Almost.

"Are you awake?" I asked.

"Sorta," she answered, her head on my chest, her leg locked over mine, one of her hands up at my face with her fingers tangled in my hair.

"You okay?" I asked.

"My legs are still shaking. And my bum hurts," she said softly and then she started to laugh. I laughed a little and then we were both laughing, holding each other, kissing one another, and then she had tears in her eyes, a beautiful smile on her face. I kissed the tears away and held her tighter.

She snuggled into me and whispered, "I think you totally destroyed my ass."

I laughed a little. "It'll feel better tomorrow."

She let out a dreamy sigh. "I love you."

"I love you, baby. Thank you."

"No, thank you," she answered and I squeezed her tighter.

"I'm sorry," she whispered.

"Don't," I said.

"No, I am. I just... I went backwards when I found all that out and just shut down, I..." she trailed off.

"It's okay," I whispered and kissed her forehead. "You've been through a lot."

We lay still together for a long time and neither of us spoke. Finally, when it was obvious we weren't going to sleep, she looked up at me and ran her thumb across my lower lip.

"Tell me about your trip."

I leaned sideways and shifted and then reached into the sheets and pulled off three or four sticky pieces of puffed wheat cereal that was stuck to my thigh. I gave her a funny look.

She laughed, cackled even. Laughed for so hard and so long she made me remember her age. Barely an adult, still young enough and still *Tia* enough to giggle uncontrollably like that. It was cute.

Maybe all was not lost. Not yet. I tossed the cereal on the nightstand and when she regained her composure I dug into my story.

"Dare and I went to see his mother."

Her expression went serious.

"She wouldn't tell us shit. We tried to dig into the past and she wouldn't talk. She was like a cornered animal. Dare got pissed. But then as we were leaving, her husband stopped us, and we went for a drive with him. He knew what my father had put her through, he knew a lot of shit. He said it took him years to earn her trust and that she was that broken from Pop. The guy's just headed into end stage Cancer so he told us he has nothing to lose and that it'd give him some degree of peace to tell us things that might mean change for the family, for Annette's kids and grandkids. My father was looking responsible for the death of his third wife. He almost killed Annette, too. Annette escaped with the kids because he was a sadistic psychopath. Used to beat her. Used to tie her up during sex."

I stopped and swallowed, letting that sink in for her, before continuing.

"And because she got the real idea of what he got up to in his business life she decided to run. He tracked her down in Italy, hauled the kids back and left her there threatening to kill her if she turned back up. He allowed her to see the kids once a year but that was it. He's responsible for the death of your uncle, too. It was a power play. It got him Joe's end of the profits and let him take the business to the next level and it was supposed to get him your mother, too. They split because of his temper and because of what he was getting up to in business. But then he sweet-talked her into leaving your father and somehow she found out about Joe and that's when she left and had the abortion, an abortion she chose to have, not was forced to have. Your father might not even be aware of it.

She confided in Annette that the pregnancy by my pop was a product of rape. They traded war stories, stayed in touch almost until your mother died. It was like therapy for the both of them. I still don't know if he killed her or not. We know the doctor who did the abortion was killed in a car accident after my father found out, too. Pop had a thing for killing people in their cars. I'm out, baby. I'm out of this life. I just need to make a few moves and it's over."

She was quiet. All traces of her comical outburst gone. Way gone. "Babe?"

She looked contemplative. "Are you confronting him, are you–"

I cut her off. "No fucking way. He would not hesitate to snuff me out."

"Tommy, surely not..."

"Yeah, Tia. Surely so. My father believes that without 100% loyalty, you're an enemy. Blood means nothing in the face of betrayal. I found out he killed his cousin a few years before Joe, too, over a stupid business disagreement. He knows I'm digging around. I've found out more shit than I wanted to even know. Stuff that would make your stomach turn. What I do about it is what'll be the ultimate test. You know how I've tested you a few times? Guess I learned that from him; learned too much from him. You have no idea how many times he tempted and tested me and my brother over the years to make us prove ourselves. Would you trust your father after all you've found out?"

"Point taken."

"I'm gonna try to get him to retire. Dare and I are making a few key moves, and then we're out of 30% of the lines of business we're in right now. That's the stuff that has risk, anything illegal whatsoever. Pop's moving outta the country. He doesn't like what we've done, we deal then. This is gonna take time, but we'll be working our exit strategy pronto. We'll end the shady relationships as soon as is feasible."

"Dario's on board?"

"Yep."

"The idea of you without the crime, Tommy? That's just...it's amazing." Her eyes were glistening with happiness.

I gave her a squeeze. "It won't be overnight but it will happen. I don't need the risk. The business can be run without it. And if Pop can't deal, I have enough dough put away to do something else, without him."

She snuggled into my shoulder and traced my tattoo lines with her fingers. I loved when she did that. We were quiet for a while. I ran my fingers up and down her arm. Then I heard her breathing even out.

She'd passed another test, one I didn't really realize I'd been giving her at first. I lay there most of the night, absorbing the feel of her, knowing bone deep that even if she'd started to run when I got even to two or three, I'd have stopped her. As much as I wanted her safe, her pain gone, there was just no way would I have ever let her go. I was too fucking selfish. That she didn't wanna go was a soothing balm for my pain. That she wanted me to chase her down and show her I'd never let her go made my heart sing. I knew that soulmates were real. I had rock solid confirmation that she was made for me. Pop got one thing right, even if it was pure evil that he'd done it at all and even if I was wrong to take it.

My brother wasn't as surprised as I expected him to be when I had finally talked to him about my findings. Turns out he had been noticing things over the years, too, things that didn't add up. He had an okay relationship with his mother but said she was always on edge whenever they saw each other. He said that it wasn't a natural relationship, and he knew Pop had her afraid of her own shadow. I needed to make sure that I didn't become the man Pop was. I was worried I was close. Dario felt the same.

The night we got the truth from Annette's husband, Tony, we sat and got drunk and talked all night about it. My brother said he saw Pop backhand his ma one night when me and the girls were asleep. He'd come out for a glass of water and saw Pop send her flying across the room. Dare said that when Debbie had cheated on him his first instinct was to beat the shit out of her, but instead he beat the guy because he'd decided as a little kid that he'd never hit a woman.

My brother was closer to me than anyone in the world and I couldn't believe that with all the talks we'd had about how we'd run the company once Pop retired that we never once sat and talked in any depth about Pop's violent streak, about how demanding of a prick he was, about suspicions that the man was darker than anyone knew. We were raised to be loyal to him and that always seemed to win out.

Dare said he thought Pop was running some side businesses underground and had thought it for years, thinking it was because he didn't wanna jeopardize some of his important relationships with influential people so kept shadier stuff secret. Dare thought Pop was too greedy to not profit off the heavier drugs. He didn't need the money, but he wanted it. I hadn't noticed some of the things Dare had noticed because I was too busy trying to prove myself to the megalomaniac.

"Tommy," she whispered to me while I was deep in thought.

"Yeah, baby?" I'd thought she was asleep.

"I moved your guns."

"You what?"

"The guns under the bed were freaking me out. I gave them to James. He's not working tonight, so I wanted to tell you."

"Baby, guns protect you. You shouldn't be afraid of them." Why hadn't Jimmy told me? I'd seen him on my way in today, had a fifteen-minute debriefing with him.

"I was…afraid of myself," she said quietly.

"Oh, babe." I kissed her. I was going to be the ruin of her. She was better off without me. Too bad I didn't have the decency to make her go.

"I just wanted to tell you so that if someone came to hurt you… you wouldn't reach and have nothing to defend yourself but the knife."

"Don't stress. Go to sleep, baby girl." I gave her a squeeze and got out of bed. "Be right back."

Tia

When I woke up in the morning, Tommy was gone, I vaguely remembered him kissing me goodbye. I woke up to the sound of the phone text alert.

> **Tommy:** Baby, I'm busy with stuff today so I won't see you till late tonight. My sister wants to pick you up and take you to the salon for nails & then lunch. If you want to go, tell Nino. Let me know. Love you. Xo.
>
> **Me:** Yes! Thanks, baby.
>
> **Tommy:** Shit, I'll have to get you a debit card & copies of my credit cards made. I'll have cash dropped off for you.
>
> **Me:** It's okay, I have a bit in my account and I have my Lost Wages money in your underwear drawer.
>
> **Tommy:** Oh that's what that was? I saw that and thought you were paying me for sex.
>
> **Me:** LOL. $5K isn't enough for the awesome sex you give me. Esp. last night. Oo
>
> **Tommy:** I'll give you a discount. Fiancée's rate.
>
> **Me:** Haha. Any requests from the salon?

Tommy: Requests?

Tommy: Wait! Don't cut your hair short!

Me: No, just a trim but I was thinking maybe I'd get my first Brazilian.

Tommy: mm...but not much of a trim, k? It needs to be long! Your hair on your head, I mean. haha.

Me: Don't worry, I'll make sure there's enough left for you to grab onto. On my head, I mean. lol. ;)

Tommy: Mmm. Making me hard here and I'm in public. I might have to spank you for that.

I chewed my lip. Sexting was fun. I was beaming at how fun and easy these texts were today. So different from the tone around here lately. As I was closing the message, I got another message in from a number I didn't recognize.

Hey Tia, it's Tess. Wanna go with moi for a mani/pedi? I have Sarah watching the boys ALL DAY :) We can have lunch, too. Tommy wants Nino to drive us.

I replied.

Hey and YES, absolutely! What time should I be ready?

Then I wrote back to Tommy,

> **I look forward to it. G2G get ready now. Love you. <3!**

> **Tommy: Be safe, baby girl. XO. Love you too.**

Tessa wrote back for me to be ready at 11:00. I asked her if they could do a trim and some waxing, too, and she wrote back it was her friend who owned the salon so she was sure it'd be no problem. It was now 10:15, so I zipped downstairs and made a coffee. I spooned my 3 sugars in knowing Sarah wasn't here to judge and then went upstairs to get a shower. I was excited about getting out of the house.

The phone blooped with another text and it was another number.

> **It's Nino. I'm outside and will text you when Tessa gets here so you can meet us at the car.**

I saved his contact info and sent him a reply.

> **Okay, thanks.**

* * *

Tessa was excited to get out, too, and told me she hadn't had a day without her boys in a few weeks. She said she was going to get all gussied up tonight for a dinner date with James. He had to work tonight at our house, but they'd go to dinner and hopefully have a quickie before he had to leave for work.

Sarah was at her house today with the boys. She said she and Sarah were in talks about her sharing the load between her place and Luc's place since Tommy didn't want a live-in any longer. She seemed happy about it, as Sarah had been like family to them and was great with the kids.

We pulled up to the salon and Nino followed us in. Tessa had linked arms with me and told me Tommy insisted Nino drive because I was cargo that was too precious to be subjected to her crazy driving. Aw! (He was right. Nino called her Tessa Andretti, teasingly.)

I was glad she didn't joke about it having anything to do with me taking off. We laughed and then as we stepped inside, Nino grabbed and then was kissing a girl behind the counter. She was tall, brunette, beautiful.

Holy crap, this was my cousin. She and I had the same hair. And I could see my mother in her eyes. It was faint, but it was definitely there.

"Tia, this is Bianca. This is her shop."

I was dumbfounded.

She gave me a knowing smile. I could tell she knew who I was. She reached out and pulled me into a tight hug.

"Nice to meet you," I said softly, almost numbly.

"C'mon girls, let's go have a cappuccino and a natter and then I'll make you both even more beautiful."

* * *

Bianca was awesome. She was smart, together, fashionable and it was obvious that she was like a big sister to Tessa. They'd grown up together on the same street. Bianca and Nino had a six-year-old son. She told me she was an only child and had no other cousins on her dad's side of the family, but lots on her mom's side. We had no living grandparents on our side, either. But I had her and that was at least someone. I liked her a lot.

We didn't talk about anything heavy, like her deceased father or my deceased mother, but she told me about our Nonna, who'd died about a year before my mother died. She said she was an old battleax who was super-strict. Bianca said she remembered my mother from when she was small, but that she hadn't seen her since she was about eight or nine years old and that her name wasn't mentioned much because of some family fall-out that no one wanted to discuss.

Her salon was cute. It was small, only had three stylist chairs and she was working alone today, only had one part time employee, said she was just getting started but was doing okay. She was skilled, gave my hair a trim, adding some long layers, then did my nails, and we talked about waxing.

"So, I didn't know we were related when I decided to ask for a Brazilian," I said, blushing with embarrassment.

She laughed. "I'm a professional, I can handle it. But have you had a Brazilian before?"

I shook my head. "No, I usually just, err, shave. All of, um... it."

"It's gonna hurt," Tessa said with a wince.

"And you shouldn't have sex till tomorrow if you do," Bianca added.

Tessa laughed and made a gag motion with her finger in her mouth.

"Oh, I don't know if I should, then. Tommy's got a very, uh, voracious, appetite."

"I can't hear this." Tessa raised her hands with her still wet nails and left the back room we had gone into.

Bianca laughed and whispered, "So I hear."

I blushed. "What have you heard?"

"I know a few girls who've been with him. Two. Both just one nighters but yeah, I hear he's got quite an appetite. And that he's pretty aggressive about it." She winked at me. "If he wasn't like a cousin to me I'd have gone for him years ago."

I didn't know what she knew and the idea of him with other girls made me feel queasy and I wasn't about to spill any beans. "I'd better just call him."

She laughed. "That's cute." Then I heard the jingle of the chimes at her front door and she left me alone in the room.

I hit his contact info on the iPhone.

"Hey, baby," he answered.

"Hiya. How's your day?"

"It's good. Yours? Having fun?"

"Yeah, Bianca is… she's great. I feel like we're related, if that doesn't sound too weird."

"She's like a cuz to me so I get it. Bee's cool," he answered.

"Okay she's my cousin and like a cousin to you so that'd make you and me like cousins and that's just…"

"Wrong," he said.

We both laughed.

"So, I told you I was gonna get a uh…Brazilian, for you," I started.

"Mm hm." He sounded like he was all dreamy-eyed.

"But Bianca says if I do we can't have sex till tomorrow. I thought I'd better check with you before going ahead."

"Awesome, baby."

"No sex is awesome?"

"Checking with me for permission before closing your body down for business is awesome." He laughed.

I was glad he was in such a good mood.

"I hear it's quite nice, the effect…" I said softly.

"It absolutely is."

I deflated. "Gah!"

"What?"

"I don't want to know how you know that it absolutely is. In fact it makes me very growly that you know that it absolutely is."

"Oops sorry," he said softly but I could hear that he was amused and maybe even enjoying my jealousy.

There was silence for a second while I pushed away thoughts of him with someone else. I heard the door chimes again, then he spoke.

"Tell ya what, you wanna do it, that's fine. You can just take care of me tonight. I can wait till tomorrow to take care of you if I must."

I laughed. "Oh, if you must, huh? How chivalrous of you."

"I try."

"Hmpf."

Bianca and Tessa came into the room at the same time. They both looked freaked out.

"The police are here for you, Tia," Tessa said.

"What?"

"Tia!" Tommy boomed. He'd obviously heard them.

"The police are here for me," I whispered. "I didn't call them, Tommy. Honestly, I didn't."

The girls were looking weirdly at me.

"Go see what they want. Don't hang up. Give the phone to my sister."

"Kay." I passed the phone to Tessa and then walked stiffly out to the salon where two uniformed officers stood at the front desk.

Tommy

"What's going on?" I asked my sister.

"Two cops came in and they asked for her."

"Where's Nino?"

"Sitting out front, reading a magazine. What could he have done?" Tessa was snarky.

"Fuck. What's going on now?"

"I'm in the back room, hang on while I go see. They're leaving with her."

"Hang up and then give her the phone. Nino's calling on my other line. I'll call you back."

I linked over. "Nino!"

"T, the cops have her. They told her they wanted to ask her questions at the station. She said they should ask her here, but they insisted. She said she programmed my number in her phone and will call me to come get her when she's done. Tessa just gave her the phone. They asked who I was to her and she told them I'm her cousin's husband. I'm following the squad car to the station and I'll wait there for her."

"I'm meeting you there. Which one?"

I hung up after he told me and got into my car.

Tia

Was this another test? It couldn't be after our talk last night. Couldn't be. Could it? Let me out of his sight and then arrange for me to sit down with the cops to see what I'd say? I knew that the Ferranos had some cops in their pocket because of what Rose had said to me at the grocery store that day.

When I got into the station, the male and female officer led me to a small, windowless interview room, containing a circular table with chairs around it.

"Is Tommy Ferrano holding you against your will?" the male cop, who'd introduced himself as Officer Francis, asked. He was a tall, older Black man. His partner was a thirty-something pretty blonde named Officer Spence.

"Tommy Ferrano is my fiancé," I said, looking at them like they were crazy.

"He's not holding you against your will?"

"What? No!" I exclaimed.

"Is Tommy Ferrano involved in illegal activities, organized crime?"

"Huh?"

"Mobster-like activities. You know: guns, prostitution, drugs, loan sharking? That sort of thing?"

"Tommy's family owns a construction company, some restaurants," I answered.

"Your father was arrested the day before yesterday," the female cop said.

I blanched. "He was?"

"Trafficking crack cocaine, methamphetamines, DMT, MDMA. He tells us he's selling drugs for the Ferrano family, that he has no choice because they are holding you for ransom. He wants to go into witness protection and wants you safe and he's willing to testify to facts related to illegal activities by..." She reached into her pocket and pulled out a small spiral notebook, "Thomas Ferrano Sr., Thomas Ferrano Jr., Dario Ferrano, James Michaelson, Edward Nichols, Nino Rossi, and several others." She flipped the book closed and looked at me expectantly.

I shook my head. "My father has been acting strangely. We suspected he was using drugs. I really don't think this has anything to do with my fiancé."

I felt like I was going to hurl the contents of my stomach all over her shiny black shoes. Luckily, I had nothing in my stomach other than two cups of coffee.

The male officer leaned over and put his hand on mine. "It's okay, you're safe. You can tell us the truth."

I pulled my hand back and shook my head. If this was a test, I wasn't failing it. Maybe this wasn't a Tommy test. Maybe this was his father testing me. Seemed like just the sort of thing he'd do. If this wasn't a test, I was not giving them anything. There was no way in the world my father was selling drugs for the Ferrano family. No fricking way.

"I'd like to make a phone call, please."

"Why do you need to make a phone call?" the female cop asked.

"To call a lawyer," I said.

"You aren't under arrest," the male cop said.

"Then I'd like to leave," I answered. My phone was ringing from my pocket, it was Tommy calling.

Tommy

Tia's phone rang twice and then went to voicemail. Fuck. I was sitting in the coffee shop across the street from the cop shop. I'd sent Nino away so he and Bee could take their son Joey to T-ball. I called Pop's lawyer and left him a voicemail. I called Pop and he said he'd try to find out what was going down. And I sat. And sat.

I texted her.

I'm in the coffee shop across the street when you're done. xxx

An hour passed and I texted her again.

I'm going home. Call me when you're done and I'll come pick you up.

Two more hours, nothing. No read receipts on my texts, even.

Pop and I talked, and he told me that he had word Greg O'Connor had been arrested. I knew there had to be a connection.

"Did you do this to O'Connor, Pop?" I asked.

He was quiet on the other end of the phone.

"Pop?"

"Maybe," Pop answered.

"Fuck, Pop."

I hung up and hit the wall with my fist. Was Tia gone? Had she been presented with a way to escape me and taken it? No. There was no way. I wanted to believe that what she and I had was real. It felt real. It felt completely fucking real. She wouldn't leave me. Would she?

Tia

For hours, they interrogated me, left me waiting in that room, came back and asked the same questions again with different phrasing. And then repeat. All day.

They started to talk about the rap sheets of some of the people in Tommy's father's "organization" as they called it. They talked about murders that they couldn't pin. They'd said that the Ferrano family was suspected of a lot of different illegal activities. They told me they were even linked with slavery trade overseas, with cocaine crops in

South America, with mass murder down in Mexico where Earl Johnson, a Ferrano "foot soldier", was found with a gunshot to the face and three gunshots to his genitals. At the same site, they'd said, a cartel leader had been found decapitated and castrated, his own genitals stuffed in his mouth. I threw up into the waste basket, just some liquid because I hadn't eaten, and of course that made them even more suspicious about whether or not I knew anything about that situation.

They also carefully watched for reactions as they talked about how that cartel's compound had been found with eight murdered men in addition to Earl and Juan Carlos Castillo. Four women had been set free and had ID'd someone matching the description of Tommy Ferrano as having been there with guns, urging them to leave.

They said a woman matching my description was reported as being there as well. I shrugged it off, saying I hadn't ever been to Mexico, and didn't know what they were talking about. There had been no record of Tommy landing there or of him leaving the country but there were eyewitness accounts initially. I was told that those had since been retracted.

I continued to tell them that I knew nothing about what they were talking about. They asked me personal questions about Tommy. They asked when his birthday was. I didn't know the answer to that; we hadn't gotten there yet but I said March 1st. They told me his birthday was April 5th (I was close. He'd told me that he turned 29 a few months ago when his father bought him the house) and then asked me if I'd think it was strange that two people were engaged but that one didn't know the other's date of birth. I shrugged and said he hated birthdays so maybe he lied when he told me his birthday.

They countered by saying perhaps I was afraid to reveal that I was really a prisoner, not his live-in girlfriend. I clammed up and told them that they needed to either arrest me or let me leave. That was when the door opened and Susie, my social worker, came in. Shit. And then it went on and on, with Susie trying to get me to talk.

She put her hand on mine, asking them to leave us alone for a minute. I hadn't seen her since my graduation day. She was such a sweet lady, had always been nice to me. I knew we weren't really alone. It was obvious that they were watching us through the mirrored glass.

"Tia, they've told me that you're saying that you're with Tommy Ferrano of your own free will."

"Yes," I answered.

"That's not what I heard, honey. Are you scared? You don't have to be. The police want to help. They can help you. I can help you."

"I don't need their help, Susie. I'm fine. I told Rose and Cal I'm fine. I'm telling you, I'm fine."

"I've known you for over half your life, Tia. Meeting some guy who's known for being connected, for being the son of a crime Don? Moving in with him and cutting off contact with everyone other than a few quick conversations that are obviously designed to make people believe you're okay? Come on. This isn't you. What's really going on here?"

I shook my head. "Susie, I'm fine. I love him. He's not mafia, that's ridiculous. His father may be, I have no idea. But, he's not. I know nothing. Can I go?" I got to my feet.

"Tia, I'm here to help you. The police are here to help. Let us help you."

I dug my heels in and she finally relented, giving me her home phone number and her cell number so that if I needed her, I could reach her.

An hour later they finally told me I could leave. My cell phone was dead, so I couldn't call Tommy as I had no idea what his number was. I called a taxi. I didn't know what the address of Tommy's house was. I knew where it was, by intersection, so I guided the cab driver until we pulled up in front of the gate. I paid the driver with my debit card and stepped out in front of the gate and pushed the buzzer. Dex was already opening it to let me in.

"You okay?" he asked. "Need me to pay the cab?"

I blew out a long breath. "I paid already and yeah, I'm okay, thanks, Dex."

"Next time, the cab gets inside the gate before you get out, okay, Tia?"

"Okay, Dex." I hoped there wouldn't be a next time.

I walked up to the house and he opened the front door with a key. The house was dark. I looked in Tommy's office and he wasn't there. I went up to the bedroom. He wasn't there, either. I went downstairs and found him beating up the punching bag.

I hesitated in the doorway. "Uh, hi."

He didn't hear me. Or he was ignoring me. I stepped around so he could see me if he simply hadn't heard me. He stopped and caught his breath and pulled the gloves off.

"Baby!"

"Hi," I approached him cautiously and he grabbed me and pulled me tight to him. He was drenched in sweat. I didn't care. I put my arms around him, relieved he was putting his arms around me, not angry with me.

"You okay? How'd you get here?" he asked, caressing my face.

I nodded. "I'm okay. Cab."

"Let's go upstairs and you can fill me in. I'll grab a fast shower. Join me?" He grabbed a bottle of water from the floor and took a glug. "I was going out of my mind not hearing from you so I was just killing time." He motioned with his chin toward the punching bag. I was surprised he looked so calm.

I followed him to the bathroom and got out of my clothes. He looked down at me. "So, too bad about that Brazilian."

I looked down at my naked lower half and started to laugh. We both laughed hard and he pulled me into the shower and against his body. He got my face into his hands and kissed me deeply, passionately. My arms wrapped around him, then I pushed him against the tiled wall and then I was devouring him. He reached behind us and turned the shower on, not breaking lip contact, and at first the water was freezing. He adjusted the temperature.

"At least we don't have to wait till tomorrow," he muttered, my earlobe in his mouth.

"Yeah, and now I know when your birthday is," I answered, and he released my lobe and looked at me with a tilted head. "And I don't think I could've waited. I need you," I added, and put my hands on his rear and ground my hips against him, up on my tippy toes trying to get better contact. He bent his knees while he lifted me onto his shaft, sliding right in. He turned us and got my back against the wall, and whoa... it was just what I needed.

*　*　*

We were in bed, lying face to face on our sides naked, one of my hands was flat against his chest, the other tracing the lines of the ink on the other shoulder, trailing down his arm, as I told him all about my day.

He listened, while sifting his hands through my hair and up and down my back, his lips against my forehead the whole time. I could feel his expression changes, smiles, lips tightening, soft kisses, or tightening of his whole body alternately while I told him all about meeting my cousin and how it felt really nice to have family, when I told him how much I liked his sister, when I told him the things the cops said, though he didn't deny or confirm some of the bad stuff.

At the end I said, "At first I thought it was a test."

He loosened his grip on me and I saw his smile instead of felt it. "That would've been the ultimate test."

"Mm hm," I answered with disapproval. "Don't get any ideas."

"I'm done testing you, baby. And I never would've done that sort of test."

"My dad, Tommy; that's fucked." I couldn't believe how calm

he'd been about all of this, how trusting he'd been of me. It was such a relief.

"Yeah, you know what else is fucked?"

"What?"

He was thoughtful for a beat, then said, "Forget about it; you don't wanna know." He got up and got into a clean pair of boxers and then poured two glasses of wine.

"What? Tell me, please. Wait I don't think I should have a drink yet. I haven't had a single thing to eat today."

"I'll order pizza." He reached for his phone. "Greg O'Connor just signed his own death warrant."

"No."

He raised his index finger to me as he started to talk on the phone and placed the order for an extra-large double cheese, pepperoni, bacon, and mushroom pizza with someone he obviously knew. When he ended the call, he resumed the conversation. "People'll want him dead."

My expression dropped. He paused a conversation talking about my father getting dead so he could order a pizza? How messed up was his life to even make that sort of thing seem so casual?

"Sorry, Tia, but this is it. When certain people get wind of this, that's it." Tommy motioned by drawing a horizontal line across his neck with his index finger.

"Shit." I put my hand over my mouth.

"'Fraid so."

"Fuck!"

I took the wine glass and I downed half of it. "I can't let that happen."

Tommy looked at me like he felt sorry for me. "Easy with the wine. The pizza'll be here in half an hour."

"He's my dad." I passed the glass back.

"Your father knows the price of what he's done. It'll happen."

"But Witness Protection..."

"He has nothing. They're not gonna protect him when he has

nothing to give them but rumors, babe. He's goin' to jail for the drug charges and then someone inside'll get him. He was hoping you'd rat, that's why he sicced the cops on you."

I hugged my myself, feeling a chill, and shook my head.

"He knows the price of his actions, Tia." Tommy shrugged.

"Don't be so cold."

"So cold?" Tommy started to look pissed. "He just tried to fucking take you from me!" came out with a roar.

I flopped down and stared at the ceiling. Tommy downed his wine and then got his cell and dialed a number.

"Pop," he said as he left the room.

I stared at the ceiling for a long time. After a little while I got up and washed my face and then plugged in the cell phone. As I did that, the house phone rang from my nightstand.

I let it ring three times in case Tommy was going to get it, but when the fourth ring started, I picked it up. "Hello?"

"Tia, Sweetpea?"

My dad.

"Dad?" How did he get this number?"

"You have to help me," he whispered. "You have to tell the cops what you know about the Ferranos, about what they've done."

"I know nothing, Dad. Nothing. What the hell did you do this for?"

"I needed to save you."

He sounded like he was crying.

"You needed to save me? Save me? You needed to try to fucking save yourself, Dad. Like always!"

Tommy was coming into the room. His eyes burned with rage as he snatched the phone out of my hand.

"Fuck off, Greg. You're done fucking with her life, you hear me?" He hung up and pulled me to him.

I was bawling.

He wrapped his arms around me. "Baby, he's fucked."

"I know," I said.

"You don't. Sit."

I sat.

"I just got some info. He owed a lot of money to another crew, not one of ours. When he came here, he was hoping to work for me for Ferrano protection against that other crew. Figured if he got in good with us, he'd get off the hook with them. This witness protection bullshit has gotta be his last kick at the can to save his own ass. Pop won't have to give any orders; Greg'll be gone fast if he's in gen-pop because of the shit he's pulled with people that have zero to do with our family. He was determined to get into this life and he got in with someone else. In over his head."

The iPhone started to ring and it was an unknown number. Tommy picked it up, listened for a second after saying *Hello*, then said, "Fuck off, O'Connor." And ended the call.

"How did he get the stupid iPhone number?"

"That's what I'd like to fuckin' know. No one outside of my family has that number. Stupid iPhone?"

"I hate that phone."

"Pick a new one. I'll get it for you."

I gave him a half a smile. Something seemingly insignificant amid a day that was total chaos, but it was sweet.

We polished off most of that extra-large pizza; I was totally starved, ate four pieces, poured another big glass of wine, but then I crashed.

* * *

I woke up alone. It was still night. The lamp was still on, the two wineglasses beside me (Tommy's empty one and my full one). It was warm, but I drank a few sips of it anyway. I got up and saw his black t-shirt on the floor beside the pizza box. I threw it over my tank top and inhaled it deeply. I was wearing a pair of boy short underwear but the t-shirt covered my booty. I lifted the box to take it to the kitchen and went in search of my fiancé.

I found him sitting in the backyard by the pool in just his boxers, his feet in the water, smoking a joint. I frowned. I'd never seen him do that before.

"Hey." He looked up at me and looked around, "Fuck, where are your pants? There are guys around." He picked up his phone from the pavement beside him and dialed, then demanded, "Steer clear of the pool area till I tell you; tell the guys!" He practically barked those orders.

"Sorry." I spun to head back in the house.

"Don't go; sit."

I sat beside him and put my feet into the water. It was warm; felt nice. He passed me the joint. I took a puff and then a second puff, then gave it back.

"I don't smoke much. Just once in a while at night when I can't seem to chill," he explained and took another haul off it and then put it out in an ashtray beside him.

If pot chilled him out, maybe he should smoke it more often. I decided not to share that info at this particular moment. I put my head against his arm. He put his arm around me so I nuzzled into him, looking up at the sky. It was a nice night. Too bad so much was fucked up for both of us right now.

"Why aren't you asleep? It's late. Trouble shutting your mind off, too?" he asked, kissing the top of my head.

"I guess," I said. "I think I'd sleep better beside you."

He leaned down and kissed me. I held tight to him.

"Let's go put you to bed," he said softly and got to his feet. He touched his phone screen and then put his phone to his ear as we walked hand in hand back inside. "You're good. Off to bed. Yep." He ended the call.

The pot definitely made me sleepy. My body felt all loose and gooey. I fell asleep running my fingers through his hair.

15

Tia

Tommy was shaking me.

"Baby, c'mon and move! We gotta bounce!"

I sat upright in bed, feeling groggy. "Huh?"

"Move!" He pulled me by the hand and was throwing a bundle of clothing at me. "Pack a couple changes of clothes for both of us and bathroom shit, whatever you can fit in that bag. And your laptop and phone and charger. Hurry."

"What's going on?" I felt so groggy.

"I'll explain on the way. We gotta hurry, Tia. Hurry!"

I sprang into action, trying to shake off the grogginess and grabbed underwear, socks, jeans, t-shirts, shorts, bras for me then jeans, socks, underwear, t-shirts, and long- sleeve shirts for Tommy. Then I grabbed my train case in the bathroom and threw our toothbrushes and toothpaste and Tommy's razor and shaving cream into it. In three minutes flat I was ready, wearing sweats and flip flops. I threw a pair of sneakers into the bag. He was dressed in jeans and a t-shirt and he grabbed the bag, my train case and purse, and then he ushered us to the Jeep.

"Something's fucked up," he said, as we pulled out onto the street. He hit a button on a small remote and the gate closed.

"What do you mean?"

"My guards disappeared. Jimmy is AWOL. We're going to the safe house."

"Jimmy disappeared?"

"He took off. Or got taken. Don't know yet."

"What?"

"He didn't show up tonight for a dinner thing with Tess. She hasn't heard from him. He was supposed to be here at midnight to pull night duty and relieve Dex. Dex had to split, so I got someone in to cover when Jimmy didn't answer his phone but he's been acting weird. It's possible he's flipped. Or someone has him. It could have something to do with the cops picking you up today. That he didn't tell me about the weapons you gave him isn't cool, doesn't look good. He didn't know I was armed under the bed. No one but you knew that. Did you tell him where you got them?"

"No, I just carried them out to him in a plastic grocery bag and said, can you please put these somewhere? Tommy left them. He just took them from me and said okay."

"He has all the codes to get in the house and I've changed everything, but I won't have us be sitting ducks. I don't know where the guards are all gone. I woke up out of nowhere, feeling like something wasn't right and no one's here. Shoulda been two guys. Phones all go to voicemail."

"And you think it's James?"

"I dunno."

"But he's your brother-in-law, he's..."

"Dare's moving Tess and the boys to his place while we figure it out. He's either been taken or gone rogue. My guards are gone, Tia. Gone. Two guys just vanished and the gate was closed but unlocked. Something is fucking very wrong and we're not sitting around to wait to find out what that something is."

We pulled into the driveway of an industrial plaza and then

behind to a gated mini storage place. Tommy's cell blooped and he looked at it.

"Fuck. Luciana's in labor."

"Should we go to the hospital?" I asked.

He shook his head. "No. Ed'll text me with news."

Tommy stopped at the storage place, a big, long alleyway of orange garage doors. He replied to his text then got out, leaving the car running, opened one of the orange doors and shut the door behind him. Then he came back out with a black backpack slung over one shoulder.

He drove us the rest of the way to the farm and when we got there we headed up the stairs in the barn and dropped our bags and I flopped into bed. It was 4:20 AM. I wasn't sure I could sleep, though. He wasn't sleeping. He sat at the table thumbing away on his phone, drinking a beer, the backpack on the floor beside him. I didn't wanna know what was in it, though I could guess.

I lay there for a long time watching him and eventually he got in beside me and pulled me to him.

* * *

He woke me up. "Baby, let's go get coffee."

I groaned, then asked, "Is the baby here yet?"

"No. Get up; I have to talk to you."

I sat up, "What time is it?"

"8:15."

"Argh, didn't we just fall asleep?"

"Tia."

The seriousness of his tone snapped me out of my sleepy, grumpy haze. I got to my feet and reached for a pair of yoga pants in the bag I'd packed, which was lying open on the floor beside the bed.

He continued. "Luc isn't in labor. That was a fake text. Someone was trying to coax me to the hospital."

"What?"

"Yeah."

"What's going on?"

He shook his head. "I need coffee. Let's go please, I'll explain. This place needs a fucking coffee pot. We'll get coffee and then you get supplies in for us to do us a week or so here." He ran his fingers through his hair in frustration and picked up his keys.

I grabbed an elastic from my purse, threw a hoodie on, and tied my hair up in a ponytail as I ran into the bathroom, quickly peed, washed my hands, quickly brushed my teeth, swished some mouthwash, and splashed water on my face, then met him down at the jeep.

"What took you?" he snarled.

"I had to pee, honey, holy shit; relax." I put my seatbelt on.

He made a growly sound and backed out of the barn.

* * *

Twenty minutes later he had coffee in him and he sat in the Jeep in the local country department store while I went in, his credit card in hand, and bought a coffee maker, a toaster oven that had two hot plate burners on top, plus a broom and a mop and bucket.

He was talking on his phone, well mostly listening and "Yeah, yeah" 'ing as he drove me across the street to the grocery store. I went in and per his directions bought enough food to feed us for a week.

When I got back out, he got off the phone and we loaded the groceries into the back and then he drove us back to the farm. He blasted Metallica all the way back. It was loud, and he drove too fast, bordering on reckless. By the time we got back, I was feeling kind of grumpy, too.

He helped me get the groceries up the stairs and then he mumbled he'd be "back in a few" as he left, dialing while going down the stairs.

I lit a few scented candles, put the groceries away, and then swept the floors in preparation for mopping. If we were staying here for a week, it certainly was a little dusty and dead buggy, so I was going to give it a thorough cleaning. I saw him out by the pond on his phone and he looked like he was reading someone the riot act. I couldn't hear him and didn't really want to, anyway. If he'd wanted me to hear the conversation, he'd have made the call from here.

When he came back in, I had the single serve coffee maker set up, I had the place smelling better, looking cleaner, and then I offered to cook breakfast for him. He nodded and sat on the sofa and put his head in his hands. He looked exhausted and stressed.

I cooked him an omelet and some toast. He ate and then he passed out on the couch, his phone lying on his chest.

* * *

Almost two hours passed before phone rang. He bolted awake and grabbed it.

"Dare!" His expression dropped and he was silent for a few minutes, listening, but his eyes were intense and his jaw was tight. "Seriously? Okay, yep. Right. Call me later, Bye."

He put the phone down.

"Sit," he said, patting his knee. I hesitantly walked over and he pulled me into his lap and kissed my head.

"This is further blowback from Mexico. There was a relative of Castillo that's local. We thought we got him but that was a decoy. He's the one who arranged the shootout in the house the day we came home from here last time. Jimmy was shot last night; he's in the hospital in intensive care."

"No." My heart sank.

"We had the security footage checked and some chick at the gate coaxed our guys to open the gate and then two other guys showed up and abducted them. I got us out of there just in time. Another few minutes and we'd have been shot up in our sleep. Someone cloned Eddy's phone after he left it on the bar at the restaurant, and so they texted me like Luc was in labor. They were just trying to get us all to the hospital, planning a shoot out there, since they didn't get me at home and couldn't get into Pop's. They got into Dare's apartment but he shot their guy. He, Tessa, and the boys are fine. But..." Tommy took a deep breath, "Pop and Lisa, they were asleep when the text came through but Lisa's phone was dead and Pop never checked his voicemail or texts. She got the texts this morning and they drove to the hospital before talking to anyone. Pop got shot twice in the hospital parking lot. Once in the shoulder; once in the gut."

I gasped.

"He's in surgery."

I put my arms around him and squeezed. He hugged me back.

"My two guys watching our house last night, found dead. Jim in ICU, Pop in surgery right now, my sister and her kids in hiding. Pop's wife beside herself. We got her with Tessa and the kids."

"Luc and Eddy?" I asked.

"Eddy got them out of town at his folks' cabin. He's trying to keep my sister calm. He's bringing her to Tess and Lisa today."

"Shit."

"Yeah, it has hit the fucking fan. I've got a few of our guys dealing with things. Dare and I have cleanup in progress."

"What does that mean?"

"It means we're safe here and that I won't bring you home until it's safe."

"Okay."

"Tia?"

"Yeah?"

"Your father was moving drugs for someone affiliated with these guys, owed them a lot of money."

My hand came up and covered my mouth.

"Your father has hours, days at most. He might already be gone."

I pulled away from him, ran to the bathroom, and promptly hurled my omelet into the toilet. After I finished brushing my teeth I heard Tommy's phone ringing.

When I came out, he wasn't here. I looked out the screened-in doorway and he was outside by the pond again, talking on the phone, pacing. He looked up at me and jerked his chin in a "You all right?" kind of way. I wiggled my fingers in a wave and blew him a kiss.

He walked toward the barn, so I sat on the sofa. He was with me a minute later.

"How's everything?" I asked.

"Same," he answered. "I feel fucking helpless right now. Sitting around waiting is not something I do well."

"Tommy."

"What?"

"Can you please hold me?"

He grabbed me and held me tight, then took me to the bed and we got under the covers and cuddled close for a long time. His phone rang after a while and I saw it had Dario's name on the screen as he lifted it to his ear, swiping the screen with his thumb.

I got up and filled the kettle and turned it on to make tea.

"Fuck. Okay," I heard him say, "Fuck! Yep."

He got to his feet, "Do you drive?"

"Drive?"

"Do you know how to drive a car?"

"I only have my learner's permit, but I can drive, yeah."

"Okay, I'm taking the Harley. I'm leaving you the Jeep keys and I'm leaving you a gun."

"No."

"Yes. Here."

He showed me how to take the safety off and lifted the screen on the back wall of the loft and then pointed the gun out the back doors and taught me how to shoot.

Afterwards, he put the gun down on the table and took me by the shoulders.

"Jimmy didn't make it," he said.

My hand covered my mouth.

"I have to go deal. I want you to stay here. Here's a phone, it's a burner. Don't turn your iPhone on." He reached into the knapsack from the storage garage, "I'll program burner numbers for me, my brother, and Nino." He looked at the flip phone in his hand and started hitting buttons on the new flip phone. If you need them 'cuz you can't get me, call one of them. I should be back tonight. If I'm not back by tomorrow morning I want you to call my brother for instructions and he'll get you with the other girls. Don't turn on your regular phone until I tell you it's okay. It's over there with the card pulled." He motioned to the counter, "And don't use your computer online with either phone as a hot spot or anything. I don't know if anyone is tracking your social media accounts to try to figure out where you're logging in from."

I started to cry. Poor Tessa. Those poor baby boys.

"Athena, don't, don't fall apart. My girl is tough enough to handle this, okay?"

I nodded solemnly. "I'm just thinking about your poor sister, your nephews. Your whole family. You. Don't get hurt, Tommy. Please."

"Baby. I'll be fine," he said, with conviction. "You're safe here. No one knows where this place is; not even my family. I'll be back as soon as possible, okay? Sleep with the gun under your pillow. Do not hesitate to use it. It's not scary."

I squeezed my eyes shut tight. He took my face into his hands. "It's not. Look at me. It's not scary; it'll protect you."

I nodded. "I won't sleep until you're back. Don't get hurt."

"Don't be afraid to sleep. This is a safe house, baby. I'll hurry back to you. I'll call when I'm on my way back." He kissed me hard and I sank against his body and wanted to memorize the feel of it. He gave me two keys. One to the Jeep and the other to the padlocks downstairs. He backed away, grabbed the backpack, and went down the stairs. I followed and watched as he pulled the motorcycle out. He kissed me again, and told me to lock the door. After I locked up I watched him drive away from a stall window and then went back upstairs. I wanted him to be okay with every fiber of my being.

Tommy

Jimmy was shot three times and didn't survive. But the thing was, I still didn't know what side he was on when he died. He acted like he'd forgotten she'd given the guns to him and he'd been sketchy when I'd asked him. He'd put them in the gun safe in my office, he'd said. They were there when I'd looked, but I'd still thought it was strange that he'd acted that way and that he hadn't mentioned them. Now, knowing I was supposed to be taken out in my sleep, I wondered if he'd neglected to tell me about it on purpose. Was he in on it? He was a friend of mine and Dare's, had been good to my sister, was dad to my two nephews, for fuck sakes, but he was ambitious. Was he so ambitious that he wanted to take me out? I didn't wanna believe it.

Pop was just out of surgery; he had serious injuries and the prognosis wasn't great. We were getting news from Sarah because if a Ferrano stepped foot on hospital property they'd likely get shot. We were worried they'd target her because of her association with us, but she insisted on being at the hospital. Pop's room was under guard by a security company we hired through Zack, my PI. I was meeting my brother and we were going to end this.

Tia's father was just a pawn. He was probably approached and likely offered some deal or something if he double crossed us. Or maybe he was just selling the drugs for them as a coincidence. I didn't know yet what the deal was, and obviously it backfired. Pop had something to do with O'Connor getting busted, for sure. I didn't know how it all factored in with Jimmy, Pop, and the two guards at my house getting shot and I didn't know how Tia's cell phone number had gotten out, but I knew it had to all be connected.

It took a lot to leave Tia by herself. If I hadn't been 100% confident that no one knew about the farm's existence I wouldn't have done it. If I hadn't been 100% confident that she'd listen to me and stay put, I wouldn't have done it.

I was wrong. On both accounts. She wasn't safe and she didn't listen. Thank God she didn't listen.

Tia

As soon as he left, I was pacing the hayloft and felt like I was going to crawl out of my skin, so I decided to take a walk. I went for a wander of the property and kept the flip phone in my pocket. I walked for a while, until I found what appeared to be the property line, a small wooden fence that bordered a thick and dense forest. Up until that point, it'd been woodsy but not dense. I decided to walk back.

As the barn and house came into view, ice pierced my veins because I saw two men approaching the house on foot.

Oh no!

I dropped into the tallish grass, I was still hundreds of feet away, and I stayed put.

Damn. The gun Tommy had left me was under a pillow, inside the pillowcase. Not that I felt like I wanted to use it, but at that moment it'd make me feel better to know I could at least point it at someone and get them to leave. The keys to the jeep were in my pocket right now because as I'd come out, I unlocked the door and stuffed the keys in my pocket with the flip phone. I hadn't re-locked the door.

I thought about the upstairs. Anyone going inside would know we were there. Beyond the Jeep being parked there and the refrigerator full of groceries, was a bag with mine and Tommy's clothes lying on the floor beside the bed. Damn. Tommy had a complete false sense of security about this place.

I dialed his number. He didn't answer. I dialed Dario's number; it went straight to voicemail. I called Nino.

"Yeah?"

"Nino, it's Tia."

"Hey, Doll. You okay?"

"No. I'm crouched in a field at Tommy's safe house and there are men approaching it." They had scoped out the house and obviously determined it wasn't inhabited so approached the barn.

"Shit," he answered. "Where's Tommy?"

"I don't know. On his way down there, I guess. He left me here."

"Stay hidden, I'll call you back. Turn your phone to silent."

"Okay." I hung up and turned the ringer off. The men had gone inside the barn.

Time ticked by slowly until I saw them come back out and talk for a minute by the door. Then one man headed toward the road and the other went back into the barn. Fuck. One was leaving and the other was waiting, presumably, for Tommy to get back.

My phone lit up. Nino calling. I answered it with a whisper.

"What's happening?" he asked.

I told him, in a low whisper, about the fact that two had come but one had left and that the other was inside. I told him the guy had a gun and that there was also a gun up in the loft in the pillow.

"I can't reach T or Dare. I should come get you. Where, exactly, are you?"

Damn. Tommy said no one knew where it was. I mean, obviously he was wrong, but should I tell Nino? Nino was practically family to me and obviously Tommy trusted him, but Tommy already suspected James had defected and there was what Earl did. Was Nino loyal to the Ferrano family? Tommy obviously believed in him enough to put his number on my phone. What should I do?

"It's okay, Tia. You can tell me. I promise you, you can," he said softly, breaking the long silence on the line.

So, I made a judgment call and told him what I knew of where we were, which I only really knew from remembering that map with the old lady and old man that day Tommy had tested me. It was actually a good thing he did do that, or I'd have no idea where I even was. I knew the nearest intersection and I described the barn and the house. He told me he was coming, he had guns, and that I should stay hidden until he'd eliminated the threat. He said that if I thought I could get to the Jeep I should run for it and drive out of there, but if someone continued to stay inside, I should try to stay hidden.

An hour later, I was still in the tall grass and I hadn't heard back from Tommy or Dario. That had me more than a bit stressed out. No one had come and the guy inside hadn't come out. He was obviously waiting for us.

Finally, I saw a black hatchback car drive by. It didn't slow, just kept going. It was the first car that had gone by so I wondered if it was either more bad guys or maybe Nino scoping the place out. A few minutes later I got a text from Nino asking me where the door was on the barn and asking me if any downstairs windows were open. I wrote back describing it as best I could in quick order.

Fifteen minutes later, I saw Nino and Dex coming from the pond side toward the barn. They were on foot, sneakily making their way to the barn, guns drawn. Thirty seconds after they were inside the barn, there was gunfire. Then thirty seconds after that, Nino was calling my phone.

"Come quick and careful. I'll cover you from the stall window in case anyone approaches."

When I finally got to the barn, heart hammering in my chest, Nino was in the doorway.

"Get into the Jeep." Nino handed me a small handgun and my

purse, which had been upstairs. "Listen. We found a tracker on it. I got it off. We're putting it on my ride so we can see if we can lure whoever it is. I'm taking that, Dex is staying here to see what comes, and we got more guys on their way. Put this under your seat and drive to the city. Drive to my wife's shop and she'll meet you and take you to her mother's place until we get shit sorted. You remember where Bianca's shop is?"

I nodded and thanked him profusely and got into the Jeep and drove out like a bat outta hell.

It'd been a while since I'd driven and I can't say I was all that great at it, but I got out of there, quickly. I drove the opposite way that we usually came in, figuring I'd figure the rest out later and also figuring if the other guy wasn't far, he'd come from the other way.

Ten minutes later I was kind of lost, but I was pretty sure I hadn't been followed. Fifteen minutes after that, the flip phone was ringing and it was Dario.

"Dario!" I answered.

"Tia! What's your status?"

I spoke fast, "I got Nino to the safe house because these two guys were there with guns and Nino got one, I don't know where the other is, he left before Nino got here and I got into Tommy's Jeep and I'm maybe about thirty minutes away from Bianca's salon where Nino said to meet her. There was a tracker on the Jeep so whoever put it there knows where the safe house is!"

"Okay, yeah, I just got off the phone with him. Change of plans," Dario said. "Are you being followed?"

"I don't think so. I'm on a dirt road alone. Haven't seen a car for the whole time I've been driving. Where's Tommy?"

"I'll explain after. Get to 15 Sweet Avenue as fast as you can. Don't put 15 Sweet into in the GPS in the Jeep in case there's a hack on the GPS. I will give you directions."

He gave me directions and let me go.

I got a text and it said Tommy.

Where r u?

I pulled over and dialed his number. No answer. I answered back.

Trying to call!?! Urgent

Him: Can't talk live. Text me where u r.

Me: I'm driving to meet Dario. Someone came to the farm!

Him: Were ru meeting Dario?

Something wasn't right.

Me: Where are you? Is everything ok?

It dinged with,

Im ok. Were r u goign?"

I suddenly had this sinking feeling, remembering the text that came through that was a fake about Luciana's labor. How did I know whether or not this was Tommy? I wrote,

I need to talk to you. I need to hear your voice.

Him: I cant talk 2 u. Need u 2 tell me were u r so I cna meet u. its urgent.

My gut told me it wasn't him.

I wrote:

What's OUR favorite ice cream flavor?

The answer:

Strawbery. Were r u honey plz

The answer came after a long time. Strawberry? Honey? All those typos? Not Tommy.

I called Dario back and told him someone was texting me from Tommy's phone or that Tommy's phone was cloned and he told me to just hurry to meet him. I ignored the next three texts that came from whoever was pretending to be Tommy.

It was nighttime when I pulled up to 15 Sweet Avenue. It was a small run-down looking house on a small and quiet street . All the lights were off. I parked and put the gun into my waistband under my shirt at the back. I knocked on the front door. I saw a figure move behind the curtains on the window adjacent to the door.

Finally, the door opened a little and Dario pulled me in by the wrist.

"We gotta move!" He said, looking angry and tweaked. He walked me through the house, holding my elbow. It was a sparse run-down place with no furniture and everything was in rough shape. He went down the stairs to the basement and now I knew it was Dario's safe house. The basement apartment was totally redone, high tech, every modern convenience. No one appeared to be here but him. I used his bathroom and then he grabbed a duffle bag and we went back upstairs.

"Stay here!" he said and I waited by the top of the stairs as he headed toward the front of the house. He was gone only about 30 seconds, then he rushed me through the back door where there was an alley with a separate garage. Inside was a black SUV. He ushered me into it. This looked like the same SUV I'd been picked up from my grad in.

"Gimme the phone?"

"Where's Tommy?" I asked, handing it to him.

He did something on the phone while shaking his head. "I don't know."

"He said someone faked a text from Eddy so I was wary."

"Good." He pulled out and was driving crazy-fast.

"Where are we going?" I had no idea what that place even was.

"Bianca's ma's house, where I've got the girls and the kids."

"Luciana?"

"She's there, too."

"How's your dad?"

"Pop's hanging in, last I heard."

"When did you last see Tommy?"

"I haven't seen him. He was supposed to meet me this morning. He never showed."

I felt sick to my stomach.

My phone, sitting on the seat between us, rang. It said Tommy on it.

"Tommy!" I looked to Dario.

He jerked his chin at the phone. "Answer it. Careful. Gimme the phone if it's not him."

I answered it. "Tommy?"

"Not Tommy," said a male voice, "But we have him. Get to where Tommy's brother is and call this number back."

"What do you want?" I looked at Dario with panic. He took the phone from me and pulled over to the side of the road.

"Who is this? This is him; what do you want?" Dario held the phone for a minute. Then after a minute of listening, he said, "Put him on the phone." A minute later he said, "Hey. You alright? Yeah, man. Yep, she's with me. Right. Right." Then he hung up.

"What do they want?"

"Money," Dario said, pulling back onto the road.

"Money?"

"Yeah; they want a million cash. That's it. These guys are small time, guys hired by Castillo's nephew. They were hired to take out a hit on Tommy but decided to sell him back. They want you delivering the money. Pop has enough money in his vault. I'll get it and we'll make the drop."

I was speechless. Dario pulled around in a U-turn and drove in the opposite direction. Ten minutes later we were at their pop's place and Dario pulled in and made me follow him inside.

"Why do they want me delivering the money?"

We were in Tom's office and Dario was opening a safe in the wall behind a family photo of Tom and the four grandkids.

"They probably figure you won't shoot them; you'll give them the money and they can get outta there clean. They'll figure if I'm in there it's a big chance that I'll be carrying and it'll go south."

Dario pulled out ten stacks of bills and then put them into a duffle bag that he'd fetched from a closet.

"But what if they just take the money and shoot me? What if Tommy's already... already..." I was panicking, big time.

"I'll have you covered. We'll have the place crawling with men. Let's go. They're calling in fifteen minutes with the drop location.

"You sure they've got Tommy?"

"They put him on the phone."

The idea of Tommy being taken seemed all but impossible to me. He was so strong, had such a presence, it was hard to imagine him being overpowered. The idea that they'd found his safe house and could've shot him...

Dario interrupted my thoughts, "This crew is small time. We give them the money, get Tommy, Tommy and I eliminate the bigger threat, and we send some of our guys to get our money back and take these guys out. It'll all work out. Don't stress."

Don't stress? Easy for him to say! There was so much going on here. Tom Ferrano in a hospital bed, my father in jail and a sitting duck (or maybe by now a dead duck), Tommy kidnapped for ransom and not from the bigger threat but some other new threat, the rest of the family in hiding. Tessa's husband dead. And me: expected to do a money drop to get Tommy back?

All while wondering if my own dad was alive or dead.

Dario pulled into a coffee shop drive thru and ordered a coffee and looked to me. "Just water," I muttered and he ordered for us and then parked in front and stared at the phone.

Tommy

They'd tracked me somehow to the farm and waited. They ran my bike off the road just down the road and I'd gotten knocked out cold. When I came to, they had disarmed me and had me cuffed in the back of their covered pickup. Now we were in a motel room. I knew this motel. It was two minutes from my condo, where my brother now lived. I knew the décor because I'd fucked a girl here a few months ago and then one of the guys had come in from outside and I recognized the neon diner sign across the road.

These guys were trying to be up and comers, subbing work for Jesse Romero, Juan Carlos Castillo's nephew. They were stupid. They were careless. And I didn't like that I'd heard them demand my girl make the drop for the money. I was relieved that my brother had Tia with him, but Dare had better find another way. There was no way he'd send Tia in here. Would he?

I didn't know how she'd wound up with him, but that was a relief. I didn't want to think about what they'd have done to her if they'd caught her back at the farm and the minute I woke and knew they'd found my safe house I'd been sick with worry about her being there, vulnerable. There were two of them, one had junkie written all over him. The other guy, a jock type, started chirping at me, asking me what my girl looked like, why there were no pics of her on my phone, talking about how maybe he'd get a taste before they let me go. I sat, not giving them anything, no words, no looks, just dead eyes.

All that was wrong right now with me was a bit of road rash, a kick to the ribs, and I'd been hit in the face when they asked me her ice cream question and asked what my pet name was for her. When she stopped answering their texts after my face made them think they knew what the right answer was based on the answers they were running through, they knew they were skunked. I was proud of my girl for suspecting it wasn't me texting her.

These guys weren't smart or sober enough to win at this game. They were out-of-towners who had no idea how connected my family was, but they would soon find out. Dare would deal with this shit and get me outta here so we could finish dealing with Romero.

There was a digital alarm clock on the nightstand beside me. I was sitting on the floor against the wall. I watched time tick by and about an hour passed and then my burner phone rang. The junkie answered it,

"You got the money? Have the bitch bring it. Room 302, Knight's Inn on Lakeshore. She comes alone or we put a bullet in your brother and then in her."

Fifteen minutes later, there was a knock at the door. Jock opened it with a gun behind his back and Junkie stood with the gun pointing at me.

After the door swung open, I saw a female figure step into the room carrying a backpack. I was fuming. How could Dare send her in here? Then I realized something wasn't right. She was taller than Tia. The light caught her face and I saw that it wasn't Tia. Who was it? It was Bianca. Good thinkin', Dare. I hid my smile.

Bianca grew up with us. Her pop was as bad a bad ass as they come. Bee was badass herself. We used to practice together on the gun range. Her, me, and Earl. She could shoot better than most men I knew. If she'd been a boy she would've been right in there with Dare and I running things. If her pop hadn't been taken out by mine and she'd been a boy, she'd be running the show; we'd all be working for her. Knowing her like I did, she could run the show, female or not. She was happy to be a mother and run her salon, but the chick was smart, cunning, and she was good with not just a gun but her fists and her feet. She'd taken martial arts as a kid and she once beat the shit out of Dario for dumping her best friend's little sister for another girl. Gave him two black eyes and then cracked a rib with one of her roundhouse kicks.

"Here's the money. Please let him go," she said softly.

Junkie took the bag and opened it. Jock started circling her.

"Damn, girl. You got a fine ass on you," he said.

Bee rolled her eyes at me.

He leaned over and touched her face. "Maybe you need to pay just a little more, a tax, to get your boyfriend outta here."

She gave me a scared look, a fake scared look; I could see the devil in a twinkle in her eye. I held my gaze steady and said, "Don't you fucking dare," to the guy.

He snickered, looking over his shoulder at me and the second he did, Bee's high heeled boot came up and kicked him square in the mouth. As she did this, she also pulled a gun and pointed it at the junkie.

Atta girl, Bee; always loved Charlie's Angels. The junkie dropped the bag of money and his gun and put his hands up.

His eyes were fucked up and I knew the guy'd been dreamin' of his fix as he'd eyeballed all the money in the bag, so he'd be extra dangerous.

"Take him out, sweetheart," I told her and she immediately shot him in the leg and then kept the gun pointed at him. The guy screamed his head off. "You fucking cunt!"

"Uncuff him," she said to the jock, who was rousing, pointing the gun back and forth between the two of them. Jock groggily got to his knees and cautiously pulled a key from the junkie's jacket pocket, worried we'd shoot him. He shakily undid my cuffs. The second he did my elbow came up backwards and hit him square under the jaw hard enough that he was on the floor on his back and out again.

I cold clocked the junkie and kicked the jock in the head and then grabbed the bag of money and Bianca passed me an extra gun from under her jacket at her back. I put two bullets in one and then two in the other.

She and I got out of there, hopping into a waiting car where Nino and Dex waited. Nino was looking at Bee with pride as we got in. I heard him call JC, head of a clean-up crew we used, and give a few key but cryptic details.

Tia

I was sitting in the back office of a coffee shop; one that Tommy's family owned. Dario was out front talking to a few burly-looking guys that had to be enforcements for the family. I was freaking right out, wondering if everything was okay. Bianca had insisted on doing this and they'd pulled me out at the last second. She hugged me hard before going in, saying, "We're family. I'm here for ya, babes! And your man is familia, too, so there's no way I'm not helping. I can do this."

Dario had assured me that Bianca would be fine. Said she could double as a paid assassin if she wanted to, she was that tough. I laughed, like it was a joke, but neither of them laughed. She gave me a serious look, as if to agree. I prayed she'd be okay. She had a son to think of. And she might be or could soon be my only living relative, unless I counted Aunt Carol – which I did not.

The door swung open and there was Tommy. I jumped to my feet and threw myself at him. He looked fine, totally fine, except for a bruise on his cheekbone.

"Hey, baby," he breathed into my hair.

"You okay? Thank God!" I wrapped my arms around his neck and he lifted me and held me tight. I wrapped my legs around his waist and he sat on the desk and kissed me roughly, deeply, possessively.

I heard a throat clearing noise and looked over my shoulder and Dario was in the doorway. He jerked his chin up at Tommy. Tommy returned the chin jerk, then turned and set me down on the desk. "Okay, baby. Gotta go end this. Bee's driving you to where the girls are. Be back soon."

I winced. "I so want this over."

"It ends tonight," he said firmly and kissed me quickly on the mouth and then turned and he was gone.

Bianca popped her head into the office. "Ready?"

Trembling, I nodded and followed her out.

* * *

That night was like an eternity: the night that wouldn't end. When I got to Bianca's mother's house it was about 10:00 and it was like a locked down fortress. It was a gated place just at the outskirts of town and there were half a dozen men guarding the place.

Inside the big, warm, welcoming house was Lisa, Tess, Luciana, the kids, Bianca's mother Marie and Bianca's Aunt Joanne. The five kids (Luc's, Tessa's, and Bianca's) were in their pjs, getting put to bed by Bianca's mom who waved at me as I came in, but ascended the stairs with the four tots and one older child. Luciana looked tired and ready to pop any second. Tessa's eyes were red and puffy. Lisa looked pale and sickly. I hugged each of them and when I got to Tessa I whispered in her ear. "I'm so, so sorry."

She nodded, her chin trembled, and she put her arms around herself and just curled into a ball on the sofa and closed her eyes.

Bianca's mom had come back from putting the kids all in her bed with a Disney movie on, and then pulled me into an embrace and told me it was nice to meet me and that she had thought very highly of my mother. Then Bianca's aunt put a big plate of pasta in front of me and told me to eat. Food was the last thing on my brain at that moment.

"How's Tom?" I asked Lisa, who'd sat beside me at a breakfast bar in the big open kitchen that had a big island surrounded by stools. To the right was a sitting area, where Luc and Tessa were curled up on opposite ends of a big sectional sofa.

She shrugged. "It's breath by breath. Tommy okay?"

I nodded. "Just a bit banged up. He's okay."

She nodded and sipped from a big glass of wine.

"I'm going to bed," Luc announced and left the room.

I tried to eat a few bites but really wasn't hungry. I didn't want to insult them, so I sat at the plate for a long time, moving food around with my fork, while Bianca talked with her mother and her aunt in Italian.

Bianca sat beside Tessa and put her arms around her. Tessa cried softly into Bianca's shoulder and I felt her sorrow, the whole room would've felt it.

"Athena, you wanna get a bath or something? I'll get you some towels."

I nodded at Marie. She took me upstairs and showed me to a

guest room and pointed out the bathroom next to it and said she'd get my bag, that Nino had brought the bag with my and Tommy's clothes from the barn as well as my make-up case.

I took a long shower and then got dressed in yoga pants and a hoodie, tied my hair into a braid, and went downstairs. Tessa had gone to bed. Bianca, Lisa, Bianca's mom, and Aunt Joanne were watching TV. Sarah was sitting there, too, having just arrived. She pulled me into a hug and then she told me that Tom was hanging in there and then in hushed whispers they all sat and talked about the fact that the boys were ending things tonight and that everyone would be back here afterwards. Marie told me to go to bed and sleep in the room she'd put my stuff in whenever I was ready, that Tommy would find me when he arrived.

I didn't think I could sleep and being there in that group felt comforting, so I curled up on the sofa with them and we watched the rerun channel with all the old comedy shows on it until well past 4:00am when I noticed that Lisa had fallen asleep. Bianca's mom and aunt were sitting at the table talking softly over mugs of tea, and Sarah had fallen asleep sitting up beside me.

I just kept staring at the TV, not really paying attention, just mulling everything over. It was nice to be part of this group, to have these other women to lean on. And Bianca was family. Her mother was my aunt by marriage. And now Lisa, Tessa, Luciana...they were family too because they were Tommy's family. It felt good to belong. Amid the stress, the worry, the tragedy, it really felt like I belonged here with these people, despite what I knew of Tommy's father.

As I pondered the group around me, I heard noise and then Nino, Eddy, Dario, and Tommy were here. I'd been holding my breath watching the guys enter in single file and when I finally saw him, I bolted to my feet and ran to him. He gripped me tight.

"Is it over?" I asked into his ear.

"Yeah," he answered.

Dario spoke to the others and then Tommy looked to Bianca's mother and spoke to her in Italian. She motioned toward the fridge and was talking with her hands gesturing. He shook his head and said some more in Italian. And then she motioned toward the stairs. Tommy took me by the hand.

"Goodnight everyone," I said. "Thank you so much for everything." I looked to Bianca, her mom, and her aunt and they all smiled at me.

In the bedroom, Tommy shed his clothes and took off mine and then just held me tight, my naked body against his. I could see in the dimness of the room that his lower back and thigh were badly scraped.

"What happened?" I asked.

"Road rash," he said. "It's fine."

"I should put some ointment on it, bandage it."

"Leave it. It's fine."

"What about the other stuff?"

"Can we just go to sleep? Talk later," he spoke softly into my throat as he nuzzled closer. "I just needed to feel you against me. So fucking tired."

"Kay," I answered and closed my eyes.

"Love you, baby girl," he whispered.

"Love you, too, baby," I said as my eyes drooped and I fell asleep feeling warm, feeling safe, feeling immensely relieved. Everything wasn't totally over, there were a lot of unanswered questions, but I was relieved that progress had been made and that he was here beside me.

16

Tia

I woke up to Tommy's hands and mouth on me. My back arched as his fingers prodded between my legs and I let out a little moan. Then I heard squeals of laughter outside the door, and he put his hand over my mouth and winked. The kids were awake and sounding like a herd of elephants running down the hallway. Tommy ignored their ruckus and kept at me, hand over my mouth the whole time.

When, I wasn't too far off an orgasm, the door burst open and Luc's two girls and Tessa's older boy all barreled in and were on the bed with us. Tommy had been on top of me, thankfully we were covered by the blankets, but the three of them were jumping on the bed, "Uncle Tommy, Auntie Tia! Breakfast is ready!" Tommy blew out a slow breath and said, "Okay, guys. Get downstairs and tell them to pour coffee. We'll be right there."

The kids all scattered. I felt my heart warm at being called Auntie.

He looked at me with a wicked grin. "To be continued," he said, then got up and we both got dressed.

"What happened last night?" I asked.

"We'll talk later. Let's go down for breakfast. I smell bacon and I think I can hear it calling my name. And if I can't be inside of you hearing you call my name then I need to answer to the call 'o the bacon."

I giggled and pushed away annoyance at not being answered. But, maybe it was better that I knew as little as possible. Plausible deniability and all. I followed him down thinking that maybe the one threat was done with but that there was at least my father to still worry about, not to mention Tommy's father. Was my dad still alive or was he gone?

The mood downstairs was strained. Obviously a cloud still loomed. Coffee was handed to me and to Tommy as we entered. Tessa was sitting on the sofa in a bathrobe with her hair up in a towel turban with Luc and they were talking quietly. Tessa still looked awful. The kids were all eating pancakes and bacon. Nino, Eddy, and Dario were eating. The other women were all busying themselves in the kitchen, buttering toast, washing and drying frying pans, another putting clean dishes away from the dishwasher.

Tommy and I sat at the table with Dario and Nino.

"Pop's showing signs of improvement," Dario said to the group, then added, "After I finish my coffee, I'm takin' Tess to make arrangements for James. We don't want the whole family in one public place at one time for a while until we know things are settled down so he's being cremated, and we'll do a memorial service later."

Tommy and Dario exchanged looks and I suspected there was more to it. Fear prickled the back of my neck. What now?

I heard a phone ringing and Tommy reached into his pocket and answered it before he stepped away from the table and outside with the phone.

I drank my coffee and managed to get a piece of toast into me, and then was helping by drying dishes when Tommy got back.

"Wanna grab our stuff and say bye? We need to go." He grabbed a piece of bacon off the platter in the center of the table and sipped his coffee while I made the rounds, thanking Marie for her hospitality, hugging Marie's sister, getting a big hug from Bianca and thanking her for her help last night. We said we'd get together soon. Then I said goodbyes to the rest of the ladies as well as the kids, who all gave me hugs. I told Tessa if she needed anything, for me to help with the boys, or anything like that to just call me. She nodded solemnly. When I hugged Luc, I felt her baby kick me through her belly and I told her that it felt like a he, like a soccer player. She hugged me hard. I hugged Tommy's brother, Eddy, and Nino, thanking them for all their help, too.

I dashed back upstairs and made the bed and then got our things and when I got to the door, Tommy was standing there talking to his brother quietly. They separated as soon as I got there and Dario pulled me in for another quick hug and kissed the top of my head as Tommy reached for the bag from me. As we left, I saw there were six men mulling about outside. We got into Tommy's car, the convertible; I didn't know how it got here, where the Jeep was, or where the Harley was, either.

When we pulled out past the gates and were on the road, he reached across and held my hand as he drove.

"They ran me off the road on the Harley just up the road from the farm. Knocked me out and took me and when I came to all I could think of was you and how I'd fucking left you a sitting duck. Nino told me you'd gone on a hike and came back to them coming in. They were gonna grab you and after they'd ransomed me out with Dare they were gonna ransom you out with me. Bunch of fuckin' chuckleheads. No idea who they were messin' with."

"That Bianca is badass," I said.

He nodded. "That was smart thinkin' on Dare's part."

"He was gonna send me in right up to the last minute. He was trying to coach me, but he'd been in touch with Nino and Bianca got wind and lost it and insisted she go in instead. They insisted it be a girl and we both have straight hair so..."

Tommy raised his brows. "Can't believe Dario was gonna send you in." He looked pissed.

"It all worked out," I said.

He nodded and squeezed my hand but he still kinda looked pissed.

"And like you said, I'm strong enough. I'm your girl."

He gave me a thin smile and then said, "Not 100% but leaning in the direction of lookin' like Jimmy might've double crossed us. Tessa knows. Devastated. Lost her husband, her kids' father, and she lost respect for the man she thought loved her. If so, Jim was expendable to the other side, they got rid of him, but if it was him that'd given them valuable intel that led to Pop getting shot, to putting everyone else in danger, to me being taken from you and leaving you vulnerable? Fuck." He shook his head.

"I'm so sorry, baby," I said.

"Yeah," he said softly but his eyes were blazing with anger.

"What's the status with my father?" I asked quietly.

"No news," Tommy answered and then he pulled up to the gate of his house and hit a button on the remote and someone moved into our view as it opened. After we got on the other side I saw a guy who'd been here a few times before; I didn't know his name.

"Boss, the house has had a full sweep. We found two bugs but all good now."

"Where?"

"Your office and the staff room. The office one was broken, though."

Tommy's jaw tensed. "Right. I'll be out to chat with you and get a brief in an hour," he said and then took my hand and we went inside.

He walked me directly upstairs, directly to the bedroom, and then as he shut the door his hands went to the fly of his jeans and I backed up slowly until I was standing against the foot of the bed.

"I need you. Lie down. Spread," he demanded, his eyes ablaze.

I obeyed, feeling a gush of warmth down below.

He yanked my pants and undies down at once and was inside of me in record time, his eyes not releasing mine while he took me hard and fast. The muscles of his jaw were hard and tense and his eyes were steely hard, too.

His phone rang. He ignored it. Someone knocked at his bedroom door and he snarled, leaned back, broke our connection, and threw his zipper back up.

"Under the covers and wait. Do not move. Unless this house is on fire, you stay right there!" He left the bedroom, looking pissed.

I waited.

And waited.

And I waited...

Finally, I was thirsty and hungry and wondering what was keeping him. I got out of bed and reached into my purse and found the flip phone. I didn't know if the iPhone was still at the hayloft or not. I texted him.

> **Hi. Since you're obviously not in a hurry to finish what you started, can I please leave the bed, Master? I'm very thirsty and hungry and you've left me all alone for so very long :(**

A few minutes later I got a reply.

> **Sorry baby! I'd like nothing better than to come and finish! Go & eat. I had to run out for a bit. You're under 3x security. You're safe. I'll be back ASAP. This phone almost out of juice so use my reg. number. We'll grab your reg phone tomorrow from the farm.**
>
> **Me: stupid Phone. LOL. <3 U. IDK your reg number off by heart so text it to me. Be safe!**

He replied with a happy face and x's and o's plus his other number. Sheesh, how long would he have left me here? I had to give him a break; he obviously had a million things on his mind. I found my way downstairs and decided to pop one of Sarah's frozen lasagnas in the oven. I drank a tall glass of water and then went back upstairs to get a shower.

Tommy hadn't turned up by the time the lasagna was ready and it was big enough to feed a dozen so I cut off a piece for me, wrapped up a piece for Tommy for later, tossed a big salad and served two bowls out, then put the rest of the lasagna and salad in the fridge in the security team's break room and stepped out to the patio where Dex was standing, talking on a cell. When he saw me, he put it back to his waistband. "Everything okay?"

"Sorry to bug you..." I started.

He waved his hand. "It's what I'm here for. What do you need?"

"Nothing, I just wanted to tell you and the other guys that I put a lasagna and salad in the fridge in the staff breakroom."

His eyes lit up. "Thanks, that's awesome," he said.

The other guy who'd been at the gate when we came in was approaching and I could tell he'd heard by how his face lit up. I decided then that I'd continually put food into the staff room fridge for these guys who were working so hard to keep us safe. It couldn't be easy being in their shoes after knowing guys were killed while on that same job the other night. It was just food, but at least it was something to show my appreciation.

After I ate and watched TV for a bit, I was pretty tired. It was only around 9:00, but I decided to crash early. I texted Tommy from the flip phone.

I'm going to bed. Hope you're okay. Love you. Xo

I got an almost instant reply.

I'm fine. See you soon. Love you. xxx

Tommy

My plan was to go home, make love to my girl, sleep for a few hours, and then find out how Pop was doing. Instead, I had to meet with my PI and my brother, to get more intel on where things were at.

On my way to get Dare from the hospital, I got a returned call back from a connection that helped me get Tia's father moved. He was safe. For how long, I didn't know. Did he deserve it? Fuck, no. But, he was her father and I didn't want her to have to deal with his death on top of everything else so he was on simmer for the time being.

Turned out that Dare talked to Pop, who'd woken up. Pop had Jimmy doing double duty for insight with his enemies related to the group Romero was part of; he wasn't really stepping out on us. Pop wasn't coherent enough to get too into detail so we had to guess at a few things. We guessed the thing with my weapons happened because it'd fallen in his lap while he'd been wearing a wire for the other guys when he was found shot so we assumed he'd been dodgy with me because of the wire. The whole wire thing made sense, too. Jimmy had really been keeping his distance the last few days before he was shot. They'd probably told him to leave me a sitting duck.

It seemed like he'd been on his way here, probably to help or warn me, when things went screwy. If that's what he intended, it didn't happen because he'd been shot instead. Dare and I planned to talk to our sister and we hoped it'd bring her a little bit of peace that her husband had been loyal, too loyal. Fucking Pop.

She wouldn't be best pleased with Pop for putting her husband in that position, getting him killed. None of us were pleased with him after the things we'd found out.

Pop was in deeper with illicit drugs than we'd imagined. And it was that depth that had created the whole rift with Juan Carlos Castillo in the first place. Many lives had been unnecessarily lost as a result of Pop moving in on Castillo's territory. But Romero didn't have the clout alone needed to take Pop out so at first, he participated in recruiting Earl and they tried to use Tia as a bargaining chip. Not only did Pop refuse to back off but as a result, I'd killed Castillo and worked with Castillo's arch nemesis to wipe out the Castillo cartel.

This had, of course, trickled back home with Jesse Romero getting desperate to hang onto his business but without the strength of his uncle he had started trying to expand his team, to swell his ranks, bringing in new guys, careless and / or inexperienced guys, making alliances. The whole thing had been a gaggle fuck. Stuff we'd agreed to with Castillo down south had less to do with what we thought we were working toward and more to do with Pop's drug deals. Now Romero and most of his crew were gone. Castillo was gone. And Pop was in a hospital bed showing signs of improvement. Big moves almost always result in a trickle effect, and I wanted to do some serious damage control.

Pop had plans to move to the islands, yeah, but retirement wasn't looking like it'd factor into those plans. My PI dug up evidence that he had plans to have me and Dare look after business here while he expanded some seedy business to do with women, drugs, and guns into Honduras, El Salvador, and Nicaragua. Pop didn't want to retire; he wanted more power, more control, and it was out of hand. One of his enemies was doing well in that part of the world and Pop wanted to take it all away from the guy.

Clearly it was out of hand if he had this secret life. Here it was about construction, the bookie business, loans, and that trickled down into a few other areas, like stolen goods, sex, a little weed. And yeah, some was illegal but where he'd sunk to seemed to me and to my brother to be worse than that, much worse than that. We knew sometimes we had to dabble in those areas, but Pop wasn't dabbling, he was deep sea diving in the cesspool.

What I now had to decide was, how was I getting out without making an enemy of my father? I called Dex to check on things at home and the fuckin' guy was talking with his mouth full.

"Can't understand what you're saying man. What are you doing? Blowing someone? Spit or swallow, man."

"Sorry, Tommy. Your girl put dinner out for everyone. Everything's cool here. No problems at all."

I hung up, shaking my head. Then I got a text from Tia that instead of crashing early it looked like Tessa's boys were being dropped off at our place for a few hours.

Tessa was overwhelmed and her mother-in-law couldn't watch the kids tonight. Luc was at the hospital with a bit of spotting so Sarah was with her. I shook my head. Feeding my men, babysitting my nephews? My heart swelled for her. I needed to give her a good life. I needed to keep myself in the right headspace to be good for her. And for that, I needed out of this life.

Tia

I'd gotten the call as I was falling asleep and I told Sarah I'd happily keep the boys overnight if she wanted me to but she said Tessa didn't want that. They knew Tommy's house was extra secured so they wanted them here but it was just for a few hours. She had

Bianca's Aunt Joanne drop them off on her way to work (she was a nurse at a hospital on the nightshift) and was going to have Sarah pick them up in a bit. I put movies on and built Lego structures with them.

I let Antonio, the older of the two, play on Tommy's laptop on a kids' game website and Lucas was content in my lap with a pop-up book. The time went by quickly and I gave them a bubble bath and put them in their PJs and around 11:00 Sarah got there to pick them up. They were quiet and subdued, not like the typical active baby and toddler. They must've sensed something was amiss. They didn't really know me, and it was probably way past their usual bedtimes, too.

Apparently, Tom had woken up and Lisa was by his side. Luc was being put on bed rest. As I was helping Sarah put the boys into their car seats in her van, I saw Tommy's car pull in and Dario's car behind him.

When Dario got out of the car, he pointed at me accusingly. "You! Follow me. We need to have a conversation."

My brows shot up in surprise. I glanced at Tommy. He narrowed his eyes at me. He motioned toward his brother with a hard expression on his face, so I said bye to Sarah and followed.

Dario marched downstairs and directly to the games room and the Ms. Pacman machine. He was giving me an incredulous look and pointing at the high score list and my #2 spot.

I started to laugh, feeling immense relief. Mr. Angry Intense brother was back, but this time, it was funny. I stepped up beside him. I was only a few hundred points shy of his high score. I'd beat out everyone else, taking the previous spot #2, which had said Marco. Spot #3 had said Polo. And now those were spots 3 and 4.

Tommy was behind me. "Dex ratted you out."

Dex was coming down the stairs.

"See if I feed you dinner again!" I harrumphed.

Dario waved his index finger accusingly at me while Dex laughed and pouted simultaneously.

"I'm hot on your heels, boy!" I teased Dario and took off up the stairs behind Tommy as he called out to me.

"Tia, c'mere here baby."

I saw Dex challenge Dario to foosball as I followed Tommy upstairs. He pulled me close once we got to the kitchen.

"How are you?" he whispered in my ear.

"I'm okay. How 'bout you?"

"I'm good. I just want to tell you a few things, then I'll order us some dinner. Chinese okay?"

"I ate already but I saved you some food."

"Dare wants Chinese. We have to work late and sort some shit out. You gonna be okay?"

"Yeah."

"What'd you make me for dinner?"

"I made one of Sarah's lasagnas. You can eat it for lunch tomorrow, maybe?"

"Sounds good, babe, even if your lasagna's better. You gonna cook me dinner every night?" He was nibbling on my earlobe and sending shivers up and down my spine.

"Yeah, most nights. If you want. We can do one takeout night a week, maybe a pizza night, one eat out at a nice restaurant together, and the rest I can cook."

"Oh," he chuckled. "Laying down the law, huh?"

"Yeah," I giggled.

"You're the boss," he said as he kissed my throat. "Except I'll cook Sunday mornings."

I laughed. "Deal. And the boss? Me? Yeah, right."

He laughed and winked at me. "You can be the boss of the food. What'd you do with the boys?"

"I'll take the power where I can get it." I winked. "I played Legos with them, did some coloring, we read a bunch of books, and I gave them a bath. What do you need to tell me?"

I hoisted myself up to sit on the countertop.

He looked at me warmly. "Thanks for that. I'm sure Tess appreciated it. I appreciate it."

"I'm happy to help. I can't imagine what she's going through."

He stared at me for a second, then said, "I, uh, had your father moved. For the moment, he's safe. I can't make long- term promises, but I got him moved for now."

My eyes widened. "You did?"

"Yeah. Called in some favors."

I threw my arms tight around his neck and whispered, "He doesn't deserve it. But thanks, Tommy."

"Mm hm," he said, his voice laced with skepticism.

I knew my dad really didn't deserve it, but Tommy was doing it for me. That counted.

"Anything else?" I asked.

"I've decided to put the farm up for sale so maybe tomorrow or the next day you and I will go up there and pick up whatever else we left there the other day."

My expression dropped.

"It's not my safe house anymore. I need to find us something else."

"I love that place," I said and pouted.

He frowned. "You want me to keep it?"

I nodded, "Can you?"

"I can," he said and kissed my nose. "If that's what you want."

"It is. It's where you told me you were in love with me."

He smiled.

"It's where you played our wedding song for me."

He smiled bigger and stroked my cheek with his thumb, his other fingers woven into my hair.

"It's where sun rays shot out of your head when you made love to me when I was wrapped in clover," I whispered.

He looked at me like I'd lost the plot. "Sun rays? Out my head?"

"Yeah." I squeezed him tight against me.

"Okay, I'll keep it. But we need another safe house."

"Okay," I said. "Can we spend the night there tomorrow night?"

"Let me see what's on the agenda. Maybe. I'm gonna go order that Chinese. There are menus in the office."

"How's your father?" I asked.

"Getting there," he mumbled and then I followed him down the hall to his office and he muttered to me that James hadn't double crossed his family after all, but that he was just another pawn in one of his pop's games. My heart sank. Things weren't getting any better for Tommy and I knew this meant it'd be even more complicated going forward.

Tommy

She sat downstairs on the arm of the chair I was in while me, Dare, and Dex all ate. She said she didn't want any but kept snagging food off my plate while we were there. Anyone else stuck their fingers in my food they'd lose said fingers. I just kept giving her looks but she was totally oblivious. Dare, however, wasn't. I could tell by his smirking he found it comical because he knew me and saw I was letting her away with it despite being mildly annoyed about it. As mildly annoying as it was it meant there was a level of relaxation and familiarity between her and I that had come and I didn't want to mess with that.

There were two other guys outside on patrol. We'd decided to move Dex and Nino up. Dex to Nino's old job (previously Earl's job) and Nino to Jimmy's post, which was mixed security for the family and other shit that we needed someone we could truly trust on. Dare was briefing the security team at Pop's house later.

When Nino arrived and reached for one of the XBOX controllers

Dare said to him, "We've gotta talk business with you. No gaming right now."

She just got up and cleared the food, kissed me, and then headed upstairs. I didn't have to get her to leave the room. It was like she was made for this life. But I wasn't keeping her in it. It was ending and tonight was going to be the beginning of that.

After a productive meeting with the guys, Dare and I strategized some more. We pulled an all-nighter and then Dare and I went to see Pop at around 7:00 in the morning. I drove us down there and then afterwards dropped Dare off back at the office where he was gonna take care of a few things and then crash on the couch for a few hours.

As I came into the bedroom at around nine o'clock in the morning, I found Tia still asleep. I climbed into bed with her. She squirmed into me. She was naked.

"You're naked," I muttered into her ear.

She sleepily answered, "You weren't here to give me a shirt. And so are you."

"Good girl," I said and pulled her tight against me.

She was breathing slow and steady and I decided to just let her sleep. I had a lot of shit on my mind.

I thought back to Dare and I going to see Pop.

"Boys," he'd said hoarsely when he saw us.

"Pop," we'd said in unison.

I sat in the chair beside the bed and my brother was leaning against the counter off to the side of the bed.

"What happened?" he asked.

"Romero's dealt with," I stated.

He nodded a little.

"Yeah," I nodded, too. "They got Jimmy. He's dead."

"Dario told me yesterday," Pop replied.

I knew he knew this but I needed to lead with that.

"Listen, Pop. I need autonomy. Now. You good with that?"

He nodded a little. "Of course, my boy. I can't exactly do much from here."

"For good, Pop."

He winced and shifted a little. "For good?"

"Yeah, Pop. See, we found out some stuff we're not too thrilled with. There's a mess on our hands. My sister's a widow. We need to clean up. You good with that?"

Pop swallowed hard and closed his eyes.

"We're done dipping into the business you were in on in Morelia. We know it's gone on elsewhere, too. It's bad news. You interested in continuing that from your retirement villa, so be it. Me and Dare, we're out. It has zilch to do with Ferrano Enterprises."

Pop had looked to my brother and my brother nodded.

"Two against one, uh?" Pop snickered.

Dare piped up. "We don't like some of what we found out, Pop. But we're happy to continue with the existing business structure for now. Tommy and I have a few changes in mind but slowly we'll make those changes so it doesn't hurt the company and so it preserves relationships that have been built that we still need. We think it's best we get you to sign over with lawyers. And you retire. Or, you don't retire but we part ways with the business here. You made a deal that he got married he'd take over. He's getting married so it's time."

I added, "You got a problem with us running things the way we want to run them, clean, we part ways now businesswise. You give us the reins you continue to get residuals of everything we decide to keep doing. You don't, we leave it in your hands and we go do something else."

Pop gave a slight shrug without looking us in the eyes, "We'll talk after. Let me think about it."

I didn't like that one bit. It felt like a game I wasn't interested in playing.

"All right, Pop. Dare and I, we'll be back in the morning. Sleep well. Glad you're all right."

Pop closed his eyes and my brother and I made our way out, nodding at the on-site security guard stationed outside his door.

Dare and I exchanged knowing glances on the way out. We didn't like his attitude. He, clearly, hadn't been thrilled with ours, either. He was a man used to calling the shots, a man who thought of his sons as his right and left hands, not as men who would pull a mutiny over on him.

Tia

When I woke up, Tommy was watching me sleep.

"Hey," I greeted.

"Hey," he replied and his eyes twinkled.

"Isn't it kinda creepy stalkerish that you were just watching me sleep?"

His mouth quirked up into a lazy smile. "I'll stalk you to the ends of the earth, baby girl."

I curled into him, knowing it was true, but for the first time, not really feeling creeped out by it.

"I smell bacon," I jolted upwards.

"Sarah's here today," Tommy said. "You go. I gotta sleep for a few hours. Wake me at two?"

"How do you want me to wake you?" I squirmed against him friskily.

"Why don't you try a few things now and I'll pick my fave?" he suggested. I disappeared under the blankets and took his cock with my mouth. He let me finish him that way and it was empowering to watch and feel him shatter like that, his hands in my hair, his body trembling as he came. It was rare that he didn't look after me in return, so I didn't feel slighted when he almost immediately fell asleep afterwards. He'd been running his fingers through my hair while my head rested on his belly and his hand just sort of flopped. I kissed his abs, kissed his chin, and then covered him up and headed to the bathroom for a shower.

A little while later, I found my way to the kitchen and sure enough, Sarah was making breakfast. She poured me a coffee and I sat at the breakfast bar and took a sip. I'd only seen her put one sugar in it. She just wasn't giving up, was she? When her back was turned, I put two more sugars in. She saw me do it and snickered.

We chatted amicably while she kept cooking and she smiled big at me when I got in there and started popping bread into the toaster. Tommy had come down, talking on the phone and walked into his office. His arm went around my waist as I was buttering toast and he scooped me against him, my back to his front, and leaned down and kissed my temple. "It's only 10:00, honey, you should be sleeping!"

"Yeah, something's come up. Looks like I'll have to sleep when I'm dead." He reached and snagged a piece of toast, "Call you later."

"Kay." I nuzzled back into his warmth. "Don't get dead." How this man could seriously function on zero sleep so often was beyond me.

"I won't. Love you," he said huskily into my ear and then kissed my lobe, leaned over and kissed me quickly on the lips and I told him I loved him too, and then he was gone.

Suddenly, it was like the life was being squeezed out of me. Sarah Martinez had her arms around me and she was shouting in Spanish while hugging me, hard.

"Whoa," I laughed, taken totally aback, dropping the butter knife to the floor.

She was shouting to the ceiling in Spanish and then she kissed both of my cheeks and my forehead with a flourish.

The toaster popped again so she let go of me, I got a fresh knife, red-faced.

She wiped up the floor with a soapy paper towel, saying, "I never thought I'd hear that boy tell a woman those words. You've been the prescription, Chiquita, the prescription."

"Yeah, well it's not all ice cream sundaes and walks on the beach, lemme tell ya," I started and then stopped myself. I bit my tongue.

She gave me a knowing smile. "Peaks and valleys exist in all relationships. All marriages."

Yeah, the peaks were high, the valleys deep. Dark and deep. Tommy and I being married would mean I really did have to take my 'for better or for worse' promise to heart.

Since it was just me, Sarah joined me for breakfast, teasing me about making eight pieces of toast for the two of us (but I was used to the bustle in the Crenshaw kitchen so had done that out of habit) and then I helped her clean up while she went over a bunch of stuff with me about running the household.

She gave me her cell phone number and we talked about her coming by twice a week for half days to do some deeper cleaning but we figured I could handle the rest and if I couldn't or wanted to change things, she was open to it. She also promised that when she did freezer meals for the girls, she'd make batches for Tommy and I. She did a day of cooking once a month to put several entrees into everyone's freezers.

She was here to pack her room up as she was moving into Tessa's to help out and would be working between here, Luc's, and Tessa's. I offered to help her pack up her room. I had nothing else to do, really. We had a nice afternoon together.

* * *

Tommy texted me that afternoon and told me we'd have to wait until the following day to go to the farm. He said he'd be home late and told me not to wait up.

The next day we left to spend two nights up in the hayloft and filled our time, making love, fishing, hiking, making love some more. He'd been sweet and attentive and we avoided talking about touchy subjects. We just took those few days to de-stress and it was mostly vanilla and totally...well...wonderful.

But the next day when we'd gotten back to the city Tommy told me that he had to take off for about a week to clear up some stuff to do with his father. He wouldn't tell me very much, just packed a bag, made love to me, and then he left. He told me he'd text me daily. He told me his brother was staying at the house while he was gone to keep an eye on things and keep me safe.

I stayed home the whole time, other than hanging by the pool. I baked, I watched Tessa's boys one day, I played Ms. Pacman, I burned through a half a dozen romance novels on my reading app on my phone, and not much else. Dario and I had a few meals together, but he seemed pretty busy, pretty preoccupied, mostly spent his time in Tommy's office.

Tommy and I had texting conversations daily. Most of it was just quick check-ins from him. On the fifth night I was in bed and hadn't heard from him all day so texted.

Hope you're okay.
Love you.
Miss you. Xo

When I got his message back a few hours later, it woke me up,

Tommy: Hey

Me: Hey

Tommy: Whatcha doin?

Me: Zzz'ing. Dreaming about you. Missing you. You?

Tommy: Send me a pic of your face.

Me: I've been sleeping. I'll look all sleepy and messy.

Tommy: Don't care.

I snapped a selfie with my lips puckered. Gah! I looked more than sleepy. I looked like something the cat had dragged in. I sent it anyway.

Me: You asked for it.

Tommy: Gorgeous.

I smiled and cuddled into the pillow.

Me: Send me your face.

Tommy: Send me a pic of your boobs first.

I laughed out loud and snapped a picture of my chest with a bit of cleavage and the use of my arms to squish my boobs together and up but I had a tank top on. I sent it.

Tommy: Naked boobs please

I giggled.

Me: I'm not that kind of girl. Send yours first and maybe a dicture (lol) I'll think about it. <wink>

Tommy: Dicture?

Me: Dick picture. LOL.

Tommy: You first.

Then it hit me. What if this wasn't him? I cringed and thanked my lucky stars that I hadn't sent a naked picture.

Me: Gimme the code word. So I know it's really you

Five minutes passed. I started to feel sick. It'd been instant replies up until that point and now nothing. I dialed his number.
 He answered. "Tia?"
 "Hi!"
 "Hey, Baby. It's late. You still up?"
 "I'm so happy to hear your voice." I started to shiver.
 "Me too. Miss you. Sorry I haven't texted you today yet. Been a bit nuts. I should be home in two, maybe three days, though. Why you up so late?"
 "Tommy."
 "What?" His voice changed. He knew something was wrong. "What, Baby. What?"
 I told him what'd happened.
 "Fuck! Fuck, fuck, fuck!" He growled, "I'll deal. Go to sleep. Don't stress."

"Don't stress?"

"No. I'm calling Dare. I'll get to the bottom of it."

"Kay," I whispered.

"Tia?"

"Hmm?"

"Love you. Good catch."

"Yeah. Love you."

"Save the messages. My brother might need to look at your phone."

We said goodnight. I didn't sleep a wink the rest of the night.

Who now? I couldn't wait until all of this was over, until he got us out and away from the danger.

* * *

It was embarrassing when Dario went through my phone in the morning. Him seeing the banter and my silly kissing photo, not to mention the tank top with the cleavage and references to Tommy's dick. Ugh. He took my phone while we were at the island in the kitchen, perused the messages, his jaw got tight, and then he disappeared into Tommy's office with the phone. I didn't hear anything else about the matter and he gave me the phone back and told me to keep being vigilant about messages.

* * *

The night before Tommy was scheduled to come home, I woke up to an alarm blaring the house down. Burglar alarm?

I jumped out of bed and threw my robe on and climbed under the bed. There was only the knife strapped, Tommy hadn't replaced the guns. My heart hammered in my chest and I wasn't sure if by this point I should be permanently traumatized or starting to get numb to this sort of stuff.

When the alarms stopped, I heard the bedroom door open and

my hand went to the knife. Then I heard Dario's loud and panicked-sounding voice. "Tia!"

"Under the bed!" I called out.

"Come out," he told me.

"What was that?" I rolled out, then scampered to my feet.

He had a gun in his hand, pointed at the floor and a ferocious-looking expression on his face. He walked over to the patio doors and checked the knobs. They were locked. He moved the blinds aside and looked out. Then he opened them and looked out. His whole body tightened for a second and then he turned around and looked at me. I was standing there, arms wrapped around myself but trying to get a read on his expression, which looked absolutely murderous.

"Dario?"

"Get dressed." He motioned toward the closet absently with the gun. I frowned, looked at it, then went in and put on a pair of jeans, a hoodie over my tank top and sleeping shorts. I slipped on my leather flip flops. I fastened an elastic band around my gathered-up hair into a messy bun as I walked back out.

"Follow me," he ordered.

I followed him down to the office where a guy I didn't know personally but had seen at Tom Sr.'s house stood. He looked alert and at Dario, his arms folded across his chest. He gave me a polite nod.

Dario put his gun into the back of his suit pants. It was three a.m., but he was still fully dressed. He motioned toward a chair.

"Relax a minute, Tia. We just need to make sure the house is secured. Someone tripped the burglar alarm and the land line isn't working. He dialed a number on his cell. "Status update?"

I sat and rubbed the sleep out of my eyes.

"Get to the balcony outside the master and do a sweep."

I frowned. What the heck did that mean?

I sat for about an hour in Tommy's office with the guy who looked ready to kill. Dario finally came back and told me I could go back to bed.

***

Tommy was in bed with me, all over me. Fingers, lips, tongue, cock. He devoured me like it hadn't been a week; it'd been more like a century.

"Missed you so much," he breathed against my ear while he was thrusting his cock into me hard, so hard. So good…

"Why are you back early?" I rasped. "And did you get a lot done?"

Then my head was banged a little against the headboard with the force of his hips against mine. He rubbed my head and took the brunt, shielding my head with his hand, his knuckles hitting the headboard a few beats, before he grabbed a pillow and shoved it behind my head to shield it, still without missing a beat, without breaking our connection, without stopping his rhythm.

"No one is going to fuck with what's mine," he grunted angrily and then he slowed and deepened the driving into me, taking us both to orgasm.

He rolled and I fell asleep on top of him, him still inside of me.

Later on, he told me someone had been on the balcony outside our door and that something had been left. He wouldn't say what it was, but his eyes were filled with wrath when he said he suspected they were there to hurt me as a message to him. I didn't know what was going on now, but suspected it was huge. I didn't know if it was an old threat or a new one. He didn't want to discuss it and asked me to have faith that he'd protect me.

17

Tia

A Week Later...

We were getting ready for Tom Sr.'s welcome home dinner. He'd been released from the hospital several days before and now that it was Sunday, the usual Ferrano family Sunday dinner thing was on, though grander in scale. Lisa had called and told me to make sure we came, that extended family would be there, too, to welcome Tom home. Tommy told me things were tense with his father and that some shit was going on in the business, but said we'd go for the sake of appearances.

The past week had largely consisted of me and Tommy seeing very little of one another. He was closed-lipped about things going on businesswise and hadn't said anything, really, about his time away. He was gone a lot. When he was home, he was affectionate and sweet, if quiet and preoccupied.

I watched Tessa's boys a few times and Sarah and I watched Luc's girls together the day she gave birth to their baby, a 5-pound 2 oz. slightly early but healthy bouncing boy they'd called Nicholas James.

The house security had first been beefed up since the night Tommy came home but then it dropped off, which I found odd. Security dwindled to just Nino during the day and Dex at night, which I asked Tommy about and he said that things weren't cool with his father and that many of the usual guards were reassigned to other Ferrano projects by his father. He had hired private security to guard the perimeter but had an intense vetting process because of the problems in the past little while so they were all outside the gates.

My first outing in a while was on the Friday before the dinner at Tom and Lisa's. I'd been taken to a shooting range where Tommy got me more comfortable with a gun so that he could leave a gun here knowing I'd know how to use it and knowing I wouldn't be afraid of it being here. Tommy hadn't said anything further about his exit plan and I didn't want to press him, knowing there was a lot on his mind.

* * *

The air was thick with tension for the whole welcome home dinner. Bianca and Nino, her mother, her Aunt Joanne and Aunt Joanne's husband Al were there plus a few other people that were considered extended family. It was catered affair. Tessa was somber and Tom was edgy and terse with everyone.

Tommy and Dario hung back for the most part, in conversation with one another rather than their father and the rest of the room.

Tommy whispered to me to say my goodbyes right after dessert. As I was making the rounds to say goodbye , I awkwardly approached Tommy's father. I leaned in as he'd motioned to hug me but then he hooked his hand around the back of my neck and pulled me to him. He kissed me on the mouth, forced his tongue into my mouth, and then looked at Tommy with ferocity on his face. The whole room seem to be stunned and the electricity coming off Tommy...he was wired.

Suddenly I was pulled back and they were chest to chest, both glaring at one another. Dario grabbed my elbow and then ushered me out of the room. The whole room then emptied, leaving Tommy and his father in there. People spilled out into the backyard. Dario put me into Tommy's car. "Two seconds, Tia," Dario said and then ran back into the house.

My heart was hammering in my chest. I looked at the house and Lisa and Luc were standing there talking and they were staring at me. I opened my mouth, still in shock, and shrugged at them. Lisa had tears in her eyes and Luc looked like she wanted to spit venom.

Suddenly my door opened and a tall and husky neckless guy pulled me out by the arm. I didn't recognize him. He wore a men-in-black suit and dark glasses. Security?

"What are you doing?"

"Come with me," he said, and he put me in the back seat of a black car parked behind Tommy's. Luc and Lisa were still staring, open-mouthed, so were some other people. The doors opened and two more burly goons got in on either side of me and the car drove away from the house. This was reminiscent of my graduation day.

What on earth?

Tommy

I was steaming fucking mad. My Pop wasn't happy about what'd happened at the hospital that day and hadn't taken our calls or seen us since. He knew I was still digging into his activities and that I was finding out shit that made my skin crawl. My father was more power-hungry, more ruthless, and more evil than I had ever realized.

He'd frozen us out. He'd frozen company accounts and was taking legal action to lock Dare and me out of the business, even though we owned shares on paper. He'd put a lawyer in charge. Lisa didn't know squat about it all so of course she invited us to Pop's big surprise welcome home dinner and Pop hadn't looked at us once all day until he put his hands and his mouth on my girl and looked right at me and that's when I was ready to fucking lose it. I'd been behind Tia and immediately ripped her out of his arms and got in his face.

Dario took her away and the room cleared out.

"What in the fuck was that?" I demanded after a stare down that went on until the French doors to that room and the sliding doors to the outside all clicked shut and it was just us two in the room.

He said nothing, just looked at me with cold dead-looking eyes.

"Pop!"

"Everything you have, my boy, everything you have is because of my blood, my sweat."

I raised my brows. "You haven't made me work for everything I've got? You haven't made me prove loyalty and worth to you every single fucking day of my life? Your kids, everyone who has ever loved you haven't all paid a heavy price for being your family, your wives?"

Pop snickered.

"You don't put your fucking hands on her again," I warned. "If you weren't who you are to me you'd be in the fucking ground for that shit."

He didn't reply, just kept looking at me with hatred.

"I guess Dare and I have your answer," I said as my brother re-entered the room.

"You might wanna rethink this, boys." He gave me a sick smile.

"What's up your sleeve?" Dario asked him.

"Re-think this," Pop threatened.

I shook my head. "No. I'm done."

I walked outside.

I walked by my two sisters who were huddled with Lisa by the gazebo near the door.

"Three of Pop's men drove off with her, Tommy," Tessa whispered. "Lisa said they pulled her out of your car and left in a black Impala."

I ran back into the house toward the room I'd been in with Pop and Dare. Dario met me in the hall.

I pushed past him, "Where the fuck?"

The room was empty.

"Where'd he go?" I yelled at my brother.

Dario looked back, "I dunno. He left the room after you. I made a call."

"He fucking took her!" I snarled.

I tore through the house looking for Pop, but he wasn't here. I finally found Nino, who'd been in the garden off that room and he'd seen Pop come outside and head toward the driveway. He had been watching his son play with the other kids while Bianca was in the kitchen with some of the other women, so he hadn't paid attention. Most of the men were still on Pop's payroll. The house security had been part of that until last week when he cut me off. Nino and Dex stayed with me; I was paying them myself.

I got on my phone and dialed Pop's cell.

"You're in time out, my boy," is how Pop answered the phone. I tried to get a lock on the rage that was building in me but no, it wasn't happening,

"Where the fuck–" I started but he cut me off.

"I'll call you later and we'll discuss the extra payment you'll have to make if you want her back. Like you've changed your mind about loyalty to me, I've changed my mind, too. I've decided that thirty-five k for Athena wasn't quite enough."

He fucking hung up on me.

Tia

"I almost kept you for myself, Athena," Tom said to me. "Almost. Now that… that woulda been the ultimate *fuck you* to your father."

We were in a living room of a cabin in the woods where we'd been dropped off by his three thugs. It was just the two of us in there; the thugs were mulling about, armed, outside. Tom was pouring a glass of wine.

I visibly shuddered.

He continued talking. "Saw you on that street and it felt like I could have a do-over with Carlita. But then I remembered you clutching your little dolly in my car that night, begging to go home to your mommy. If it weren't for that image burned in my brain, I wouldn't have given you to my son."

I tried to hold my emotions in check, but he went on, "Your father, piece of shit moron that he is, he thinks this was all his idea. I told him it was time to pay his debts, planted a few seeds, and he practically offered you on a silver platter."

My armor split right down the middle and I started to lose my foothold, started to lose my foothold on everything.

"He'd have agreed to it being me, being Tommy, or you could've been given to my pool guy if it'd mean saving his ass."

I was going to throw up.

"Dario has a thing for you. Wishes it were him. I know how he feels. I wish it was me." He downed his drink, put his glass down, and then he started to walk towards me.

"He's here, Sir," a gruff voice announced, then I heard a gunshot and a thump. The goon who'd announced that was down on the ground, bleeding from his head. I heard rapid fire outside the cabin. I turtled on the floor and scampered backwards against a wall.

Tom Sr. advanced and got right in front of me. He was an inch from me when I heard Tommy's voice and then saw him. Tommy was in the doorway and the gun in his hand was pointed at his father. On his face was a hard, stony, hateful expression and it was trained on his father.

"Back away," he told him.

Tom sneered at Tommy, then reached, grabbing me, yanking me to my feet, then spun around so that he was in the corner of the room and my back was against his front. Tom's arm was around my neck, my throat in the crook of his arm; his fingers digging into my shoulder.

Tommy didn't look me in the eye. He was looking at his father.

"You let her fucking go, Pop. Now."

"I gave her to you!" Tom shouted. "She saves your soul from hell and you thank me by pointing a gun at me, boy?" Tom started to laugh.

"Let. Her. Go."

I'd never seen Tommy's face like that. In all the moments when he'd frightened me, in all the times I thought his anger couldn't be any scarier, nothing had prepared me for the emanating anger that was coming off of him at this moment.

"You letting me walk out of here, son?"

"No." Tommy's eyes were cold. Stone cold.

"Then why would I let you have her back?"

I felt Tom shuffle behind me.

"Don't move!" Tommy hollered but Tom was quick. There was something cold against my temple. His gun.

Tommy's jaw tightened.

Then Tom cocked the gun. "Drop your gun or there's a bullet in her brain."

Tommy didn't hesitate, he dropped his gun and it slid across the floor. The cold steel left my temple.

"The love of a good woman, huh?" Tom said softly. "It does a lot to a man. I hope you appreciate that I gave this to you. But I'm surprised you're so weak to choose her over yourself. Thought I raised you better." He pushed me forward and I landed on the floor. I looked back and he had his gun trained on Tommy.

"Protecting what's mine isn't weak, Pop. It's what a real man does. He prioritizes his family above all else."

"Yeah? So why are you betraying me, my boy?"

"You're wrong, Pop. You've chosen wrong. You've chosen power and ego over family. You taught me wrong. You bred anger and hate and rage into me. Somehow that beautiful girl on the floor at your feet, she changed all that for me. Made me want to put her first. She's my family, my future. She and I won't raise our kids the way I've been raised, Pop."

He shook his head. "You think it's been easy for me? Keep my family safe? Build this business for you and your brother? You think I haven't had to make some gut-wrenching decisions in my life? You think I'm gonna let you shit on it? You turn your brother against me?" Tom was shaking his head in disgust. "How'd it feel when I took her? You like having something of yours taken away? You're trying to take my company away from me, the respect your brother has for me. I don't know what happened to your respect. I tried to get her last week, you know? Disarmed your house. You're lucky I've had a chance to calm down since then or I might've shot her dead right in front of the whole family."

The rage emanating off Tommy intensified. "We both know that was a game, Pop. I saw what you had your guys leave. And was that you fucking with my phone, too? Trying to get Tia to send nude pictures?"

Tom Sr. snickered. "Yeah, my boy. You been digging round in my business, you think I don't know all you've found out? You think I haven't been a step ahead of you every step you've taken? There's something you haven't figured out yet, son. A kitten can't fuck a tomcat."

"So, what now? You ending my life, Tomcat?" Tommy shrugged. "That's how little I matter to you? What about Dare? What's his punishment gonna be? Gonna fuck with the brakes in his car?"

Tom Sr. snickered again.

I stared at Tommy's gun that he'd dropped. It was two feet from me. I could lunge for it and put a stop to this. I looked up at Tommy, tears in my eyes. He still wasn't looking at me. I wanted to get a message to him with my eyes, to tell him I could grab for the gun, but he wasn't looking at me. It was like I was invisible. Tom and Tommy were in a faceoff and they were staring one another down.

"You out of the picture, your brother'll come back into the fold." Tom shrugged.

"He's no puppet," Tommy answered.

"He looked up to you, but he was jealous of you. Jealous you were my namesake, jealous you were getting the keys to the kingdom. Jealous you got the girl," Tom Sr. motioned to me with his chin. "You outta the way, he'll be happy with all he'll get. Maybe I'll gift her to him."

Tommy glanced at me and I glanced at the gun. I saw something in his eyes shift, a flare of his eyes in warning. He didn't want me reaching for it. But how else were we getting out of this?

Tom casually wandered over to the bar and as he did I inched a little toward the gun. Tom didn't seem to notice. He poured another drink and drank some, his gun still pointed at his son.

I looked at Tommy's face and he didn't look at me but he jerked his head in a 'no'. He knew my plan to reach for the gun. I moistened my lips and decided on another tactic.

"Tom?" I called out. Tommy's father's attention snapped to me. I shifted ahead on my knees and sat back on my heels. My back was to Tommy and now the gun was behind me, between Tommy and me.

"Did you kill my mother?" I asked.

The color seemed to drain out of his face.

"No," he said softly. "I did not. She won the game the only way she knew how. I refused let her go so she took herself from me."

I covered my face with my hands and pushed away my emotions. The look of pain on his face when he'd said those words made me think it could distract him.

"I loved her like no other woman, would've forgiven her for anything. I forgave her for leaving me, for your father, for the abortion. She was it for me. Everything. But she didn't feel the same. She couldn't take me as I was."

A chill slithered up my spine. The silence in the room was near deafening.

"I love your son unconditionally," I whispered, taking my hands off my face, tears burning in my eyes, my chest, my throat.

Tom looked at me and shook his head, with pain, with skepticism, jealousy; I didn't know. I couldn't read his expression.

"Let us go. Don't take it from him. You said you wanted to give him what you didn't have. If you meant that, really meant it... he has it. He has it. Let us go. Maybe in time you and your family can heal from this."

"Tia, don't," Tommy answered behind me but his voice was hoarse.

Tom looked at me with tears glistening in his eyes and after a moment, he said, "Go."

He shrugged. The hand with his gun in his hand dropped to his side but as I got to my feet a sneer spread across his face and he raised the gun in my direction.

"Tia; fuck!" Tommy's voice was urgent behind me and suddenly he hauled me behind himself and at the same time produced a gun from somewhere on his body and he fired in his father's direction.

Tommy

A split second after I fired my gun and hit my father in the forehead with a bullet, Tia went almost limp in my arms. I knew my speed and my aim was better than his. He always had others do his dirty work, so he was out of practice. I also had two guns on my body, not just the one in my hand when I walked in.

She was staring at my father's body there on the floor in a pool of blood.

I jerked her out of the daze by pulling her hand. "C'mon."

We left the building. She looked numb, looked like she was in a trance. I led her outside toward the Jeep where Nino, Dario, and Dex sat. The guards were all dead on the front porch.

I got into the back seat with her; my brother was back there, too.

"Call JC for cleanup," I told Nino, who was in the passenger seat. Dex drove away. Dario and I exchanged looks. My brother's expression softened for the first time in weeks and then he looked out the window.

She didn't completely lose it until we were back at the farm. I had the guys drop us off there, knowing it's where we'd need to be.

When we got up the stairs, she walked ahead of me to the sofa and sat down on it stiffly, staring off into space.

I went to the fridge and pulled out two bottles of water and then sat down beside her, putting the bottles on the floor in front of us.

"Baby?" I whispered and her eyes traveled up my body to my face. The fog seemed to lift and when she fell against me, I crumbled.

18

Tia

2 Weeks Later...

I woke up and my head was on his chest, on his right peck and in my line of vision was ink on his left peck. I lifted up on an elbow and looked closer. It was surrounded by skin that was reddish, a tiny bit swollen-looking due to being new. It was shiny, probably with some sort of ointment, and it was beautiful.

He'd gotten in last night late, after I'd been asleep. Over his heart was a tattoo that very much looked like the tribal art on his shoulder trailing down his arm, but this was a small owl on an olive branch, the Greek mythological Athena symbol I'd seen a million times in my life.

Below the olive branch, it said my name, but instead of my given Goddess name, it said Tia and it looked like my own handwriting, like I'd drawn my name on myself. A lump formed in my throat and tears filled my eyes. His eyes opened and he saw what my focus was on. He looked at me lovingly and caressed my cheek.

"The forgiveness you've shown me for all I've done to you, baby? It means everything." His voice was sleepy, sweet. "You've written your name on my heart, so I wanted it visible. I saw the artist who did my other ink. I think he integrated it all really well."

"It's beautiful, Tommy."

He kissed my cheekbone, kissing a tear away. "The way you trace my ink all the time after we make love, I want you tracing your name on me, too. So, I had it written just the way you'd do it. Went through your boxes to get a writing sample. I'm branded. You own me, baby girl. Body and soul."

"Will you marry me?" I asked, through tears, looking at my Ice Cream Parlor Hottie, my dream man.

Every time he gave me a big smile, I thought it was the most beautiful smile I'd ever seen. But right then, lying together in the little bed in the hayloft where I'd truly fallen in love with him, he gave me the most beautiful smile I'd ever seen yet and then he said, "I'll think about it."

I scrunched my nose up at him and he leaned over and kissed it.

* * *

Later that morning we drove back to the city to finish packing our things. We were starting over somewhere else. We didn't want to live in the house Tom bought, the house that I now knew was bought because it was my own mother's dream house. Tom's distorted entitlement put all this in motion and we wanted nothing to do with it. We were getting on a plane and taking some time for one another before the family flew down to meet us for our wedding.

I went into the kitchen and Sarah handed me a cup of coffee. When I took a sip, I could swear there was not a grain of sugar in it. My eyes narrowed at her and she gave me a sly smile and turned around and resumed packing a box of dishes. I was about to reach for the sugar but noticed the sugar bowl had already been packed away. I sat down at the island and decided to see if I could live without my three sugars. I took a second sip and really, it wasn't all that bad.

Epilogue

Tia

We planned to get married in Costa Rica with Tommy's siblings, Eddy, Bianca and Nino, Sarah, Lisa, and all the kids. Tommy and I are moving there for now.

I haven't said goodbye to my old friends and my old life; I just can't go there right now. It's too raw and I'm too different.

My friends are in school, dating, working part-time jobs, and being teenaged girls. I've changed so much in the last few months. I wrote Rose and Cal a letter, it was vague but heartfelt. I mailed it to them before we left. I do hope I can see them again.

Dario's taken the company reins and he's going to transition it into something clean and wholesome and then he says he's going to sell it. He's thinking of becoming an airline pilot. That's what he dreamt of ever since he was a small child. I asked Tommy what he dreamt of. He never answered the question honestly, gave me a storybook 'happily ever after with my ice cream parlor maid' kind of answer. I know that's not true, because he never envisioned himself settling down before he met me. I know he envisioned himself at the helm of Ferrano Enterprises.

I don't know what he'll do with his life, but I know he is too driven and too smart to stay idle for long. He needs time to heal, to figure out what he wants. We both do. Then we'll see what pearls life's oyster offers us.

My father is still incarcerated, but at least he's still alive, thanks to Tommy. Tommy's father's death along with the death of the guards that were also there was reported in the newspapers as having to do with mafia business gone wrong and related to a cartel in Mexico. I guess JC, whoever he is, has good clean-up skills. Thank God Tommy had the foresight to put a GPS in my engagement ring. It was crazy stalkerish of him to do it, but it probably saved my life. Would Tom have killed me to teach his son a lesson? We'll never know.

Since we've been here in paradise, Tommy's been having nightmares and I finally convinced him to get therapy after he woke up in the throes of one of those nightmares with my throat in his hand as I began turning blue. He agreed, after a big argument where I stood my ground and won, to start video counselling sessions with a therapist in the UK that has excellent credentials and experience in helping men like Tommy come to terms with their dominating personalities.

I don't know if it's the counselling, the guilt, or the grief over all that happened but he hasn't wanted to play any sex games. I've tried to initiate them for stress relief, or thinking it'd help bring his spark back but right now he's quiet, subdued, reflective, and seems to be all about the vanilla. He's sweet and attentive, but he's also sad and troubled and he's not the same. I'm missing the blackjack berry thunder. We just have to give it time. I hope. I know he feels regret for all the pain and hurt and I know he loves me but I kind of miss my dominator. Yes, he's possessive and protective but he's trying to be too... vanilla.

Tommy

We got married at sunset on a beach in Costa Rica with our family around us. We were both dressed in white. I danced with her to our song and she put on the ring with the gold and black knots. And I was in heaven, for she was truly mine at last. I didn't deserve her, but she gave herself to me anyway. She'd stared into my eyes and promised to love, honor and obey, which made me smirk, which then made her smirk. I gave her a look of promise and her gaze went heated. The justice of the peace that married us had to clear his throat to get our attention back on the ceremony.

When the song ended and another one began, I whispered into her ear,

"Wife, when your husband takes you to bed to consummate our marriage, he's going to rip that fucking vanilla dress off you and fuck you like you've never been fucked."

I continued, but looked into her eyes; they were huge and she was panting.

I told her, "I've got handcuffs and a spreader bar, some toys, and a tub of blackjack berry thunder ice cream."

She had a full body shiver.

I'd gotten a local chef to recreate that ice cream flavor from the approximate recipe of the brand back home.

I was ready for our life together to truly begin and while I had a long way to go with therapy and making sure that I never went overboard with her again, and while I'd decided to give up my birthright as mafia crime boss I had not given up the right for my life to have flavor.

The End
Or is it?

Nope, it isn't!
This story continues with Truth or Dare

The Dominator Playlist

Breaking the Girl - Red Hot Chili Peppers –
Wild Horses - The Rolling Stones
Iris - Goo Goo Dolls
Holding back the Years - Simply Red
Wicked Game - Stone Sour
At Last - Etta James

End of Book Notes:

I started working on The Dominator when I was 15 years old. I could never seem to finish it. Through my teens and early 20's I stopped and restarted and started over multiple times. The idea for this book got put away until finally, in my early 40's, I sat down and re-started and then finished it. It feels great to have finally closed this chapter. It feels like it needed to happen in order for me to move forward and share the other stories that have been brewing in my brain all this time.

There are a lot of people who have cheered on my writing in my lifetime. Teachers, co-workers, friends, family, loves. Thank you all!

I hope you'll continue the journey with Truth or Dare and Unbound.

I hang out regularly in my Facebook reader group, DD's Chickadees, where there's lots of fun, book teasers, giveaways, and shenanigans. I hope you'll join me there.

About the Author

DD Prince has been writing ever since she learned she could put pen to paper and create with words. She has a passion for faith, family, friends, food, and words. Born and raised in Toronto, she has over twenty five books that were written with views of a lake, then near the waterfalls of Niagara Falls, and she now writes from the Maritimes near the Atlantic ocean.

She loves to read and write dark, contemporary, and paranormal love stories, especially when love – whether dark, sweet, or co-dependent is the anecdote.

Follow Me

Follow DD Prince on most social media sites as ddprince or ddprincebooks

Facebook: Facebook.com/ddprincebooks
Website: ddprince.com
More: https://linktr.ee/ddprincebooks

Subscribe to the free newsletter, The Scoop, at http://ddprince.com/newsletter-signup to be notified about upcoming releases and books sales.

Thank you very much for reading my books! A review is a huge help, as is a recommendation to friends who love this style of story.